All the Missing Children

All the Missing Children

ZAHID GAMIELDIEN

ultimo press

Published in 2024 by Ultimo Press,
an imprint of Hardie Grant Publishing

Ultimo Press
Gadigal Country
7, 45 Jones Street
Ultimo, NSW 2007
ultimopress.com.au

  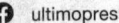 ultimopress

All rights reserved. No part of this publication may be reproduced, stored in a retrieval system or transmitted in any form by any means, electronic, mechanical, photocopying, recording or otherwise, without the prior written permission of the publishers and copyright holders.

The moral rights of the author have been asserted.

Copyright © Zahid Gamieldien 2024

 A catalogue record for this book is available from the National Library of Australia

All the Missing Children
ISBN 978 1 76115 318 1 (paperback)

Cover design and illustrations George Saad
Text design Simon Paterson, Bookhouse
Typesetting Bookhouse, Sydney | 12/17 pt Baskerville MT Pro
Copyeditor Ali Lavau
Proofreader Rebecca Hamilton

10 9 8 7 6 5 4 3 2 1

Printed in Australia by Opus Group Pty Ltd, an Accredited ISO AS/NZS 14001 Environmental Management System printer.

 The paper this book is printed on is certified against the Forest Stewardship Council® Standards.
Griffin Press – a member of the Opus Group – holds chain of custody certification SCS-COC-001185. FSC® promotes environmentally responsible, socially beneficial and economically viable management of the world's forests.

Ultimo Press acknowledges the Traditional Owners of the Country on which we work, the Gadigal People of the Eora Nation and the Wurundjeri People of the Kulin Nation, and recognises their continuing connection to the land, waters and culture. We pay our respects to their Elders past and present.

For K, who already knows

Part One
Ilene

I

Days before her children went missing, Ilene Gajdos-Little gnawed on the dry skin of her bottom lip and reclined in her low-backed stool and felt, deep in her bones, that she was due a change of fortune. She reached out and pressed the poker machine's backlit button again. Once more, the machine played its jaunty tune of anticipation. Once more, it scrolled through its motley images—casino cards, jade turtles, gold lions—and once more, it settled on a combination that was literally within an ace of winning.

Ilene threw her head back and groaned. The ceiling was adorned with circular mirrors framed by fluorescents the hue of sundown, and she was down to sixty-seven cents' credit. When her credit was exhausted, she decided, she'd top it up with the twenty she'd pilfered from the till at work. But she glanced at her Casio watch: soon she'd have to leave the Casus Hill Workers' Club to pick up Jack and Lonnie from school. She didn't have time to spin through twenty extra dollars, unless she accepted that she'd be late.

Somewhere to her right, a machine paid out and blared its festive ragtime melody. That machine was called Horseshoe Saloon. She knew it; she'd won and lost on it plenty of times before. Her machine for the day, Jewels of the Orient, was due to pay out any second. If she didn't stay until she at least broke even, the next punter would reap all the luck she'd sown.

She picked up her schooner and moistened her lips with the tepid froth that remained. Then she knuckled the backlit button. Rapid-fire, the digital reels wound themselves into another losing pattern. Now she had forty-seven cents' credit left, which was twenty-three-and-a-half for each occasion she'd been late to pick her children up this month.

The previous Tuesday, she'd arrived to find them loitering on the pavement by the school gates. Neither of them approached her battered orange Datsun. Jack, who was eight, watched a magpie wheel low overhead, while six-year-old Lonnie slipped her thumbs beneath the fraying straps of her backpack. Ilene hooted, but they eyed the car as if it were a foreign object. Then the school principal, Ms Subraman, shuffled past the two pine trees and out through the gates with her Peter Pan collar flapping in the breeze.

Ilene played another spin, and this time she came close to the change of fortune she'd anticipated. Pretty close, she corrected herself—a single jade turtle shy of winning twelve free spins. She scratched her crown. It wouldn't matter to her children if she were late. They'd be safe. They'd probably feel safer with the principal than with her. What she didn't want to deal with was Ms Subraman's mouth, which she'd hold on that commiserative angle, as if Ilene wasn't even worth scolding.

From her right, the ragtime melody blared again, and she scowled at the row of pokies perpendicular to hers. Most of the gaming stools were empty, but a lone woman hunched on the stool in front of Horseshoe Saloon. She sat unnaturally still, and the glow of her machine formed a pale nimbus around her. Her hair was woven into a volute bun that reminded Ilene of a severed ear. She could not look away. The melody slowed its tempo, and the only movement was the plume of light enveloping the woman.

When the melody finished, Ilene dragged her gaze to her knuckles. She whistled cool air onto them and, too afraid to watch, played her final spin. In turn, the machine played its jaunty tune, and she imagined the images on-screen jostling for position. She willed the victory music to follow. But nothing followed. Her credit was down to seven cents, which was not enough for another spin.

She exhaled through her nostrils. Then she dug the fingernails of her right hand into her upper left arm until she made herself wince. There was only one way to break even now. She had to use the stolen twenty. She had to re-disappoint Ms Subraman. She had to make her children wait.

But she may as well make them wait. They didn't trust her, let alone love her. She could tell this from the way Jack rolled over in the upper bunk when she greeted him in the morning. She could sense it whenever Lonnie hugged her from behind, or the side—never from the front. The reflection of the stars in the bore water tank's murk glinted in Ilene's memory, and her pulse crashed above her ears.

She felt as if she were submerged, and only her yearning for another spin brought her back to the surface. Her handbag lay on the bus seat–patterned carpet at her feet. She dragged it onto her lap and guddled through it in pursuit of the twenty-dollar note. When she found it, her pulse eased up, and she peered to her right. The row of pokies there was unoccupied. The woman with the volute bun must have taken her winnings and left.

A cloud drifted across the afternoon sun, and from the corridor of the main school building, Ilene watched its shadow fall upon the classroom in which her children waited. Seated at a wooden desk, Jack scrawled something in a dog-eared exercise book. Lonnie crouched beside a cabinet and poked a short straw through an egg carton. The sun returned and illuminated the stains on the yellow t-shirt of her uniform; it brightened the shade of Jack's grey hoodie, which Ms Subraman had explained was from lost and found.

In the circumstances, Ilene imagined that other children would've glanced around in anticipation of their mother. Hers hadn't even noticed her belated arrival. She rested her shoulder against the wall of the corridor. Then Ms Subraman re-emerged from her office with Jack's bloodied shirt in one hand and a form of some sort in the other.

'He won't tell me or the counsellor who the fight was with,' she said. 'Or what it was over. But it was not trivial.'

She handed the shirt to Ilene, who pinched the yoke either side of the collar and held it up for inspection. The cotton was sheer, and near the hem three tears ran through a blotch of dried blood that looked like a Rorschach test. There was something of the scarecrow about it, Ilene thought. She imagined hay protruding from the rents in the fabric, but that image soon gave way to one of deep talon wounds on Jack's abdomen.

'How bad is it?' she asked.

'The shirt came off worse than the boy, fortunately.' Ms Subraman smiled without showing her teeth. 'We bandaged him in sick bay—he's all right.' Her smile faded, and she gripped the form with both hands. 'You didn't check on him while I was in my office?'

Ilene draped Jack's shirt over her arm. She peered into the classroom and almost followed her gaze inside. Lonnie had taken a seat next to Jack and was waving the egg carton under his nose. He ignored her and poured his concentration into the exercise book and raked his angry pencil over the page. Ilene longed to comfort him, to hug both of her children, but she feared that they would stiffen in her embrace—and that Ms Subraman would see.

'Jack won't dob in the other kid?' she asked.

'Perhaps you can get it out of him.' Ms Subraman did not seem as if she were being sarcastic. She appeared merely distracted, skim-reading the form in her hands and clearing her throat. 'My staff attempted to contact you after lunch, after we wrote up the incident report.'

'That the report?'

Ms Subraman shook her head. 'When you didn't answer, we tried your husband. He told us he couldn't come.'

Ilene caught the upward inflection in Ms Subraman's voice, and the hallway seemed to tilt. The thought spiralled through her mind that Jack and Lonnie had told the principal about what had happened that night a year earlier, or perhaps Carl had let something slip over the phone.

She blinked hard, and the school corridor righted itself. 'My husband's been sick,' she offered. His sickness, if that was the right word, had actually begun two years earlier, after he'd lost his job as a brink-of-the-city farmhand; he'd been accused of slitting a sheep's throat when in truth, he'd claimed, all he did was shepherd a couple of workers into a union. 'He's not in the kids' lives for now. We made that call together.'

Ms Subraman folded the form in half. Deliberately, she flattened the crease in the paper between her thumb and forefinger. 'Here.'

She passed the form to Ilene, who unfolded it and scanned its text. It was an application for after-school care, and a hot flush rose from Ilene's chest to her neck. 'I don't need this. I work shifts at the supermarket, yeah.'

'Ilene, you've been late three times this month. According to the rules—'

'But I can drop them off, pick them up.'

'According to the rules, I should've sent them already.'

Ilene sighed, and Ms Subraman's mouth shifted to that commiserative angle. 'It only costs twenty-five dollars to get on the waitlist, and the council gives special consideration to low-income earners, as you'll see.' She pointed at the form. 'And to sole carers,' she added.

Ilene stuffed the bloodied shirt and form into her handbag. 'Anything else?'

She stared at Ms Subraman and tried to force the principal to avert her gaze. But the principal looked resolutely back at her. 'If Jack tells you who hurt him, please let me know.'

Ilene entered the classroom, and Lonnie ran to her and embraced her—albeit from the side. Ilene stroked her daughter's matted curls and glared at her son. Jack remained seated and flicked his exercise book shut. On the wall above him were paintings of sunflowers and animals and happy families. She prised the egg carton from Lonnie's grip.

'It's a bus,' Lonnie said.

'It's excellent.' Ilene glanced at Ms Subraman, who waited in the corridor, and relaxed the muscles of her face. 'Now go sit next to your brother again. You both look *so* beautiful.'

Her tone verged on insincerity, and Lonnie withdrew from the embrace. 'We do?'

''Course you do. In fact, let me get a photo of you two before we go.'

'Oh-kay.'

Lonnie dragged her feet back behind the desk, and Ilene tossed the egg carton aside. It ricocheted off the cabinet and rolled along the floor. She didn't check Ms Subraman's reaction. But the hot flush returned to her neck, and she busied herself with her phone. Its camera lens and screen were cracked, although she could see she had a message from Carl and missed calls from the school. She cleared the notifications and raised the phone and lined up a photograph.

'Ready? Three, two, one—smile.'

Jack and Lonnie did not smile. They sat there with serious expressions and their heads slightly bowed. Ilene tapped the button for the camera anyway, and the flash went off. She checked the photo on her phone. It'd come out grainy, the children's features partly obscured by shadow. She should take another photo, she thought. Then she looked to the corridor and realised that Ms Subraman had ended her watch.

'It's a good one,' Ilene said.

Lonnie half-rose. 'Can I see?'

'Later, maybe. First I need to ask you some stuff.'

Ilene put her phone away and took a few paces forward. Lonnie adjusted herself in her chair, and Ilene couldn't help feeling that she'd positioned her children for an interrogation. This sense was exacerbated by a thought she rarely had: while she was pale and freckled, her children's skin tones were closer to Carl's. She resisted the urge to drop to her haunches.

'What?' Jack said. 'I didn't do anything.'

Ilene raised her eyebrows. 'Then who did?'

'No one.'

'No one?'

He exchanged a look with Lonnie, who puffed out her cheeks as if to keep the answer from escaping her mouth.

'You want to tell me something, Lonnie?' Ilene asked.

Her daughter gave two big shakes of her head. She let air seep out between her lips, and Ilene folded her arms and nodded at Jack's stomach. 'Show me.'

He wiped his septum with the heel of his hand. Then he got to his feet and lifted the grey hoodie's hem to reveal his abdomen. Taped over his kidney area was a napped white bandage, stained with a pink shiver of blood. Above the bandage, his rib cage was that of a prisoner on a hunger strike. Ilene's arms fell to her side, and she stuttered another step in his direction. She wished she could go to him and hold him. But his mouth was set hard and his eyes narrowed, and he tugged at the hem of his hoodie.

'You won't tell me who did that to you?' Ilene said.

'I already told you.'

Jack took his seat and rested his forearms on the closed exercise book before him. Lonnie patted his shoulder—an acquired adult gesture, Ilene figured. The sun had started to take on the hue of the gaming room's fluorescents, and she checked that the corridor remained empty.

'Well,' she said, 'then can I see what you wrote in that book?'

'No.'

'Why not?'

'It's private.'

Lonnie's eyes were enormous. 'Some things are private.'

Ilene flinched. She'd said that to her children once, on her haunches, in an anteroom that reeked of disinfectant. They were to be interviewed by a government psychologist at the hospital where Carl was being treated, and she didn't want them to speak a word about how he'd ended up there.

'There are no secrets between children and mothers,' she replied. Then she dropped her voice to a murmur and asked, 'Did you say something to Ms Subraman? About something private? Or maybe you wrote it down somewhere?'

Lonnie blinked repeatedly; with some effort, Jack kept himself stationary.

'Lonnie?' Ilene said.

'No, Mum.'

'Jack?'

'I didn't *say* anything.'

He balled his fists over the exercise book. Ilene caught the movement, and her hot flush made its way to her face. Blood sloshed through her temples, and she lunged for the book and grabbed it. Jack shifted his weight. He pushed down. But he didn't have the heft to stop her, and she wrenched the book out from under his fists.

Ilene turned side-on to her children and flicked through the pages. They were filled with maths homework, notes on the Earth's crust, a book report. An unfinished short story, without full stops, filled the last page on which Jack had written. *The children went into the cave and smashed up some stars*, Ilene read. She flipped through the pages a second time. Then she closed the book, and her children's gazes stung her cheek.

Without meeting their eyes, she laid the exercise book on the desk in front of Jack. It occurred to her to apologise. But a subtle tremor in the shadows of the corridor diverted her attention. Ms Subraman was staring into the classroom, so Ilene helped her children pack their bags and ushered them off the school grounds.

Heat snaked from the electric coil of the stove to the blackened pan, in which eight store-bought meatballs hissed and spat. Ilene raised one and checked the underside. The mince was well done but not as dark as the pan, and she decided to let it crisp up a little more. That was how Jack and Lonnie liked it, and she hoped that her children might accept her burnt offering in lieu of an apology.

When the meatballs were done, she scoffed two down and unglued her feet from the linoleum floor. She arranged the remaining meatballs on dinner plates with Smith's chips and bread rolls and the last couple of squeezes of tomato sauce. Then she carried the plates past the faded red polo of her cashier's uniform—which was draped over a chair at the dining table—and into the living room.

On the sofa, her children sat together and watched television at full volume. Lonnie had her legs crossed and her finger on her chin. Jack's mouth hung open. On TV, women wore gold dresses and gold nail polish and gold lipstick. Muzak blared, and one by one they opened gold briefcases to reveal random words.

'Who wants meatballs?' Ilene singsonged.

Jack and Lonnie gave no sign that they'd heard, and Ilene stepped between them and the TV and slid the two plates of meatballs onto the coffee table. It bore water stains from glasses and mugs, circles of different sizes, and her eye settled on a smaller ring within a larger one. This put her in mind of the hunched woman from the gaming room and the plume of light surrounding her; Ilene recalled her own paralysis and withdrew to stand behind the sofa.

'I burned them just how you like.'

On TV, a woman opened a briefcase with the word 'blowfly' in it, and the male game show host shouted the house down to announce that the contestant had won.

Ilene yawned. 'I'm gonna catch some sleep before work. Don't stay up too late, okay?' She leaned over and kissed Lonnie's head. Lonnie stiffened but did not flee. Her hair smelled of beeswax and wet soil. It wasn't the fragrance of clean hair, Ilene thought, yet it wasn't unpleasant. 'Okay?' she repeated.

'Okay, Mum,' Lonnie replied.

Ilene shuffled across to kiss Jack's crown. Before she got to him, he scrambled to the floor and knelt in the gap between the sofa and the coffee table. He dunked his bread roll into the tomato sauce and took a great bite. Lonnie slid to the floor beside her brother and stuffed a whole meatball into her mouth.

Ilene yawned again and brought tears to her eyes. 'Night,' she said.

This time she didn't expect a reply. She moved from the living room to the hallway and past the two bedrooms and into the dingy bathroom. The leaking showerhead was pressed against the wall, and behind the sink the bristles of three toothbrushes pointed in every direction. Next to them, a tube of toothpaste lay flat and used-up.

She stared at herself in the mirror and splashed her face with water. A droplet fell onto her foot. It felt as jagged as broken glass, but the pain wasn't in the present. Not long after Carl had lost his job, not long after the bills had begun to go unpaid, she'd run into the bathroom to find his lip burned and his tongue bleeding and the smoking fragments of a pipe on the tiles. She'd cut her sole helping him and tramped bloodied footprints along the hallway, right past her children's bedroom.

II

The pneumatic timer switch clicked and extinguished all the lights in the stairwell. On the third-floor landing of Carl's apartment building, Ilene stood in the precipitate dark and knocked on his door. It was verging on midnight, which was when her shift started, and she was already in her uniform—black pants and the faded red polo she'd plucked from the chair in the kitchen. After dinner, she'd caught a few hours' sleep. She'd awoken to discover Jack and Lonnie dozing in front of the television; she'd hustled them into their bunk bed and sped away from the otherwise empty house.

Carl's apartment may have been empty as well. From within, there was no response to her knock. In the darkness, she shifted her weight from foot to foot. Her mind conjured an image of her holding Carl's hand in the dusty field, of Jack and Lonnie holding hands up ahead. The scruff of her neck tingled. She scrabbled along the wall for the timer switch and pushed it in and knocked on the door again. This time, a creak sounded from within the apartment, and she stepped back.

Through a gap in the handrails, she spied the grimy entryway and its sickly green tinge. The last time she'd stood down there, Carl had said they shouldn't see each other for a while. He hadn't specified how long. Still, she'd respected his wishes. For months she hadn't come. The only reason for her visit now, she told herself, was to tell him about Jack's injury—and maybe to ask what he'd said to Ms Subraman on the phone.

Inside the apartment, the footsteps trudged towards the door. Ilene's pulse faltered for a beat before it hurried on. She tried to recall how she'd appeared in the bathroom mirror, whether she'd been haggard or stooped, whether her fresh worry lines had aged her. But all she could picture were the broken shards of the pipe.

On the other side of the door, the footsteps paused. She licked her chapped lips and wiped her hands on her polo, but what the hell was she thinking? If her main purpose for being here was to tell Carl about Jack's injury, she'd show the bloodied shirt to him upfront and be on her way. She reached into her bag and took hold of it.

The lock turned; the door opened. Carl appeared at the threshold of his dark apartment. Ilene removed the shirt from her bag and held it mutely before her. For an instant she perceived her husband as he was: raw-boned, exhausted, with charcoaled recesses beneath his eyes and an oleaginous amber undercoat to his brown skin. He had an unkempt beard and a crooked nose that had never been reset after she'd smashed it with a shovel.

Then the stairwell's lights went out, and Ilene could perceive nothing. Her lips quivered, and desperately, with so much force that it stung, she mashed them against Carl's. He kissed her back, grabbed a fistful of her hair. They collapsed, grappling, onto the floor of his unlit apartment. Her handbag slipped off her shoulder, and the bloodied shirt left her grip. She kicked the door shut and forced her shoes and pants off. She moved astride him, and the sharp of his hipbones dug into her thighs.

Almost as soon as he entered her, though, his body slackened. She leaned forward and tried to kiss him again but found only the rough warmth of his cheek. For a few seconds, she sat there, unsure of herself. Then she pushed down on his chest with both hands, as if she were performing a compression, and rolled off to the side.

She lay supine near the apartment's entrance and caught her breath, along with the odour of baked beans and sour milk. The bathroom tap dripped. In the gloom, she could barely see Carl's silhouette, although now she heard him sobbing.

'The children,' he whispered.

He was curled up beside her on the carpet, yet it sounded as if his voice had been filtered through a phone line. Unsighted, she fixed herself up and collected her bag and felt around for the bloodied shirt. It wasn't far off, scrunched into a ball and gossamer to the touch. She put it back in her bag and exited without a word.

Behind her register near the cigarette counter, Ilene picked up her iced coffee from the hidden shelf beneath the till. A couple of customers flitted through the aisles, and her eye twitched at them. She felt as if the grime from Carl's apartment building had settled on her corneas. Her polo smelled of cooking oil, and she also reeked of sex, although she only knew this because of what the evening manager, Stefan, had said at the end of his shift. He'd blushed and told her she looked nice. But as he left, he muttered an aside to another staff member—all Ilene had caught were the words 'stinks of a good time'.

She yawned and slurped at her iced coffee and tried to shake off all that'd happened before she'd started work. Soon the sun would rise, and her shift would be over. Until then, she had to remain alert for the right opportunity.

Over her shoulder, she checked on the position of the security guard, Marco. He pushed himself off one of the closed roller doors that, at night, separated the supermarket from the shut-up shopping plaza. His black shoes squeaked, and he sauntered along the path that led to the after-hours exit. Yet he didn't head out to the car park.

Instead he approached Tandy, the other cashier on shift, and looped his arms around her waist. She feigned an attempt to wriggle free and rolled her eyes at Ilene, who raised her drink to toast the happy couple.

'Did you see we have hula hoops?' Tandy called out in her Singaporean accent.

Before Ilene could answer, a strung-out teenage girl in a tracksuit steered a trolley towards Tandy's register. Tandy shrugged Marco off. He withdrew but kept an eye on the teenage girl.

Ilene stared at the apples shimmering in the fruit section. Something about having to witness the spark of her friend's relationship had caused a knot of electrical wire to form in her mind. Through that knot slipped the memory of Carl sobbing in the post-coital gloom of his apartment. Then she pictured him with a smile on his face, his nose unbroken, his ear on her bulging belly in which Jack was taking form.

'Ilene . . . Ilene?' The teenage girl had left, and from behind her register, Tandy beamed and beckoned. 'Come here.'

Ilene sipped at the last of her iced coffee and ambled past the unpeopled registers to Tandy.

Marco smirked and leaned against the roller door nearest the exit. 'How long you reckon Tandy can keep a hula hoop going?'

'No idea.'

Tandy's grin widened. 'Marco bet me I can't do it for more than a minute. I bet he can't either.'

'If I can't last for more than a minute—' Marco began. Tandy chuckled, and he snorted and shook his head. 'I swear to God, you're a child.'

'Your money's on me, right, Ilene?'

Ilene shrugged. She'd intended for this to seem playful, or at least challenging in its nonchalance. But she knew it probably appeared sullen. Tandy's smile failed her for an instant before she wagged a jovial finger at Ilene and Marco. 'I'll show you. I'll show you all!'

She faked a maniacal laugh and jogged out from behind her register and disappeared into the aisle that housed the meagre toy collection. Marco trailed his girlfriend, although he stopped by a display of mouthwash at the aisle's entry to nod at a woman in yoga pants. She tipped a bottle of mouthwash into her shopping basket and strode to Tandy's register.

Ilene positioned herself behind it. She rested her iced coffee on the hidden shelf, where she noticed four rolls of coins wrapped in cardboard. They should've been in the till already, she thought. She caressed one, and adrenaline rushed to her fingertips. 'Evening,' she said to the woman.

'Well, technically morning.' The woman placed her few groceries onto the conveyor belt and handed Ilene a reusable bag. 'Hard to find anything twenty-four hours in Sydney. Especially here out west.'

Ilene scanned and bagged a pack of diet bars. 'Not enough demand, I guess.'

'Oh, and the rent and the bloody penalty rates.' The woman waited by the credit card machine.

Ilene kept scanning and bagging groceries. 'You're not from around here?'

'Melbourne. One more day and I get to go home, thank Christ.'

Ilene scanned and bagged the mouthwash, which was the last item on the conveyor belt. 'Paying with card?'

The woman nodded and glanced at the after-hours exit. In front of the mouthwash display, Marco chatted with Tandy, who held a yellow hula hoop and frowned an apology in Ilene's direction. Ilene scratched her throat. The CCTV camera watched her. 'The machine's tap thingy is broken,' she said in a low voice. Her chipped nails rested on the buttons of the register. 'You'll have to insert . . .'

The woman sighed, but she slid her credit card into the machine.

'Cash out?' Ilene asked.

'No—you still do that?'

Lightning-fast, Ilene added twenty dollars to the total on the register. 'Pin?'

The woman squinted at the credit card machine, and Ilene prayed she wouldn't check the total displayed there. In her experience, most people didn't, and even if this woman did, at this stage Ilene could probably play it off as an error.

The woman covered the number pad with her hand and keyed in her pin. Tandy's register printed a receipt, and the till pinged open. Ilene knocked it shut with her hip. 'You want a receipt?' she asked.

But the woman was already striding out with her reusable bag of groceries, and Ilene tossed the receipt into the bin. She felt shiny and self-conscious under the supermarket lights. Her fingers trembled, but she had to keep going. From the hidden shelf, she collected a roll of twenty one-dollar coins and tipped it into the open maw of her iced coffee carton. It disappeared completely, and she lifted the carton to her lips as if she were drinking from it.

At the mouthwash display, Tandy and Marco whispered to each other. Their expressions were blank, and Marco looked at Ilene as he had the teenage girl. She froze. The carton of iced coffee shook in her hand. Then Tandy smiled and stepped into the hula hoop to see if she could keep it spinning for more than a minute.

When her shift ended, Ilene wandered out to the plaza's car park and got into her orange Datsun and sank into the spongy foam of the driver's seat. To her right, cars dotted the space between her and the supermarket's twenty-four-hour entrance; to her left were asphalt and paint and a suburban street embellished with an overhanging sun. There were no people about, so she reached into the iced coffee carton and extracted the roll of dollar coins. Its cardboard wrapping was gluey. She squeezed it in her fist and inhaled the ultra-sweet coffee on her skin.

Pleasure purled through her, and a sleepy smile crossed her face. She let her eyelids slowly close. What she felt was not unlike winning on the pokies, although the other day, when she'd been at the workers' club, she'd lost and lost and seen the hunched woman with the volute bun.

Ilene's face straightened out, but the minor thrill of her thievery continued to burble away in her veins. Ready to drive home, she placed the carton and roll of coins on the passenger seat with her handbag. Then she caught sight of a miniature ziplock bag wedged, almost hidden, against the side of the centre console. She understood what it was, and some instinct screamed at her not to examine it more closely. But she picked it up anyway.

The ziplock bag was coated with fine powder that, in the daylight, took on a reddish hue. It'd belonged to Carl and slept undisturbed in the centre console since that night, a year earlier. Ilene had followed Jack and Lonnie out of the Datsun and into the dusty field; Carl had lingered in the car a while, his features distorted by the lighter's flame licking the bowl of his pipe.

Ilene fluttered the ziplock bag as if doing so would shake off the recollection. But it only made her aware of the thrill in her veins ebbing further. When Carl had finished with the pipe, she'd held his hand and walked with him through the dusty field. The Datsun's headlights had shone cold on their spines, and under their shadows Jack and Lonnie had traipsed on ahead. Beyond the children loomed the bore water tank, glimmering in sections, rusted in others, and at its base grazed a sheep shorn of its wool. Carl had let out a mad whoop of warning and pegged his pipe at the tank; the sheep had scampered off into the black—and Ilene had realised where they were.

In the shopping plaza's car park, she shuddered and stared at her fingers and expected them to be stained with powder. All she saw were her coffee-coloured fingerprints. The whorls of them made her woozy, and she could hear the roar of an ocean she knew wasn't there. She put the ziplock bag on the passenger seat with the other items. Her head lolled in the opposite direction, and she squinted at the street and the accusatory sun.

A moment later, Ilene was startled by a knock on the front passenger window. She turned to it, and Tandy's countenance skated into focus. Tandy held up a hand in greeting. Not far behind her, Marco folded his arms and scuffed his soles on the ground. Panic rushed through Ilene. The roll of coins sat on the passenger seat, along with the ziplock bag and empty iced coffee carton. She swept the lot onto the floor and, feigning clumsiness, reached across and wound down the window.

'Tandy,' she said. 'What's up?'

'Nothing much.'

Tandy leaned forward, and her gaze roamed the crumb-covered interior of the car. From the driver's seat, Ilene spotted the carton tipped over and leaking iced coffee. She wasn't sure where the roll of coins had gone, and she followed Tandy's eyeline to check if she'd spied it. 'How are Jack and Lonnie going?' Tandy asked.

'Fine.' Ilene shrugged. 'Both doing good. Why?'

Marco coughed, and Tandy looked over her shoulder at him. Ilene clocked the thin line of his mouth. She pressed the brake down with her foot and considered whether he and Tandy had discovered they were short a roll of coins. But she reminded herself that the cash in Tandy's till would've balanced and that Tandy probably hadn't spotted the stolen roll in the car.

When Tandy turned back to Ilene, though, her expression was grim.

Ilene breathed out a laugh. 'What is it?'

'What about Carl?' Tandy asked. 'Has he moved back in after his . . . sickness?'

'No, not yet.' Ilene contorted her dry lips into a smile. She hadn't told Tandy much more than she'd told Ms Subraman about

Carl's affliction. The most she'd ever said was that he had a prolonged stay in hospital to deal with 'some heavy stuff'. She never used the medical term or the words *drug-induced*, and Tandy never asked follow-up questions. Now Ilene nodded reassuringly. 'Things are right, Tandy. I'm doing all right.'

Tandy held her gaze. 'Okay. But if you ever need anything—'

'Thanks.'

'—babysitting, a movie night, Solnox? You call me.'

Ilene started the car and put it in reverse. 'I'll call you, yeah.'

'Wait a second.' Merrily, Tandy swung a hula hoop up before her. The hoop was vivid and yellow, yet the inky arc of its shadow fell on her face. 'A gift for Jack and Lonnie,' she said.

III

Hoop in hand, Ilene arrived at the front door of her house and pressed at it with the side of her fist. The door didn't budge, and she lowered her head. She always feared that one day she'd arrive home to find the wood splintered, the lock forced, her children gone. Beneath that fear, there lurked an undercurrent that she barely wished to acknowledge. If Jack and Lonnie disappeared, she'd cry a flood and scream until she lost her voice. When she could speak again, though, she'd feel so unburdened.

Ilene drowned this notion and unlocked the door and went into the house.

In the kitchen, the aroma of stale oil hung in the air, and she placed the hula hoop on the table. She leaned over a sink full of dirty dishes and gulped water from the tap. Then she positioned Jack's shirt in the middle of the hoop—a question and a reward lying in wait for her children. The blood on the garment caught her eye, and she hurried to fold the shirt so as to obscure the tears in the fabric.

She took off her shoes and headed to Jack and Lonnie's room. They were asleep in their bunk bed, Jack on the edge of the upper bunk, Lonnie sprawled on the lower one. Ilene sniffed at the dank. She squatted and woke Lonnie by kissing her on the cheek.

Lonnie's eyes opened wide, her toothy mouth less so. Her breath smelled of hunger, and Ilene combed aside the brown hair pasted to her daughter's brow. Then she realised that she'd done this in the wrong order. First she should ask Jack for the name of whoever hurt him. No, that was terrible as well. Surely a caring mother would first want to inspect the wounds on his abdomen.

Ilene touched her forefinger to her lips and stood. Jack remained asleep. He hadn't showered in days, and his body bore it worse than Lonnie's; Ilene would have to remind him to rinse his hair and wash his armpits. She lifted his pyjama top to expose his abdomen. The bandage was larger than she recalled. His unstitched cuts must have been long and shallow—less like talon wounds and more like furrows in farmland. Tenderness flowed to her fingertips, and she reached out and began to peel the bandage away.

'Jack,' Lonnie warned from the lower bunk.

Jack jolted awake and kicked at the sheets. He wrenched down his pyjama top, and Ilene held her hands up in surrender. She stepped away and looked at Lonnie, who'd propped herself up on her elbows.

'What are you doing?' Jack asked.

'Just wanted to check if your cuts are right.' Ilene's brow spasmed, and she put her nails against it. 'And to ask . . .'

Jack scowled and sat with his legs dangling over the side of his bed. He gripped the bunk's frame and bent forward to check on his sister. She met his gaze impassively, and Ilene was unable to fathom what passed between them.

A heaviness descended on her chest. She couldn't bring herself to push her children for a name yet; they didn't even trust her to inspect Jack's wounds. But at least Tandy had given her something positive to offer them this morning. 'And to ask,' she continued, 'if you want to play with the present I got you. It's in the kitchen.'

Immediately, Jack leaped from his bed and sprinted from the room. Lonnie chased after him. The weight remained on Ilene's chest, yet she followed her children to the kitchen.

Near the table, Jack and Lonnie stared in awe at the hula hoop. They both grabbed hold of it, and Jack pulled it towards him. 'Give it,' he said.

Lonnie yanked at it and let out a guttural screech. 'It's mine!'

They wrestled over the hoop, and for a fraction of a second they held it upright. Ilene saw their heads just above its circumference—Jack facing her, Lonnie looking away. Onto this visual, her mind projected an image: the reflection of the stars in the murk of the bore water tank.

'Stop fighting,' she said.

Lonnie loosened her grip on the hula hoop. Jack took it from her and stepped through it and positioned it around his waist. She pouted, and he stood still as if waiting for Ilene to order him to give the hoop to his sister. Ilene knew she probably should. But the distance between her and Jack was becoming more and more difficult to bridge.

'You're next,' she told Lonnie.

'Oh-kay.' Lonnie came and waited beside her mother. 'My turn next,' she said to Jack.

He exhaled with the calmness of an archer, and his face grew sombre. Then he sent the hoop spinning around him and waggled his hips. Instantly the hoop slithered down his legs and ended up on the floor. Lonnie looked to Ilene, and Jack repositioned the hoop around his waist. 'I can do it,' he said.

Ilene nodded, and he had another go. His technique was unchanged, though, and so too the outcome. He smiled sheepishly, and Ilene managed to smile back at him. 'Give Lonnie a go.'

He passed the hoop to Lonnie, but he didn't come and stand beside his mother. Rather, he leaned against a dining chair to observe; behind him, the shirt with its hint of a bloodstain resembled a shroud of some sort. Lonnie positioned the hoop at her waist. She paused and let out an archer's breath, same as her brother.

Then she wobbled, absurdly, head to toe, and the hoop clattered to the floor.

Jack grinned; Ilene couldn't help laughing. 'Try again.'

On her second go, Lonnie gyrated in a more controlled fashion—too controlled. Her movements were fitful and robotic, and the hoop caught at her knees and wormed down to her ankles. At least she was trying, Ilene thought.

'My turn again?' Jack asked.

Lonnie said nothing. She stepped out of the hoop and threw her arms around Ilene, from the front. Jack took over the hula hoop and made an attempt to keep it spinning. Ilene rubbed her daughter's back. She wouldn't ask her children for a name at all, she decided. She'd simply get them ready to be at school on time.

In the Datsun's side mirror, she saw the principal waiting for someone at the school gates. She looked over her shoulder. In the back seat, Lonnie unclipped the harness of her booster, and Jack shoved the kerbside door open with the holey sole of his sneaker.

'Bye, kids,' Ilene said.

'Bye, Mum.' Lonnie shuffled across the back seat. 'Thanks for the hula.'

She scrambled out onto the pavement next to Jack and adjusted her uniform. He slammed the car door, and he and Lonnie, backpacks bobbing, scurried past the parents and the other children to the school gates, where Ms Subraman greeted them. She asked them a question and gestured at Jack's hoodie. Then she scanned the cars, and her eyes locked on the orange Datsun.

'Fuck,' Ilene whispered.

Ms Subraman strode towards the car, and Ilene faced the road and sought to pull away from the kerb. But a green LandCruiser had double-parked beside her, and a tiny girl was making her laggard way out. In the kerbside mirror, Ilene watched as Ms Subraman was waylaid by another parent—an old man with a young son. Ilene flicked on her indicator and rocked, agitated, in her seat. Ms Subraman touched the old man's elbow and marched on.

Then the tiny child appeared in Ilene's kerbside mirror, and the green LandCruiser drove off. A red Mazda was on its tail, but she nosed the orange Datsun into the gap between the vehicles and got away scot-free.

The backs of her eyelids bright with the morning sun, she lay on her side in briefs and a white tee and no bra. Dust and dead skin had accumulated at the foot of her bed; she could smell herself, too, or at least the self she'd been overnight. The reek of sweat and stale oil reached her nostrils, along with Carl's faint scent. Her thighs ached with the memory of him, and she balled her fists between them. But she didn't open her eyes. She was determined to slip back into her routine, which usually involved a nap and a shower and a postprandial stint on the pokies.

Today, though, after she'd dropped Jack and Lonnie off at school, she'd detoured to her husband's latest workplace: a graffiti-encrusted warehouse that specialised in packaging and delivery. She'd parked the Datsun and spied a hard-hatted worker, driving a forklift, who might have been Carl. But when she'd waited to cross the road, a truck had sliced the light from her shoes. She'd recalled the darkness of the third-floor landing and Carl's body going slack in his apartment—and she'd gotten back into her car and driven away.

In her bedroom, her eyelids flickered open. Removing her fists from between her thighs, she rolled onto her back. She'd wanted to eyeball Carl when she told him about Jack's injury; she'd wanted to see his reaction when she asked what he'd said to Ms Subraman, but she was too afraid of what his broken face might convey.

She grabbed her phone from the bedside table and shut one eye and typed out a vague text message: *Hey, you say anything to Subraman?*

She thumbed the send button. There was a satisfying *swoosh*, and the message turned blue. Almost instantly, a grey box appeared beneath it with three dots line-dancing inside. Ilene writhed in bed to scratch her back. Dust and dead skin pasted itself to her feet, and her nipple chafed against her t-shirt. She covered it with her fingertips, and her heart thumped out of sync with the pulse in her hand.

When she focused on her phone again, its screen had dimmed. But she could see that the grey box had shrunk and now contained only a single punctuation mark: *?*

It wasn't much of a reply, yet Ilene figured it was enough. She plucked her t-shirt away from her nipple and returned one fist between her thighs. Her fist began to unclench. Then she thought better of it and undimmed her phone screen and navigated to the grainy photograph of her children. They sat in the classroom with their heads bowed and their faces partly obscured by shadow. It really was a good photo, she decided.

By the afternoon, she was back in the swing of her routine. She sat in the perennial golden hour of the Casus Hill Workers' Club and let Horseshoe Saloon's festive ragtime melody wash over her. On the poker machine's screen, the digital reels had come to a standstill, and a flashing line connected four grinning horses. This meant Ilene had won again. Her stomach rumbled, and she glanced from her empty schooner to her Casio watch. It was almost time to pick up Jack and Lonnie from school, and she was ahead for the day: she had twenty dollars and sixty cents' credit remaining. To stay ahead, all she had to do was leave to fetch her children on time.

She still had minutes and credit to spare, though, and she punched the backlit button on the console. Horseshoe Saloon strummed a quiet digital mandolin and shammed the ticking over of reels. While the reels spun, Ilene thought about Jack and Lonnie playing with the hula hoop. Her son had grinned, and her daughter had hugged her without reservation. That was what mattered, she told herself.

On the poker machine's screen, the reels revealed cowboys and gold bars and horseshoes. Yet no items matched, and Ilene's recollection turned to her children wrestling over the hoop, its circumference cutting across their throats. Quickly, she played another spin and shepherded her mind back into Carl's apartment. She could almost feel his skin against hers, and with her middle finger, she caressed a tiny laceration on her lip.

But this only made her wince, and when her machine fell silent, she played her final spin. The reels rotated. The mandolin jangled. Then she heard the celebratory tune of Jewels of the Orient—the machine she'd played on the other day—and all at once, she pictured herself in the dusty field. Ahead of her, Jack and Lonnie held hands; she was holding Carl's hand. In her other hand was a shovel, and even in her memory, she hated the splintered feel of its handle.

In front of Horseshoe Saloon, she shivered and exhaled. She was back down to twenty dollars' credit. If she left now, she could break even and just about be on time for school pick-up. Instinctively, though, her hand drifted like a crane machine's claw towards the backlit button.

Then she pictured Ms Subraman waiting outside the classroom, waiting at the school gates—waiting for Ilene to screw up—and to her own relief, she shimmied her hand away from the button and set the machine to cash her out. She got to her feet and paused for the machine to print her a ticket.

'Lucky cunt,' she heard a woman sneer.

Ilene spun around and caught sight of the speaker, who occupied the low-backed stool in front of Jewels of the Orient. It was the hunched woman. Her outline shimmered and pulsed, and around her the light curled through the air like smoke. Ilene had no glimpse of her face or mouth, yet she could not look away. All she could see was the woman's strange glister and, from an angle, the white spiral of the bun on the back of her head.

'What'd you say?' Ilene asked.

'Oh, I was just remarking'—the woman pressed the backlit button on the console, and the reels on her screen ticked over—'that you know exactly how to get away with it.'

'What do you mean by that?' Ilene's stomach lurched, and her fingers went cold. She wondered what the woman knew—how she could know it. 'Are you . . .?' Ilene swallowed and took one step towards her. 'Are you following me?'

Jewels of the Orient blared a winning tune, and the light enveloping the woman buzzed and shook and changed chroma from white to grey and back again. Ilene took another step towards her. But the woman inclined her head, and Ilene's stride faltered. Unhurried, the woman turned to peer at Ilene. Her pallid face was wrinkled, and a skin tag dangled over her left eye. Her expression was vacant and her blinking slow and deliberate.

A mild tremor seemed to rock the gaming room's floor, and Ilene's legs felt weak. Her mouth opened, but she struggled to shape words. 'Just leave us alone,' she managed to say.

IV

On the sofa in her living room, Ilene concertinaed the last morsel of her dinner—a sandwich of Smith's chips and margarine—into her mouth. She chewed and watched a reporter on television sprint after a tradie while screaming questions about a burning barn. Both of Ilene's children were present and accounted for: Jack knelt at the coffee table by her feet, his mouth full of sandwich and eyes glued to the TV; Lonnie stood beside the table and tried to keep the hula hoop awhirl around her. Her latest attempt was all jerky hips and adorable failure, and the hoop dropped to her feet.

Ilene had been on time to pick her children up from school. She'd avoided Ms Subraman altogether. Yet after the incident at the workers' club, she wondered whether she remained ahead for the day. She gulped, and unchewed chips scratched at her throat. Then she pictured the spiral bun on the back of the woman's head, the light curling around her.

Six months after Carl had lost his job, she'd comforted him while he sweated and shivered during a blazing electrical storm. Afterwards, he'd said the storm told him that to save the children, he and Ilene had to give them to the light. In reply she'd whispered, *I think I heard it too.* But as she replayed this memory, what she could hear was the crunch of her shovel against flesh and bone.

Lucky cunt, the woman had sneered.

Current affairs music from the TV caromed around the room, and the hoop clattered to the floor at Lonnie's feet. Goosebumps spread along Ilene's arms. She watched her daughter raise the hoop around her waist, as if it were a skirt she'd dragged through the mud. At the coffee table, Jack swept up a smear of margarine from the wood and licked it off his finger. Ilene's gaze flitted from her daughter to the wispy hairs on her son's nape.

She leaned forward and ran her nails through them, her touch as tender as when she'd tried to peel away his bandages.

Jack straightened. He tensed as if he were about to jerk out of her reach. Then his shoulders relaxed. He finished his sandwich while she caressed the scruff of his neck. She wove her fingers through his hair as if she were conducting a slow-motion orchestra. Her goosebumps flattened out, and any thought of the hunched woman from the gaming room faded.

Beside the coffee table, Lonnie giggled. She kept the hoop spinning for about ten seconds, and Ilene nodded at her daughter. She looked back to the TV and smiled. A sob escaped her mouth, and her vision blurred. She kissed Jack's filthy crown and stood and carried three dirty plates to the sink in the kitchen.

Before her sight could clear, she grabbed the bloodied shirt and tossed it into the overflowing bin. She corralled the rest of the rubbish—the tomato sauce bottle, the empty chip packet—into the bin bag. Then she lugged that out the back door and through the long grass and into the sumptuous moonlight.

A minute into the witching hour, Ilene walked through the capacious storeroom and along an aisle flanked by metal shelves and towards the staffroom in the back corner. It was located opposite the manager's office, in which a light burned. This was unusual: Stefan's shift ended before hers began, and the only reason he ever stayed late was to smoke out in the car park. But Ilene ignored the vague flutter of her gut. She clung to her handbag and the soothing recollection of caressing the scruff of Jack's neck.

Averting her gaze from the manager's office, she entered the staffroom. Against one wall was a rudimentary kitchenette; on the counter, a plastic kettle cooled next to a microwave with its door ajar. She walked past a shivering bar fridge and a table and arrived at the pigeonholes at the rear of the room.

Tandy's bag occupied a pigeonhole in the middle, and with the merest glimmer of intention, Ilene eyed the wallet that poked out of it. She arched her back. There'd be more forgiving opportunities, she told herself. Then she yawned and slipped her handbag off her shoulder. She'd slept between taking out the bin and experiencing the low-level panic of leaving her children in the empty house. Still, she'd need to grab an iced coffee to get herself through the night.

Behind her, a door clanged shut, and she was instantly wide awake. She spun around. Stefan stood at the staffroom's entrance with the strap of his messenger bag digging into his torso; on one hand he balanced a new red polo shirt, wrapped in plastic, as if it were a silver platter. A flush crept up Ilene's chest. The staffroom door was open, though; the door he'd slammed belonged to the microwave.

'Sorry.' Stefan rubbed the back of his neck. 'I didn't mean to startle you.'

Ilene forced herself to smile. 'You didn't, Stefan. Are you on your way out?'

'Uh-huh. Shift's over.'

'Cool. I guess I'll see you later?'

She turned away and arranged her bag in the pigeonhole beside Tandy's. Then she pretended to rummage through it. For a moment, she expected to find the roll of dollar coins she'd stolen. But it remained somewhere in the front passenger footwell of the Datsun, along with the carton of iced coffee and the ziplock bag.

'That the same shirt you were wearing yesterday?' Stefan asked. The flutter of her gut became more definite, and she pinched her handbag closed. Again, she turned to meet his gaze.

He grinned sheepishly. 'Smells like the same shirt, Ilene.'

'Does it?' She sniffed the collar; she'd meant to wash the shirt, meant to get her children to shower, but she hadn't gotten around to either job. What she had done was break even on the pokies and told the hunched woman to leave them alone. She'd received a carefree hug from Lonnie and caressed Jack's wispy hair. 'I washed it,' she said.

Stefan raised his eyebrows. He tossed the new polo onto the table, where it landed with a slap. 'Change into this, please.'

Ilene swallowed, and the flush climbed from her chest to her neck. She made no move to collect the polo, and Stefan didn't retreat. Neither did he advance. He slipped his thumb beneath the strap of his messenger bag and peered at her with an expression of polite expectation.

'Right now?' she asked.

He started at the sound of her voice. 'Oh, of course. Sorry, Ilene, I'll, uh, I'll give you some privacy.'

Stefan didn't leave, though; he swivelled and folded his arms. The saliva Ilene had swallowed lodged in her throat, and she stepped towards the table. Beyond Stefan, the entrance to the manager's office was out of sight, yet she could tell that it'd gone dark.

'You still with Carl?' Stefan asked, with his back to her. 'Or did you guys finally call it quits?'

'We're still together.'

Ilene freed the new polo of its wrapping and laid it on the table. The plastic crinkled, and she saw Stefan's ears twitch. His lobes had grown as red as the polo before her. 'It must be more of a casual thing now,' he said, 'since he doesn't live with you and all?'

'I guess.'

She paused to make sure Stefan wasn't about to turn around. Then she took off her faded old polo and abandoned it on the table. She clenched her abdomen—now she was down to her bra. Its twisted straps dug into her skin, and some of the underwire was jagged and exposed.

'What are you up to on Friday night?' Stefan asked.

'The usual.' Ilene snatched up the new polo. She glanced from Stefan's earlobes to the wrinkles that ran across her belly. Her arms found the polo's sleeves, and she made a swimming motion to pull the shirt over her head. 'Dinner with the kids, sleep, work.'

'Oh, I've got the day off. I thought maybe we could, uh . . .'

The shirt snagged on the underwire of her bra, and he began to turn towards her. Her heartbeat scurried like a child's footsteps, and the flush was in her cheeks. Her hands grew clumsy. But she managed to yank the fabric free of the underwire before Stefan's eyes fell on her.

He looked her up and down. 'Name tag and you're perfect.' He sauntered towards her, and she tucked in her new shirt. Close by, he picked up her old one from the table and removed her name tag from it. Then he dropped the faded shirt onto the floor and held the tag up before him. 'May I?' he asked formally.

Every pore in Ilene's skin was leaking. She bowed her head, and for a reason she couldn't fathom, she nodded. She didn't look Stefan in the eye. His squarish fingers approached her chest with the name tag. They pinched her new shirt and lifted it gently away from her bra. Then they forced the pin through the fabric and closed the clasp.

The fingers retreated, and Ilene lifted her chin. Stefan returned to the staffroom's entrance, where he loitered once more as if attempting to remember what he wanted to say. He gave half a shrug. 'You look nice,' he said. 'I might see you at work tomorrow.'

'Yeah,' Ilene replied. 'Tomorrow.'

He turned on his heel and left for the night, and she picked up her old polo from the staffroom floor.

By the tiny hours of the morning, Ilene's interaction with Stefan seemed almost like a story she'd overheard about someone else. Yet the vivid red of her new polo caught her eye under the supermarket lights. She glanced at the CCTV camera and unclipped her name tag and put it in her pocket. Then she leaned against her register.

At the register furthest from hers, Tandy chatted with Marco. They clasped hands loosely; they seemed to be making promises again, and Ilene yawned. Carl had held her hand like that when he'd proposed to her. They had been walking down an alley, and his tongue was coated with McDonald's soft serve. She'd laughed at the casualness of the proposal. He'd laughed too, and they'd shared a kiss—her answer was never in doubt.

Tandy cupped her free hand around her mouth. 'Almost home time, Ilene.'

Ilene nodded, and a young man emerged from an aisle with a loaf of bread under his arm and a bottle of methylated spirits in hand. He paused before the registers as if unable to decide which to choose: Tandy's, which was nearest the exit, or Ilene's, which was next to the cigarette counter.

Marco retreated from Tandy, and she stood to attention. But Ilene inclined her head to beckon the young man to her. The gesture undid his paralysis. He walked over to her register and dumped his bread-and-spirits dyad onto the conveyor belt.

'Good morning,' he slurred.

Ilene faked a grin. 'Yeah, morning is what it is.' The conveyor belt buzzed and brought his two items to her, and she scanned them. 'Plastic bag?'

'Why not, eh?' He grinned back at her as if they were sharing a private joke. 'And a pack of Rothmans Blue.'

Ilene dumped the bread and spirits into a plastic bag. 'What size?'

'Gimme Thirties. Please.'

She sidled past him and sniffed the air and caught no whiff of alcohol. Behind the cigarette counter, she unlocked the Rothmans compartment and retrieved a plain packet. The young man swayed on his feet: if she overcharged him by twenty, she doubted he'd realise.

She returned to her register and scanned the cigarettes. Marco wandered alongside the closed roller doors to monitor the transaction from a distance. But his gaze was firm on the young man and slack on Ilene. She felt herself sweating, layering salt on salt, and sensed that she was shining again under the supermarket's glare. 'Paying cash?'

'You betcha.' The young man squinted. 'What's the damage?'

Ilene clocked the total on her screen: $65.90. In her mind, she rehearsed saying, 'Eighty-five ninety,' so she wouldn't trip over the words. She licked her lips and parted them to speak.

Before anything came out, the young man's knees buckled slightly. He rebalanced himself and readied his fat canvas wallet. Ilene's eye twitched, and she observed him more keenly. His top was a rugby league jersey from the nineties, and his blue jeans seemed a couple of sizes too large. This made her picture Jack in his grey hoodie, Lonnie in her yellow t-shirt.

'How much?' the young man asked, as if she'd told him and he hadn't listened.

'Eighty.' She hesitated and read the total on her screen. 'Sixty-five-ninety.'

He removed a wad of hundreds from his wallet. 'Bargain,' he said.

When he'd paid and shambled off, Ilene stared at the display of Smith's chips that were on sale at the front of a distant aisle. The squeak of Marco's sneakers reached her ears as he made his way back to Tandy. Ilene sighed; her shift was almost over.

In her living room, she reached into her pocket and took out her name tag and held it with *Ilene* facing up. Her old polo mimicked lava erupting from her handbag on the sofa. The coffee table's edge was smeared with margarine from her children's hands. She eyed the spot where Lonnie had played with the hula hoop and tried to reconnect with the warmth of the domestic moment. But she remembered Stefan's fingers poking the name tag through her shirt, and a less pleasant warmth filled her body. She tossed the name tag into her bag and shed herself of her new polo. Then she yawned a distracted path past the children's room and along the hallway.

Morning light filled her bedroom, and her white tee lay at the foot of her unmade bed. She grabbed it and dragged it on and strode back to the children's room to wake them.

She entered their room and came to a sudden halt. The lower bunk was empty, and on Lonnie's bed the duvet was curled like a wave captured in a photograph. Ilene let its implications crash over her. Her knees buckled slightly, and she experienced an odd sense that she and the wasted young man in the supermarket were one. She ran to the bunk bed and uncovered a boyish lump under Jack's duvet. But it wasn't him. It was his pillow, marbled with drool.

Ilene's ears hummed, and she hurried back to the hallway. 'Lonnie,' she called. 'Jack?'

Over the hum, a morning vehicle groaned on its way to work. The house itself stayed quiet. She jogged to the bathroom, where the three toothbrushes remained on the sink. A flare of mould beneath the leaking showerhead caught her eye, and she rushed to the living room.

'Jack!' she yelled. 'Lonnie!'

The TV wasn't on, and the margarine smears on the coffee table now struck her as sinister. She imagined her children trying to hold on while someone or something spirited them away. The rents in Jack's shirt bled onto the walls of her mind, and the white noise in her ears grew louder. She careened into the kitchen and stumbled over a chair leg. The utensil drawer hung open, and a long serrated knife rested on the counter.

She shut the drawer and stepped towards the knife. Clear droplets glistened on its blade, along with strange dust that reminded her of the ziplock bag. She gripped the knife's handle but didn't raise her knuckles from the counter; they tapped the blade against the scuffed laminate. Jack and Lonnie couldn't be gone, she reasoned. The front door had been intact, and she hadn't spied a broken window. But why was the knife here?

Unbidden, her mind conjured a vision of Carl—smiling, nose reset, living at home again. The white noise in her ears took on the quality of a quiet voice, and she brought the heel of her free hand to her brow.

Then she realised the quiet voice belonged to Lonnie. She turned towards the electric coils of the stove and listened. Nothing further came. But she lurched after her gut into the laundry and out the back door. In the ankle-high grass, she clutched her stomach and doubled over: her children were out here. Jack and Lonnie sat a short distance away, in the longer grass of the yard, and concentrated on something between them.

Lonnie pointed at it. 'This one,' she said.

'You reckon?' Jack asked.

They didn't seem to notice Ilene, who took a step towards them before she peered at the knife that dangled from her hand. She remembered the heft of the shovel she'd borne on that night. Then she gasped and, with a flick of her wrist, tossed the knife aside. Its blade glimmered in the dew, but it was mostly obscured by grass.

Disarmed, Ilene headed towards Jack and Lonnie. 'What are you two doing out here?'

She kept her tone light. But Lonnie's head darted up, and Jack ignored the interruption altogether. Ilene's footsteps crunched over the grass. She drew near to her children and saw that the object between them was the yellow hula hoop—or it used to be. They'd sliced it into several irregular pieces and arranged these into a haphazard helical shape on the flattened grass between them. Before Ilene could make sense of the shape—if there was any sense to be made—Lonnie scrambled it with her foot.

Ilene stood over her children and looked at the remnants of the hoop. 'Why'd you do that?'

Lonnie shrugged. 'Fun.'

Ilene glanced from her son to her daughter and back again. 'Doesn't look like fun,' she said. 'Looks like you broke your toy.'

'Good,' Jack replied.

His expression was the same as when he and Lonnie had held eye contact in their bedroom, and Ilene blinked. 'I thought you liked it?'

'Nope,' Jack said.

Lonnie rose and brushed dirt from her knees. She began to collect the pieces of hula hoop as if they were kindling. Some of the pieces appeared to be sharp. Jack joined her, and Ilene stared at the sheafs of yellow cradled in their arms. The previous day, she thought she'd made progress with the hoop. Now her children carried its ruins past the knife in the grass and to the rear of the house.

'Jack,' she called out. 'Hair and pits before school, all right?'

She had no idea what else to say.

V

She hadn't said much to Jack and Lonnie by the time she pulled the car over in a queue near the school gates. She was dropping them off on time, but it didn't matter: there was no avoiding Ms Subraman. The principal, wearing a black-and-white tunic, strode through the drop-off crowd on the pavement and halted beside the Datsun. She opened the rear passenger door and waited on the kerb with her head beyond Ilene's sight.

In the back of the car, Jack unclipped his seatbelt. He got out, and Lonnie hauled her backpack after him onto the kerb. Neither offered Ilene a farewell, and she watched them pause beside Ms Subraman. The low babel of children and parents made its way into the car.

'Morning, children,' the principal said.

'Good morning, Miss Subraman,' Lonnie carolled.

Ms Subraman crouched and helped Lonnie get her backpack on. 'Morning, Jack,' she said.

He peered away from her, into the car, with his mouth set hard and his eyes narrowed. But he avoided looking at Ilene, who caught the faintest twitch of Ms Subraman's nose. Her ears started to hum again, yet she said nothing.

'Morning,' Jack muttered.

Ms Subraman patted a strap of Lonnie's backpack, near the girl's bony chest, and smiled without showing her teeth. 'Into school with you two then,' she said. Jack and Lonnie strolled away, and Ms Subraman's eyes raked over the crumbed carpet of the Datsun. 'Ilene?' she said.

She gestured for Ilene to get out and eased the rear passenger door shut. Ilene gripped the parking brake. Then she unbuckled her seatbelt and got out of the car and slammed her door. 'I'm on time,' she called over the Datsun's sunburned roof. 'Been on time the last couple of days.'

Ms Subraman nodded, and Ilene joined her on the pavement outside the school. Children in uniforms and their uniform parents swarmed about; Jack and Lonnie passed an on-duty teacher and through the school gates. Ilene watched them until Lonnie's yellow t-shirt and Jack's grey hoodie—under which he wore nothing but a bandage—disappeared behind the main building.

'Did Jack tell you who injured him?' Ms Subraman asked.

'Nope.' Ilene licked her teeth. 'Reckon he'll tell you?'

Ms Subraman shook her head. 'But he seems fine at home? After a traumatic incident such as that?'

'He's a tough kid.' Ilene thought of her children collecting shards of hoop from the grass and conveying them inside. On that night a year earlier, she'd cradle-carried sleeping Lonnie out of the house and loaded her into the car while Carl coaxed Jack to climb in the other side.

Ilene glanced over her shoulder at the window of the orange Datsun, and a bolus of truth reached the back of her throat. 'I mean, he—'

She was interrupted by a hubbub that arose from the school gates, where the on-duty teacher tapped at his phone; next to him, a group of year-six boys yelled and jostled one another.

'Mr Jute?' Ms Subraman called out. She redirected the teacher's attention with a sweep of her finger. He pocketed his phone and clapped amiably at the boys and ushered them onto the school grounds. Ms Subraman half-smiled at Ilene as if inviting her to continue speaking. But the moment had passed, and the principal cleared her throat. 'Did you change his bandages?'

'Haven't had a chance.'

'The nurse will change them today—although you might need to redo them, after you give him a bath this evening.'

Ilene pinched the skin of her neck. She rubbed the salt-on-salt between her thumb and forefinger and eyed a sweatless mother strolling past. 'I will,' she said.

'He can't keep wearing that hoodie to school. You know that.' Ms Subraman sought out her gaze. 'You'll have to buy him a new uniform.'

'Right.'

'When you're able,' Ms Subraman added. 'And, Ilene, please do consider after-school care if—'

'I'm on time,' Ilene interjected. She backed away to the driver's side of the Datsun. 'I'll just keep being on time.'

Ms Subraman twisted her mouth into that commiserative angle. 'There's zero shame,' she said haltingly.

Ilene grimaced and opened the driver's door. 'You sure about that?'

She ducked into the car and took a deep breath. Ms Subraman walked away. Ilene grabbed her phone and texted Carl to say she missed him. Then she drove home to bring the knife in from the dew.

The rest of the day passed without incident, and with midnight on her Casio, she walked through the supermarket's twenty-four-hour entrance and raised her hand to greet Tandy. But Tandy wasn't operating her usual register. In her place, a gaunt older woman scanned and bagged a box of Stevie-brand menstrual pads. She pursed her fuchsia lips at Ilene in some form of greeting—and Ilene, who'd met the woman once or twice before, lowered her hand and didn't break stride. Ahead of her, Marco pushed himself off the roller door against which he'd been leaning. He folded his arms and scuffed the soles of his sneakers.

'Tandy off sick?' Ilene asked.

He shook his head as she passed. 'Don't say anything,' he murmured, mostly to his shoes.

'What?'

Ilene cast a bemused glance over her shoulder. Marco strode out to the car park, and she continued into the supermarket on her way to the staffroom. The checkouts she passed were cordoned off and unmanned; a plastic divider spanned the breadth of the conveyor belt of Ilene's usual register.

Behind the tobacco counter, Stefan finished paying for his cigarettes and emerged to stand before her. His earlobes had a pinkish tinge, and the strap of his messenger bag, tight across his torso, betrayed his heightened breathing rate. He flipped a packet of cigarettes over, and over again, and knocked it upright against his palm as if straightening a deck of cards.

Ilene adjusted her bag on her shoulder. Belatedly, she realised that she was wearing her old polo. 'What's going on, Stefan?'

'Not here,' he replied. 'C'mon.'

He unlocked one of the roller doors and let it rattle towards the ceiling. Then he stood aside and invited her to set foot in the shut-up shopping plaza. She made grave eye contact with him and tried to ponder the meaning of Marco's murmured imperative. But a memory of Stefan's squarish fingers pinching her new shirt blocked her train of thought.

She stepped from the supermarket into the shopping plaza and heard the roller door crash to the ground. Stefan overtook her, and the surrounding quiet made her heartbeat echo through her head. The escalators were at rest, the clothes stores and electronics shops shuttered. The food stalls were dark, and most had emptied out their display cabinets; a sushi stall hadn't, or hadn't entirely, and its splayed prawns on rice resembled children's toys.

With the roller door at her back, Ilene stayed put. A short distance away, Stefan passed a potted fern and took two chairs off a table outside a closed cafe. He positioned the chairs either end of the table and dumped his messenger bag onto the flecked white floor. Then he frowned at Ilene. 'Back to your old shirt, eh?'

She wiped her palm on her sleeve. 'I had to put the new one in the wash.'

'Uh-huh, I see.' Stefan ripped the cellophane from his cigarette packet. 'Did you wash this one?'

''Course I did.' Ilene inhaled through her nose. She couldn't smell herself anymore, but she did wonder why she'd worn her old unwashed polo rather than her new unwashed polo.

Stefan flicked the cellophane from his packet and let it feather its way onto the table. 'I'm guessing you heard about Tandy? Take a seat, please, Ilene.'

He spoke it all as a single nervy sentence and lowered himself into a chair. His back was to the cafe, which was obscured by a metal grille. Ilene glanced at the roller door behind her; beyond its glaucous horizontal panels, the aisles of the supermarket swam like lanes of a pool. Her gut fluttered, but she walked towards Stefan. 'What about Tandy?' She sat opposite him and placed her bag in her lap. 'Is she okay?'

'Oh, I—I thought you would've heard. I had to send her home.' His eyebrows grew serious. 'Pending.'

'Pending what?'

'It's a weird business, really.' Stefan rested his forearms on the table and held the naked cigarette packet in both hands. He stared at it. 'So this lady rings me from Melbourne, okay? And she says one of our cashiers stole twenty dollars off her card.' His eyes darted up. 'How often do you fail to wear your name tag, Ilene?'

Under his gaze, she felt shimmery and on edge—and some combination of perspiration and pulse caused her hair tie to slip a fraction down her ponytail. She resisted the urge to fix it. 'I always wear my name tag. I've got it in my bag.'

'Hm.' Stefan returned his gaze to his cigarette packet, which he thumbed open. 'Anyway, with this Melbourne lady, I do my thing and trace the, uh, the issue to Tandy's register.'

'How do you know the lady didn't get twenty dollars cash out?' Ilene blurted.

'True.' Stefan took out a cigarette from the packet and scrutinised it. His hand trembled. 'I went to find the spot on the DVR to check for myself.' His voice trembled as well. 'The footage was gone.'

Ilene winced, very slightly, and covered up by thumbing her septum. 'How could it be gone?'

'It's an old system.' Stefan abandoned the packet on the table with the cellophane. Shakily, he put the cigarette in his mouth and lit it and took a drag. 'I assumed Marco erased the footage to protect his girlfriend. Then Tandy comes in, pays the money back, admits everything—long as we don't get police involved.'

He got to his feet and stepped off to the side; the chair he'd vacated was adorned with a flare of fresh damp that reminded Ilene of the mould beneath the showerhead. She could sense Stefan looking down at her, but she kept her eyes on the empty chair and scrambled to work out what Tandy and Marco wanted her to do or say.

'I called the Melbourne lady again,' Stefan continued, 'and I told her there'd been a tech error. Apologised, refunded the money et cetera, et cetera.' He wandered behind Ilene, and she listened to him taking another drag on his cigarette. 'Here's the weirdest thing: she described the cashier to me.'

Ilene's heart hammered against her rib cage. The flutter in her gut felt as if she'd swallowed a hummingbird. Bile rose to her throat, but she kept her mouth shut.

Stefan's voice floated to her: 'Dirty brunette ponytail. Pretty. White.' His footsteps drew closer. 'It was you, Ilene,' he said.

'We both know it.' The heat of his torso arrived at her back. 'Why does everyone want to help you? Why do *I* want to help you?' He rested his hands on her shoulders, and smoke curled around her face from the cigarette between his fingers. 'Do you deserve help?'

The question jounced around her skull, yet it failed to animate her body. On that night in the dusty field, the stars had reflected off the murk in the bore water tank. But they must have been in her children's eyes as well: by choice or otherwise, Jack and Lonnie had been staring at the sky.

Stefan's cigarette remained at her shoulder, while the fingers of his other hand crept beyond her clavicles. She knew she should take a deep breath. But she felt as if she couldn't inhale.

Across from her, the flare of damp on the chair receded. Then her mind summoned the whip-crack of Carl's face breaking. She almost experienced his pain herself, yet she'd been on the other side of the equation. The memory jolted her, sent adrenaline hurtling through her veins. 'Get off me!' She shrugged herself free of Stefan's hands and jerked to her feet. 'Get *off* me!'

Her voice was an octave higher than usual; her handbag and chair fell to the floor. She twisted around to face Stefan, who raised his palms in surrender. Only the fallen chair separated him from Ilene. The potted fern was at his back, the splayed prawns on rice further away. 'I'm just saying,' he stammered. 'You should talk to me, Ilene. I'm a good listener, and I really do want to help you.'

Patches of sweat stained his armpits, and his earlobes became the colour of the blood on Jack's shirt. His eyes flitted about in their sockets and settled on Ilene's. Breathing hard, she glared at him. She blinked back tears and gritted her teeth. 'I don't need your help,' she said.

With an exaggerated sweep of her arm, she scooped up her handbag and strode back towards the roller door.

In the morning, in her children's room, she drew an unsteady breath. Lonnie slept on the lower bunk with the dirty heel of her foot elevated against the wall. On the upper bunk, Jack lay on his side; a string of drool stitched his mouth to his pillow, and he rested his cheek on his fist. Ilene squinted. The sight of her children in repose eased her torment, but she had to wake them for school.

Then her eye was troubled by a speck of sun that passed through a gap in the venetian blind. On the floor beneath the blind, the grey hoodie and yellow t-shirt lay in crumpled heaps, and between these ghostly items of clothing, the hula hoop shards were stacked in a tight pile.

The smell of dank hit her nostrils, and she decided to open the window. Quietly, she twirled the wand for the blind. The plastic slats tilted and allowed the morning into the room. Jack let out a groan; Lonnie didn't stir. At Ilene's feet, the pile of hula hoop shards sparkled in the striated light as if it were a campfire. She stuck her hand through the slats and unlocked the window and pulled it open.

Outside, she saw the wooden fence and painted bricks of the house next door. She leaned forward to glimpse the wilted dreamcatcher that hung on her neighbour's porch and the vine that curled around the wooden pillar there. She only had an oblique view of a porch-framed section of the street, but she was almost certain that she descried, on the pavement in the distance, the woman with the volute bun.

The woman had her back to Ilene and stood at the kerb as if she were waiting to cross the road. The street seemed devoid of cars, though, and the woman made no attempt to go anywhere. She swayed and gave off a gentle glow like the flame of a votive candle. Ilene's eyes burned. She felt as if she couldn't look away, couldn't even blink.

The morning sun made the woman appear alien and attenuated. Then the sunlight enveloped her, and Ilene blinked.

Jack stirred, and she glanced at him with bleary eyes. He sat up in bed and wiped his mouth with his hand. She turned back to the window. But her neighbour's porch now framed only the deserted suburban street. The woman was gone.

It was not yet midday when, on her way to the Casus Hill Workers' Club, Ilene pulled over on a narrow avenue and stumbled out of the orange Datsun. The cladded duplex before her, of which Tandy occupied half, was portly and dwarfed by the double-storey homes either side of it. Ilene's sneakers sank into the boggy grass of the nature strip. She hadn't slept or showered after dropping her children off at school, and she still wore her old polo. What she yearned for was a moment to collect herself. But Tandy, barefoot, in flannel pyjamas, had already emerged onto her porch.

'Your car's too *loud*,' she called out. The Singapore in her accent always seemed more pronounced when she raised her voice. 'I heard you coming a mile away.'

Above the roof of the subdivided house, thready streaks of grey darkened the blue. Ilene approached the duplex along a paved path and stopped at the bottom of three steps. At the top of the steps, Tandy stood beside the single-brick wall that cleft the porch and the property in two.

'Did you get fired?' Ilene asked.

Tandy chuckled grimly. 'Ilene, how could I not get fired?'

'Sorry.' Ilene scratched her neck and almost felt the heft of Stefan's hands on her shoulders. 'You all right?' she asked.

Tandy fiddled with a button on her pyjama top. 'You know.'

Behind her, the duplex's tiny interior was visible through the doorway. Ilene watched Marco, in a singlet and trackpants, wander off between a glass dining table and a shabby couch. He shot her a sidelong glance and in an instant was out of sight.

Ilene swallowed. 'Tell Marco I'm sorry, too.'

'Aargh.' Tandy swatted the air, although the gesture lacked the insouciance that would've made it convincing. 'Don't worry about him. He hated that job—the pay was bad, they were stiffing him on super. He would've quit ages ago if we weren't a thing.'

'And what about you?'

'I've got some savings and stuff. I'll be okay.'

Ilene placed the toe of her shoe on the bottom step and shifted her weight onto it. Her gaze settled on the creases that ran across her sneaker, which were much like the wrinkles on her belly. 'How long have you been covering for me?' she murmured.

Tandy shifted her stance, or at least, Ilene heard a rush of flannel. 'Two months, maybe.'

'Why?'

'What do you mean?'

Ilene tried to reply, but she was starting to lose control of the muscles of her mouth. The contrast between the tangerine of the paving and the black of her shoe diminished. She looked up at Tandy, who now leaned against the dividing wall in imitation of her boyfriend against the roller door. 'Why did you help me?' Ilene asked.

Tandy folded her arms. 'I saw you steal money from the till one time. And I knew, I *knew*, you were going to get caught.' Her face tensed, and she blushed. 'Your plan was stupid, Ilene. Too risky. But'—she sighed, and her voice assumed a gentler tone—'with Carl's sickness, I thought you must need the money. For your kids.'

Ilene returned her gaze to the creases in her shoe. She pictured Jack and Lonnie at school, the former in his grey hoodie from lost and found, the latter in her threadbare yellow t-shirt. 'I did, but that's not what I spent it on.'

'What did you spend it on?' Tandy asked.

'I lost it.' Ilene's knees almost gave out, and she put all her energy into forcing her mouth to do as she commanded. 'I lost it on the pokies,' she said. 'I'm on my way there right now.'

A motorcycle sped along the street and filled the air with its roar and whine. Ilene's lip quivered almost uncontrollably. 'You regret it now?' she asked. 'Helping me?'

In the silence that followed, pins and needles spread over her skin. She took a shallow breath and raised her imploring eyes to meet Tandy's.

'I'm a useless person, Tandy. I don't deserve help.'

Tandy peered in the direction of the orange Datsun. Her cheeks retained a trace of the blush that'd shaded them when she'd scolded Ilene. She unfolded her arms and descended the steps. On the path, she stopped and faced Ilene. She raised her arm, and Ilene braced for a slap. Then Tandy rested a graceful hand on her shoulder. 'Anyone can have a bad year,' she said.

Ilene dropped her chin. Her lips would not stop quivering. 'But I almost did something terrible.'

'Almost?' Tandy snorted. 'Ilene, I helped you because you're my friend. I knew what it would cost—Marco knew what it would cost. We can afford it for now, okay?' She brought her forehead towards Ilene's. 'Okay?'

Ilene let out a single sob. 'Okay.'

Abruptly, Tandy pulled her in for an embrace; Ilene stumbled and settled into the hug. Tears ran down her cheeks, and she sniffled. The scent of Tandy's hair reminded Ilene of Lonnie's, and she drank it in. For a while, she rested her jaw on the soft flesh that curved Tandy's shoulder into her neck.

'You should have a shower, Tandy,' she said.

'Like you can talk.' Tandy grinned and half-shoved Ilene free from the embrace. 'You should stop stealing from the register, Ilene. And invite me and Marco round for dinner sometime.'

"Course.' Ilene wiped her tears away. Her phone vibrated in her pocket, and she took it out and looked at it. The number on the screen belonged to the school. 'I should take this,' she said.

She strode back along the paved path with the vibrating phone in her hand.

'Hey,' Tandy called out. 'Did Jack and Lonnie like the hula hoop?'

Ilene smiled over her shoulder. 'They loved it.'

Then she answered her phone and heard the guttural omen of Ms Subraman clearing her throat.

VI

Ilene carried the evidence bag—a clear sandwich bag from the school canteen—over to the open window. The breeze whiffled the flyscreen and perfumed the principal's office with the scent of pine. In the courtyard outside, the trunks of two evergreens loomed while their fallen needles decayed on the grass. She plucked anxiously at a loose flap of beige paint on the windowsill; the coat beneath was prison grey, and she wondered whether it was leaded. The notion made her queasy, or perhaps she was already queasy: behind her imposing desk, Ms Subraman had just asked Ilene to identify 'the weapon'.

'Jack and Lonnie refuse to tell us anything,' the principal prompted.

Her swivel chair creaked, and Ilene peered down. The evidence bag contained a hollow shard of the hula hoop Jack and Lonnie had knifed into pieces. Where the plastic tube had been eroded, it had the texture of brittle bone, and a drop of blood had leached into its razor-sharp tip. In spite of this, the object retained its childish aspect. It resembled a banana-shaped novelty pen more than it did a weapon.

'It's part of a hoop,' Ilene muttered.

'I'm sorry?'

'It's part of a hula hoop,' she said, more loudly. 'I came home from work yesterday morning, and they'd chopped it into bits, but I had no idea.'

She shook her head at Ms Subraman, who creased her brow and lowered her gaze. The way Ilene pictured the assault that'd been described to her, Lonnie sprinted up to the boy—the one who'd cut Jack's abdomen—and tackled him to the asphalt. Jack helped pin the boy down and readied the yellow shard. The boy screamed and wriggled free, maybe swung his fist, and Lonnie tore a chunk out of his cheek with her teeth. The boy screamed more desperately, and Jack sliced his abdomen in the same spot he himself had been cut, all before Mr Jute got off his phone to rush over and break things up.

Ilene forced herself to blink. Her eyes stung from the tears she'd shed with Tandy, and she narrowed them at the wall that separated the office from the corridor in which Jack and Lonnie waited. 'What're you gonna do with them?' she asked.

'Do with them?'

'Yeah.' Ilene conveyed the evidence bag back across the office and positioned herself between two visitor's chairs. 'What're you gonna do with my kids?'

On the desk before Ms Subraman was a manila folder at forty-five degrees and, to the side, a computer screen and mouse and keyboard on the same angle. The screen cast its light on her face and illuminated her pained expression. 'Given the severity of their conduct, the fact that it was premeditated revenge—unfortunately, I don't see that I have many options.'

'You're not getting the cops involved?'

Ilene's head spun, and she recalled kneeling before her children in that dusty field and explaining their fate. Later, during Carl's stay in the hospital, she'd waited every day for the arrival of a police car—or, worse, a government sedan with two social workers inside. But no official vehicle had ever parked outside the house, and she did not now yield to the temptation to lower herself into a chair across from Ms Subraman. To keep herself upright, she rested her fist on the desk.

Ms Subraman mustered a smile. 'I already called the Youth Liaison Unit for advice. Thankfully, they do not want anything to do with this.'

'So what happens is up to you?'

The principal ironed out her expression. 'Well, I am subject to policies, procedures, community expectations.'

'Even still, it's your call?'

'Ultimately, yes.' She sighed and allowed a deliberate silence to fall. 'And I am afraid I will be expelling both of your children.'

Ilene bit her lip. She didn't want Jack and Lonnie to be expelled—of course she didn't—for their sake. Plus, if they were expelled, it'd take her some time to find them a new school. In the interim, they'd lurk around the house, unbalancing her, blaming her, preventing Carl from coming home.

'Please don't do that,' she murmured.

Ms Subraman entwined her fingers. 'I'm afraid I cannot make any other decision here.'

'You can.'

A draught blew in through the window, and a shiver of resentment towards her children travelled along Ilene's spine. When the air stilled, though, tears of maternal love pressed at her eyes. She felt as if she were in the same place as she'd been on that night when she'd released Carl's hand to grip the shovel with both of hers.

In the principal's office, she swayed on her fist and anchored herself by focusing on the textbooks on the shelves behind Ms Subraman. 'Look, I know they did a bad thing,' she said. 'A really bad thing. They're not bad kids. They've just had a rough time of it.'

'They have.'

Ms Subraman's reply had the contours of an accusation, and Ilene took in the principal's navy dress, the white collar of which accentuated the narrowness of her shoulders. Ilene wasn't in rags, but her skin was still covered in salt-on-salt and her bra was jagged and her polo unwashed. She gripped the evidence bag with both hands as if she were holding a soup bowl. 'Don't expel them.'

Ms Subraman shook her entwined fingers up and down. 'If I could make any other choice here, believe me, I would.'

She dropped her fingers onto the manila folder, and Ilene was reminded of Jack weighing down his exercise book with his fists. Then she thought about him reluctantly displaying the napped white bandage, stained with blood. 'Did you expel the other kid?' she asked.

'I cannot talk about disciplinary matters related to other children.'

'Because you didn't, did you?' Ilene said. 'You're only expelling my kids.'

'Yes, but that's not because . . .' Ms Subraman trailed off. Her shoulders slumped, and her mouth shifted to that commiserative angle. 'For what it's worth,' she said, 'I am very sorry about Jack and Lonnie.'

There was no changing Ms Subraman's mind, Ilene figured, and the apology she'd been offered struck her as something else. Blood sloshed through her temples, and the evidence bag felt slippery in her hands.

'What do you mean you're sorry?' she asked.

Ms Subraman's brows went circumflex. 'Only—'

'Sorry my kids were born into a shithole family?'

'No.'

'Sorry that Carl's their father? Sorry that I'm their mother?'

The principal untwined her fingers and raised a stop sign of a hand. 'That is not what I said.'

'Isn't it, Miss? 'Cause I reckon it's exactly what you said.' Ilene's voice cracked. 'I reckon it's what you've been saying to me this whole bloody time.'

She flicked the evidence bag across the desk, and it skimmed like a stone towards Ms Subraman. A collision seemed unavoidable—and yet, with surprising swiftness, the principal slammed her hand onto it and stopped it dead at her rib cage. The clap echoed, and she lifted her hand to uncover the bloodied shard of hoop.

'Who looks after your children at night?' Ms Subraman asked.

Ilene stumbled half a step backwards. 'What?'

'You said you came home yesterday morning.' Ms Subraman's expression had gone blank, and no trace of commiseration remained on her lips. 'Who looks after your children in your absence, Ilene?'

Ilene's eye twitched. She glared at the principal and blinked hard. 'None of your fucking business.'

In the corridor, Lonnie sat swinging her feet in a broken classroom chair while Jack idled, hooded, against the wall; Ilene careened out of the principal's office and rushed right past them. But she knew by the leporine pitapat of their footsteps that they'd hauled their backpacks onto their shoulders and hopped into pursuit. She strode out to the playground, where it was darker than she'd expected. Thunderheads had formed, and paler clouds drifted among them like riders on horseback. The orange Datsun was parked across the road from the school gates, and she headed straight for it.

'Mum,' Lonnie called out.

Ilene ignored her. She marched out of the school and paused for a mere heartbeat at the kerb. Left and right there were no cars, and she walked onto the road.

'Mum,' Lonnie called out again.

The child's voice sounded distant and mewling, and Ilene didn't break stride. She thrust her hand into her bag in search of the car keys. Then she winced and came to a halt near the Datsun. Her knuckles had brushed against something that felt like dry skin. She dropped her head and stood panting on the asphalt.

Her fingers curled around the object in her bag, which had the same approximate shape as a shard of hula hoop. She brought it out into the stormy light and saw that it was a scroll of some sort. The scroll wasn't made of skin or animal hide, though; it seemed to be a weather-beaten sheet of canvas, rolled up and thick with paint. She bit her lip. But she hesitated only a moment before she unravelled the scroll.

She held it before her like a treasure map, and the first thing she noticed was the damage. The canvas had chaotic red-rimmed gashes running through it as if it'd been burned or stretched to breaking point. She focused on the coagulated paint, which formed an artwork that was divided into two panels and done in a simple folk style.

In the left panel, a woman wielding a bloodied shovel stood over a seated man with a profusely bleeding nose. Above them was a round tank, in which two small, solemn faces could be seen in the water. The panel on the right, which was at once eerier and more innocuous, showed two children holding hands before a tree that wept blood and was haloed with gold.

'Mum?' Lonnie's voice was uncertain.

Ilene turned to where her children lingered on the pavement. The school gates and evergreens and main building served as their scenic backdrop.

'You did this, didn't you?' Ilene said in a quaver. She turned to them and showed them the canvas. Then she scrunched it up. 'Why are you here?' She pushed the thrum of her voice out with her tongue. 'Why are you *still* here?'

Jack had his hands in the pockets of his hoodie. Lonnie's eyes were huge, yet they were not innocent. She and Jack could not have done this painting. But Jack had carved a boy's abdomen open,

Lonnie had bitten his cheek, and neither child had love or sympathy for their mother—or their father.

Ilene laughed bitterly. 'Right,' she said. 'All right.'

She crammed the painting into her handbag and turned around. Walking back towards the car, she found the keys. Then something glinted overhead. She threw her hands up protectively—and a bolt of lightning zigzagged from the sky to the earth. White with a bruised outline, the lightning branched and came back together and crashed into the roof of the Datsun. A thunderclap resounded like an explosion. The asphalt rumbled, and the lightning shattered into embers and disappeared.

When everything fell quiet, Ilene caught her breath and glanced at her children. Now they idled in the middle of the road and watched her. She turned from them and ran her eye over the Datsun. The car didn't seem damaged, save perhaps for a charred circle on the roof, but that might have been there for years.

She walked around to the driver's side and ducked into the car. Then she turned the keys in the ignition. The engine sputtered and came to life, as it always had, and Ilene clipped on her seatbelt. Through the passenger window, she saw that her children remained in the middle of the road. She could've driven off. Instead, she punched the horn to hurry them up, and they sprinted to the car.

The tyres must have been bald, because Ilene didn't think she was speeding and yet the Datsun skidded to a halt in the driveway of Carl's workplace. She unclipped her seatbelt and grimaced at her children in the back seat. Then she hustled out of the car and slammed the door on them. Immediately, a man with a clipboard came towards her. His hard hat wobbled on his head, and he wore a hi-vis vest over a collared shirt unbuttoned to his sternum. 'You can't park there,' he said.

He held the clipboard at Ilene's elbow and attempted to guide her back into the Datsun. But she stood her ground and stared past him into the warehouse, from which emanated a hot industrial wind. 'I need to talk to my husband,' she said.

'You need to move your car.'

Towards the front of the warehouse, the concrete of a truck turntable reflected the hanging pendant lights. Deeper within were boxes wrapped in plastic and skeletal shelves and pallets stacked upon pallets. A woman in a hard hat yelled at a forklift driver; Ilene caught a glimpse of him, but his skin was too pale for him to be Carl.

She sidestepped the clipboard, and the man beside her grasped her arm. The straps of her handbag tumbled off her shoulder and slid towards his fingers. They were unlike Stefan's fingers, stubby but not square, yet they sent a rush of indignation through her nonetheless. She was about to wrench herself free, or knock his hand away, when the man let her go.

'Okay.' He sighed. 'Who's your husband?'

'Carl.'

'Carl?' He raised his eyebrows. 'I'll go get him. Then you have to move your car.'

The man jogged off and went behind some taller shelves, where there must have been another section of the warehouse. Ilene fixed the straps of her bag and retied her hair and straightened her polo. She was no longer panting, but her breath wasn't controlled, either. The forklift beeped, and the woman who'd yelled earlier yelled again. A moment later, Carl strolled over the turntable towards Ilene while the man with the clipboard hung back and folded his arms.

'Boss says you won't move your car?' Carl called out.

His eyes remained sunken and his nose unfixed. There was a fragility to him that gave her the impression he might melt down like candle wax. This impression reached back in imagined time and altered her memory of holding him, six months after he'd lost his job: he seemed less solid in her arms—in her mind—as he shivered and sweated and muttered covenants to the electrical storm.

Still, when Carl emerged from the warehouse, he appeared healthier than when she'd last seen him. Having shaved, he looked like someone who might function in the real world, and remorse hit her even before she reached into her bag and thrust the canvas under his nose. 'Look at this.'

He straightened out the painting, and Ilene watched him take in the left panel—the man with the bleeding nose, the woman with the shovel, the faces in the tank. She saw his eyes drift to the right panel, with the children and the haloed tree, and his face took on its night-time disposition. 'Who did this?' he asked.

'Dunno. Could be Jack, could be Lonnie.'

'They can paint like this?'

'No. I dunno, but if it's not them, and it's not you—' Ilene lapsed into silence.

Carl shook his head at the painting. 'I never told a soul. Not even the doctors.'

Ilene wondered if this could possibly be true. Then she reminded herself that she'd believed it wholeheartedly until a few days ago.

Carl glanced at the Datsun, parked askew no more than a few footfalls away. He flinched, and she followed his gaze. In the back seat, the children peered out at their parents. They were almost silhouettes, which made them seem like spectres. Ilene dug the nails of her right hand into her upper left arm. She fixed her eyes on Carl, who'd returned his to the canvas.

'They got expelled from school today,' she said.

'Why?'

'They attacked a boy who hurt Jack. They cut him. Bit his face.'

Carl continued to stare at the painting. His Adam's apple bobbed, and he let out a sharp breath. 'I almost made us . . .'

Ilene thought of what he'd said they had to do to save Jack and Lonnie. Then she shoved the thought aside. 'Least you can say you weren't yourself.'

'You weren't yourself neither.'

Thunder rumbled above him, and her mind looped back to the night of the electrical storm. In her memory, Carl remained as candle wax in her arms. He'd told her the storm said they had to give the children to the light; she'd embraced him and kissed his brow and confessed that she'd heard the command as well. But whether this was true or not, she'd never been quite sure.

'But I was myself.' She brought her husband's broken face into focus. 'Carl, I need you to take them.'

He blinked back tears. 'If you hadn't clocked me with that shovel—'

'Take them,' she said.

'—I would've done it. To save them. To save all of us.'

'*Take* them.'

Carl pressed the painting to Ilene's chest. 'I can't.'

He returned to the warehouse, and Ilene watched him lumber past the man with the clipboard and behind the shelves to the section that was hidden from her sight. She clutched the painting and faced her children, who waited for her still in the back seat of the car.

VII

At a set of traffic lights, Ilene brought the car to a stop in the right turning lane. Why she'd chosen that lane, she wasn't sure, and it occurred to her that she didn't know where she was going. Beneath that thought, though, lurked another that was more like an atavistic drumbeat than anything to do with words. She looked up at the storm clouds. Then she adjusted the rear-view mirror and caught Lonnie's doleful gaze. Jack's was beyond the scope of the glass, and she didn't seek it out. Instead, she tilted the rear-view to keep both her children below her line of sight. This was where she wanted them, at least for the afternoon.

She wished Carl had been able to take them. But he'd flinched at their silhouettes and pressed the painted canvas to her chest. Now, a cold bead of sweat ran down her back, and she shuddered. Then she leaned over and jammed her hand into her bag and scrabbled beneath the canvas for her mobile. She scrolled through her contacts and dialled Tandy's number.

Ilene tapped her thumb against the steering wheel, and the phone rang and rang—until it stopped. *'Hi, you've reached Tandy,'* a recorded message said.

A car behind the Datsun blasted its horn, and Ilene ended the call. The traffic lights must have been green for some time, for they were already changing to orange. Panic coursed through her, impelled her forward. She stomped on the accelerator, and the bald tyres screeched. But the car went nowhere until the rubber found purchase on the asphalt. Phone in hand, Ilene steered the Datsun around the corner in a wide, reckless arc. The car fishtailed. She felt as if she were about to lose control. A second later, though, she was doing sixty on the straight of the highway—the only vehicle to have made it through the lights.

She eased up on the accelerator, and in the back seat, Jack murmured to Lonnie. Ilene had heard him murmur like this on the night they drove to the dusty field. She glanced at the radio dial and then in the rear-view, where she half-expected to see the reflection of the shovel's handle in the middle seat.

The highway curved, and without indicating, she let the car drift into the lane closest to the kerb. She scanned her surrounds as if she still wasn't sure where she was going. The Datsun sped through a couple of sets of traffic lights. Her gaze rested on an abandoned fridge on the pavement, and her foot shifted to the brake.

At the next cross street, her knowing hands pulled the car through a sharp left turn, and the atavistic drumbeat in her mind echoed through her chest. Up ahead, the painted concrete monolith of the Casus Hill Workers' Club loomed by the roadside. She sucked in a breath. The air felt thin.

She cruised into the half-empty car park and slotted the Datsun into the first available space. Then she cut the engine and took the keys from the ignition and tried Tandy again. The phone gave a shrug of a ring before the recorded message hit its first syllable, and Ilene hung up.

The engine cooled; the sweat on her back warmed. She waited for the drumbeat in her chest to hush, and as it did, the last question Ms Subraman had posed ran through her head. *Who looks after your children in your absence, Ilene?*

She refused to glance at Jack and Lonnie. Rather, she pulled her handbag up to her lap and dropped her phone into it. 'Wait here,' she said.

'Where are you going?' Lonnie asked.

'She's leaving,' Jack replied.

'I'm not leaving.'

'Where are you going then?' he said.

Ilene gestured towards the tinted doors of the workers' club. 'In there.'

'You're leaving us?' Lonnie said.

Ilene craned her neck. Her daughter's face was dirty, and her irises were bigger than they'd been in the rear-view; her son had lowered his hoodie, and his eyes seemed sunken. He looked so much like Carl, she thought. They both did. Her mind dragged her unwillingly to that night, to the moment she'd entered the children's room behind her husband. He'd stood Jack up and patted his solar plexus. Ilene had lifted sleeping Lonnie from the lower bunk and carried her out of the room.

She forced a white flash through her mind, and the memory erased itself.

'Listen,' she said. 'I'm the only one who gives a shit about you, all right? I'm the only one who's ever looked out for you, ever cared for you—ever *wanted* you. Understand?' She drew a breath. 'I'm your mother,' she said, 'and I am not leaving.'

Lonnie stared at her; Jack turned his cheek. 'Just go.'

Ilene glanced from him to Lonnie. With some effort, she reached out and thumbed the dirt from her daughter's face. Then she climbed out of the car and locked it behind her.

In the gaming room of the workers' club, she chose Horseshoe Saloon over Jewels of the Orient. One of her hands was flush with cash; the other gripped a gin and tonic that the bartender—a sympathetic woman with a severe underbite—had given to her for free. She sipped at it and slammed the glass down on a coaster near the console. Then she hauled herself onto the low-backed stool and dropped her bag at her feet. The light of the poker machine's horizontal slot winked at her. A minute later it was winking still, yet her hand was empty, and the screen showed that she had three hundred and forty dollars' credit with which to play.

That was all the money the ATM would let her withdraw. It was all the money in the world that she'd earned rather than stolen. Her gin and tonic perspired. Frozen in its ice was the golden hour hue of the circular fluorescents above. She shivered. Then she pictured Jack, in the car, turning his cheek and urging her to go. Lonnie's eyes had glistened in her dirty face. The children had reminded Ilene of Carl, who'd been unable to offer them more than a glance full of remorse.

On the poker machine's console, the play button addressed her with its glow. She let her hand hover over it, let its light touch her fingers. Then she diverted to her gin and tonic and took another sip. The ice jangled whatever strings connected her teeth with her brain, and she put the drink down. Still, the memory of Carl in the children's room scuttled to the front of her mind.

Ilene thumped at her brow with her wrist and became aware of the drumbeat that'd shifted from her head to her chest. Her molars ached; her breath came swiftly. But despite the sensory noise, the memory remained at the forefront of her thoughts—and to rid herself of it, she jabbed at the glowing button.

Horseshoe Saloon's digital reels ticked and spun and came to a halt. A flashing line connected four matching horses, and the machine played its festive ragtime melody. Her credits counted up. The same rush that'd made her stomp on the Datsun's accelerator surged through her, and she hit the play button again.

Once more, the ragtime melody blared; once more, her credits counted up. That made three wins in a row, she figured, if she included the free gin and tonic. Reflexively, she slurped at it. Her brain freeze returned, and with it came the memory of Carl in the children's room. How assured his hands had been when he patted Jack's solar plexus. She'd hung back; Carl had smiled. Her doubts had spiralled. But she hadn't seen Carl so himself in years, and she smiled back at him and lifted Lonnie from the bottom bunk. Then, husband and son in tow, she carried her sleeping daughter out into the hallway.

In the gaming room, Ilene blinked at the reels rotating on the poker machine's screen. She wasn't sure how many spins she'd played. But she couldn't have won any of them or the ragtime melody would've blared. The gin and tonic sweated in her fingers, and she brought it to her lips. Then she paused. There was a black speck floating in her drink. She raised the glass to eye level. The speck was an inverted fly: there was an upside-down blowfly trapped under the ice of her drink.

Her stomach quaked, and she couldn't stop herself: she recalled carrying Lonnie out into the pleasant cool of the night. Her daughter had awoken as Ilene loaded her into the Datsun. Jack had climbed in willingly, although he'd looked perturbed when he spotted the shovel in the middle of the back seat.

The poker machine played its jaunty tune of anticipation. Then it fell silent. Ilene had no recollection of pushing the button. She put her gin and tonic down on the coaster and, with some force, pressed the button again. A jagged line connected four cowboys, and the ragtime melody played. She tried to lose herself in the music. But it hit a glitch and faltered, almost imperceptibly—and the spin yielded only more recollections of that night.

With trembling fingers, she'd twiddled the radio dial in the orange Datsun. In the passenger seat, Carl's voice grew manic yet his words were garbled in her memory. He nodded at her beseechingly, and she returned her eyes to the ripcord of road pulling ahead of them into the darkness. In the back seat, Jack murmured to Lonnie—it sounded like a warning. Ilene tried to find her children in the rear-view, but they were below her line of sight, and all she could make out was the splintered handle of the shovel.

Horseshoe Saloon's melody tugged her back to the present. She'd won twelve free spins, although she couldn't be sure how many she'd lost. In her throat, her breath felt serrated; she dug the nails of her right hand into her upper left arm. Then she punched the play button with the side of her fist.

On that night, she'd retrieved the shovel and wandered out into the cold beam of the Datsun's headlights. Carl had remained in the passenger seat, his face smoky and illuminated by a lighter; already out of the car, Jack and Lonnie trod uncertainly ahead of Ilene through the dusty field. Jack offered Lonnie his hand, and she took it. She stumbled and glanced back at her mother, who swallowed and gestured for her to keep walking.

Then Ilene heard the car door slam, and Carl appeared beside her. He took hold of her free hand, and the pair of them stalked after their children. Ilene's vision was stippled, but beyond Jack and Lonnie she could spy the bore water tank, glimmering in sections, rusted in others, brimming with murky water. A lone sheep, shorn of its wool, grazed in front of it. When Carl whooped and hurled his pipe to scare the sheep off, the children flinched. But it was the realisation that they were at Carl's old workplace that frightened Ilene. She looked at him and noticed a mad neon sheen on his face.

In the gaming room, a snake charmer's melody blared. Ilene blinked at her screen and expected to see a flashing line that indicated a win. But she was playing Horseshoe Saloon, not Jewels of the Orient, and the melody came from behind her. The reels of her machine ticked and spun and stopped silently. All she could hear was her own breath, which now made the sound of a knife slicing through the brittle bone of a hula hoop.

She dug her nails deeper into her upper arm and cast a longing glance at her gin and tonic. Its ice had almost melted and, still upside down, the blowfly floated just below the surface. A feverish shiver overtook her, and she hit the backlit button. The spin was not a winning one. She hit it again. A loss. Again. A loss. Again.

Another loss.

And in the dusty field, she'd stood beside Carl in the diffused glow of the car's headlights. Then, near the bore water tank, she'd knelt before Jack and Lonnie. Her white knuckles had gripped the shovel's handle, and she heard herself murmuring as Jack had in the back seat. She was explaining to her children what Carl had told her: that they had to do this to save them—to save them all.

Another loss another loss.

And Ilene had hugged her daughter. She'd wiped Lonnie's tears and helped her into the tank. Too deep for the children to stand, the water was streaked with rust, yet it managed to reflect the stars when Jack and Lonnie lowered themselves in right up to their necks. Their thin fingers curled over the rim of the tank, above which their heads were visible. They'd never been taught to swim, and they kicked their feet feebly. Ilene retreated to where she'd knelt and held on to Carl's hand.

Another loss another loss another loss.

And the children called out for her, desperately. They clung on for so long. They should've been able to climb out, she thought. But it was as if they were waiting for her to give them permission. They cleaved to the edge, and to each other, for what seemed like hours before they let go. For an instant, Ilene saw only the panicked masks of their upturned faces above the waterline. The stars must have been in their eyes. Then they slipped under.

Another loss another loss another loss another loss.

And pins and needles stabbed at her skin. Tears begged her ducts for release, and she peered across at Carl, who was watching the bore water tank with grim determination. When he turned to her, the neon sheen of his face broke into a wistful smile. He was so sad and beautiful; she loved him so much. But her eye fell on the burn on his lip, and she realised she'd been wrong. He wasn't himself, and in his state, he'd try to stop her from undoing this. She returned his smile. Then, all in one movement, she released his hand and gripped the shovel with both of hers and swung it at his face with all her might.

Another loss another loss another loss another loss another loss.

And she could scarcely remember what happened next, but she somehow managed to haul Jack and Lonnie out of the tank. The next thing she recalled was leading them, sputtering and drenched, towards the Datsun. They walked past Carl, who sat in the dirt and clasped his knees with his elbows. He stared at Ilene and the children and cried, while blood streamed from the broken nose that he later refused to have reset.

In the distance, and then close by, Ilene heard her own ragged breathing. Tears carved a path down her cheeks. Before her, the screen of Horseshoe Saloon showed that she was down to seven dollars' credit. She could barely see, could barely control her hand. But she pressed the backlit button again and again until the reels stopped spinning—and even then, she kept pushing the button.

In her gin and tonic, the ice had melted completely, and the blowfly was no longer inverted. It was still alive, or perhaps it'd come back to life. By its front legs, it hauled its bedraggled body up the inside of the glass. The blowfly got to the rim and balanced there as if it were about to topple back into the beverage. For several seconds, she watched it shake itself dry. Then it took flight. It zipped by her ear, and she followed its path with her eyes.

The blowfly buzzed over the stools in front of the dormant poker machines and headed inexorably for Jewels of the Orient. On that machine hunched the woman with the volute bun. A nimbus of light swirled around her, and she pressed the play button on her console. Her reels ticked and spun, and the blowfly landed on her crown. Exhausted, it crawled to the back of her head. Then it burrowed into the centre of her bun and disappeared into that spiral of white hair.

The snake charmer's melody played, and Ilene felt a wave of nausea.

The woman turned towards her, and the light curled and hung in the air. A faint smile crept across the woman's face, and she hunched further, as if she were greeting a child.

The pain in Ilene's throat intensified. 'You,' she said.

She would've said more, would've made her accusation more precise. But she was out of breath, and all she could think was that Jewels of the Orient had credit—and she wanted to keep playing the pokies. Seized by this impulse, she stood and advanced. She drew closer and balled her fist, yet the woman kept smiling, kept blinking, and the skin tag on her eyelid fluttered up and down.

Ilene stood over her and raised her fist. She was about to swing it when the circular fluorescent pulsed above her. Suddenly bathed in golden hour light, she recalled the lightning that had struck the Datsun, and a hazy sense of deja vu formed in her mind.

The woman lifted her eyes to the ceiling, and Ilene did likewise. She gazed up into the dark mirror overhead, which was circumscribed by the pulsing fluorescent tube. Rather than seeing her reflection, though, she saw a blurry rust-coloured disc that spun around and around. She pictured the night sky reflected in the murk of the bore water tank. Fleetingly, she thought of Jack and Lonnie. Then she thought that the disc resembled a dollar coin, and she'd left a stolen roll of those in the Datsun.

She strode from the gaming room and hurried by the bar, where the drinks on the shelf sparkled each alone. The sympathetic bartender caught her eye as she passed. 'Excuse me, miss, are you okay?' she called. 'Do you need help?'

Ilene didn't respond; instead, she picked up her pace. The tinted doors of the workers' club opened, and Ilene exited to the car park. Outside, the storm clouds had cleared, and the sun was low on the horizon. She squinted; she could feel the arid tracks that her tears had left on her cheeks and the humidity of her sweat, which rose off her as steam.

She spotted the Datsun with its front passenger door hanging open. All thought of the roll of coins fled her mind, and she went numb. She couldn't feel her feet, but she heard her footsteps on the asphalt. Her vision juddered each time she pushed off the ground.

She heard the bartender call out behind her, and the world listed. Ilene was falling, she realised, and caught herself on the Datsun's bonnet. She stared into her car. It was empty. Where Jack and Lonnie had been, there was nothing but the frayed fabric of the car seats and a pair of open backpacks. She scrambled around the side of the car to inspect the footwells. But her children were not there. She stood up straight and cast her frenzied gaze around the parking lot. There was no movement that she could see.

She ran between the rows of parked cars. 'Jack!' she called out. 'Lonnie?'

Then she turned and ran in the other direction. She crashed straight into the bartender, who clasped her by her shoulders and asked a question. The bartender's forehead was creased with concern. Ilene lowered her eyes. She expected tears to fill them and fall in a torrent upon the ground; she expected a scream to build in her throat and shred her vocal cords. But without the children, all she encountered was silence.

Interlude

Nonna Oscura

Thirty-six years earlier, a bell rang at a shop's entrance, and in the back room, the owner—who was called by her professional name, Nonna Oscura, far more frequently than her real name—put her salami sandwich down on the table. She finished chewing and stood and gathered up her jowls. Then she swept aside the curtain separating the back room from the shop and sailed theatrically beyond it.

Near the entrance, a young man smoked at a flat top lectern that only passed for a counter because it bore a cash register and an ashtray. He exhaled a thin plume. 'Hi, I'd like one of your letters, please,' he said. 'One with my fortune on it?'

Nonna Oscura nodded and cast her heavily mascaraed eyes at the window, where the obligatory neon sign buzzed above a row of chairs upholstered with green vinyl. Outside, boxy sedans and station wagons streamed past. 'Please sit,' she said.

Her voice was resonant and her accent Italian, and she gestured not at the vinyl chairs but at the round table in the centre of the shop. The young man dragged on his cigarette; she sat on the side furthest from the lectern and placed her foot on a pedal hidden beneath a rug.

Before her was the grand prop of a winged Oliver typewriter, and to her left was a decorative crystal ball. To her right was a pile of paper and envelopes and a quill that might have come from a rainbow lorikeet. At the lectern, the young man stubbed out his cigarette and struggled to light another. Nonna Oscura frowned at his bouffant hair and overlarge short-sleeved shirt and sensible black sneakers.

'You are in health?' she asked. Finally, he lit the cigarette, and she raised a bejewelled finger to prevent him from speaking. 'No,' she said. 'You are in health *care*?'

'Yes, I will be. Soon.' He brought the ashtray to the table with him and eased himself into the seat across from her. 'Do I pay now or later?' He bounced his knee up and down. 'I'm sorry. I've never done this before.'

'Later.' Nonna Oscura placed her palms on either side of the typewriter. A beat of silence fell, and the young man blew smoke through it. But he steadied his knee, and she fed a sheet of paper into the typewriter. 'Who do I address my letter to?'

'Nasser—Nass. That's me.'

Gentile Signor Nasser, she typed, and straightened her back. 'Tell me what it is you wish to know about your future,' she said. 'What questions would you like to ask?'

'Oh, all of them.' He tapped his cigarette twice on the rim of the ashtray. 'Like, do I spend my entire career in health care?'

Nonna Oscura took a breath and mouthed words and let her eyelids flutter. She opened her eyes and began to compose a letter on the typewriter. 'You do,' she said. 'It is your calling, your *passione*. You care deeply about people who cannot for themselves.'

'Do I meet a girl?' he asked.

'You will meet a woman, and you will love her more than anything in the world. And she will love you almost as much.'

Nasser grinned and toked on his cigarette. 'Will we have children?'

'You will experience children'—Nonna Oscura typed furiously— 'with the woman you love.'

'Do we spend our whole lives living in Sydney?'

'You do.'

'I don't ever get to live on a farm?'

'No.'

'What, never?'

'Wait.'

Abruptly, Nonna Oscura stopped typing and started mouthing words again. She tapped the pedal with her foot as if she were sewing, and the lights in the shop flickered. Nasser blew smoke at the ceiling, and Nonna Oscura allowed the lights to steady. '*Sì, sì*,' she said, in an even more resonant voice. 'You will one day be on a farm with children and the woman you love.'

She resumed typing. Nasser knocked a curl of ash into the tray and swallowed audibly—*glug*. 'How do I die?'

Nonna Oscura typed out a complimentary close to her letter and sat back to regard him. 'No,' she said firmly. 'You are still such a young man.'

She dragged the letter out of the typewriter and signed it with the quill. Then she folded the letter and slipped it into the envelope, on the front of which she wrote his name.

On the pavement beyond the window, Nonna Oscura's six-year-old grandson—carrying a backpack and wearing his school uniform—waved goodbye to a girl with curly brown hair. The girl walked on, her feet dirty and shoeless, and he made his way into the shop; the bell rang, and he lingered near the row of chairs.

Nonna Oscura glanced at him and led Nasser to the lectern, where he paid in cash. She handed him the envelope, which bore her italic script on the front. 'You spelled my name right,' he observed. 'Thank you, Nonna Oscura.'

'*Prego*,' she replied. 'And maybe we'll see you again . . . in the future.'

Nasser grinned and whacked his palm with the envelope.

When he'd left, Nonna Oscura dropped to her haunches and kissed her grandson's brow.

'Nonna,' he said, 'why do you put on that voice for the customers?'

'It's a funny thing, Beniamino,' she replied in her Australian accent. 'People seem to pay more attention when there's a bit of theatre involved.'

Her grandson shrugged off his backpack. He circumnavigated the table, and she watched him eye the typewriter and return to her. 'Can you tell me my future?' he asked.

She stared daggers at his discarded backpack. Then she ran her fingertips tenderly over his hairline. 'Forget about it,' she commanded.

Part Two
Omar

1

The children had not yet been missing seventy-two hours when Omar Dualeh's phone pinged with a message. He rubbed the screen on his linen shirt, over his heart, to remove his fingerprints. Outside, heat wafted off the asphalt of the Coff-n-Snax forecourt and the conterminous petrol station. Beyond that, a concrete barrier obscured a highway that was clogged with early morning traffic and gurgled like a garbage disposal. Its noise had jarred his bones on the six-hour drive from his hometown of Belli to this truck stop on the city's rim. Now he sat alone in a booth and nursed a coffee. He'd come here to meet with Detective Inspector Sue Maric, but either she was thirty minutes late or she'd spoken to the Professional Standards Command and decided not to come.

Unsmudged, his phone winked up at him. He'd presumed the message to be an encrypted one from the detective inspector, cancelling their meeting, yet the sender's name made him conscious of the heavy percussion in his chest, and he sipped at his coffee in a vain attempt to relax himself.

Sure come on by, Camille had written. *Would be nice to catch up.*

His phone pinged again: she'd sent through her address in the inner city. Then it pinged a third time: she'd be available until 4 pm, she wrote, and closed with a smiley face.

Omar struggled to bring her messages into focus. The previous day, he'd texted her to say he'd be in Sydney on the chance she was off work and free for a visit. It'd been eighteen months since her wedding to a man Omar had never met—eighteen months since Omar had sent them a gift wrapped in his apologies—and he'd thought he was ready. But her replies were so feather-light that they floated over his irises and had him inventing excuses not to visit.

He gulped another mouthful of coffee and made a bargain with himself: if Sue didn't show, he'd head straight home; if she did, he'd visit Camille, then head straight home.

No sooner had he made this bargain than the door of the Coff-n-Snax swung open. He lifted his eyes and almost laughed at the hope that rose with them. But the detective inspector had not arrived. Rather, a young couple had wandered into the shiny new cafe. They'd been driving all night, Omar guessed, probably at the insistence of the man, whose hand rested on the small of the woman's back. Omar caught her eye and smiled, and she cast her gaze over the dark skin of his face. Then she averted it.

He stared out at the petrol bowsers and went to run his hand through the tight curls on his head. But he'd razored his hair the night before—he'd forgotten—and the shock of the stubble against his palm sent his mind reeling back to his PSC interrogation. One of the internal affairs officers had asked him who else had motive to install listening devices in Bruno Metcalf's house. Omar had refused to speculate, and the officer had smacked the back of his head.

The unanswered question was damning enough, though. It condemned Omar to a suspension and potential dismissal. But it was more worthy of condemnation, he reasoned, that he was the only detective still trying to prove that Bruno had abducted Patricia and Freeston Reeves. That was why he'd arranged to meet with the detective inspector: to see if her investigation was connected to his. It was why, on the heels of his PSC interrogation, he'd crouched in Bruno's driveway and attached a GPS tracker to the golden-brown Mercedes parked there.

The cafe's door swung open, and Omar blinked at it. Again, it wasn't Sue who entered. A workman in cargo shorts strode to the counter to examine the muffins and pastries and sandwiches on display. He had a limp and a surgical scar under his patella. Omar wondered if his injury had occurred on the job—whether he'd been compensated for it. Unlikely, he figured, although at least the workman had a wound he could display to shame his bosses.

Omar sculled the rest of his coffee and decided he'd waited long enough. The detective inspector wasn't going to show, and he wasn't going to drive to the inner city to visit Camille. He left his empty cup alone in the booth and exited to the forecourt.

On the highway back to Belli, a siren blared behind Omar's grey Ford Fairlane. He was travelling at 130—twenty kilometres over the limit—and he tapped the brake. The speedometer's dial drifted anticlockwise: 125, 120. In his rear-view, he watched an unmarked police motorcycle weave through traffic and tailgate him. Blue lights strobed on the motorcycle's front and rear, and the female rider, in head-to-toe black, jabbed a finger to indicate that Omar should pull over.

He clenched his jaw. Trucks and cars zoomed all about him; surely he wasn't the only one speeding. Still, he brought his sedan to a halt on the shoulder of the road beside a hill of patchy grass with a cluster of fume-stained dandelions. The motorcycle pulled over a few metres behind him, and the rider flicked out her kickstand and stepped off the bike.

Usually, in a situation like this, Omar would show his police badge and be done with it. But he didn't have a badge for the moment, or indeed a gun, and he reached into his wallet and readied his licence. The officer, though, had not approached along the driver's side of the Fairlane. Without removing her helmet, she yanked at the handle of the front passenger door. A sense of panic spread over Omar's skin, and his dilatory hand shot towards the lock button.

But the rider had already opened the door. She leaned forward and peered at him through her tinted visor. Omar could see the lines on his forehead reflected in its plastic surface. One of the officer's hands was at her hip, and he kept both of his stationary and within her view. Then she removed her helmet, and he recognised her.

'Sorry I'm late,' the detective inspector said.

Omar nodded and feigned equanimity. The residue of his panic remained on his skin, and he switched on the air conditioner. Sue unzipped her black jacket to reveal a collared shirt that was similar in colour to a police uniform. Omar had never met her in person, and the shirt tallied—far more than her motorcycle gear—with the impression he'd formed from her appearances on the news.

'I didn't think you were coming,' he said.

'I've got a lot on my plate right now.' Sue ducked into the car and placed her helmet on her lap. Then she slammed the door. 'And you were speeding.'

'You wanna write me a ticket?'

He offered her his licence, mostly in jest. She snatched it from him, and her eyes flitted from the youthful photo on the card to his freshly shaved scalp. 'The haircut to commemorate your suspension?' She handed the licence back to him. 'Goes with your nihilistic chic, I guess. My twelve-year-old would love it.'

He laughed and replaced the licence in his wallet. Then he cleared his throat. 'I don't know how much you know about the case I'm investigating—'

'That's a question I have for you, actually,' she interjected. 'Are you investigating, Detective Constable, or are you being investigated?' She raised an eyebrow at him and gave a lopsided grin.

Omar took in her aquiline nose and the freckles showing faintly through her foundation. 'I was pretty upfront about the PSC's inquiries,' he said. 'I am suspended, but I'm still investigating.'

Omar blinked earnestly at her; otherwise, he kept his features under control. But his mind wandered to a memory of Camille. She flickered, and the edges of her blurred and warped the background. Their old bedroom with the cracked wooden dressing table: that was where he pictured her standing. He had yet to reply to her text message, he realised.

'We'll come back to that,' Sue muttered. 'So what is it you want, exactly?'

'My case,' he began. 'I've got two missing kids, a girl and boy: Patricia and Freeston Reeves. Five years ago, they disappeared from a car park while their mother was at a pub. I sent you my original report and the report from the strike force, as well as my additional notes.'

'I looked at the file. Slim pickings.'

'You got the same sort of facts from three days ago, right?' He angled his body towards her and rested his wrist on the steering wheel. 'With Jack and Lonnie Gajdos-Little?'

Sue drummed her nails on her helmet. 'Your kids are older, First Nations, snatched from outside a country hotel.'

Omar touched his sternum. 'Maybe that's why a local detective's left carrying the case and not a . . .' He gestured at her.

'You got your strike force.'

'Belatedly.'

'My kids aren't white either.'

'I know.' He'd seen a photo of the kids, along with press conference footage of their unspeaking parents: a pale, put-upon mother and a brown-skinned father with a busted nose. 'Maybe that's another connection.'

Sue scratched her eyebrow and nodded, more at something she seemed to be thinking than at what he'd said. He straightened in the driver's seat and tuned his ears to the aircon. A truck sped by and shook the car. Then Sue reached into her jacket pocket and took out a square photograph and gave it to him.

'What's this?' he asked.

The photo paper felt tacky between his thumb and forefinger. He brought it towards his face. It was a photo of a simple two-panel painting, marked as evidence. The left panel depicted a woman holding a shovel and standing over a man with a profusely bleeding nose. The right panel showed two children holding hands before a bloodied tree that wore a halo. If Omar were to guess, he'd say it was something from Spain or Latin America, but he was no art expert.

'See the kids in the tank?' Sue prompted.

Omar studied the left panel and saw 'the kids in the tank'. That wasn't how he would've described it, though. Above the bloody man and shovel-wielding woman were two faces floating in the opaque water of what looked like an above-ground pool. They could have been children, he thought. 'This part of your case?'

Sue shrugged. 'The mother found it the day Jack and Lonnie disappeared.'

'What is it?'

'We think a potential threat. The situation with the parents is'—she let out a groan—'obscure.'

Omar examined the haloed tree again. 'Looks like a religious offering.'

'Have anything like it in your case?'

He looked across at her. 'My suspect did a stint in jail for possession of child pornography. Jail records show that he was repeatedly visited by a defrocked priest named Urbain Urrutia.'

'And?'

'Urrutia lives in Sydney now. The two of them might have links with a wider paedophile ring.'

'Might have? Unfortunately, there are loads of "might haves" on our radar.' She switched off the air conditioner. 'Look, none of our suspects have any links to yours. Despite the circumstantial similarities, our cases don't appear to be connected.'

'Are you sure?' he said.

Sue nodded. 'I'm sorry.'

She motioned for him to return the photograph. But the painting in it fascinated him, or unnerved him, and he wanted to keep staring at it. He wanted to see the original. Reluctantly, he gave the photo back to her. 'Why did you agree to meet with me then?'

She slipped the picture into the inside pocket of her jacket and gilded her face with another lopsided grin. 'Tell me about your suspension, Omar.'

'Why?'

She rolled her eyes. 'Okay, I'll tell you about your suspension. The PSC probably won't find you guilty, due to lack of evidence. But they know you're guilty. I know you're guilty; *you* know you're guilty. You broke into Bruno Metcalf's house and, without a warrant, you planted listening devices. You probably did worse.'

Omar directed his gaze at the speedometer; he wasn't budging. He recalled going over the recordings he'd made. They'd yielded only a scrap of potential evidence before Bruno had found the listening devices and handed them in to the PSC. *How are the kids?* Bruno had murmured to someone over the phone.

Then Omar's mind turned to the undiscovered GPS tracker beneath the Mercedes and the spare one in the glove box above Sue's knees. He watched her shift them, along with her shoulders, so that she was facing him.

'Here's the bit that might surprise you.' She drummed on her helmet again. 'I don't give a shit. You did what you did because you were investigating. No ulterior motive. You know the bastard's guilty and you want to get him. And I looked at some of your other files—you've got half-decent instincts. I could use you.'

Omar winced. 'What could you use me for?'

'I want you to follow someone for me. Unofficially.'

He didn't respond.

'It might have to do with that painting,' she added.

'Might have?' He scoffed, but he almost asked if he could see it one more time. Then he made a line of his lips and shook his head. 'I'm sorry,' he said. 'I've got my own investigation to pursue.'

When Sue had ridden off, Omar turned his car around and made the journey to Sydney's inner city. He parked outside Camille's house and rang the doorbell. Then he waited on the pavement with his back to the house and held his hand horizontal to check if it was shaking. It wasn't; it only felt like it was. He wiped his palms on the sides of his pants and placed the sole of his boot on a circular concrete pit cover. Along the street, the homes were a mixed bag: terrace houses, townhouses, California bungalows. But the gardens were all well-tended, and leafy trees dappled the late morning sunshine. He heard movement from behind him, and he turned around.

Between him and the house was a sliver of pavement and a tiled path with a bed of rosemary on one side and a frangipani tree on the other. Camille emerged onto the path, barefoot, in trackpants and a loose t-shirt. Her face was free of make-up, and her sole piece of jewellery was her wedding band.

'Hey, Camille,' Omar said.

She appeared older than his mental image of her. The laughter lines around her mouth had deepened, and her eyes conveyed a greater sense of melancholy. Despite this, a slow smile crept over her face. 'Omar,' she replied.

He tried to smile through whatever his own eyes were conveying, and she stepped from the tiled path onto the pavement and embraced him. For a moment, he remained rigid in her arms. Then her scent got to him: the familiar oils of her hair and the floral notes of her deodorant—along with something vague and new. He relaxed into the hug and draped his arms around her. Words that he could only ever whisper reached the tip of his tongue, and he swallowed them. It was too early, he thought. Far too early.

She withdrew from the embrace.

'House looks good,' he said.

She glanced at the bland modern facade. 'It's smaller than you'd get back home, but we like it.'

From the garden bed, she collected a frangipani flower that'd got caught amid the rosemary. Omar watched her and pictured their house in Belli, which was ramshackle but spacious. For some reason, he imagined it empty, from the perspective of a presence that drifted over the country-style kitchen and through the tiny bedrooms. Whether it was empty because he and Camille hadn't moved in yet, or because they'd vacated it after years of living there, he couldn't say.

She put the frangipani flower to her nose. 'How come you're in town?'

'An investigation.'

'In Sydney?' She let her arm drop to her side. 'Were you seconded to that missing children case? That one just fucks with me. Like history repeating.' Then she measured him, from his shaved head to his scuffed boots. 'You're not here to talk to Mick Metcalf, are you?'

Omar hemmed. Mick was Bruno's estranged son, and the thought of reinterviewing him hadn't crossed Omar's mind. But in Camille's unswerving gaze was a truth: Omar's investigation of Bruno wasn't the entire story of why she'd left him, but it had played a major role in the denouement. After being released from jail, a drunken Bruno had knocked on their door, and despite Camille's protests, Omar had invited him in. On their leather sofa, he'd almost coaxed a confession out of Bruno. Then Bruno had noticed Camille weeping in the shadows, and he'd fled into the night.

Omar cast the regret from his mind and started to reply, but the wail of a newborn struck him dumb. Camille dropped the frangipani flower and darted inside. The door remained open, and Omar stared after her, although all he could see was a bare hallway.

The baby's wail grew louder before it dipped below the roar of a jet engine. He dragged the exhaust into his lungs. The vague new scent he'd detected on Camille, he realised, was regurgitated breast milk. Nobody had told him she'd had a baby. She hadn't told him herself, but they hadn't communicated much since her wedding—and what did he expect?

The wail drew closer, and Camille appeared as a shape at the end of the hallway, out of focus yet unmistakable as a woman with a child. 'Omar?' she called out.

He willed his body to return to his Fairlane and drive away. Instead, his boots carried him into the house and along the hallway. In the living room, he stood in front of Camille, who cradled a swaddled newborn and rocked the child back and forth.

The child kept bawling, pausing only for breath, yet Camille brought the newborn to Omar. 'His name's Oscar.'

'Oscar?'

Omar pronounced the name to rhyme with his own and sought out Camille's eyes. Her attention was elsewhere. She kissed her baby's temple and let out a quiet snort that might have been a chuckle or a sob. 'You want to hold him?'

Before Omar could decline, she foisted the crying child onto him. Her movements were jerky, and he stepped away to soften the handover. Oscar's delicate head settled on the inside of Omar's elbow. The child's hairless fontanelle pulsed, ever so slightly bluish. His face was the same cedar brown colour as Camille's; his skin seemed as soft as chamois. He peered up through lidded eyes—not at Omar exactly but above his head, at his outline or atmosphere—and fell silent.

As if by transference, Omar felt tears forming somewhere in the chasm he imagined existed between his eyes and his brain. He could sense them, even though he was in no imminent danger of crying. This child could have been his and Camille's. Their lives could have been so different. That was reductive and ridiculous to think, he told himself, yet he stroked Oscar's cheek and thought it anyway.

'He looks like you,' he offered.

'Most people think he looks like Dev.' Camille had backed off towards the three-seater sofa. 'I wanted to tell you about him, but it's been so hard. And I didn't know if you and I were ever going to—'

'It's okay.'

Oscar's face crumpled, and he let out a wail. Camille pressed her hand to her hairline. 'He cries for five hours every single day,' she said. 'Sometimes I have to just drive around.'

Omar rocked the baby back and forth, but Oscar's crying intensified.

Camille eased the child from him and into her own arms. 'Are you sticking around for that missing children investigation?' she asked. 'Maybe we can catch up for dinner before you leave? I'll text you?'

Omar grimaced, yet he didn't trust himself to speak. All he could bring himself to do was nod.

In the ensuite of his motel room, Omar placed a glass on the corroded rim of the sink. He ripped a fresh toothbrush from its wrapping and dropped it into the glass. He did likewise with a razor. Then he realised he'd forgotten to buy toothpaste. His encounter with Camille had thrown him into disarray. Her demeanour and his connection with Oscar had burnished his hopes. But she was married, with a newborn, and the absurdity of his position wasn't lost on him. He pursed his lips and spiked the plastic and cardboard wrapping into the bin.

Exiting the ensuite, he shut the door behind him. The sordid bedroom went dark, although midday limned the musty curtains and crept through the undercut of the ensuite door. This lent a glow to the carpet, and he could just about see the leaves on the wallpaper and the mould blooming in the upper corners. He took his phone out of his pocket. Already he'd sent Sue an encrypted message asking for the details of whom he should follow. She'd responded with a question about where he was staying. He'd replied, and now he had to wait.

While he waited, he tapped the app for the GPS tracker. A blurry map of Belli loaded, with a blue dot pulsing in its centre. The map grew more detailed, and the familiar shapes of the police station and pub and goldmine museum came into focus. He zoomed in on the blue dot until he could see that it was where it often was: in the driveway of Bruno's house.

Omar put his phone on the bed and picked up one of the new shirts he'd tossed there beside his new socks and underwear. Shirt in hand, he turned to the mahogany wardrobe beside the ensuite's entrance. His eye lingered on it. With its tendinous legs and twin bevelled doors, the wardrobe seemed out of place in the room. He moved closer. The patterns in the wood reminded him of the photograph of the two-panel painting he'd seen that morning. Two knots on the left were like drowning faces, and an arc of pastel discolouration on the right was akin to a halo.

He grasped the metal key in the wardrobe's lock and turned it anticlockwise, carefully, as if it were a suspect to be coaxed into a confession. The lock mechanism creaked, and Omar thought he heard something from within the wardrobe—a keening on the brink of earshot. He stilled himself and listened, but he couldn't identify what it was, or even whether it was.

A knock on the motel room door jolted him from his concentration. He locked the wardrobe and opened the door. In the courtyard, standing by the bonnet of his Fairlane, was the woman he'd met at reception—a weather-beaten chain-smoker who probably owned the motel. A cigarette waited patiently for her behind her ear, and she carried an A4 envelope.

'Is that laundry for me?' she asked.

Nonplussed, she gestured at the shirt dangling from his hand. He'd forgotten he was holding it. 'Uh, no. Thank you.'

'Someone tried to slide this under your door,' she said.

She offered him the envelope, which was sealed and unmarked, and he took it. 'Was it a woman on a motorcycle?'

The motel owner shifted the cigarette to her mouth. 'Nah, it was a young bloke with glasses.'

'A delivery guy?'

She shook her head and lit her cigarette with a transparent lighter. 'He was one of you fellas.' He thought about querying whether she meant that the guy was Black or blue. But she toked on her cigarette and smiled. 'Have a nice day, officer,' she said.

He hung up the DO NOT DISTURB sign before he closed the door to his room. With a glance at the wardrobe, he dumped the shirt in his hand with the others on the bed. He threw open the ensuite door to let more light in and tore across the top of the envelope.

Inside was a colour copy of a driver's licence. Its photo was of a woman with white hair and a skin tag on her drooping left eyelid. Her name was Amma Corban. Her car's numberplate was typed in all caps along with the polite imperative: *No records. Dispose of thoughtfully.* Omar took down the relevant details in his notebook. Then he crumbled the photocopy under the ensuite tap and let the lumpy pieces flow down the drain.

II

Omar yawned and adjusted his position in the driver's seat of the Fairlane. It was humid in his parked car. He'd been assiduously bird-dogging Amma for more than forty-eight hours, and he was already sweating through another of his new shirts. With one hand he rubbed his head, which was prickled and greasy; in his other hand, his phone displayed a map of Belli with the blue dot in its centre. The dot pulsed from a spot near the railway station. Was Bruno on the train? Omar wondered. Then his eye darted to the bottom corner of the screen, where a gauge showed that the GPS tracker's battery was low.

Omar tongued the plaque on his front teeth. From the glove box, he took out the spare GPS tracker from behind his police torch and an old pair of binoculars. He switched on the metallic black device and loaded a fresh map. This one was blurry and had a red dot pulsing in its centre. It soon cleaned itself up, though, and the red dot found his current location: the car park of the Casus Hill Workers' Club.

He scowled at the tracker and the use to which he was thinking of putting it. Yet his notebook was filled with Amma's comings and goings, which were barely worth recording. Indeed, for a third consecutive afternoon, he was sweating it out in the car park while she played the pokies in the comfort of the club. Next, she would go to the shopping plaza. Then she'd head home. She seemed a creature of such banal habit, he thought, and he was puzzled by why Sue wanted her followed at all.

He got out of the car with the tracker in hand. Two rows over, Amma's silver hatchback glimmered near a pedestrian walkway that led to the club's glassy entrance. No people walked that route; no one else was around. He pictured Jack and Lonnie's mother in the gaming room, the glow of a poker machine's screen coming right off her face. Then he imagined Jack and Lonnie being lured away from the car park with no witness to the tragedy. But he wasn't thinking of Jack and Lonnie at all, he realised. He wasn't even positing himself as a witness. In his mind, the children had become Patricia and Freeston Reeves, as they were five years before, and he'd taken on the perspective of the formless thing he'd imagined drifting through the house he'd shared with Camille.

He stared at his boots—she still hadn't texted him about dinner. Then the asphalt's warmth reached his soles, and he refocused on Amma's hatchback. He'd attach the GPS tracker to it for a couple of days. That'd make trailing her less onerous. After that, he'd have to retrieve the tracker and use it to replace the one dying under Bruno's Mercedes.

Omar strode to the silver hatchback and scoped out the car park one last time. It remained bereft of people. All the cars were unmoved and unmoving. He squatted and cached the GPS tracker near the car's rear wheel well. The magnets attached themselves with a clank, and he tugged at the tracker to test its resolve.

Satisfied, he ambled back to his sedan. He was almost there when he saw Amma emerge from the workers' club. She marched along the pedestrian walkway and headed towards her hatchback. A minor sense of fret stirred in his gut, but she didn't so much as glance at him. Instead, she glared at her car as if she sensed something about it was awry. He observed her over his shoulder and ducked into his Fairlane.

The glove box remained open, and a pair of cable ties had fallen to the front. He shoved them back in and slapped the glove box shut. Amma hadn't sensed anything, he told himself. She hadn't seen him, either, and even if she had, he'd have been no more noticeable than a cigarette burn in the upper corner of a cinema screen.

She drove out of the car park, and he bowed his head. Then he mounted his phone on the dash and watched the red dot of her hatchback traverse the map. It glided to the highway, in the opposite direction to the shopping plaza, and stopped at a set of traffic lights. Omar waited a minute before he turned the ignition and followed.

The red dot came to a standstill in a cul-de-sac, and Omar brought his Fairlane to a halt on the perpendicular street. On the corner, a give way sign had collapsed or been run over; it lay flat with its conical concrete base uprooted from the nature strip. Notebook in hand, he climbed out of his car and walked towards the sign. He tried to exhibit a professional curiosity in the hope that anyone observing him might mistake him for a council worker.

As he hoisted the sign vertical and drove it into the earth, he peeked at Amma's hatchback. It was parked, driverless, about fifteen metres away, outside a property with a front garden overgrown with jungle verdure.

Omar released the give way sign, which remained upright for a second before lying down to bask in the golden hour. He jotted the time and name of the street in his notebook. Then he made his way to the overgrown property.

The front path was marked by a gap in the greenery and an unvarnished wooden arch with a crescent moon and star chalked onto its apex. Beside this, four holes in the shape of a diamond made him suppose that a cross or crucifix could once have been nailed there. The supposition brought to mind a memory of his father, in a *thawb*, explaining that Muslims regarded Christians and Jews and perhaps even Zoroastrians as 'People of the Book'. According to his father, though, it was holier to be a lone person of faith than a member of a congregation. He blinked the memory away. Nailed to the side of the arch was a wooden board advertising the sale of pet rabbits.

From somewhere to his left, he heard the hiss of spraying water. At the cul-de-sac's keyhole-shaped terminus, a bald man in a singlet had come out of a townhouse to hose his front lawn. The man side-eyed Omar, who acknowledged him with a nod and strode back to his Fairlane. He wrote a note about the arch and the advertising board, yet left off any mention of faith.

When Amma departed, he'd come back and see if he could confirm with the homeowner why she'd been there. He'd do this for completeness—for the no-records verbal report he'd give to the detective inspector—rather than because he was invested in the answer. His stomach rumbled, and his thoughts returned to the fading prospect of dinner with Camille. In a roundabout fashion, she'd been right about Bruno's case: for completeness, he should reinterview Mick Metcalf. But now he needed something to eat.

At a Turkish takeaway joint, he slurped at a kebab and a Coke and flicked between the maps on his phone. The afternoon ticked away, and the blue dot of Bruno's Mercedes still pulsed from the railway station. Ominously, that GPS tracker's battery had dropped by another percent. The other tracker's battery was at ninety-nine, and the red dot of Amma's hatchback remained stationary on the dead-end street.

The maps disappeared, and Omar's phone vibrated with a phone call. It was from Angus Troy, a straightish arrow who'd been Omar's police partner for the last two years; technically, he had carriage of the Reeves case, although he'd never actually worked it. Omar picked up.

'How's the big smoke?' Angus asked.

'Bloody smoky,' Omar replied.

'Just don't inhale, mate.' Angus chuckled. 'What're you doing there anyway?'

Behind the counter, a heavyset man used an electric carver to hack at a rotating cone of kebab meat. Omar watched the meat fall into the tray like frogs from the sky. 'Waiting around,' he said, distracted.

'Fair enough.' Angus cleared his throat. 'Listen, Omar, I just wanted to let you know that, uh, the toecutters are due to deliver their findings next week.'

Omar sipped at his Coke. Next week: that was when the PSC would decide whether he was fit to stay a cop, as if they were qualified to make a call like that, as if a call like that meant anything. He felt tears forming in the chasm between his eyes and his brain—a void that seemed somehow less imaginary than it had before.

'You there, mate?' Angus asked.

'Yeah.' Omar burped silently. 'Thanks for the call, Angus.'

He hung up. Then he flicked across to the map with the pulsing blue dot and the tiny icon of a dying battery. Bruno hadn't shifted, but when Omar checked on the red dot, he saw that Amma was on the road again.

Out the front of the overgrown property on the cul-de-sac, a young woman in jeans and a hijab used the claw of a hammer to lever the final nail from the advertising board. She dropped the hammer with all the nails on the pavement. Then she lowered the board from the arch, and Omar stopped his Fairlane at the kerb behind her. He wound down the passenger window.

'Salaam, sister,' he called out in a jovial tone. 'Don't tell me you just sold the last rabbit?'

The woman flinched, either at the bass note of his voice or its falsity. She swivelled and clocked his visage and held the board in front of her protectively. Her eyes were wide and unblinking, and her waxy face wore a mournful expression. Omar felt his eyebrows betray his confusion, and he strained to keep them under control.

'Did you just sell the last one, sister?' he asked in the same jovial tone.

'I sold the last two,' she replied in a monotone.

'To the woman who left a minute ago?' He was out on a limb and smiled to disguise it.

The woman in the hijab gave a nod, and he shook his head amiably. 'Oh, sister, my kids are going to be very upset with me.'

Her eyes glistened, and she blinked and looked away. 'Your kids?' She picked up the hammer and nails from the pavement. 'Tell them you left things too late.'

Without waiting for his response, she walked beneath the wooden arch and evanesced among the verdant shade of her front garden. Omar's smile slackened. At least he was certain Amma had bought a rabbit. Two rabbits. This was a deviation from her routine and an almost-interesting fact he'd be able to relate to the detective inspector. He scribbled it in his notebook and pulled away from the kerb.

Around the corner, he checked his phone for the location of Amma's hatchback. The red dot pulsed from an arterial road, and Omar followed in his Fairlane until the dot settled at the shopping plaza. With Amma back in her routine, he veered off in the direction of his other case.

By the time he arrived at Mick Metcalf's house, all that remained of the day were thready striations of pink on the horizon. Omar stood on the porch and pressed the doorbell. The in-built video camera switched on, and he stepped back. Then he stepped forward and stared into the fisheye lens, a mirror that dragged at his cheeks and exaggerated the downturn of his mouth. The house stayed quiet, and he jabbed at the doorbell again.

He retreated over the green velvet grass of the lawn to the letterbox. From the slot, he withdrew a stack of envelopes. One was addressed to Mick's business, Metcalf Builders. Another was from the Fraternity of Retired Police, which wouldn't allow Omar to become a member if internal affairs found him guilty—and might not welcome him even if internal affairs did not.

He frowned and fed the envelopes back into the letterbox. Maybe Mick wasn't home from work yet; maybe he wasn't even in town. Omar gazed at the sky-blue facade of the two-storey house, which somehow struck him as a display home rather than an occupied space. On the right, a paved driveway sloped down to an underground garage.

His curiosity sent him left, where he peered into a recycling bin. It was half-filled with pizza boxes and empty beer bottles and milk cartons. He shifted a layer of these out of the way, and his eye settled on an empty blue box of menstrual pads. So Mick had a long-term partner, he figured, although she didn't seem to be home either.

Beside the bins, a wrought-iron gate guarded a passage that ran between the fence and the house, and on the street, a sudden string of headlights cruised by. Omar closed the recycling bin's lid and dropped his chin to his chest. He waited, in case one of the cars was Mick's or a neighbour's.

When the string of headlights moved on, he elegantly hurdled the gate. Soft-shoeing it over the paving of the passage, he tried to peer in through the windows. Blinds blocked his view, and he walked on.

He arrived at a courtyard at the rear of the house. A corrugated iron fence, lined with bushes, lent privacy to the space; between the bushes, mossy water features—styled as clay urns—burbled away peacefully. Omar approached the French doors at the house's rear and searched for a glimpse inside, but all he could see was the fabric of the floor-to-ceiling blinds.

He hemmed, and a dog barked from behind the corrugated iron fence. The owner mollified it, her words tinged with suspicion, and Omar decided it was time to leave.

In heavy traffic, he mounted his phone on the Fairlane's dash and navigated to the GPS tracking app. He noted with some relief that the blue dot of Bruno's Mercedes no longer pulsed from the railway station; it had returned to the driveway of his house, where it belonged. But the red dot was not at Amma's house; it was on the highway, speeding towards the CBD, with at least a half-hour's head start. Omar steered his car into a gap in the next lane and accelerated in the red dot's wake.

When he arrived at its destination—a quiet street in an industrial zone adjacent to the city centre—the last scraps of pink on the horizon had faded to the blue-black of urban sky. The streetlights had not yet come on, and the buildings were grey or red-brick warehouses from the late twentieth century, with one exception. Amma's hatchback was parked outside the exception: a dilapidated Victorian manor that seemed to have been converted into a warehouse and then left to moulder. If Amma was inside, which seemed probable, he wondered what the hell she was doing there.

Down the street, he pulled his Fairlane over in front of a lonely four-wheel drive. He got out and sauntered past the hatchback and peeked into it. The boot and cabin appeared empty; there were no groceries, no rabbits. He crossed the road and positioned himself in the shadow of a shuttered clothing wholesaler and took in the abandoned Victorian.

At the front of the manor, temporary chain-link fencing on cinder blocks formed a gapped boundary. Graffiti covered the facade in all its human-accessible places, and in lieu of doors, barricade tape fluttered in the shape of an X. All the windows were smashed, or otherwise glassless, and one of these drew his gaze.

Near the pitched roof was an oculus without a pane, and through the empty circle shone an inconstant light. The light gathered itself and grew more intense. Then it dimmed, before it gained intensity once more.

Omar guessed that the source of the light was closer to the floor than the ceiling. He tried to picture it, but he couldn't quite—and he felt faint, as if he were the formless thing of his imagination. His form remained, though. A fine mist of dread collected on his skin, and he reached back and flattened a palm against the day-warmed bricks behind him.

Circumscribed by the window, the light made him think of the photograph of the painting Sue had shown him—an object twice removed from any reality. In the painting's left panel, two faces had floated in the water; in the right, two children had held hands in front of a haloed tree. He stood transfixed by the circle of light and thought of Oscar, the way the newborn had quietened when he looked not at Omar but at his atmosphere. Then he remembered Camille, sobbing, on the night he'd let Bruno into their home.

A deep breath, like a prolonged gasp, haled itself into his mouth. The light in the window flared and reduced to a candle's flicker and snuffed itself out altogether.

III

On the pavement, Omar leaned against the passenger door of his Fairlane and eyed the abandoned Victorian on the oblique across the road. Amma had left empty-handed a while ago. He'd watched the red dot of her hatchback wend its way home while he stayed put, in case someone else emerged from the old manor. No one did. The streetlights had switched on, and one of them burned overhead. Yet whenever he tried to picture the source of the other light—the inconstant one that had unmoored him at dusk—he felt dizzy. But, suspended or not, he knew it was his role to investigate.

He reached into the car to retrieve his police torch from the glove box; his fingers brushed against his pocketknife, but he decided to leave it behind. Then he locked the car and crossed the road. He sidled through a gap in the temporary chain-link fencing and stopped at the X that feebly sought to bar his way. The barricade tape flapped and fluttered, and he pointed the beam of his torch through its upper half.

He'd meant to illuminate the ground floor. But unlike the building's facade, the other walls were mostly missing, and the torchlight wandered out back and stopped at a tussock of pampas grass that grew to the height of the timber fence. He dragged the torchlight back indoors, where bricks lay in crumbling piles and whatever was left of the walls heaved with must and cockroaches and graffiti. Termites and time had worn through the floorboards, and someone had laid down a warped plank between the entrance and a staircase on the right.

Omar sniffed at the putrefaction in the air. He peered behind him at the chain-link fencing and the street and the shuttered clothing wholesaler across the road. Then, careful not to snap the X, he slipped through it. The torch lit up the plank at his feet and caught a cockroach scurrying across the warped surface. The hair on Omar's neck bristled, and he considered retreat. But Amma must have come this way, he told himself, and at least there were no rats. So, cautiously, he walked the plank, which swayed and clunked yet bore his weight without trouble.

At the base of the stairs, he aimed his torch at a busted baluster that marked out the first floor. He let the beam descend the staircase like a finger over piano keys. Two steps had sawtooth holes in them; a few others had rotted away and seemed about to give in. He settled his boot on the first step, and it went concave and let out a prolonged creak.

When the creak stopped, he thought he heard a faint high-pitched whine. His heart sent mortar fire against his rib cage, and he swished the torch around. The beam hit only the minor apocalypse of rubble and cockroaches he'd already encountered, and the whine became neither louder nor softer. It continued keening on the brink of earshot, as it had from the wardrobe in his motel room—as it would if it were an auditory hallucination.

Accompanied by the noise, he manoeuvred his way up the stairs. He avoided the middle of each step and instead eased his weight onto the edges—one foot on the next step, one foot on the next step—until he reached the busted baluster.

He pushed off it and explored the first floor by torchlight. The ceiling was lower than the one on ground level and the floorboards and walls more intact. Taking up much of the area was the serpentine fossil of a collapsed conveyor belt. He circumnavigated it and imagined the workers who might once have toiled in the space.

They would have punched in and done their job—whatever that was—and then punched out with a meagre paycheque to spend on their lives.

At least there was delineation, he thought; at least they had lives. He pictured Camille in the bedroom of their house in Belli, standing in front of the cracked wooden dressing table. Then he remembered Bruno murmuring, *How are the kids?* to someone over the phone. The high-pitched whine intruded on his consciousness, and he shivered his way back to the present: he was one floor below the oculus.

In the rear corner, he discovered a staircase. Its steps betrayed no signs of decay, and he jogged up them to the second floor. He slowed when he arrived in a featureless space where he could see only what his torch showed him. Dust drifted like ancient confetti through its beam; otherwise, the space seemed empty and reminiscent of a ballroom. At the front of the ballroom, where a stage might have been, an unpainted plasterboard wall had an arched doorway cut out of it.

Omar made his way towards the plasterboard. His footsteps echoed, and the whine grew louder and developed the sandpaper texture of a siren or alarm. He shivered again, and the fine mist of dread that'd settled on his skin earlier returned. But his footsteps did not falter, and he shone his torch at the arch and followed his conviction through it.

He entered a room that was indeed shaped like a stage. His torch revealed the cobwebbed rafters overhead and the hollow innards of the pitched roof. High on the wall before him was the oculus through which he'd observed the inconstant glow. In the night sky outside, he could see wisps of cloud that reminded him of smoke from his mother's cigarettes. Then his gaze descended to a vague object in the middle of the room, and he shone the torch at it.

Resting on ornate legs, the object was a bowl-shaped fire pit with a square cage soldered to its top. The golden bars of the cage's base had melted away to leave a round gap, and the charred remainder of the underside drooped as if it were a wire model of a wormhole. Amma must have burned something here to cause the light, Omar surmised, and the residue of whatever she'd burned was at the bottom of the wormhole—in the bowl of the pit. He braced himself for the discovery: a blackened and bloodied pelt perhaps, or a singed item of children's clothing.

As if in response to this logic, the keening grew even louder, its texture even more abrasive. He ignored it and inhaled and stepped forward to see what Amma had burned. But the light of his torch crept beyond the fire pit and revealed something else: a disembowelled rabbit, lying on the floor beneath the round window. The rabbit's head, severed or twisted off, remained attached by cables of flesh, and an infinity-shaped pool of blood surrounded the carcass.

Omar recoiled, and the mortar fire in his chest rumbled under the unceasing high-pitched noise. His head growled at him to leave. He had an obligation to look, though, and with both hands he wrestled the torchlight into the bowl of the fire pit. Then he exhaled sharply. Beneath the cage, the fire pit contained nothing, not even ash—nothing at all except the Doppler echo of the high-pitched whine.

IV

Later, in his motel room, Omar paced and fumbled with his phone. Twice he'd tried to call the detective inspector from the industrial street. She hadn't picked up, and now he read the umpteenth encrypted message he'd composed to her without sending. This one was overlong and mentioned the fire pit and disembowelled rabbit; it mentioned everything he'd jotted down in his notebook bar the inconstant light and the high-pitched whine. No records, he thought. He deleted the message and replaced it with a shorter one. *Can we meet? It's urgent*, he typed, and hit send.

At the foot of the bed, he stopped pacing. Agitated, he sought a place to put his phone down and slid it on top of the wardrobe and surveyed the room. The leaves hadn't fallen from the wallpaper; the mould in the upper corner hadn't spread. His bed remained unmade thanks to the DO NOT DISTURB sign, and his shirts and socks and underwear were still strewn across the floor beneath the musty curtains.

He stepped out of his boots, and his phone vibrated; without looking, he reached on top of the wardrobe to collect it. His fingers failed to grasp it and instead flicked it behind the wardrobe. The device skittered down the narrow strait between the mahogany and the wallpaper. It hit the floor with a cushioned thud. He sighed and dropped to his hands and knees. Then he put his temple to the carpet and peered under the wardrobe.

Screen alight, the phone had settled in a spot equidistant from each of the wardrobe's four legs. Omar remained still, as if he were making *salah*. He kept his eye on the phone and listened, but there was no sound except his own breathing and the distant burr of traffic. He reached out and snatched up the phone.

In the morning, Sue had replied.

Omar raised his head, and his eyes drifted from the dismissive message to the patterns on the wardrobe. From his low angle, they resembled the two-panel painting more than ever. The knots on the left had become more face-like and the arc of discolouration on the right more coronal. He rose to his full height. The wardrobe, with its ornate legs, shared the approximate shape of the cage and the fire pit.

For an instant, he felt as if he'd never left the abandoned Victorian—as if this were a room within it—and he wondered if he'd be able to sleep here. Then he tossed his phone onto the bedside table and pulled the duvet from the mattress. Swiftly, he wrenched free the top sheet, which was so lacking in thread that he almost tore it. He flung it over the wardrobe and adjusted it to cover the furnishing from head to toe.

The wardrobe now resembled a Halloween ghost, and although the patterns in the wood still haunted the diaphanous cotton, the sheet obscured the faces and halo and cage-on-fire-pit shape enough for him to pretend they didn't exist. He swept up his phone and lay on the stripped bed. *Okay where?* he wrote to Sue.

Then he tapped the GPS tracking app. He checked on the red dot, which pulsed from outside Amma's house in Casus Hill. But he fell asleep staring at the blue dot and picturing the golden-brown Mercedes with the tracker beneath—its battery on the very verge of death.

In the morning, there was a knock on Omar's motel room door, and he gave up refreshing the map on his phone. He'd woken to find no blue dot pulsing on it. The battery in the tracker under Bruno's Mercedes had died while he slept. When he tapped on 'show last location', a message informed him that the function was coming soon to mobile; for now, it was only available on the desktop dashboard.

The ensuite door was ajar, and in the sunlight the Halloween ghost that he'd crafted seemed transparent and ridiculous. Omar strode to the motel room door and considered taking the sheet down so no one else would see it. But he decided not to bother; he was in his socks and had no intention of letting anyone into the room.

When he opened the door, it was no surprise to find the detective inspector out in the courtyard. What did surprise him was that she hadn't removed her motorcycle helmet—although an explanation lurked nearby. Beside a parked lime-green station wagon, the motel owner puffed on a cigarette and leered at his room without shame.

'I'll just get my boots on,' Omar said to Sue.

He pushed the door to shut it. It would not be hurried, though, and Sue shoved it open and bustled her way into the room. Omar let the door ease closed, and the space gloomed slightly. 'Why does it matter if she sees your face?' he asked.

Sue took off her helmet and rested it atop the ghostly wardrobe. She tucked her hair behind her ears. 'She strike you as the discreet type?'

'Doubt she'd recognise you from the news. And anyway, your guy left the envelope where she could find it.'

Sue nodded, and her eye flitted from the stripped bed to the clothes on the carpet. She jabbed her thumb over her shoulder at the wardrobe. 'What's this about?'

Omar tensed. 'I got bad vibes from it.'

'Bad vibes?' Sue gazed at the rest of the room. 'How much sleep did you get, Omar?'

He forced a chuckle. 'Probably not enough, but who gets enough these days?'

She took a couple of contemplative steps towards the curtains and ran her fingertips along the top edge of the wardrobe, over the sheet.

'I've been following Corban,' he said, 'like you asked.'

'Did you learn anything interesting?'

'She's a woman of habit.' He retrieved his boots and perched on the side of the bed that faced the exit. 'She goes from her home to the pokies to the grocery store. And back to her home.'

'Uh-huh.'

Sue opened the ensuite door wider. The room brightened. He figured she'd only see his razor and the bristles of his toothbrush that were already starting to wilt. Still, he felt intruded upon, doubly so now, as if one shameful aspect of his character were embedded in the room and another in the ensuite. Idly, he wondered if he could share his personal space with anyone ever again, or if he'd become wedded to his solitude.

'Then yesterday,' he said, 'she visited a woman who sold rabbits. And she bought two.' The laces of Omar's right boot were knotted, and he rested it in his lap. 'After dark, she entered a derelict warehouse near the city centre.'

Sue's posture grew more rigid. 'Say more about that.'

'Why am I following Corban?'

'Why'd she go into the warehouse?'

Omar picked at the knotted laces.

'Fuck's sake,' Sue exclaimed. She strode to the side of the bed and snatched the boot from him. 'You're following her because she's not officially on our radar. Her alibi's solid. Her history's clean. But the children's mother claims Corban slipped her that painting as part of a campaign of threat and harassment.' Sue plucked violently at the knot. 'Now, there's nothing at all to back this claim up . . .'

'Except your gut feeling?'

'Except my gut feeling.' Sue nodded. 'We're under-resourced, Omar. And Corban made my guy.'

Omar gave a tight smile. 'Your guy who delivered the envelope?'

'Well, now you're my guy.' She returned his smile with a lopsided grin and lobbed the unknotted boot towards him. 'So do you have something for me or not?'

He caught the boot. 'I'm not sure. I followed up at the warehouse. I believe Corban slaughtered a rabbit there. On the second floor. There was also'—he slipped the boot onto his foot and flattened his tone—'a fire pit thing with a melting cage attached to it.'

'A what?'

He shrugged. 'That's why I tried to call you.'

Sue glared at him. She touched her jaw and turned away.

Omar tied his bootlaces. 'Does that mean something to you?'

She walked towards the ensuite. 'What was burned in the fire pit?'

'I don't know. Nothing, as far as I could tell.' He recalled the inconstant light and having to use both his hands to force the beam of his torch into the bowl of the fire pit. Then he swallowed and dragged his left boot towards him. 'But I can't say what happened to the other rabbit she bought.'

Omar put on his left boot. Sue wandered in front of the wardrobe and stood with her back to it. 'Did you take photos?'

In the hum of what passed for silence in the city, Omar tied his laces. He thought he heard the keening from inside the wardrobe, and his gaze drifted to its veiled form. At Sue's back, the sheet rippled with such subtlety that it looked like sand being swept off a dune.

'I thought I wasn't meant to produce a digital trail,' he said. His hands felt as if they were shaking. But they weren't, and he finished tying his laces and sat upright. 'Besides, I didn't know the status of the property, and I didn't have a warrant.'

Sue snorted and folded her arms. 'Did you have a warrant for Michael Metcalf's house?' She met Omar's surprised gaze. 'I set up an alert for him, just in case. And some passers-by saw a "Black man"'—she put the identity in air quotes—'going through Michael's rubbish. Naturally, they called the police.'

Omar got to his booted feet. The keening from the wardrobe had stopped, if it'd ever started, and he tried to calculate why Sue thought she could use his particular help on this case. 'I rang the bell,' he said. 'Twice.'

'You sure? Michael was home when two uniform cops arrived. Said he'd been home all day.' She took down her helmet from the wardrobe. 'He's not even a suspect, is he?'

Omar stuffed his hands into his pockets. 'Not exactly.'

Sue passed him her notebook. 'Here, write down the address of the warehouse. I'll get someone to check on it.' When he'd done this, she snapped the notebook shut and put her helmet on. Then she walked to the door and reached for the handle. 'Just forget your personal stuff for a couple more days, will you?'

He wanted to tell her that it wasn't personal stuff—it was work. But she was already gone, and he was alone again with his razor and toothbrush and the Halloween ghost of the wardrobe.

In the evening, Omar stood in the hallway of Camille's house and rubbed the stubble on his head. It was greasy once more from a workday tailing Amma, and his face remained unshaven. Ahead of him, Camille leaned against the wall beside a framed wedding photo of her and Dev. She shuffled the bottle of shiraz Omar had brought with him out of its paper bag and inspected the label. 'Do you drink these days?' she asked.

'Still no.' He'd never drunk on account of his parents' faith, which lay dormant within him, and he turned his gaze to the wedding photo. 'I brought it for you guys.'

'Thanks.' She wrestled the bottle back into the paper bag. 'I'm not drinking right now, and Oscar's asleep, so he definitely won't be having any.' The hint of a smile played at the corners of Camille's mouth. 'Dev's working late,' she added, wrinkling her nose. 'He might not be home for a while.'

She padded barefoot towards the living room, and Omar let out a contented breath. When she'd finally texted to invite him to dinner, he'd wanted to ask if it would be with or without her husband. There'd been no reasonable way of phrasing the question, though, and it pleased him now to discover the answer. 'What does Dev do, anyway?'

'Project manager,' Camille replied. Ahead of him, she trailed her fingers over the contours of a closed bedroom door. She wore a beachy pair of shorts, and her legs were brailled with eczema. 'We used to work together but now he works for an NGO.'

Omar passed the bedroom door, behind which Oscar snuffled and wheezed—and the thought he'd had in his motel room came back to him: could he share his personal space with anyone ever again? With Camille and Oscar? The notion seemed less fantastical than it had before, and he found himself wishing that Dev did not exist. Nonexistence was a cruel thing to wish upon the man, he knew, yet it was not as cruel as his hope.

In the living room, Camille gestured for Omar to take a seat. 'Where are you staying?' she asked.

He gave her the name of the motel and overtook her and surveyed his seating options. They were a lone recliner, off to the side, and a three-seater sofa that faced both an overlarge television and the small screen of a baby monitor on the coffee table. For the moment, he made no move towards either.

'And how's work for you?' she said.

'It's work.' Omar shrugged. 'I'm trying to finish some things up. Make space for better things, you know?'

He wondered whether this were true and tarried in the spot in which he'd held the newborn. Oscar had peered up at him—had peered at his atmosphere—and quieted. The memory sent warmth flowing through his body.

Camille cleared her throat. 'You don't want to tell me about the case?'

He glanced at her. 'You really want to know about it?'

'You never used to give me a choice.'

She cast her eyes down, and the warmth gathered itself in his cheeks. He followed her gaze to the flecked mauve polish of her toenails. 'I'm not exactly the same as I used to be,' he said.

'Neither am I.' She raised her eyes. 'I'll grab you a Coke.'

She spirited the shiraz into the kitchen, and he sat on the sofa, in the seat closest to the recliner in which he assumed Camille would sit. On the baby monitor, he could see a bundle in a bassinet and a volume gauge that filled and emptied to the rhythm of Oscar's breathing.

Camille returned with two glasses of Coke. She handed one to him. 'So, are you going to tell me?'

'About the investigation in Sydney?' He watched her nod and weigh up where to position herself in the room. 'Well,' he continued, 'I'm following a person of interest, and . . .'

Instead of sitting in the recliner, Camille eased herself onto the sofa beside him. She left a space between them, yet she tucked her legs beneath her body and pushed her mauve toenails towards his thigh. This was how they'd often sat on their leather sofa in Belli, except that he used to rest his hand on her ankle. The temptation to do so now reached his fingertips, and he tightened his grip on his perspiring glass.

'And?' She put her glass on the coffee table. 'Are you any closer to finding the guy who killed them?'

For a moment, he thought she was asking about Bruno—Omar figured that Patricia and Freeston were almost certainly dead. Then he reminded himself that she would not be. 'We don't know that the children are dead.'

'I mean, surely.' Her gaze grew dolorous, almost desperate in its melancholy. 'Are you at least following the main suspect?'

'I'm following an older woman who's a person of interest.'

Camille hemmed and caressed her throat, and Omar felt as if he were seeing a mirror of himself. 'Was she the one who did it?' she asked.

'There's no evidence of that.'

His mind flashed with a recollection of the torchlight hitting the empty bowl of the fire pit, and through the baby monitor Oscar let out a short burble of dissatisfaction. Omar glanced at it. Camille continued to stare at him, and he felt unsteady. But he managed to meet her gaze without flinching. It was Camille who looked away and fixed her eyes on the television. Then her hand moved towards his thigh. She gripped her toes and flexed them, and her fingertips came to a gentle rest on the nub of her ankle. 'Do you remember the time when we trailed that arsonist together?' she murmured.

Omar sensed the warmth still in his cheeks. The time they'd trailed that arsonist together, they'd fucked in the back seat of his Fairlane—and then found a rock in a field under which the arsonist had secreted an inculpatory USB drive. He wondered which of these moments she was bringing to mind, or whether she'd forgotten the specifics and abstracted the memory into a montage.

'Camille?' he said.

He placed his glass beside hers on the coffee table. She blinked rapidly and began to turn towards him. Then the front door slammed, and his attention swung in its direction.

'Sorry,' Dev called out from the hallway.

He'd woken Oscar, who let out a piercing cry. The newborn squalled in his bassinet, and an anodised version of the noise echoed through the baby monitor. On the small screen, the bundle writhed as if it were about to split down the middle.

Without a word, Camille rose from the sofa and dashed to the bedroom. Omar stood too. On the monitor, he watched Camille pick up Oscar and cradle him to her chest. She rocked the baby back and forth, back and forth, yet Oscar kept bawling.

Dev, who was dressed in a suit, entered the living room and clocked the screaming monitor and the two glasses of Coke side by side. He strode over to Omar and extended a hand in greeting. 'Omar?' he said. 'Camille's told me so much about you.'

There was no malice in the cliché or the man's smile. Camille's husband seemed at ease with the dissonant situation.

Omar shook his hand. 'Yeah, likewise.'

The squalling on the baby monitor stopped. 'I didn't mean to wake him,' Dev said. 'The damn door used to have this hydraulic closer.' He gestured towards the hallway. 'Did you order food already?'

'Not yet.'

The small screen distracted Omar, and Dev joined him in watching. Her back to the camera, Camille had offered Oscar her breast, and the newborn alternately suckled and whimpered. But the volume gauge registered a cry more plaintive now, and on the screen Camille shuddered with sobs.

'Excuse me,' Dev said.

He joined Camille and their child in the bedroom, and Omar saw him enfold them both in an embrace. They lingered like that, a young family in a private moment. Omar could hear that Oscar had stopped whimpering; he could hear Camille's quaky breathing.

'I love you so much,' Camille whispered.

'I love you too,' Dev breathed, and kissed her.

In the living room, Omar felt woozy. More than that, he felt as if he were the formless thing once more, adrift, a phantasmatic interloper there simply to bear witness, and it occurred to him that perhaps his wish for Dev not to exist was directed at the wrong man. He thought of Bruno fleeing the house in Belli. Then he fled himself, and he only felt corporeal again when he parked his Fairlane outside Mick Metcalf's house.

Omar wandered past the emptied letterbox and over the velvet grass to the porch. He pressed the doorbell, and the camera drank in his visage. Almost immediately, Mick appeared on the threshold. Half a head taller than Omar, he wore a checked shirt and an ironic but not unfriendly smile. 'Figured you'd be back.'

Omar tried to arrange his countenance to match, but he felt as if an optogram of the baby monitor was on his retinas, and he wasn't sure if his smile convinced. Camille had tried to call him repeatedly; he'd texted her to say that something urgent had come up with his case. 'Well,' he said to Mick, 'I still have some questions for you.'

'Fresh questions?'

'Yeah.'

'Like what?'

Omar shifted his weight; he only had two fresh questions of any substance. One was whether Mick had had recent contact with his father. The other was whether Bruno had any acquaintances whose children he might ask after over the phone. But Omar would go over stale questions as well—all that awaited him in his motel room were ghosts of his own making. 'Like why didn't you answer the door the other night?' he said.

Mick scanned the pavement behind Omar. 'Wasn't home.'

'Uniform cops said you were.'

'Uniform cops, huh?' Mick said. 'You want to come in, Detective, or do you want to go through my bin again?'

Mick gestured for Omar to walk ahead of him into the house. On the left was a carpeted staircase that disappeared into the dark of the first floor; to the right was a home gym with another staircase that Omar presumed led down to the garage. As in Camille's house, there was a closed bedroom or bathroom door towards the end of the hallway.

'Right on through,' Mick said.

Omar continued on to an open-plan area that encompassed a stark white kitchen and commodious living-and-dining space. A television, far smaller than Camille's, was mounted high on a wall; below it, a record player sat atop a bookcase lined with vinyl record sleeves.

Mick headed into the kitchen. 'Where do you want to start?'

'Let's start with this.' At the bookcase, Omar blinked at the spines of the record collection. 'Have you spoken to your father lately?'

'My father?' From the fridge, Mick grabbed a bottle of Pepsi. 'We're more or less estranged; I've told you this.'

Omar plucked a cardboard sleeve at random from the bookcase—a Joni Mitchell LP—and heard ice tinkle into a glass in the kitchen. 'Tell me again.'

'It's a boring history,' Mick said. 'Small-minded man unhappy with his life. Turns to drink. Wife leaves.'

Omar inspected the album cover: a painting of Mitchell with bluffs for cheekbones, existentially smoking a cigarette over a glass of red wine. If he shifted the colours and swapped the wine out for coffee, the image could almost be his own mother—a sharp woman with disapproving cheekbones that always seemed to glisten behind the smoke of her cigarette.

Mick was still talking, Omar realised, and he heard liquid dribble into the glass. 'Son gets the living shit beaten out of him every day,' Mick said. 'But he thinks: silver lining—he's not a daughter.'

Omar raised an eyebrow, and in turn Mick raised a tumbler of rum and Pepsi in a toast. 'Cheers.'

'That's why you joined the police?'

'High-minded. Like you, I figure.' Drink in hand, Mick walked towards the bookcase where Omar stood. 'Probably also explains why I quit.'

Omar nodded. His mother's one-way flight to Somalia had precipitated his joining the police—the only Black officer for a country mile—and, as if in protest at this, his father had abandoned small-town New South Wales and taken his sister to live in smaller-town Queensland. Omar pressed at the sides of the cardboard sleeve he was holding. It opened like a fish's mouth: the Joni Mitchell LP was missing.

'That one's gone.' Mick loitered at his shoulder. 'Quite a few of them are, but the ladies love a record shelf that's full.'

Omar thought of the empty blue box of menstrual pads in the bin. 'I thought you had a partner?'

'No one exclusive.' A smile flashed across Mick's face, and he took the empty cardboard sleeve from Omar. 'Want me to play something?'

'Sure.' Omar stepped away. Behind him, a slimline couch looked like a slice of display furniture; behind that was a nondescript dining table. Mick rested his drink on the bookcase between the record player and a triangular block of wood veneer. An identical block was affixed to the wall on the other side of the player—they were like a pair of implacable bookends.

'So you haven't spoken to your father?' Omar said.

Mick slid the Joni Mitchell sleeve back onto the shelf and thumbed through his collection. 'I more or less stopped speaking with him after he went to jail.'

'What's he say, though,' Omar persisted, 'when you do speak to him?'

Mick held up a different cardboard sleeve—*The Freewheelin' Bob Dylan*. 'He told me he was sorry for everything he put me through. He looked at child porn—he admitted that—but he said he didn't kill those two kids.'

Omar perched on the arm of the couch. 'You talk about the Reeves children with your father?'

Mick slipped the vinyl out of its sleeve. 'No.'

'About the day it happened?'

'No.' Mick frowned over his shoulder. 'The day it happened I was in Sydney on a shift with my police partner.'

'I know.' Omar folded his arms and considered some of the evidence against Bruno. 'I'm asking if your dad's ever said anything about that day—why he lied about his alibi, why a witness saw him in a white VW van near the crime scene.'

Mick tossed the cardboard sleeve onto the bookcase. '*I'm sorry, I didn't do it.*' He lifted the record player's lid and positioned the LP on the turntable. 'That's as far as the conversation gets with him.'

'And you believe him?'

'I don't know.' The vinyl spun silently, its grooves awaiting the hovering needle; Mick nudged it into the right place. 'If my dad's guilty, he's gotten off lightly,' he said. 'If he's not?'

He lowered the needle onto the vinyl. There followed a couple of scratchy seconds that put Omar in mind of Oscar's receding whimper and Camille's quaky breathing. *I love you so much*, she'd whispered. Then an acoustic guitar kicked in, and Dylan distracted him with a pair of apocalyptic questions.

Omar asked a question of his own: 'Do you know if your father has any friends with children?'

Mick sighed. 'Is that your fresh question?' He collected his tumbler and finished his drink and headed back to the kitchen.

Omar unfolded his arms. 'I have evidence that he communicated with someone who has children.'

'And would it matter if he has friends with children?'

'It might matter.' Omar stood from the arm of the couch. 'Might matter even more if he doesn't.'

'I don't know who my father's friends are,' Mick muttered. On the counter before him were his tumbler and ice and bottles of Pepsi and rum. He flattened his palms either side of the deconstructed drink and bent his shoulders inwards. 'The internal affairs allegations against you are true then.'

It was more a statement than a question, and Omar lowered his eyebrows. 'Did your father tell you about that?'

'No.' Mick snorted. 'I still have mates in the police, Omar. Do you?'

The LP spun on the turntable, and Dylan circled around to variations of his opening questions. The cardboard sleeve lay on the bookcase, near the wood veneer block on the left. One of the block's screws was almost stripped, Omar noticed. He thought of the call he'd received from Angus to let him know that the PSC might soon strip him of his job. 'At least one,' he replied.

Over the music, he heard something clatter and jangle—or he thought he did. He glanced in the direction of the closed door he'd passed on his way in. 'Is someone else here?'

In the kitchen, Mick gripped the Pepsi and canted his head. 'Maybe.'

Omar heard a second clatter. 'Who else is here, Mick?'

Mick returned the Pepsi to the fridge. 'Maybe it's my father?'

He scooped up the bottle of rum and unscrewed its cap. Omar made a line of his lips. He didn't believe Bruno was in the house, but he could no longer track the man, and he didn't want to be the idiot detective who failed to follow up. 'Do you mind if I take a quick look?'

'Of course not.' Mick refilled his tumbler with rum. 'I'd expect nothing less of you.'

He swigged from his glass, and Omar strode to the closed door. The one in Camille's house that'd separated him from her family loomed in his mind. He recalled the arched doorway inside the abandoned Victorian, with its fire pit and disembowelled rabbit. Then he drew a breath and shoved the door open.

In front of him was an empty bathroom—fresh tiling, spotless sink, a rainwater shower dripping over a bathtub. The main thing out of place was a stopper attached to a short metal chain. It must have tumbled off the edge of the tub, and a bottle of conditioner had been unable to resist the urge to dive in its wake.

Omar looked back towards the open-plan area, where the record was still playing. Beside the kitchen counter, Mick watched him with a vacant expression on his face. He tipped the rest of his rum into his mouth and chewed on a shard of ice.

Afterwards, Omar pulled his Fairlane into the parking spot that faced his motel room. He pictured again what awaited him inside: an unused razor glinting in the ensuite and a wilting toothbrush in its glass and a wardrobe veiled with a sheet. Then he opened the encrypted messaging app. *Anything from the warehouse?* he wrote to Sue. *And can you give me whatever you got on MM?* He climbed out of his Fairlane and glanced up at the firmament and walked towards the room.

Close by, an engine idled, and in a parking spot across the courtyard, an SUV's headlights came on. Omar bowed his head and fiddled with his room key. The car accelerated and turned, somewhat recklessly, not towards the exit but in his direction. Its headlights struck him like a match, and the car came to a haphazard halt behind his Fairlane.

Camille peered at him through the smudged driver's-side window. Omar pursed his lips; heat radiated from his scalp. She cut the headlights, but she left the engine on and clambered out of the car. 'Where'd you run off to tonight?' she asked.

'Camille.'

He heard his own penitence, yet he didn't know how to follow it through. There was one thing he wished to say and so much he didn't.

'You know,' she blurted, 'it's very—'

She swallowed and narrowed her eyes at his room. He slapped his palm with his key and followed her gaze to the DO NOT DISTURB sign dangling near his hip. He yearned to let her into his life. But how could he when he couldn't even bear to invite her into his room?

'It was very rude to run off before dinner like that,' Camille managed to say.

'I'm sorry.'

'I thought we were going to catch up.'

'Didn't you get my message?'

She cupped her left elbow with her right hand. 'Yeah, I got it.'

Omar surveyed the courtyard. There was a sedan parked askew by a rushed driver and a couple of rooms with their lights on. 'Are you okay?' he asked. 'Earlier tonight—'

'I'm fine.' Her cheek twitched. 'It's just been really *fucking* hard. Do you understand?'

'I don't, but I can, if you tell me.' In his peripheral vision, the motel owner's cigarette glowed orange; near the front office, halfway up the outdoor stairs that led to what Omar assumed were living quarters, she leaned against the railing and gawked at him. He took a couple of steps towards Camille. 'Does Dev know you're here?'

Camille glanced at him. 'Like I told you, sometimes I drive Oscar around for hours. It helps him sleep.' She let go of her left elbow. 'I didn't plan to end up here.'

He stepped towards her again so that they were standing face-to-face with each other. 'How did you end up here?'

She let out a sob that had an undertow of self-deprecation. Then she gave an uncontrolled shrug. 'I don't know.'

He sought out her eyes, as if to pick up from the instant before Dev had arrived home. 'I do remember the night we followed that arsonist,' he murmured.

She let out another sob. 'That was before . . .'

She trailed off. He allowed himself a smile and ignored the remorse gathering in his throat. Then he took hold of her hand, grasping only her fingertips. He stared down and marvelled at the contact. Her wedding band encircled her finger, yet it felt like this was the moment. *Speak*, he urged himself.

But rather than speaking, he leaned in to kiss her. Their lips touched, and a shiver of electricity ran from the base of his skull to the bottom of his spine. The remorse in his throat dissolved, and everything else seemed soluble—a future with Camille, his twinned cases, the situation with internal affairs. The feeling lasted a single second before Camille pulled away.

Their faces remained close, and her gaze flitted from one of his eyes to the other. 'Where'd you go tonight?' she whispered. 'Really?'

He eased back and released her hand. Her focus shifted from his eyes to his unshaven chin, and he retreated further. He glimpsed Oscar in his capsule in the back seat and wished he could hold the newborn again. 'I went to reinterview Mick Metcalf,' he confessed. 'I'm here on a different case but I'm still investigating Bruno. But I'd stop if—'

'Then stop,' she said.

Her eyes were tearful, yet her mouth betrayed no sentiment, and he offered her no declamation or promise or invitation. Instead, he watched her turn from him and climb into her SUV. She switched the headlights on, and he observed the SUV jerking into reverse and braking hard and accelerating away. He saw a plume of smoke curling from the motel owner's cigarette.

Then he let himself into his room to ignore his ghosts and nurse the soupçon of hope that lingered in the aftermath of the kiss. The time had come to retrieve the tracker from beneath Amma's hatchback and go back to Belli.

V

In the early morning, Omar was on the highway, accelerating beyond a corroded sign that informed him he was leaving Sydney. He wasn't heading back to Belli, though. Onto the foot of his stripped bed he'd piled his socks and shirts. He'd almost taken the sheet down from the wardrobe and checked out of the motel. Then he'd spied Amma's location on his phone—the red dot skidding west across the map—and he'd rushed to his Fairlane to do his duty.

Now he drove beneath an overpass, and his phone vibrated on the dash. Angus Troy's name appeared on the screen. Omar was about to pick up when he spotted a police car stowed away in the overpass's shadow and a uniform cop firing a speed gun at him. He was travelling a tick over the limit, and his foot retreated from the accelerator. But he touched neither his mobile nor the horizontal pedal lest his skin colour and brake lights combine to act as a lure.

The police car faded into the distance behind him, and his phone stopped ringing. On the screen, the red dot replaced Angus's name and travelled along a highway in the Blue Mountains. Omar chased after it through small towns and bushland, past grey hotels and greyer nomads. His collar felt damp, and he pumped up the aircon.

Beyond the Mountains, he passed trees burned and cracked and genuflecting. He noted a rainbow chart that said the fire danger was as high as the danger of a storm. By the roadside, sunlight shimmered in the leaves of a gum beside a water tank and put him in mind of the halo of the two-panel painting. He rested his elbow against the driver's window and wondered how much longer he'd follow Amma. Then he kept going.

After four hours on the road, he cruised through a dusty town which had the same Federation architecture as Belli. His mind projected an image of Jack and Lonnie, seated on the boot of a topsoil-smeared sedan. Near them, he imagined Patricia and Freeston—the same age as they were five years ago—leaning against the pillars of a country pub and watching him drive away.

Angus called again; this time Omar didn't answer because he didn't feel like it. Again, he considered turning back, but he continued on. He trailed the red dot, which drifted inland until it came to a halt in a tiny village called Morningvale.

On the main street, Omar pulled over a distance away from Amma's hatchback. A handful of country jalopies were parked around him and partially obscured his view of her—and hers of him. He'd parked next to a faded pharmacy that was merely one of the many moribund shopfronts that lined the road.

Through the gaps between vehicles, he watched Amma approach a young man who wore a baseball cap that cast his face in shadow. She gave the young man a kiss on each cheek and stepped back and handed him an object. He inspected it near the overladen tray of his maroon Dodge Ram ute. Omar watched the conversation between Amma and the young man; he heard a dog bark as if it were part of the discussion. Then his phone vibrated. Angus was calling for a third time, and Omar answered him on speaker.

'The fuck have you been?' Angus demanded.

Omar returned to watching Amma and the young man. 'I'm in Sydney. Why?'

'Because.'

Angus paused, and the phone rustled. In the distance, the young man raised the object above eye level and turned it over in his hand.

It caught the light like a block of lodestone, and Omar drummed his fingers against his lips. The object could only be one thing: the GPS tracker he'd cached under Amma's car.

'Omar,' Angus said. 'Bruno Metcalf has gone missing.'

Omar felt his entire body lurch, yet he found himself sitting still. 'What?'

'It's not in the system yet, but the guy hasn't been seen or heard from in a whole day apparently.'

'And?'

'And no, mate, there have been absolutely no reports of missing children.'

Omar heard a mechanical whirr nearby. At the entrance to the pharmacy, a bald man in a white coat was lowering the roller door.

'You said you're in Sydney, right?' Angus asked.

The roller door came to a halt about a third of the way down. Then the pharmacist raised it a little and lowered it again, as if he were adjusting it to a precise height.

'Omar?' Angus prompted. 'You're in Sydney, right?'

'Yeah.'

'What are you doing right now?'

'Some guest work on another case. Off the books.'

Angus sighed. 'Don't tell me shit like that,' he muttered.

'Okay.' Omar turned his gaze back to Amma and the young man. The roller door might have caught their attention, because they seemed to gesticulate in his direction. 'So what are you asking me, Angus?' he said.

The bald pharmacist wandered out onto the pavement. He looked pointedly at the Fairlane's licence plate and returned to his store. Omar squinted through his windscreen: Amma and the young man were heading towards him.

'Nothing.' Angus cleared his throat. 'Anyway, mate, the PSC are—'

'Sorry, Angus,' Omar said. 'I gotta run.'

Amma and the young man drew closer, and Omar hung up. He started the car and jammed it into gear. Right in front of them, he performed a swift U-turn. His eyes met Amma's, and in the flicker of her skin tag he thought he perceived recognition. Then he hightailed it out of town.

The Fairlane bobbled along a winding, potholed road that had farmland on one side and bush on the other. Amma and the young man had long since disappeared from Omar's rear-view; on his phone, the map with the red dot had been erased. But that no longer concerned him. He jabbed at the phone to refresh the other map—the one on which the blue dot used to pulse. It stayed obstinately blank.

Rapid-fire, he navigated to the option to 'show last location'. When he tapped it, a message he'd already seen appeared: the feature was coming soon; for now, it was only available on the desktop dashboard. He braked, and the car came to an abrupt halt. The seatbelt dug into his shoulder. He felt claustrophobic and breathless. Fleetingly, he thought about calling Sue. Less fleetingly, he thought about calling Angus back. But he knew there was only one person he could trust with this.

He let the Fairlane roll to a second halt on the gravel beside the bush and the charred trunk of a coolabah. Then he got out and dialled Camille's number. The phone trilled in his ear, and he paced from shade to sun, sun to shade.

'Omar?'

The sound of her voice made his throat constrict. For a moment, he couldn't speak. There was still time to stop and say something else, he thought, and he shifted his fingers to the narrow gap between his Adam's apple and his facial hair.

'I'm sorry,' he said. 'I need you to do a favour for me.'

Camille was quiet a moment. Then in a flat voice she asked, 'What do you need?'

'Are you home?' In the distance, he saw a four-wheel drive approaching at speed along the potholed road. 'Do you have your computer nearby?'

'Hang on.'

The padding of her footfalls was accompanied by air whooshing between the mouthpiece and her lips. He pictured her walking, not through her own house but through the one they'd shared in Belli. She was striding away from him, he realised, from the kitchen where he stood dumbstruck to the bedroom where she would begin to pack her things.

'Is Oscar asleep?'

'Dev's out walking him,' she replied. 'What do you want me to do?'

'Do you have a VPN? Or a Tor browser?'

'Do I need one?'

The four-wheel drive braked near Omar, and the driver—a burly man in wraparound sunglasses—leaned out the window. 'You broken down, bud?'

'Nah, I'm good. Thanks. Just, uh . . .' Omar pointed to the phone.

The driver gave a sardonic smile and accelerated to a more reckless speed than the one at which he'd approached.

'Where are you?' Camille said.

'On the road,' Omar replied. 'Don't worry about the VPN.'

He asked Camille to open the website for the GPS tracker and retreated to the mottled shade of the coolabah. The dispassionate breeze lapped at his skin. Misery stole into his chest, and all he did was give banal tech-help instructions: input a username, type in a password, enter an authentication code. 'Is there a "show last location" option?' he asked.

He heard her mouse clicking. 'I can export recent locations to a CSV file.'

'Can you do that, please?'

From the farmland over the road came the lowing of a cow, or perhaps the throaty bleating of a sheep. He wandered out of the shade and past his Fairlane and across the road.

'It's asking me if I want GPS tracker "blue" or "red",' Camille said. 'Blue.'

Before him stretched a barbed-wire fence and a sward of grass that curved up towards a hummock on the horizon. Trees grew diffidently on the hummock, and it didn't seem possible for an animal to hide there. But the sward was as empty as the bowl of the fire pit.

'I assume these are times and coordinates?' Camille said.

Omar walked back to the Fairlane and rested his elbows against its warm metal. 'What's the last set?'

'There are days of coordinates here, a set for every half-hour.'

He put her on speaker and opened the notes app on his phone. 'Is there anything recent?'

She made no reply, and he heard the keys of her laptop being pressed, one by one. He remembered her fingertips on her ankle—and then in his hand; he understood that they'd never be there again.

'These coordinates are all in Belli,' she murmured. 'You're calling me to find Bruno Metcalf's location?'

Once more, he heard the lowing, or bleating, and he stared over his shoulder at the farmland across the road. It remained desolate. In his miserable chest, his heart fired blood through his arteries, and he could almost hear the rat-a-tat of Bruno knocking on the door. 'If I hadn't invited him in that night,' he said, 'would we still be together?'

He heard Camille shift her position. Then she swallowed loudly. 'No,' she replied.

He felt tears forming behind his eyes, and he squeezed them shut.

Camille clicked the mouse. 'There's a random set of coordinates here from yesterday. Do you want them?'

Omar opened his eyes and found that they were completely dry. 'Yes,' he said.

―――

Hours later, he drove the Fairlane over a dirt road covered with twigs and dead leaves. A fresh spray of grass lined the road's centre, and macilent trees grew either side. Mounted on the dash, his phone was in flight mode, but he'd marked the GPS coordinates Camille had given him by dropping a pin on an offline map of Jemalong-Cooke National Park. His own position in Jemalong-Cooke was marked as well: he was a remorseful grey dot pulsing on the screen.

The grey dot approached the pin—and ahead of him, parked on the uphill slope between the boles of two gums, lurked the golden-brown Mercedes. Omar let the Fairlane glide past and looked into the other vehicle. It was unoccupied; there was no sign of Bruno or anyone else.

On the opposite side of the road, Omar parked on the downhill slope near an overgrown walking trail. He got out of his car and listened to the screech and whistle of birdsong. Then he went to the Mercedes and circled it to check its body for damage. The hubcaps bore scratches, but otherwise the car was uninjured.

He unbuttoned his shirtsleeve and covered his fingers with his cuff and tried the handle of the driver's door. To his surprise, it opened. He straightened and scanned the landscape to see if anyone might be spying on him. But through the trees, only the first inklings of sunset were watching.

Careful not to leave a trace, he inspected the car's seats and footwells and glove box. He found nothing of note. The boot was also empty except for a crimped receipt for groceries. Omar read it without touching. Dated the previous day, the receipt revealed that Bruno had purchased unbranded water, bread, canned tuna, toilet paper, wet wipes and tea; the only branded item was a ten-pack of something called Stevie Extra Plus, which Omar figured could be powdered milk or artificial sweetener.

He slammed the boot. The thud echoed, yet the birdsong did not even pause. Was Bruno planning on spending time camping in the national park? Why would he do that? Bruno had never been to Jemalong-Cooke before, as far as Omar knew. Besides, the unlocked car and failure to inform anyone about his impending absence suggested Bruno thought this would be a quick trip. Perhaps Omar's pursuit of him had driven him to madness and flight.

Omar considered the possibility that Bruno, like Amma, had discovered the GPS tracker. Maybe Bruno was luring him out here. That seemed doubtful, though, since Bruno's best play would've been to turn the tracker over to the PSC—as he'd done with the listening devices.

Even with those assurances in mind, Omar felt uncertain when he crouched at the rear wheel. He covered his fingers with his cuff again and felt beneath the Mercedes for the GPS tracker. When he found it, he used both hands to wrench it free. Then he stood and examined the black box. Spattered with mud, it appeared not to have been touched by a hand other than his.

He carried it towards the Fairlane. This was no setup, he concluded; Bruno was out in the national park somewhere, although why he'd come remained difficult to fathom. Omar tossed the tracker into the glove box and picked up his torch. After a moment's hesitation, he grabbed the pocketknife and pair of binoculars as well.

Vanishing point arrived a minute into Omar's trek along the overgrown trail. He glanced behind him and couldn't spy any evidence of the dirt road or the Fairlane. This was as he'd expected, yet the sense of isolation parched his throat. He wished he'd brought water. Then the breeze cooled his nape. Birds tweeted, and he comforted himself with the knowledge that his phone and its offline map could guide him back to his car. Plus, Camille knew where he was, even if she no longer cared.

He walked on, and the track curved in one direction and became rocky; it then twisted in the other direction, and the topsoil turned to dust. He wove beneath trees and glimpsed mammals and snakes at the periphery of his vision. On a steep section of the trail, he found himself in constant danger of skidding and held on to whatever foliage he could grip. At one point, he leaped carelessly onto a log that blocked the path. It rolled under his sole, but he managed to steady himself by grabbing at the limb of a young silvertop ash.

The light faded, and he came to the end of the marked trail. It led out onto a concrete platform that bore traces of a fence and overlooked a valley. Below, millions of trees blanketed the landscape. The dull sun was setting behind the faraway bluffs, and over the valley a wispy cloud had separated from the sky and made a low play for custody of the treetops.

The sight was stunning, yet it also sparked a faint terror in him. Then he reminded himself that he'd ventured into the abandoned Victorian and made his way out unharmed. He raised his binoculars and scanned the forest. The east gave up no secrets. But after a time, to the west, an animal trotted through a small clearing on the mountainside.

It was a feral pig, and a white object flashed in its maw. Omar's instinct told him this was a sneaker, and he suffered a bout of vertigo. By the time he'd steadied himself and his mind had suggested that the object might be a rabbit or a bird, the pig had absconded into the bush. But his instinct persisted: if it might have been a sneaker, he had to investigate.

On his phone, he dropped a pin with his current location on the offline map. He wandered off the trail through dense bushland

and across the mountainside. The terrain was fluctuating and unpredictable. He navigated around thickets and forced his way through foliage. Evening descended, and the lower pitch of the birdsong seemed to signify a shift change. He raised his torch above his shoulder and shone it ahead of him.

After a while, he reached the clearing and ventured into the bush after the pig. Here, the trees huddled together, and ethereal fern-like plants dotted the ground. Omar moved his torch around—there was no sign of the pig. Something drew his attention, though, and he made his way to it; it was only a shard of glass.

He heard rustling behind him, and when he turned, his police torch caught a small rodent escaping through the undergrowth. Where the animal had been foraging, the torchlight hit something else. Omar approached it and unburied it with his boot. Chewed and torn, it was the dotted toe box of a white sneaker. Mulch was pasted to it with mucus, and beneath that there was a smear of blood. The faint terror stirred within him again, and his skin went cold.

He retreated to the clearing, which was a shade brighter than the bush, and through his binoculars, he peered at the upsloping slog of the mountainside. Trees and rocky overhangs ornamented the landscape. Clouds gathered above the peak; he should head back to the car soon, he thought.

Instead, he began to walk up the mountainside and negotiated a damp clump of forest by torchlight. He emerged onto scree that led to an overhang shadowed by a vertical crag. With the torch in his mouth and the binoculars in hand, he traversed the loose stones. His boots could find no proper grip, and he scraped his knuckles on the ground.

But he persisted, panting, until he arrived at the overhang. Then he hauled himself onto the rocky ledge and paused to catch his breath. He took the torch out of his mouth and aimed it at the sheer sedimentary face of the crag. The eye-like beam resembled the round window in the abandoned Victorian, and he became aware of a vague shape on the ground before him. He lowered the torchlight to take it in.

The hair on his neck bristled a moment before he comprehended what he'd discovered. The first thing he noticed was the corpse's mangled foot, wearing half a white sneaker. The other foot had been stripped of shoe and skin and flesh. Three of its toes were missing. The corpse's legs and groin had been gnawed at and the stomach opened by pigs' teeth. Not much remained of the intestines, and the throat looked like rusted grapeshot loosed of its canvas bag.

The shadow of the corpse's chin obscured its face, but Omar knew whose body it was. Still, he stepped forward and stood over it and forced the torchlight into the dead eyes of Bruno Metcalf. Bruno's face was predominantly untouched, and he lay in an infinity-shaped pool of blood. Omar pictured the disembowelled rabbit; he listened out for a high-pitched whine, but what he heard was the bark of an owl.

He pressed his elbows against his abdomen to warm himself. His panting had not eased, and lactic acid was building up in his calves. He squatted and, with his torch, traced the crag to its top. Then he illuminated the corpse again and leaned in closer. A jagged rock formed a pillow beneath Bruno's head; it appeared as black as the GPS tracker, but in the daylight it'd be crimson. The man must've fallen to his death, probably while hiking.

Omar lit up the impenetrable foliage either side of the crag. The only way to the top, he realised, was via a steep dusty slope to his right. Unsure of his rationale, he strode to it and began to climb. Immediately, he slipped; immediately, he tried again—and slipped once more. Then he found himself madly scurrying upwards, his mind scattered, his thoughts ravenous and unfed.

His boots rebelled against the frenzy and sent debris tumbling in their wake. But they obliged him sufficiently enough that he arrived at a point from which he could see over the crag. He breathed hard. All that was there was more rock and more forest and more mountain and more sky. He pushed off desperately. Then his calf seized up, and he began to skid down the slope.

He arrested the descent near the rocky ledge and sucked in a breath. His calf kept cramping as if he'd been stabbed, and he was sure, too, that he'd torn a layer of skin off his thigh. His pant leg was intact, but it soon grew wet with blood. He shut off the torch and sat for a while in the darkness with Bruno's corpse, before he made his shambling way back to his car.

VI

It started sprinkling when Omar drove away from the national park, but it was dry by the time he detoured from the highway in the Blue Mountains to rasp the corpse's coordinates into an anonymous payphone. Having made the call, he deleted the offline maps and every pin he'd dropped. Closer to Sydney, he bought snacks and electrolytes and ibuprofen from a petrol station. Then he stopped on the outskirts of Sydney and spent an addlepated hour switching his tyres with those of a parked car. By the time he dragged his exhausted body into his motel room, dawn was far closer than midnight.

He went straight into the ensuite, where his shimmery face stared back at him from the mirror. His features drooped, and an almost imperceptible layer of dust covered the stubble on his head and the hair on his face. He shrugged off his shirt and spied a contusion on his torso. His reflection stared at it—and for the first time in years, he recalled Patricia and Freeston's mother, a Wiradjuri woman, sobbing at the station after he'd asked obligatory questions to rule her out as a suspect. He was several shades darker than she, and yet she'd called him a 'heartless white bastard' and later refused to cooperate with the strike force.

For some reason, he connected this with the PSC officer smacking the back of his head. He pressed his fist against his bruised torso and whistled air in through his teeth. Were he white, he thought, the contusion would have glowed purple, and doctors might even believe his pain. He mentally replayed the press conference footage of Jack and Lonnie's parents. The mother had agony etched into her freckles, while the father sported his busted nose as if to shame somebody. Idly, Omar wondered who. Then he slipped off his boots and socks and found that his pant leg was glued to his skin.

He let the shower warm and stepped in with his pants on. The wound on his thigh burned, and red-tinged water circled the drain. He peeled his wet pants and briefs off and winced—it felt as if he were using a jack plane on his thigh. Turning the pants inside out, he scrubbed away the congealed blood and flesh that was pasted there. He wrung out his clothes and draped them over the shower screen. His skinless thigh was stippled and nursling pink, and every touch of his fingers produced sparks of pain.

After his shower, he dried himself with the motel towel but left the wound damp. He used the shirt he'd worn that day to pat it dry, leaving a pale bloody imprint on the cotton. With the same shirt, he wiped his boots clean—he'd have to wear the incriminating shoes until he returned to Belli. Then he washed the shirt in the sink and draped it with his pants and briefs over the shower screen.

Bone-tired, he lay naked on his back on the stripped bed. Beneath its sheet, the wardrobe haunted his peripheral vision, and he eyed the mould in the upper corner of the room. A memory floated down to him, or perhaps he floated over it: Bruno lying at the base of the crag, eyes open, a bloodied rock for a pillow.

Omar left a lamp on but shut his eyes. He slid his hand beneath his head and fingered a bony prominence at the base of his skull. What the hell was Bruno doing in Jemalong-Cooke? he wondered.

Omar realised he'd fallen asleep, although he only knew this because he woke with the impression that he'd heard a noise. He bent his ear towards it and listened. Soon he could make out the familiar keening on the brink of earshot. But that wasn't what had woken him. He sat up groggily. His torso ached, and his temples throbbed. The room spun around him, and while it did, he made a quick study of it: he was alone with the lamp and whatever was left of the pre-dawn. The room slowed and stopped. Then he heard the noise that had brought him to consciousness, and he focused on the wardrobe.

A concussion reverberated from beneath the sheet, along with the high-pitched whine or wail and the sound of scuffling and scraping—as if an animal or a child were trapped in the wardrobe's mahogany cage. Omar controlled his breathing. His mind drifted out again into the national park and over Bruno's corpse; it took him further back, to the abandoned Victorian and fire pit and disembowelled rabbit.

Dew seemed to drip off the leaves on the wallpaper and cover his skin. He shuddered; the wound on his thigh felt both frozen and aflame, but he eased himself off the bed and stood naked before the wardrobe. He reached out and pinched the top of the sheet. The trapped animal sounds rang in his ears, and his hand did not move. Steeling himself, he yanked the sheet off the wardrobe and tossed it in a clean arc over his shoulder.

The discord grew more panicked, and his heart rose to his jugular. Still, he took hold of the key in the wardrobe's lock. Then he spied the patterns on the doors that he'd been avoiding for days. On the left, two drowning faces disguised themselves as knots in the wood; on the right, a halo masqueraded as an arc of pastel discolouration. He brought his cheek closer to the wardrobe, and the high-pitched wail became louder and developed a tremolo. It was the same noise he'd heard in the abandoned Victorian, yet now it echoed like a distortion of something known and familiar.

I love you so much, Camille had whispered to Dev while cradling their baby.

How are the kids? Bruno had murmured to someone over the phone.

Omar's head swam, and a sense of formlessness overtook him. He could see, but the angles of everything looked wrong: his hand extended a great distance and turned the key in the lock. He could hear, too, as the thudding and scraping and keening reached a febrile crescendo. With both hands, he flung the wardrobe open.

Inside, he discovered only silence.

Gradually, he became aware of his feet on the carpet. His breathing drew closer until he recognised it as his own, and he felt the dry-ice pain of his thigh. He was nude and shivering and peering into the wardrobe of his motel room. There was no animal trapped within and nothing that might have produced a high-pitched wail.

But there, on the wardrobe's base, was a small mound of ash. Omar dropped to his haunches. The mound had the same shape as the drooping underside of the cage—the one soldered to the fire pit in the abandoned Victorian. The sole difference, he noted, was that it was inverted.

Daylight arrived, and Omar received an encrypted message from the detective inspector asking him to meet her for 'morning tea'. He shaved and brushed his teeth and put on the shirt that stank the least. His pants remained damp even after he ironed them, but he dragged them on over the wound on his thigh. After locking the wardrobe, he threw a plastic bag full of ash and his meagre possessions into the Fairlane.

He approached the motel owner, who stood smoking at the bottom of the external stairs. When she saw him, she pinched her tongue with her fingers and snuffed out her stubby cigarette. She slotted it behind her ear, and he followed her into the reception area.

It reeked of a dwindling campfire, and the carpet was stained with motor oil.

'Checking out?' the motel owner asked.

He nodded, and she squeezed behind a counter overburdened with paperwork.

'Enjoy your stay in Sydney?'

'Not so much.'

'Was it the old wardrobe?'

Omar hesitated, and the motel owner sifted through a pile of papers. He figured she would've gone into his room despite the persistent DO NOT DISTURB sign, but he didn't expect she'd be so open about it. A note of the trapped animal and high-pitched wail wrote itself onto a stave in his brain. Then, from her perspective, he pictured the absurd spectacle of his wardrobe.

The motel owner kept on sifting. 'Last guest didn't like the wardrobe neither.'

'Oh yeah?' Omar heard the hope in his voice; perhaps his experience was universal. 'Why not?' he asked.

'Wasn't tall enough to hang a ballgown, she reckoned.'

The motel owner paused her sifting and raised her eyes. To shield his own, Omar feigned interest in a brochure for an Italian restaurant.

She moved on to another pile of papers. 'I told her, "If you want to hang a ballgown, you should stay at a ballgown-hanging establishment."'

Omar mustered an exhausted smile. 'That seems fair.'

The motel owner found what she was looking for and tallied his bill on a grimy calculator. Omar dumped his room key on the counter and glanced at the security camera trained on him. Its cable wasn't attached to anything, so it had no chance of remembering what it witnessed. 'Did you ever see anyone loitering around my room?' he asked.

'When?' The motel owner lifted her head, and the stubby cigarette feathered its way onto her paperwork. 'I mean, I saw the secret motorbike cop. And the depressed lady with the baby, the one that you—'

'What about last night?' he interjected.

'No.' She replaced the stub behind her ear and seemed to reflect on her answer. Then she shook her head. 'Nah, nothing last night. Was something stolen from you, officer?'

For a moment, he was tempted to answer in the affirmative. Instead he replied, 'No, I was just curious.'

A couple of hours shy of noon, Omar carried a tray with a chicken burger and bottle of water away from Chicken Palace's luridly promotional service counter. He lugged the tray towards a table in the corner, where Sue perched on a stool. She wore a look of disgust and watched a young man in horn-rimmed spectacles—a junior detective, presumably—wolfing down a plate of chicken nuggets beside her. Omar sat across from them, and the wound on his thigh chafed against the bag of ash flattened in his pocket.

Sue's disgusted face swung towards him. 'Jesus. You sleep at all last night?'

Omar screwed the lid off his water. 'A little.'

'What? Like one minute, two minutes?'

'Closer to two.'

'Well you resemble trampled horseshit.'

'One of the perils of an off-the-books job, I guess.' Omar picked up his burger and took a bite; it had a chilli kick to it. He watched the junior detective dunk a nugget into a small container of tomato sauce. 'This is the guy,' Omar said, 'who couldn't even slide Corban's details under my door properly?'

The junior detective swallowed as if he were about to protest. Then he double-dipped his chicken nugget.

'What'd you find in the old warehouse?' Omar asked Sue.

She brushed a strand of hair from her brow. 'First, I want to know what you've been up to.'

Omar bought time by taking another bite of his burger. He'd have to tell her about the encounter in Morningvale—the aboveboard aspects of it anyway. He swallowed a salty-sweet globule of poultry and bun and cheese. 'I followed Corban out of town yesterday,' he said. 'Unfortunately, she and her male companion made me.'

The junior detective grinned, and the detective inspector folded her arms. 'Anything else to report?'

'One other thing.'

Omar put his burger down and took a sip of water. Sue glared at him like someone waiting to play a trump card. But she probably hadn't heard about Bruno's death or even his disappearance, and there was no way she could know about Omar's detour to Jemalong-Cooke. A memory of the bloodied rock beneath Bruno's head settled at the back of Omar's. He pushed it aside. Instantly, the motel room's wardrobe filled the vacancy with its thudding and scraping and keening.

'When I returned to my motel room,' he said, 'I found something. This.'

He placed the ash-filled bag in the centre of the table. Sue ignored it; the junior detective ate his nuggets indifferently.

Omar tapped the table with his index finger. 'This goes with the fire pit, doesn't it?'

Sue's sharp attention scratched at his grazed knuckles, and he remembered how he'd felt when she'd sighted his hotel room and ensuite. This time, though, a different thought about his personal space struck him: it didn't matter whether he could share it with Camille and Oscar, for they would never share it with him. He removed his finger from the table.

The young detective picked up the bag and brought it towards his glasses. But Sue remained unmoved. 'We didn't find a fire pit in the warehouse,' she said.

Omar lowered his eyebrows. 'What?'

'We didn't find anything in the warehouse.'

He glanced from Sue to the junior detective and back again. 'Someone must've cleaned it out.'

Sue shrugged. 'Maybe.'

'No, not maybe.' Blood surged to Omar's head, and the bony prominence at the base of his skull itched. He refused to scratch it. 'Between when I left and when your people arrived, someone must've cleaned it out.'

The junior detective offered Sue the bag of ash, and she accepted it without much interest. 'Omar, there's no evidence anything was ever there in the first place.'

'There is.' He tapped his sternum. 'I'm the evidence. I fucking saw it.' His breathing went shallow, and he pictured the inconstant light shining through the oculus. There'd been a disembowelled rabbit beneath the window and a fire pit in the middle of the narrow room. Plus there was that high-pitched noise, the same one he'd heard in his motel room. 'How do you explain the ash then?' He gestured at the bag. 'I found it at the bottom of the wardrobe in my motel room.'

'This the wardrobe you covered with a sheet?' Sue replied.

Omar stiffened his jaw. He wanted to refute the implication of the question, but nothing cogent came to him.

Sue put the ash back in the centre of the table. 'Did you or anyone else see who put this in your wardrobe?'

'No.'

'You understand what I'm getting at, Detective Constable?'

He rested his fist on the evidence bag. His grazes were on display again, although whether they shamed him or the detective inspector, he wasn't sure. He shifted the bag towards his food and placed it beside his burger. In a monotone he asked, 'Do you want to hear anything further about Corban?'

Sue sighed. 'Fresh evidence has been received about the children's movements on the day of their disappearance.' She got to her feet. 'Amma Corban is no longer a person of interest. I'm sorry to have distracted you from your'—she waved her hand about as if swirling a glass of wine—'suspension.'

She nodded at the junior detective and hurried out of the fast-food joint. Left behind, the junior detective rose with an affected groan and handed Omar a sheet of paper. For some reason, Omar imagined that it was a cheque, or perhaps a timesheet for him to fill out.

'The info you requested,' the junior detective said. 'And good luck with the toecutters next week.'

Omar waited for him to leave before examining the sheet of paper. It was a report of recent interactions between police and Michael Metcalf. There were two entries. One was about the cops being called on the night Omar went through Mick's bins. The other was from dawn the next morning, when a camera had caught Mick's car speeding through the Blue Mountains in the direction of Sydney.

VII

On the pavement outside Chicken Palace, Omar tossed the bag of ash onto the passenger seat of the Fairlane. He almost climbed into the driver's seat. But his mind raced and urged his feet to do likewise. He stuffed the report into his pocket and strode away from his car and considered the details he'd discovered: half an hour after he'd sifted through Mick's recycling, Mick had greeted the uniform cops who'd shown up at his door; early the next morning, he'd sped *towards* Sydney on his way through the Blue Mountains.

At a set of traffic lights, Omar pumped the button for the pedestrian crossing. Beside him was a vacant lot, with a dirt furrow dividing the grass into two triangles. He traced it with his eye and considered a known detail alongside the new ones: the previous night, he'd stopped off in the Blue Mountains to report that Bruno's corpse could be found in the national park.

These details felt like more than coincidence, but they remained less than evidence. They didn't prove that Mick had driven the same route as Omar. Mick might have been returning from an overnight trip to anywhere within a radius of a couple of hundred kilometres. Perhaps he wasn't even the one driving his car, and a statutory declaration would clarify that one of his friends or lovers was at the wheel.

Or perhaps Mick had indeed driven to Jemalong-Cooke and back in a single night.

The light to cross went green, and Omar rushed over the road. It occurred to him that he might have missed something at Mick's house or in the national park. The mucoid toe box with its smear of blood gleamed in his mind. He recalled his own frenzy when he'd climbed the dusty slope by the side of the crag.

His thigh throbbed, and he walked through a residential area and came upon a bustling bank of shops. He passed a filthy dental surgery and a pristine bakery; he strode by a dumpling house and sidestepped people queueing on the pavement outside. At the kerb, a portly man toiled to load three bags of meat into the boot of his sedan. Myoglobin ooze sloshed against the plastic, and the man heaved the bags onto an uncovered spare tyre. Then he shut the boot.

The thunk bounced back off the rigid awning overhead, and Omar remembered slamming the boot of the golden-brown Mercedes; there'd been a receipt inside with one branded item he hadn't recognised. Its precise name escaped him, but it was the only lead after which his restless feet could chase.

A few minutes later, in the fresh fruit section of an independent supermarket, he approached a weedy kid who was stacking red apples. 'Excuse me,' he said.

But the kid just hummed to himself and polished an apple on his apron.

'Excuse me,' Omar repeated, and tapped the kid on the shoulder.

The kid jolted and dropped the apple, which rolled down the aisle of shining fruit. He glanced up at Omar, and something he saw made his eyes widen with fear.

Omar stepped back. 'Sorry.'

'That's all right.' The kid's voice shook, and he sought out the apple he'd dropped. 'You just kinda snuck up on me there. Can I help?'

'My wife asked me to get something called'—Omar rumpled his chin as if trying to recall—'Stevia, I think.'

'Stevia? Sure, I'll show you where that is.'

The kid picked up the dropped apple and gestured for Omar to follow. He led the way to the supermarket's central aisle and stopped beside a display of tea and coffee. The kid took down a tin of artificial sweetener and offered it to Omar. 'This what you want?'

Omar frowned at the tin. 'No, I don't think it's sold by weight. The thing is sold in packs of ten.'

'Yeah, probably not this, then. Stevia's sold by weight or in a pack of like five hundred.' The kid replaced the tin on the shelf. He pointed at a pack of stevia tablets, which was about the size of a matchbox. 'Can't you just call your wife and ask?'

Omar breathed out a bitter laugh. He passed his gaze over the instant coffee and thought back on the nonverbal aspects of his last conversation with Camille: the whooshing air, her laptop keys being pressed, her long silences. 'It wouldn't go down well,' he said.

Beside him, the kid tossed the red apple into the air and caught it. 'Is it something for her, for you? For your kids?'

Omar tried to picture the receipt in Bruno's boot. In his memory, it was as pixelated as a map loading on a phone. 'Stevia Extra?' he said.

The kid tossed the apple up again and snatched it out of the air. 'Could she have said Stevie Extra Plus, you reckon?'

The recollection of the receipt gained some definition, and Omar faked a smile. 'That's exactly what she said. Where can I find it?'

The kid laughed. 'That's in aisle seven—personal hygiene.'

Omar rushed to aisle seven, where he paced and regarded the products. His eye snagged on interdental brushes and cotton buds. Then he spotted a pack labelled Stevie Extra Plus. He took it off the shelf and stared at the beige wrapping adorned with a stylised picture of a butterfly. It was a ten-pack of menstrual pads. He searched the shelves and took down a blue box of menstrual pads identical to the one he'd seen in Mick's recycling bin.

Omar looked from one pack to the other. Here was another pair of details that felt like more than coincidence yet less than evidence.

Could the girl be . . .? He tried to restrain his mind from leaping too far ahead of him. It didn't make sense. Anyway, Mick had an alibi for the day of Patricia and Freeston's disappearance: he was on duty with his police partner.

At the top of the aisle, the kid with the apple stood and watched. Omar raised the pack of Stevie Extra Plus. 'Found it. Thanks.'

When the kid walked off, Omar returned both items to the shelves. Then he bought himself more electrolytes and legged it out to the street with the intention of calling Angus Troy.

Omar rushed back through the bank of shops, where the crowd outside the dumpling house had increased in size. By the time he came to the residential area, he'd finished his electrolyte drink. The pedestrians had all but disappeared, and he phoned Angus.

'Omar, you saved me a call,' Angus said. 'But maybe you've heard already?'

A plane's engine growled above the hum of traffic. 'Heard what?'

'Just tell me you're still in Sydney.'

'That's where I am.'

'Are you sitting down?'

Omar glanced up. On the balcony of a flat, a woman in football shorts draped children's clothes over a line and watched him pass. He nodded at her. She pretended she didn't notice, and he strode on. 'Not at all,' he replied.

Omar heard Angus tap a pen on his desk. 'Listen,' Angus said. 'They found Bruno Metcalf this morning. Dead.'

'Fuck,' Omar breathed.

'At least, they're pretty sure it was him. His car was there but his body was waterlogged—and his face? Apparently his face had been eaten off by wild pigs.'

Omar stopped at the lights across from the vacant lot. He pushed the button to cross the road and tried to calibrate an appropriate response. When he'd discovered Bruno's corpse, it'd already been wearing a costume of cruor. The elements and animals must have made it worse, though: overnight, they'd gnawed away its human mask. 'Is that how he died?' Omar said. 'Wild pigs?'

'The coroner will take a look, but the crime scene was a washout.'

'That's unfortunate.' The lights went green, and Omar crossed the road. He looked with relief from his boots to the dirt furrow in the vacant lot and realised there was an obvious question he should ask. 'Where the hell was the body found?'

Angus tapped his pen again, as if in approval. 'It was in a national park called, uh, Jemalong-Cooke—about halfway between Sydney and Belli. A hiker called it in with GPS coordinates, apparently.'

'So, all we can do is wait for the coroner?' Omar said.

'Seems that way.' Angus's office chair creaked. 'You're probably calling me about the PSC, right?'

Omar could hear the rapid beat of his footfalls over the traffic. He slowed his pace. The Fairlane and Chicken Palace weren't far away now. 'I'm calling for a Metcalf-related reason, actually.'

Angus snickered. 'I just told you: Bruno Metcalf is no more.'

'This isn't about Bruno,' Omar replied. 'It's about his son, Michael. About his alibi.'

'What the fuck are you—?'

'Kimber Lee.' Omar switched the phone from one ear to the other and dug into his pocket for his car keys. 'She was a constable back then, on shift with Mick. I want to look her up, but I don't have access right now.'

'They audit all our searches, Omar.' Angus lowered his voice. 'You know that.'

'It's your open case.'

'Technically.'

'And you just told me that the main suspect's body was found chewed up by wild pigs this morning.'

Angus's chair creaked again, more violently this time. 'Fucking hell!' Omar heard a pen being hurled onto a desk and skittering onto the floor. 'I thought you'd be'—Angus paused—'happy or something.'

Omar jangled his keys. 'Happy?'

'Or at least—I don't know—satisfied?' Angus let out an exasperated breath, and Omar heard his chair roll closer to the desk. 'Shit. Okay, what's the name again? Kimberly something?'

'No, Kimber Lee. L-E-E. That's the full name. She was a constable.'

Omar listened to the forceful clack of Angus's two-fingered typing, so different from Camille's.

'She's no longer law enforcement,' Angus said. 'Looks like she's got a couple of minor drugs possession charges.'

Omar unlocked the Fairlane and sat in the driver's seat. 'Anything from her police days?'

Angus made a throaty noise that suggested he was subvocalising. 'Looks like you and her have something in common.'

'What's that?'

'She was investigated by the toecutters,' Angus said. 'For dealing heroin during her shifts. Couldn't nail her, apparently, but looks like she quit after that.'

Omar wound down the window. He tallied this fact with the coincidences he'd previously noted, and his temples throbbed with such force that he worried Angus might hear. Everything he'd uncovered remained short of evidence, he reminded himself.

'An address?' he asked.

'Nothing for Ms Lee.'

Omar peered out the window and ran his palm over the stubble on his head, and his certitude about Bruno's guilt rushed through him. That certitude, rather than Camille, was why he'd come to Sydney in the first place. It was why he'd attached a GPS tracker to the golden-brown Mercedes. It was why he'd planted listening devices in Bruno's house without a warrant. Those devices had recorded only a single phrase, a single question, that'd stood out to Omar—who thanked Angus and hung up.

Not long after that, Omar was waiting in a queue for the checkout in a cavernous hardware store. In his hand, he held a roll of duct tape, as well as a paintbrush that he didn't need. Nearby, he spotted a display of white rabbit soft toys billed as a 'special purchase'. His first thought was of the disembowelled rabbit in the abandoned Victorian; his second was that he should buy a farewell gift for Oscar. But the connection between the two thoughts made him vacillate.

The woman at the register scanned the duct tape and paintbrush, and he glanced over at the rabbits. 'Do you have any other soft toys?' he asked. 'My kids aren't really *Alice in Wonderland* types.'

She shook her head. 'We shouldn't even have those, by rights.'

He stepped towards the display and hoisted a rabbit up by its ears. After he paid for his three items with cash, he drove straight to Camille's place. He parked down the road; from here he could make out her house in his side mirror. Opening his notebook, he flicked beyond the superfluous pages that related to Amma Corban.

Dear Camille, he wrote. He hesitated before he added: *and Dev.*

I wish your family nothing but the best. Here's a gift for Oscar.

All my love,
Omar

He tore the page out and carried it, along with the plush rabbit, to the path between the rosemary and frangipani. On Camille's doorstep, he set the soft toy down and slipped the note beneath it. He hurried back to his Fairlane and sent her a message asking her to come outside.

From the safety of the driver's seat, he watched her emerge onto her doorstep. She picked up the plush rabbit and perused the note he'd written. Her face betrayed nothing, and when she was done reading, she peered along the leafy street. Her eye fell on the Fairlane and seemed to catch his in the glass of the side mirror. Then she averted her gaze, and he started the car and drove away.

Omar prodded the doorbell camera into wakefulness. It would record his profile—his clenched jaw and dark-ringed eyes, the lacquer of his skin. But it'd fail to notice the strips of duct tape on the back of his pants, let alone the phone and cable ties and knife in his pockets. He wiped his palms on his hips and brought his focus to his breath. After a moment, Mick opened the front door and filled the space between the handle and the jamb. 'You're back, Detective,' he said. 'Did you find more fresh questions to ask me?'

Omar blinked and made no reply, and an ironic smile crossed Mick's face. 'What are you doing?' He opened the door all the way. 'Are you having a seizure or something?'

A question hit terminal velocity in Omar's mind, although it wasn't the one Mick had asked. Omar's heart thudded, yet still he didn't speak. He glanced over his shoulder at the velvet grass that led to the letterbox and the lull of the weekend street. Sunlight streamed through his lashes, and an SUV cruised past. He peered at his grazed knuckles before he lifted his eyes to meet Mick's.

'How are the kids?' he murmured, in his best impression of Bruno.

Mick maintained his smile. Then it slackened, only a fraction, and the pink undertone of his cheeks paled ever so slightly. He opened his mouth to speak, and Omar thought of Bruno's face when the elder Metcalf had sat, on the cusp of confession, beside him on the couch in Belli. That night, Bruno had registered Camille's sobs and fled; now, Mick regathered himself immediately.

'What are you talking about?' he asked.

But Omar had made up his mind. He jammed his boot into Mick's abdomen with all the force he could muster. Mick grunted and reeled backwards; pain shimmied from Omar's thigh and throughout his nervous system. He scrambled into the house and closed the door behind him.

Winded, Mick fell beside the staircase that led to the first floor. Omar balled his fist as if he were about to cold-cock the man. Mick flung his hands up defensively, and Omar reached between them and yanked him up by the collar of his shirt. He twisted Mick onto his stomach. Then he saddled his back with a heavy knee and held his forearm in place. Mick wheezed and thrashed about.

Omar drew the knife and brought it towards Mick's crazed eyeball. He let the blade glint, and Mick went quiet—except for his wheezing. Omar pressed the knife against the taut skin of Mick's throat. 'Hands,' he commanded. 'Small of your back.'

Mick's body slackened. Omar eased his weight off it, and Mick clasped his hands at the small of his back. Omar fumbled for the cable ties in his pocket; he kept the knife at Mick's jugular. Then he slid a cable tie over Mick's wrists and zipped it tight.

'Feet together,' he said. 'Legs extended.'

He applied a cable tie to Mick's ankles—Mick didn't fight him—and by the time he'd finished, Mick's wheeze had dissipated.

Omar stood and stumbled against the hallway wall and caught his breath. The creases on Mick's brow were rivulets, but his back rose and fell evenly. 'You've lost your fucking mind,' he said.

'Probably.'

'They'll kick you out for this, you know? They'll arrest you.'

'Like they arrested Constable Lee?' Omar panted and placed his hands on his crown. 'I suppose it depends on what I find.' His thigh had started to bleed again, and he wrinkled his nose. 'Did you kill your father?'

The creases on Mick's brow deepened.

'You don't know?' Omar said.

Omar fought back a ripple of pity and looked towards the front door. If there'd been a witness to his entry, he had between fifteen and thirty minutes before a pair of uniform cops came knocking. He returned his gaze to Mick, whose expression had swum to one of shock.

'My father's dead?' Mick asked.

Omar nodded. 'They found his body this morning in Jemalong-Cooke National Park.'

Mick didn't react, and Omar dropped to his haunches. 'Are they here, Mick?' he said. 'Or are they in the national park?'

Saliva dribbled from the corner of Mick's lips onto the floorboards. He took a quick breath, followed by a faster one and a faster one than that. Soon he was almost hyperventilating. He panted half a scream, and Omar peeled a strip of duct tape from the back of his pants and applied it to Mick's mouth.

He left Mick helpless on the verge of the open-plan area and did a cursory inspection of the upstairs. There was not much to see: rooms without character and wardrobes containing Mick's clothes and linen fit for a hospital. He jogged back downstairs, where Mick had rolled in front of the bathroom door in the hallway. Omar reached over him and opened it. In the bathroom, the stopper had been returned to the side of the tub along with the bottle of conditioner. Otherwise, it was as Omar had last seen it.

He left Mick and entered the front room—the home gym. Weights were lined up neatly on a rack, and he ran his nail over the handlebar of an exercise bike. Then he walked down the stairs to the underground garage and flicked on the light. Power tools dangled from the walls; a drill, marked by its outline, was absent. Cardboard boxes were stacked in tidy piles.

A Lexus four-wheel drive was parked in the centre of the space. Omar circled it, as he had Bruno's Mercedes, but there wasn't a hint of mud on its body. Perhaps it'd been cleaned recently, or perhaps it'd never been to the national park. He set aside his doubts and got onto his hands and knees and rested his temple against the concrete floor. Beneath the car, a grate covered what appeared to be a drainage pit.

Before he could speculate on this, though, thumping and muffled screaming resounded from above. For a moment, he thought of the cacophony in the motel wardrobe. He pushed himself to his feet and sprinted towards the noise.

In the hallway, Mick had slithered from the bathroom to the front door. He lay on his back and kicked at the door and gargled for help through the duct tape.

'Shut up,' Omar said.

But Mick groaned and gave the door one final kick.

Knife in hand, Omar knelt over Mick's visage. He cleared his throat to steady his voice. 'If you're not going to tell me where they are,' he said, 'the least you could do is shut the fuck up.'

Mick eyed the blade in silence. Then Omar slipped his hands beneath Mick's briny underarms and dragged him away from the door. Mick thrashed about and headbutted Omar's wounded thigh. Pain coursed through Omar's limbs, and he lost his grip on the knife—and on Mick. Mick's head crashed to the floorboards, and he let out a falsetto squeal through the duct tape.

Omar sighed and swept up the knife. He grabbed Mick by the armpits again and lugged his belligerent weight into the open-plan area, where he dumped him in front of the slimline couch. Mick lay there panting. Omar's muscles ached, and the wound on his thigh felt as if it were a fire burning in a snowscape. He took a breath and inspected his knuckles, which were bright with fresh blood.

Then he surveyed the open-plan area. As ever, all the blinds were shut. The furniture was as minimal as he recalled, and the kitchen seemed unused except for a set of keys on the counter.

A siren blared in the distance, and Mick mumbled something that had the cadence of gloating. Omar ignored him. He gazed from the mounted television to the bookcase below, lined with record sleeves. The siren faded away, but it forced him to wonder whether Mick had managed to attract the attention of a passer-by or neighbour. If he had, that might entail a second call to the police, which would shorten the time Omar had left to check the drainage pit. But if he hadn't, Omar thought, some covering music would not go astray.

From the top shelf of the bookcase, he picked out a cardboard sleeve for an R.E.M. album with an anvil-like object on its cover. When he reached into the sleeve, he found that it contained no LP. He tossed it onto the floor. The next one he plucked out was *Desertshore* by Nico. He tested the cardboard's resolve and met no resistance; it too contained no vinyl.

Dropping it onto the empty R.E.M. cover, he grabbed an armful of sleeves and confirmed, one by one, that they held no LPs. He discarded them and caressed the spot on his throat between his Adam's apple and his five o'clock shadow. 'Do you actually own any records?'

It was a rhetorical question, spoken to the pile of empties on the floor. Oddly, Mick felt compelled to answer. He volunteered a reply through the tape that Omar guessed was 'Linkin Park', and it didn't take Omar long to find an LP called *Hybrid Theory*. He slid the vinyl from its cardboard sleeve, which he threw with the others onto the floor. Then he opened the plastic lid of the record player and positioned the vinyl on the turntable and set it to spin.

He raised the needle, and something to his right sparkled. His eye drifted to the wood veneer block beside the record player; an identical block was to his left, and both remained affixed to the wall—as they had been on his last visit. There was a change, though. Whereas before he'd taken note of a stripped screw, now all of the screws were in mint condition.

'You replaced the screws?' he muttered.

He peered at Mick, who eyed him sidelong and strained to haul himself into a seated position. Omar took out his knife and used it to remove the screws that held one of the blocks in place. Then he tossed the block onto the pile of empties on the floor.

On the turntable, the record spun; the needle hovered, and Omar's thoughts crackled. The wood veneer block had been obscuring a black hinge that attached the bookcase to the wall. Sticking out of the hinge was a lever shaped like a soap dispenser and capped with a red button.

Omar pressed the button, and the lever clicked and slackened. Once more, he glanced at Mick, who now sat with his back against the sofa. Around the collar of his shirt, his sweat formed a dark noose, and he watched Omar without making a sound.

Omar removed the screws that held the other block in place and released the lever. Then he tugged at the base of the bookcase and guided it in a gentle arc towards the television. The L-shaped hinges rewrote themselves as Vs, and the bookcase rose beyond the horizontal like half a drawbridge. The record player's plastic lid closed and cracked, and the bookcase came to a halt with its base around head height. White acoustic foam covered its rear, and in the recessed wall behind where it had stood was a plain white door.

Omar could feel the awl of Mick's gaze prodding at his back, and he turned to look at him. 'Are they in there?' he asked. 'How do I get in?'

Mick indicated the kitchen counter.

Omar retrieved the set of keys and held them up. 'Which one?'

Mick nodded at a silver key, and Omar returned to the recessed door and unlocked it. He palmed it open, and a miasma of damp and ammonia wafted to his nostrils.

'Hello?' he called out.

No one and nothing replied, not even an echo of his own voice. Before him was a staircase that seemed the inverse of the one he'd jogged up to get to the second floor of the abandoned Victorian. This one led to a dark underground space.

'Patricia, Freeston?' Omar said, haltingly. 'I'm a police detective. I'm coming in.'

He ducked through the doorway and made his way down the staircase. At the bottom, he stepped onto a hard floor and brushed against a dangling cord. His skin tingled, and he shuddered as if he'd passed through the finest web. Then he pulled on the cord, and a naked bulb lit up.

The room he was in resembled a padded cell or the servants' quarters in the manor of a sadist. The floor was concrete, and the walls and ceiling and door were covered with double-layered sheets of white acoustic foam. Snatches of white had been clawed away, and in the far corner—where there was a filthy drain and showerhead and toilet—the foam was patchy and mouldering.

A soiled king single mattress was pushed up against one wall. Laid out on the mattress was a police uniform, and on the foam above it was the shock of a bloodstain. Bile gathered in Omar's throat, and he clamped his teeth together to hold it back. His cheeks burned with something like collective shame, and he retreated through the door to find that Mick hadn't budged.

'They were here,' Omar said in a quaver. 'Now they're in the national park?'

Mick loured at him.

'You moved them that night I snooped around your house?' He stepped towards Mick. 'Because you knew I broke into your father's house?'

Mick continued to lour.

'Are they alive?'

Mick inhaled deeply. Then he exhaled and nodded once.

'How do I find them?'

Mick gave the merest of shrugs, and Omar put the knife to his throat. He yanked the tape off Mick's mouth, and Mick flinched before he brought his features under control. 'You can't,' he croaked. 'Not without me.'

Omar sniffed. 'There's no way I'm taking you with me.'

'Then you won't find them—she won't let you.' Mick turned his cheek to Omar. 'She won't bring him out to any cop except me.'

Omar put more pressure on the knife, and blood seeped from a shallow cut on Mick's throat. Mick didn't respond in any way, and Omar was tempted to make the wound less subtle. But he pictured the bloodstain on the foam and the police uniform on the mattress and understood that Mick was telling the truth.

VIII

Omar cut the engine of the Lexus and listened out for its owner, whom he'd manoeuvred—mouth retaped, wrists and ankles cable-tied—into the boot. All he heard was the birdsong of Jemalong-Cooke National Park. Omar hadn't dared to walk out of Mick's house to his Fairlane. But Mick hadn't made a sound since they'd left his garage; he'd been silent on the highway, even when a uniform cop had signalled for Omar to join a queue for a random breath test. A second uniform cop had sauntered to the window and asked to see his licence. 'This your vehicle?' she'd said.

'Does it not look like my vehicle?' he'd replied.

She'd glanced sheepishly from his licence to his shaved head. He'd wrung the steering wheel and prayed for Mick's continued quiet. Then the cop had breathalysed Omar and motioned for him to drive on as if she wished to put the whole interaction behind her.

With the sun just below the horizon, he watched fine drizzle fall from the clouds and settle on the windscreen. Rain had muddied the dirt road before him and blackened the bushfire scars on the macilent trees upslope to his right. He needn't have worried about Mick making noise in the boot, he realised. While Omar had decided not to involve Sue or Angus, Mick must have calculated that gaining the attention of uniform cops was a low percentage play. Indeed, Mick's highest percentage play was to try to overpower

Omar in the national park, unwitnessed, and do whatever was necessary to cover his tracks.

Either that, or his silence meant he'd asphyxiated on the journey to Jemalong-Cooke.

Omar traced the contours of the knife in one pocket; he felt for his phone in the other. Then he swigged at a bottle of water he'd snatched from Mick's kitchen and got out of the car and walked towards the rear. He eyed the spot where the golden-brown Mercedes had been parked. The forensics team had wound police tape around the trunks of three trees in an attempt to cordon off the area. But animals or the wind had bitten through the tape, and it lay in the mud like a ribbon sarcastically cut at the opening of a potter's field.

The police tape to the left of the four-wheel drive had fared better. At the start of the overgrown walking trail, it fluttered in the breeze in the shape of an X. Omar recalled the X of the barricade tape across the doorway of the abandoned Victorian and felt his heart rate spike.

At the back of the four-wheel drive, he pushed a button and eased the boot open. Inside, Mick's ungainly frame was curled in the foetal position. At first, Omar thought he really was dead. Then Mick groaned and blinked. The fresh strip of duct tape was askew over his mouth, and his neck was stained with blood from the shallow cut Omar had made. His wrists remained cable-tied at the small of his back and his ankles left upon right.

Omar read thirst and fatigue in Mick's eyes. 'Can you sit?' he asked.

Mick swung his legs out of the boot and struggled into a seated position. Omar didn't help; he wanted Mick upright yet weak.

'Water?'

Mick nodded, and Omar ripped the duct tape off. Then Mick

opened his mouth like a baby bird and let Omar pour the last trickle of water into it.

Omar felt pity tug at him once more. 'I'm going to cut your ankles free,' he said, 'and you're going to take me to the children.' He tossed the empty bottle into the boot. 'If you don't, you're going to end up like your father. Do you understand?'

Omar drew the knife. The fatigue had not left Mick's eyes, and neither had the thirst. But a measure of vitality had returned to them, and with it had come animus. 'I understand,' he whispered.

Before Omar reached vanishing point on the trail, he cast a final glance back at the police tape and Mick's four-wheel drive. He rubbed the stubble on his head and found that his scalp was slick with rainwater. His mouth was parched, too, although this time not from the sense of isolation. Hands cable-tied at the small of his back, Mick rounded the bend ahead of him.

Omar followed along the overgrown track he'd traversed earlier. In the wet, the rocky parts had grown slippery, and the dusty topsoil had turned to clay. The steep section of the trail was difficult to hike, and where he could, Omar grabbed hold of the dank limbs and leaves of trees. But Mick, who had no use of his hands, wound up on his backside more than once. When he reached a level section of the trail, he stopped to wait for Omar beneath a drooping eucalyptus. He was mud-stained, but he'd regained his strength. 'Why do you always have to take the hardest fucking path?' he asked.

Omar picked his way carefully over a jutting root. 'Is there an easier way to get to where we're going?'

'Maybe you and I aren't going to the same place.'

Omar stopped a short distance from Mick. 'In the long run,' he said, 'I hope you're right.'

Mick snorted. 'You're bloody insufferable, you know that?'

'I've been told.'

Mick walked on, and Omar fell in behind. He approached the log over which he'd almost tripped before. Mick stepped on it and hopped off. A bird cooed, and Omar considered what Mick had said earlier: *She won't bring him out to any cop except me.*

He figured this meant Mick had convinced the children to trust nobody, and especially not cops. Patricia would keep them hidden, and only Mick would be able to coax them from their place of refuge—or free them from their prison. Omar had to force Mick to do that. But all he had at his disposal was violence and its threat, which reminded him of the grotesquerie of the police uniform on the mattress.

He hurdled the log without trouble. 'Why'd you wear the uniform with the kids?' he asked. 'Just to frighten them, or was it like taking a blue pill?'

'No.' Mick strode ahead of him. 'I wore it because I'm a cop—a real fucking cop.'

'You're not even on the force anymore.'

'Neither are you.'

Omar's boots slewed in the muck, and he grabbed at the sprawl of a dwarf she-oak to steady himself. Mick glanced back and smirked. Then he continued on his way. The rain became heavier, and Omar listened to it roiling a river that he couldn't see. He wondered whether being a cop was akin to being Catholic or Muslim: perhaps all you could ever become was a lapsed cop.

'Were there other cops involved?' he asked.

Mick seemed not to hear. The end of the marked trail lurched into view, and he paused. Omar stopped, too. Beyond the concrete of the lookout, the valley of trees undulated, and sombre pinstripes of rainfall obscured the faraway bluffs. Was he a lapsed cop already? he wondered. Or had he always been something different?

'Were there other cops involved?' he repeated.

Mick rested his shoe on the nub of a rock. 'No.'

'What about Constable Lee?' Omar asked. 'She alibied you.'

'We just borrowed her van for a day.'

'The white Vee Dub?'

Mick bowed his head. 'It was a brown Tarago.'

Abruptly, he shuffled off towards the bushland to the west. Omar stared at Mick's cable-tied wrists. It was such a minor error in the scheme of things: a witness had reported that she'd seen Bruno in a white VW van, when it turned out he'd been driving a brown Tarago. If Omar had known that at the time, he'd have been able to connect Bruno with Kimber, and the case might have been solved within a day. He jogged after Mick into the bushland but couldn't make him out in the darkness.

'Bruno drove them here in the van?' he called out. 'And you took them on to Sydney?' A branch of wet leaves struck his jaw, and his hand trembled. He put it in his pocket and gripped the knife. Then he caught sight of Mick in a thin place where the trees grew sparsely and the clouds were visible. Omar paused at the tree line. 'Why'd you take them?'

Mick lingered and raised his face to the sky. The rain made his eyelids flicker. 'They were a gift from my father.' He peered at Omar, his cheeks and eyes damp. 'Reparations for a shitty childhood.'

Sheet lightning flashed in the incipient night, and in Omar's gut there settled a deeper terror than the last time he'd been here. He remembered Patricia and Freeston's mother calling him a 'heartless white bastard'. Then he stepped into the thin place and heard the rumble of thunder—and he felt a tremor in his boots that he knew was of the earth rather than the sky. His temples pulsed, and he looked for Mick, who was already moving off into denser bushland.

'Wait,' Omar yelled.

But the footfalls of feral pigs drowned him out. They were suddenly everywhere in the thin place—the pigs. Their pale coats were drenched in rainwater and spattered with mud, and they were all around him. There must have been a dozen of them, yet they moved as a single being: a rabid, contortionist mass that grunted and squealed and scrambled down the mountainside.

Omar backed against the slimy trunk of a tree. His boots sank into a spongy patch of mire. The pigs paid him no special heed, though, and disappeared almost as swiftly as they'd arrived. Omar pushed away from the trunk. His thigh ached, but he sprinted through the thin place and after Mick into the bushland.

'Mick?' He fumbled to take the knife from his pocket. 'Mick!'

He kept the downhill slope to his left and the uphill slope to his right and continued to jog in as straight a line as he could manage. Then he almost pitched over, and he switched on his phone's torch to take in his surroundings. Speckles of rain dotted the knife's blade, and the territory was as difficult as he recalled. This particular stretch of bushland was unfamiliar, though, and he could spy no evidence that Mick or anyone else had ever passed through it.

In a more forbidding stretch of bushland, Omar spied a creatural shadow from the corner of his eye. He turned to confront it, but in the darkness, he could make out no movement before him. Having left his police torch in the Fairlane, he'd kept the phone's torch off to conserve the battery. Now, he flicked it on briefly to see what he was facing. It wasn't Mick, or even an animal; it was the pathetic stems of a mallee, swaying in the breeze.

Distant thunder rolled beneath his skin, and he lowered the knife and accepted that he was alone. A couple of hours had passed since Mick had disappeared into the bush. In that time, Omar had checked a map on his phone and made his way west in the hope of coming across the rocky overhang where he'd found Bruno's corpse. From there, he'd have to find the children somehow—and he had to get to them before Mick did.

He pocketed his phone and cupped his hands to collect rainwater. Then he recalled forcing the beam of his torch into the fire pit—and he drank at the water and glanced at the forest to the west. It was difficult to tell, but he could have been in the area where he'd happened upon the subsidence and almost fallen the last time he'd been here. In squelching boots, he stumbled into the forest and ran his hands through the leaves of plants. Something scurried through the undergrowth and gave him hope that he was in the right place.

Soon, though, the scrub thickened and became impenetrable, and he abandoned that path. He took out his phone and checked the map again. It was possible he'd gotten his topography wrong, that he'd gone past the rocky overhang. He about-faced and went east until the scrub became less dense. When it did, he trekked directly up the mountainside. But the change in landscape was insignificant, and a while later he realised that his fatigue had seen him trudge back downslope.

Pausing, he sensed rather than saw movement behind a curtain of leaf and vine. Lightning flashed, and the curtain took on the appearance of the wardrobe from his motel room, with its haloed tree and the faces in the wood. Thunder rumbled in the aftermath, and beneath that he thought he heard scuffling and thudding. Was it Mick, he wondered, or something worse? His stomach lurched and hurled the taste of hunger and despair into his mouth.

He slashed at the leaf and vine and shoved his way through. Behind the curtain, he found merely bushland, and he began to run. He was lost, he thought. He'd lost Camille; he'd lost the Metcalfs; he'd lost the children. Helter-skelter, his feet carried him through Jemalong-Cooke. He sprinted through the darkness and recognised nothing—until the pain in his thigh and the tightness in his calf became unbearable, and he doubled over and caught his breath. Around him, familiar trees huddled together, and ethereal fern-like plants dotted the ground.

Omar straightened. He wandered upslope and arrived in the clearing where he'd seen the pig with the sneaker in its maw. Shutting his eyes, he shook with laughter. When he opened his eyes, his breathing had settled, and he even felt as if he could see more clearly. He walked up the mountainside and through the damp clump of forest and emerged onto the scree.

Omar took a few cautious steps over the loose stones. But one of his boots sent pebbles tumbling in its wake, and the other slipped. He grazed his already abraded knuckles and found himself almost horizontal. He was positioned like a relay runner on the blocks: one leg out behind him, the knife in his hand extended like a baton.

In his peripheral vision, he caught sight of a dislimned figure hurtling towards him. His heart started its mortar fire, and he scraped himself to his feet. There was no doubt this time: free of its bonds, Mick's silhouette skittered over the scree and wielded a tree limb that bore the shape of a baseball bat. Omar lowered his centre of gravity. He held the knife at the ready.

Mick careened into view and swung the bat at Omar's head. Omar weaved, although not fast enough. The bat smashed into his left shoulder and split in two. He groaned; the pain was so intense that he almost passed out. His scapular felt shattered, and his left arm dangled limp by his side.

He lunged with the knife and sliced only raindrops. Then Mick tackled him. As Omar fell, he twisted to protect his left shoulder; his right slammed into the stones and jarred his body. He clenched his jaw. Mick pressed a knee onto Omar's right forearm and pinned it to the ground and sought to prise the knife from Omar's hand.

Omar knew that to lose the knife meant death. He tried to swing his left fist, but the ferocity of the pain in his shoulder stopped him. Instead, he did the only thing he could manage: he flicked his right wrist. The knife cut into the other man's fingers, and Mick winced and cried out and quickly recovered. Without shifting his knee from Omar's forearm, Mick grabbed Omar by the shirtfront and punched him hard in the face. Omar didn't feel the blow, but he heard a keening on the brink of earshot.

Mick punched him again, even harder.

Belatedly, the hurt of two blows caromed through his skull. His heart slowed. He saw sheet lightning in the sky above. But its flare lingered a beat longer than it should have, and no thunder followed. Perhaps he was seeing the winking moon, he thought. Whatever it was, it revealed the grim contortions of Mick's face and illuminated his cocked fist.

Omar's right arm remained trapped, and his left seemed dead by his side. Resurrecting it was his only hope. He focused on the task, and his left hand lifted from the scree. It trembled, and his shoulder sent haphazard waves of pain crashing through his system.

Mick's fist arced towards his eye, and Omar willed his left arm to keep moving. It twitched and rose, almost imperceptibly at first. He felt as if he were tearing it from its socket, but he gritted his teeth and wrenched his left arm through the rain. The physical agony seemed audible: his nerves vibrated, and he registered the keening once more.

With his left hand, Omar shoved Mick off balance; Mick's fist grazed his cheek and hit the stones beside his head. The weight on Omar's right forearm eased, and he freed himself. In one fluid motion, he plunged the knife into Mick's belly and withdrew it and stood up.

Mick lay prone, and a dark pool spread from his stomach onto the wet scree. Omar hugged himself with his left arm, which still radiated pain. He held the knife out in front of him. 'Where are they?' he breathed.

Blood dripped from the blade and trickled between the stones and joined the infinity-shaped pool forming around Mick. Mick said nothing, and his eyes closed. Then Omar realised that there was light enough for him to see.

※

Omar stared at the bell curve of the mountain's vertex. Above it were clouds bound to the earth by ropes of rainfall; the path to the peak was adorned with the same trees and rocky overhangs that he'd already encountered. But from a vague locus high on the mountain, a light was shining. It gathered itself and grew more intense. Then it dimmed, before it gained in intensity once more.

He tried to picture it—the light's source—as he had outside the abandoned Victorian. It remained beyond the bourn of his consciousness, and again he felt faint, as if he were the formless thing of his imagination. He stood mesmerised by the light and recalled the shiver of electricity he'd felt when he'd kissed Camille for the last time. He pictured Jack and Lonnie Gajdos-Little, taken from the car park of the Casus Hill Workers' Club without a witness, and wondered where they were. Then he thought of Patricia and Freeston Reeves, somewhere out here in Jemalong-Cooke National Park.

A breath shuddered itself into his mouth, and his shoulder throbbed. He was drenched in fear and salt water and Mick's blood. But he wasn't lost anymore. The light on the mountainside went out. Yet the night seemed brighter, and he could still hear the high-pitched wail. Unlike the light, it had a more definite point of emanation—a coordinate near the peak from which blared something that sounded like a siren.

His boots shifted and sent stones rolling downhill. The rocky overhang and the sheer sedentary crag were shadows among shadows upslope, and the point of emanation was beyond them. Some part of Omar's mind urged him to flee. Then he glanced at Mick—not dead but not quite alive—and he pocketed the knife and began his ascent.

He slipped and backslid and stumbled; he traversed the loose stones and made his way towards the overhang and hauled himself onto it. The sharp pain in his shoulder made him whimper, and he crawled beneath the A-frame of a police barrier to the place where Bruno's corpse had lain. He collapsed there, with the jagged rock as a pillow. It pressed against the bony prominence at the base of his skull, and he looked up at the spot where the eye-like beam of his torch had hit the crag. The world spun, and the only thing that kept him from succumbing to sleep was the unabating wail.

He stood and staggered to the steep dusty slope to the right and climbed. Immediately, he slipped; immediately, he tried again—and slipped once more. He imagined the ache in his body as an animal gnawing at his flesh. But he refused to stop, and he scurried madly upwards.

Eventually, he got to a point from which he could see over the crag—could make out more rock and more forest and more mountain and more sky. Then the keening grew louder. It became rougher and more tremulous and more familiar. He pushed off desperately. His boots skidded, but he managed to plant them on the narrow platform at the top of the crag.

Swaying with exhaustion, he caught his breath. Then he picked his way through a thicket with an incline of about forty degrees. The ground was soft dirt when he entered, although it grew rocky as he approached the thicket's end. He paused at the curled trunk of a fallen tree; it put him in mind of the collapsed conveyor belt he'd seen in the abandoned Victorian.

On the slope ahead of him loomed a gap between two smaller gums, the leaves of which touched like fingertips and formed an arch. The keening reverberated from beyond the gap. He bent his ear to the noise, and he finally recognised it for what it was: the bawling of a baby.

He shivered, and his skin erupted in goosebumps. Staring skywards, he clocked the crown shyness of the canopy, and his vision blurred. Tears formed behind his eyes. Then he made his way towards the arch. The baby's cry grew louder, and when Omar was close enough that he could see past the trees, he was baffled by the sight ahead of him. A figure appeared as a shape in the centre of a circular clearing, out of focus yet unmistakable as a woman with a child.

'Camille?' Omar murmured.

He emerged into the meridian-like clearing and blinked at the figure. When he could see properly, he understood that it was not Camille before him in the rain. It was Patricia Reeves, sallow and emaciated and five years older than his mental image of her. She cradled a swaddled newborn and rocked the crying child back and forth. On the ground behind her, at the base of a bloodwood, a sodden picnic blanket was strewn with bones that could only have belonged to her brother, Freeston.

The newborn kept bawling, pausing only for breath, yet Patricia brought the child to Omar. 'You're not a cop,' she said. 'Are you?'

Omar swallowed and shook his head. He didn't trust himself to speak.

Patricia kissed her baby's temple. 'You want to hold him?'

Omar nodded, and she eased the child into his arms. The newborn peered up, not at Omar exactly but above his head, at his outline or atmosphere. Then the child fell silent, and at last, as if by transference, Omar wept.

Interlude

Interlude

Carl

The upper and lower mattresses on the double bunk were stripped of their sheets, and the venetian blind was shut. But a speck of sunlight stole through a gap and twinkled in Carl Little's eye. He stood at the threshold of Jack and Lonnie's room. A dank odour hung in the air, and he stared at the stack of yellow hula hoop shards on the floor. He sniffled and turned his back and blinked at the napkin in his hands. Then he used it to wipe the dairy-stained webbing between his thumb and forefinger.

The living room, of which he only had a partial view, had fallen silent. He strode away from it and past Ilene's disarranged bedroom. In the bathroom, he glanced at the leaking showerhead pressed against the wall above a flare of damp. A bottle of bleach waited on the tiles; behind the sink were two toothbrushes and a razor and a box of Solnox that bore a sticker with his name on it.

He pocketed the napkin and met his eyes in the mirror. His face was clean-shaved, and there was no hint of charcoal or amber on his skin. He touched the still-crooked bridge of his nose thoughtfully and let his fingertip slide to the corner of his mouth. Then he practised a smile and turned the tap on high.

The water whooshed and gurgled and rose in the sink. Underneath the sound, it was as if a series of sibilant voices were straining to be heard. Carl's smile disappeared, and he glanced at the razor. Swiftly, he opened the box of Solnox and popped out two shell-pink pills. He tossed them into his mouth and gulped from the tap.

The rush of water smoothed itself out, and he swallowed the pills. He washed his hands with a fragile sliver of soap and turned the tap off. Then he dried himself and looked in the mirror and filled his lungs with air. He walked back along the hallway—past Ilene's room, past the children's room—and into the living room.

On the sofa, Ilene sat with her back straight and her gaze unfocused. She held a napkin wrapped around the cone of a melting McDonald's soft serve. The napkin did not protect her, though: streaks of dairy dribbled over her fingers and dripped onto the floor between her feet.

Carl approached her. 'Ilene?' he said.

She looked up at him and smiled. It was more an expression of politeness than pleasure, and she didn't seem to notice her melting ice cream. His eye fell on the circular water stains on the coffee table—rings within rings—and he sat beside Ilene on the sofa.

They stayed silent for a while. She stared into the distance; he watched the dairy drip as if it were tapping out a message in Morse code. Then he put his arm around her and tilted her body towards him. She rested her soft serve against her chest and her head on his shoulder. He kissed her crown, and they stayed like this for a while.

'Carl?' Ilene said eventually.

She reached out with her free hand and took hold of his and guided it to her belly, where her t-shirt was already cold and steeped in sweet milk. He flattened his palm and fingers on the cotton. Beneath it, her belly button seemed nothing more than a gentle depression.

Ice cream dripped from her fist and collected at the ball of his thumb. She lifted her head off his shoulder. They looked into each other's eyes, and they kissed.

Part Three
Benji

I

Five nameless lorikeets—four fledglings and their father—screeched and pecked and jostled for position in the domed birdcage. The nameless mother remained in her nesting box, situated near the top of the aviary Benji Ronzino had constructed by wrapping his own mother's Hills hoist in chicken wire. He lugged the domed birdcage over the grass of the yard and through the aviary's makeshift gate. He shut himself in. Then he planted his feet on the plywood floor, damp from the hosing down he'd given it. The aviary looked gimcrack, he conceded, like a gazebo made of knucklebones. Still, it was functional enough for an amateur breeder like him.

He rested the birdcage on the plywood, and his collared long-sleeved shirt clung to his chest. Hose water had soaked into the cotton, and the cage had branded the hem with stripes of rust. He pinched the fabric away from his olive skin. Why he'd changed into his Sunday best before cleaning the aviary, he wasn't sure. He'd have to change again if he intended to accompany his mother, Florry, to mass. But he hadn't yet decided whether he was doing that or not.

It wasn't that he didn't believe in God, or Jesus—although, if pressed, he'd have to admit he didn't. Part of the reason for this was Sondra, his best friend for most of her life. He recalled her helping him get on for the first time: her melancholy smile and curly red hair and the lavender bruises flowering around her track marks. The needle had yoked her fist to his elbow—her pain to his pain—and their lives had flowed back and forth like that for more than twenty years.

In the aviary, Benji dropped to his haunches next to the birdcage. Sondra had made it to step four with him and then died in the usual way, and he'd undergone the torturous transition to shots of depot bupe. So Jesus would have to forgive him his lack of faith, especially if he attended mass in spite of everything. Then again, it wouldn't be for Jesus' sake that he was going.

He released the lorikeets from the birdcage, and four of them fluttered out into the aviary. They perched on wooden dowels and drank water from a metal trough. One fledgling gnawed at a bottlebrush branch Benji had wedged into the chicken wire. But his favourite fledgling, which had brittle grey chest feathers, refused to be released.

'Come on, man.' Benji jangled the cage, and the grey fledgling gripped the bars with its talons. The bird bobbed and made a sound that approximated a dog barking. Benji brought the cage to his eyeline, and the lorikeet stared out at him. 'Your feathers are never gonna go technicolour, are they?' he mumbled.

It'd be impossible to sell the grey fledgling, he thought, unless its feathers brightened up. That seemed unlikely. His online research suggested the discolouration was permanent. Either he had to name the bird or be rid of it. He extended a hand to the cage, and the grey fledgling hopped onto his finger. Then he dropped the cage and tickled the bird's neck and manoeuvred it onto a dowel. It trilled a thank you with three sweet and sour notes, and its mother popped her head out of the nesting box.

On tiptoes, Benji tried to glimpse the two eggs inside. All he could see in the box was nothingness, and it was into this that the mother lorikeet retreated. He scowled. At the end of his previous stay with Florry, he'd slipped out of her unlit bedroom, goosepimpled and rattling, with her jewellery box under his arm. He'd paused to check his haul on the nature strip outside, certain that his mother had mutely watched him steal from her.

He grabbed the rusted birdcage and dashed out of the aviary. Not once had his mother reproached him for his actions; without hesitation, she'd let him move back in. This time, he was determined to pull his weight. In his colder moments, he figured that his government allowance was recognition he was already doing that. But the morning was hot, and he urged himself to change shirts and go to church—for the sake of Florry's happiness.

He slammed the aviary's gate behind him but left the padlock off. The grey fledgling, clumsy in flight, leaped onto the chicken wire. It whistled and begged Benji to turn around.

'Yeah, yeah, I'll be back in a minute,' he replied.

He strode to the rear of the house—the same brick cottage in south-east Sydney in which he'd been raised by Florry and his nonna. Mould dotted its wooden trims, and he'd repainted the back door an ugly salmon-pink because he'd found a premixed tin by the roadside. The tin was now on the concrete under the carport beside the house, along with piles of oxidising tools and sundries for which Benji had bargained or scavenged. He dumped the birdcage there and went inside.

On a hook near the back door hung the key to the aviary's padlock; on the kitchen counter waited bowls of wet mix and beans and apples. Benji took his rust-stained shirt off and reminded himself to feed the lorikeets before he left for church. At the entry to the narrow laundry, he lobbed the shirt into a basket. He continued to his bedroom, which was across the hallway from his mother's. Her door was ajar, and he could hear her talking to someone on the phone.

His room reeked of the deodorant with which he'd sprayed himself earlier. He opened the window and snatched up a long-sleeved

Henley tee from the chest of drawers. His mother was still on the phone. But she had no friends—no close friends, anyway—and he wondered who she was talking to. Without thinking, he slung his shirt around the back of his neck and strode into the hallway.

He paused outside Florry's room to eavesdrop on her conversation. It sounded secretive, or perhaps anxious. If replies came at all, they were like the susurration of dead leaves or the sizzle of a spoon, and he couldn't make out any of the words. He shoved the door open and leaned shirtless against the jamb.

Florry's phone rested against the speckled mirror of her dressing table, beside a Blu-Tacked newspaper advertisement for his nonna's old business. The sepia ad included a photograph of the grandiose proprietor above her professional name, Nonna Oscura, which was lettered in a circus font.

But Florry's phone screen was blank. Florry herself faced her wardrobe and wore a formal dress and lipstick. On the wardrobe's top shelf, Benji clocked the winged Oliver typewriter that seemed only to be gathering dust. Like the house, it'd once belonged to his nonna, and he'd always thought it resembled a 1950s automobile.

'Who were you talking to?' he asked his mother.

She took a latticed hat from the wardrobe. 'Me? Talking? Who would I be talking to?'

'That's what I'm asking.'

On the bedside table beside Florry's king single, the bulky XpressFlow machine was from a more recent decade than the typewriter. Its beige mass reminded Benji of the computers his primary school had rented in the 1980s, before some kid smashed them up with a cricket bat; that was one of Benji's earliest memories, and in it he was already seven. Thankfully, the XpressFlow remained intact. It was plumbed and plugged in and biding its time. In the evening, he'd attach his mother to it for her nocturnal haemodialysis.

Florry plucked a white hair from her hat and straightened the brim. 'I wasn't talking to anybody, Beniamino.' Her Australian accent was so broad that his full name—the name of his grandfather—sounded ridiculous rolling off her tongue.

'You got a secret lover or something—at your age?' He coughed out a couple of laughs. 'Again, Mama? Again?'

She put her hat on and turned to him with a smile. 'What happened to your nice shirt?'

Her expression did not change, but her gaze drifted to the crook of his arm, where the skin was ridged with scar tissue. Florry's arm looked the same, fleshier even, though her scars were from current and former AV fistulas. At this moment, they were obscured by her dress, as Benji's usually were by his shirtsleeves: he showed his arms to no one, not even the doctor who gave him his monthly injection of Sublocade.

'The leaky hose got me again—that's what happened.' He struggled into his Henley tee and tasted the phlegm of his coughed laughs. 'We gotta get a new hose, Mama.'

She held the white hair as if it were a spider's leg. 'Aren't you coming with me to mass?'

He caught sight of an idling ute through the lace sheers on Florry's window. It didn't matter what shirt he wore to mass: the parishioners all looked at him as if they could spy his scars anyway. They didn't judge him. Not exactly. Rather, they gazed over from their pews when they thought he wouldn't notice and projected their feelings at him—goodwill and embarrassment and sometimes even jealousy. All those surreptitious eyeballs made his legs itch.

He squeezed his right hand with his left. 'I'll meet you afterwards and walk you back, okay?'

'That will be very nice.' Florry looked at her sensibly soled shoes. 'Almost as nice as walking back with my secret lover.'

She stepped towards the dressing table and met her reflection in the mirror. Then she adjusted her hat and let the white hair float to the floor. The spot where her jewellery box used to sit remained bare and her phone blank. But the drawer was open, and from its corner she retrieved her diamond engagement ring.

Benji folded his arms to stop himself fidgeting. 'You were talking to somebody, weren't you?' he said. 'I heard whisperings, Mama.'

Florry slipped the ring onto her little finger, which was swollen with arthritis. A saturnine expression tugged at her bright mouth. 'Did you hear the latest about the children?'

'What children?'

'What children do you think, Benji?' She found her lipstick and uncapped it and applied another coat. 'That poor Jack and Lonnie, of course.'

Benji clucked his tongue. 'I'm gonna go feed the birds.'

He ambled to the rear of the house and saw, in the yard, a visitor in a suit and baseball cap loitering by the Hills hoist aviary.

※

The visitor's suit had the hue of a thundercloud, and Benji would've assumed he was attending a funeral had it not been for his workman's boots and tattered red cap. The visitor stooped at the aviary's unlocked gate and peered at the lorikeets barking and flapping about. He extended his hand as if to spring the gate open.

'Hey, man, what are you doing?' Benji called out.

He jogged towards the aviary.

The visitor straightened and stepped away from the chicken wire. 'I'm not a thief,' he declared.

'Yeah, well, you gotta be careful or you're gonna be mistaken for one.' Benji stood at the aviary's gate, and the lorikeets screeched at him for the breakfast he'd left in the kitchen. 'What are you doing out in my yard, man?'

The visitor's cap cast an oblique shadow across his face, such that it seemed to be composed of two triangles. 'I saw your invitation,' he said. 'Out front.'

'My invitation?' Benji craned his neck and caught sight of the domed birdcage and all the other junk beneath the carport next to the house. He looked back at the visitor, whose eyes did not wander. 'You mean the sign that says I've got lorikeets to sell—is that what you mean by my invitation?'

The visitor put his hands behind his back. 'I don't see what else I could mean.'

'Yeah, of course—I've just never heard anyone call it an invitation before. But if you're in the market for a lorikeet, then I *invite* you to buy one from me.' Benji chuckled in the visitor's impassive face. 'They're high-quality birds, man. Take a look.'

He stepped away from the aviary's gate, and the visitor resumed his stooped position, this time with his hands clasped at the small of his back. His suit was crimped at the shoulders, and the sun flashed in its folds like faraway lightning. The birds screamed, and he squinted to take them in. 'I'm really not a thief,' he said. 'My mum taught me to pay for whatever I want to take.'

'Your mum sounds like a good woman.'

The visitor sighed and shut his eyes for a moment. 'Fucking dumb,' he whispered. His shoulders tensed; the suit grew smoother and shinier, and Benji's pulse rumbled through his temples.

'All the lorikeets are for sale, man,' he said, 'except the mating pair—the two big ones. Actually, they're for sale too, like, as a pair, but you have to leave the mother here until her eggs hatch. She's in her box.' He nodded at the nesting box. 'And you have to pay a premium if you want the pair, because they produce really strong offspring.'

'I only need one bird from you, right? I'll get another somewhere else.' The visitor let silence fall, and again Benji squeezed his right hand with his left. Then the grey fledgling flung itself at the gate and held on to the chicken wire.

'What's the matter with him?' the visitor asked.

Benji stopped squeezing his hand. 'First of all, I don't know their sexes because I haven't had them tested. Second, nothing's wrong with that bird, man. It just has a temporary grey feather situation that its personality more than makes up for. Like, you can tickle it, teach it to whistle songs—watch.'

He moved closer to the visitor and smelled the petrichor of day-old booze. The rumble in Benji's temples grew louder. He poked a finger through the chicken wire and tickled the grey fledgling's neck, and the bird trilled the same three sweet and sour notes as before.

'Its feathers will go technicolour soon, so long as you care for it properly.' Benji withdrew his finger before the bird could bite it. 'But no returns if not. This backyard is *caveat emptor*, man.'

The visitor rose to his full height. 'How much for the grey lory then?'

'Let me calculate that for you.'

Benji turned his cheek and mouthed words as if he were doing sums. The moment of transaction had arrived too soon, and he wasn't sure he wanted to sell the grey fledgling—especially not to the visitor. Why, then, had he gone into salesperson mode? Perhaps it was habit—although, equally, he could use the money. He'd price the lory higher than what he'd last paid for a gram, he decided. That would be too expensive for the visitor to haggle over, and it would bring an end to the interaction.

'The grey bird will set you back three hundred and sixty dollars,' he said. 'Now I know that sounds expensive, but—'

'Sounds fair to me.'

The visitor extended his hand towards Benji in much the same way he had towards the aviary's gate. A groan escaped Benji's throat. He sought out the visitor's eyes beneath the brim of his cap, or maybe they sought him out, and suddenly he found himself shaking the visitor's hand.

'Do you have a cage to transport it in?'

'I'll work something out.' The visitor released Benji's hand and started to saunter off. 'And I'll get your money, too.'

'I'll, um—I'll bring the bird to you,' Benji said.

The visitor passed beneath the carport and disappeared on his way to the street.

Benji collected the domed birdcage and coaxed the grey fledgling into it. He carried the cage down the carport side of the property and walked the concrete path between the house and the paint tin and oxidising tools and sundries. Then his gaze snagged on a loose brick in the wall. The brick was mortarless and askew and directly beneath his bedroom window. He thought of his mother's door and the whispers behind it, and his step faltered. Then the grey fledgling trilled, and Benji reminded himself that the sale to the visitor wasn't yet complete.

He prodded the brick back into place and made his way along the driveway and out to the pavement. On the asphalt of the road, the visitor waited behind an imposing maroon ute and toyed with a variegated sheaf of banknotes. A red metal toolbox rested on the kerb in front of him. The ute was idling, Benji realised, and through its tinted window, he saw the panting silhouette of a massive dog.

Uncovered, the ute's tray was filled with oddball cargo—a wicker chair with snapped legs, a plastic clock with Mickey Mouse on it. Benji eyed a splintered plank of wood and an oil canister marked with an X. 'Where's your cage?' he asked.

'Haven't got one anymore.' The visitor squatted at the kerb and prised opened the toolbox. 'You can just stick him right in here.'

Benji ventured onto the nature strip and put the birdcage down. He could almost sense the heat radiating from the toolbox. Scratches in the paint glimmered, although it'd be pitch-black inside the box if it were shut. A smoky memory wafted through his mind—a young girl, her hair hanging over her face, scribbling furiously with a coloured pencil on a glinting sheet of paper. The girl had curly hair, like Sondra's, but where Sondra's locks had been red, the girl's were brown.

He batted the memory away and concentrated on the toolbox and the price he'd last paid for a gram. That amount and more was in cash in the visitor's hand. But Benji made eye contact with the grey fledgling and chastised himself for counting coin by weight. 'I can't let you take it in that,' he said. 'It's too cramped, man, too hot—the bird will die. You gotta come back with a proper cage.'

The visitor took a breath, as if to control himself. 'Fucking dumb,' he whispered again, and slipped the cash into his pants pocket. He rose, and Benji noticed patches of sweat on the underarms of his suit. 'Just put the bird in the box,' the visitor said in a low voice, 'and everything will be square.'

Benji was sweating as well. Droplets had collected like river stones at the top of his spine, and his temples had started to rumble once more. 'I'm sorry, man—I can't do it. I can't sell you this lory if you're gonna put it in that box.'

He took hold of the cage and retreated; the visitor stepped over the toolbox and advanced. 'Put the bird in the fucking toolbox, you cunt.'

Benji stumbled backwards and dragged the cage over the pavement. 'No,' he said.

Then he heard an old woman call out, 'Buy his cage.'

Her voice emanated from the ute's cabin, yet it rang with the clarity of a bell. Benji stared at the vehicle's windows. At first, all he could see was the dog's silhouette. Then, in the front passenger seat, the speaker turned her head, and he clocked the bleary lineation of her hair styled in a bun. The visitor halted and peered in the same direction. He inhaled deeply through his nose. 'I'll take your cage for an extra hundred.'

Benji ceased his retreat. No longer on the pavement, he was behind the fence line of his mother's property, albeit in the driveway. He read the sign he'd erected on the front lawn: LORIKEETS FOR SALE. COME ON IN! An extra hundred certainly would make this a significant sale. But the red toolbox sat on the kerb like a time capsule unearthed, and he shook his head. 'I'm not going to sell you this bird, man. I can't do it.'

Immediately, the visitor was on to Benji, who prepared himself for a blow. He staggered and fell onto his rump. The cage clanked onto the ground and tipped over, and he waited for the rumble in his head to become a whine—for the hurt of the visitor's fist against his cheek to ripple through his skull and finish up in his brain.

'Give him time,' the old woman's voice tolled from the ute. 'Give the junkie'—the dog's panting filled the pause—'time.'

The blow from the visitor never arrived, but the rumble in Benji's head did become a whine, and a phantom ache reached his brain. He wondered how the old woman knew anything about him—perhaps she'd spotted his scars through Florry's lace sheers. An animal barked, although he couldn't tell if it was the lorikeet or the dog. His eye fell upon a horned ram's head badge on the ute's tailgate. He could feel the onset of the rattles and tried in vain to get a better view of the old woman in the front passenger seat.

The visitor still towered over him with his fist cocked; his sweat and heavy breathing intensified the stench of liquor. 'Lucky cunt,' he sneered. 'I'm out of town for a week, but I'll be back next Sunday—at dawn.' He met Benji's eye. 'And you? You'll put the fucking bird in the toolbox, or you'll pay for what you took from me.'

The visitor withdrew and picked up the toolbox and tossed it into the tray of the ute. He got into the driver's seat and drove off, while Benji sat on his rump and watched, and the grey fledgling screeched at him from its cage.

II

Once he was certain mass had ended, Benji walked a crooked path to the suburban street on which lay Sacred Innocents' Church. The church's pentagonal facade and the cross attached to its gable roof loomed up ahead. On the laneway beside the church, Florry chewed the ear off a woman who nodded so reluctantly she may well have been disagreeing. At least his mother was occupied, Benji thought, and passed under the collective shadow of a union of terrace houses.

He scanned the thinning crowd of parishioners in the church's yard and spotted the reassuring heft of Father Paolo. Paolo was busy farewelling two young families. Then Benji saw a wiry man in a black suit—several shades darker than the visitor's—seated on a marble bench in the yard. A leather satchel leaned against the man's shins, and he rested his hands in his lap and kept his head bowed.

Benji had the impression the man was waiting for him. He expected his legs to itch, yet it was his bones that rattled again. In his ears, the voice of the old woman in the ute tolled over the panting of the massive dog. *Give the junkie time,* she'd commanded, and the visitor had obeyed. He'd promised to return in a week at dawn, and he struck Benji as a man of his baleful word.

On the edge of sunlight, Benji stopped and leaned against the fence of one of the terrace houses. He knew he wouldn't be able to bring himself to coax the grey fledgling into the toolbox. Neither could he abandon Florry to face the visitor alone. So when the two young families departed, he left the collective shadow; he made sure his mother was still monologuing and strode to the church.

In the yard, a few of the remaining parishioners cast glances at him. He sensed envy in the mascaraed eyes of a teenage girl, and he wanted to assure her that he was no freer than she. But he kept walking and fixed his gaze on a statue of the Virgin and passed the man in black on the marble bench.

By the church's entrance, Paolo threw out his arms and grinned at Benji. 'I didn't see you at the service today.'

'Yeah, well, I wasn't feeling especially, um, Jesus-y today.'

Benji stood next to Paolo, who clapped his hands together and kept them clasped. 'That's the thing about faith, Benji: you come to mass and maybe you end up feeling a little more Jesus-y when you leave, eh?'

He raised an eyebrow, and Benji lifted one side of his mouth. The laneway was behind him, and his mother's voice carried on the breeze. He glanced at the leather satchel leaning against the shins of the man in black and felt an acute yearning to grab it and rip it open. 'Can I talk to you inside, Father?' he said.

On the bench, the ears of the man in black twitched.

Paolo led Benji into the church's vestibule, where the natural light and the light from the stained-glass windows in the nave combined soothingly. The effect was ruined, Benji decided, by the enormous bleeding Jesus nailed to a cross on the wall and the tacky printed material that covered a desk to the right.

'What's the trouble?' Paolo asked from near the entrance.

Benji wandered over to the desk. 'I really was gonna come to church this morning, Father. I was dressed in a nice shirt and everything. You can ask my mum—I'm telling the truth, I swear.' He picked up a pamphlet with the Star of Bethlehem on it and pretended to read. 'Then this guy came round to the house, you know? Actually, I don't know if you do know: I've been breeding birds, or trying to breed birds, while also caring for my mother every day.'

Paolo placed a finger to his own chin. 'Florence told me. I think it's a very positive thing.'

'Yeah, yeah, I think it's a positive thing too. But this guy—he made threats against me.' Over the pamphlet, Benji tried to gauge Paolo's mien. The priest's bulk did not budge and, above his finger, his countenance remained unmoved. 'And against my mum,' Benji added. The crook of his elbow itched. 'My mama, Father, who's a permanent congregant of your, um, congregation.'

Paolo peered out into the yard. 'What exactly did this person say to you, Benji?'

Benji put down the pamphlet. He thought back on what the visitor had said and realised he couldn't recall his words verbatim. Mainly what he could recall was the old woman's voice and the toolbox on the kerb and the smoky memory of the curly-haired girl.

In the vestibule, he stroked a pile of pocket books with lambs on the cover. 'I don't remember, exactly,' he replied. 'He said he'd come back next Sunday and hurt me. And hurt Florry. And the way he said it, Father, it was like he was gonna . . .' He canted his head and made a guttural noise. 'You know? And I was just wondering if the church could help me out—help us out—with a situation like that.'

Paolo wandered towards the desk. He did not lower his finger from his chin. 'Is this person someone you knew from your life before?'

'No, man. No.' Beside Paolo, Benji folded his arms and rubbed the itching scars on his elbow. 'Father, I've never met this guy in my life or had any dealings with him or anything like that.'

Paolo picked up the pamphlet that Benji had put down. 'What does the threat have to do with your birds?'

'I mean, the guy wanted to buy a lorikeet, and I didn't want to sell—'

'This is a business dispute?'

'It's not a business dispute.'

The priest frowned at Benji's folded arms and rotated the pamphlet in his hands. 'Forgive me, Benji, but are you . . .?'

'Am I what, man?' On the cover of the spinning pamphlet, Benji read the words *We have seen His star in the East*. He scratched at his scars and sighed. 'Can't the church just be there for me, man? And for my mum?'

'The church can certainly be there for you. But, Benji, the church isn't in the business of protecting people from physical threats.' The priest took half a step forward. 'Have you told your mother about this?'

Benji shook his head.

'I think you should.' Paolo stopped rotating the pamphlet. 'And have you gone to the proper authorities?'

Benji scoffed. 'I can't go to the cops, man.'

Paolo stood vis-a-vis with him, but Benji turned his attention to the enormous bleeding Jesus on the wall. The painted droplets of blood seemed to ooze down to Jesus' elbows. Paolo touched Benji's upper arm, and goosebumps flared on his skin and ended up in the same place as Jesus' blood.

'If you need me to accompany you to the police station,' Paolo said, 'I'm more than happy to come along.'

Benji sought out the priest's eyes. 'Thank you, Father,' he replied, 'but you don't need to do that for me.'

'Are you sure?' Paolo patted Benji's arm and grinned, as he had when Benji arrived. 'Okay, then. I'll pray for you, Benji, and I hope to see you with Florence in the pews next week, eh?'

🐇

Benji sat side-saddle on the edge of Florry's king single. In a sleeveless nightgown, his mother was propped up in bed with a pillow at her back. He tried to bring the two scabbed puncture wounds on her arm into focus, but he was distracted by the Star of Bethlehem on the pamphlet in her lap. No succour would be forthcoming from Father Paolo or the church. Benji had even taken up the priest's suggestion and caught a bus to the police station. Outside, he'd spotted a cop he recognised, and a hard-wired instinct had kicked in: he'd fled without a backward glance.

Florry extended a latex-gloved hand and stroked his hairline, and he registered that she'd spoken to him.

'What'd you say, Mama?'

She smiled, although her hand retreated. 'Are you okay, Beniamino?'

'Am I okay?' Also wearing gloves, he collected a scraper from among the items and implements in front of the XpressFlow. A bag of saline dangled from a hook on the wall; along the adjacent wall ran the jumbled cave of his mother's wardrobe. He wondered whether he could pack Florry and the lorikeets up and leave town for a week. That'd involve telling her about the visitor's threat and asking her to pay for accommodation. Plus, they'd need to take her XpressFlow along for the ride—and he had no right to tax her with his problems or a request for money. 'Why are you always asking if I'm okay?' he said.

She straightened her arm to give him easier access to her wounds. 'Because I'm your mother.'

'And you always want me *not* to be okay, just so you can be my mother.' With the scraper, he picked off the scabs from her AV fistula while she breathed out a prayer he couldn't identify. Her twin wounds didn't bleed much, yet she flinched when Benji scraped away a gooey ribbon of flesh. 'Sorry,' he said. 'Anyway, that wasn't what you said, Mama—asking if I'm okay. What'd you say, really?'

She crossed herself. 'I said it's odd that the news isn't reporting what people are saying.'

'What are people saying? Huh?' Benji put the scraper down

and picked up a rainbow tourniquet. 'Probably all sorts of dumb things,' he muttered.

The words forced him to remember the cussed judgement the visitor had delivered after Benji had praised the man's mother. The visitor's hushed tone had only reinforced the undercurrent of violence, and Benji imagined the visitor's fists striking his head again and again. He pictured a galaxy composed of Stars of Bethlehem and then his whole world shrinking to the black perdition inside the toolbox. That was another of his options, he supposed: taking a beating, possibly to death.

'They're saying they left the car by themselves,' Florry said.

Benji applied the rainbow tourniquet to her arm. 'Who left the car?'

'The children.'

'What children?'

Benji stood and gave the pipes protruding from the XpressFlow a shake. From among the implements in front of it, he picked out two hypodermic needles attached to discrete plastic tubes that led nowhere. There was an easier path to take towards oblivion, he reflected, thinking of both the children and the prospect of a beating.

Florry opened and shut her fist. 'I bet that bloody defrocked priest had something to do with it.'

'Who's that, Mama?'

'The man who was sitting on the bench after mass. You must have seen him when you were talking to Father Paolo?'

Her query hung in the air, and Benji bit the inside of his cheek. He guided one needle through a puncture wound on his mother's skin and into a vein. The second needle he jabbed into the other puncture wound, which burrowed its way to an artery. His mother's bicep spasmed, and she drew a sharp breath. 'Sorry,' he said again.

He let the tubes that led nowhere fill with his mother's blood and clamped them off. Then he removed the tourniquet, and Florry made a chicken-dance motion that implied she had pins and needles. She'd never commented on his proficiency with all of this, although he knew it could not have escaped her notice. *Rattle, rattle—we snakes,* Sondra had whispered when she and he had rung the bell of their old dealer, Raymond, for the last time.

Benji taped the needles to his mother's arm. Rather than buying a gram of oblivion, he thought, he could pay Raymond for protection from the visitor. For that, he needed cash, fast—and if he couldn't ask his mother, there was only one sure-fire way to get it.

'Benji?' Florry said gently. 'You don't want to tell me what you and Father Paolo were talking about?'

'I already told you, Mama.' He gestured at the pamphlet. 'We were just talking about miracles—and all that other priestly stuff, you know? Paolo said he wants to see me at mass next week.'

She patted the bed where he'd been sitting. '*I'd* like to see you at mass next week.'

To avoid the tenderness of her gaze, he turned to her dressing table at the foot of her bed. But their eyes met in the glass. His plummeted to the spot where her jewellery box had been, and in spite of himself he noticed that the drawer in which she kept her diamond ring was not shut. Pawning the ring was too large a risk, though; it was too personal an object. It was the sole memento Florry had kept from her marriage—and besides, she wore it to church every Sunday.

'Maybe I'll come,' he said, 'if I can keep myself clean—shirt-wise, I mean.' Expertly, he injected syringes of saline into the blood-filled plastic tubes that used to lead nowhere but now led to Florry's wounds. He followed that up with heparin to stop her blood from clotting overnight. 'You, um, really think that defrocked priest had something to do with it all?'

'To do with what all?'

He checked the cylindrical filter in the XpressFlow. 'You know—the children.'

'What children?'

'The children,' he replied. 'The children you've been blah-blah-blahing about for months.'

She adjusted her pillows and laughed. 'I know what children you meant.'

'Oh, you were joking. That was a very funny joke, Mama—ha ha.' He connected the tubes in her arms to the pipes protruding from the XpressFlow. Then he tapped the bag of saline. 'I wrote down your temperature and blood pressure right, didn't I?'

'You did.'

'And your dry weight and current weight?'

'Mm-hm.'

Benji undid the clamps on the tubes, and his mother's blood seeped through the pipes towards the XpressFlow. He started the machine and removed his gloves. His mother switched on her bedside lamp, and Benji flicked off the main light in the room. Florry pulled off her own gloves, and he returned to sit by her side.

'I don't know if that priest had anything to do with it,' she said. 'He just gives me the creeps.' She handed the pamphlet to Benji, along with her gloves. 'To be honest, I think the children might have walked off on purpose, just to make their poor mother suffer.'

Benji rolled his eyes. 'I'll come back in half an hour to check on you, okay?'

He got up and glanced again at the cave of her wardrobe, in which he caught sight of his nonna's winged Oliver typewriter on the top shelf.

In the middle of the night, Benji woke in his bed with the impression he'd been shaken from a dream. Already, though, the dream was fading. He sat up and blinked at a drawer jutting from the chest like a rib with a compound fracture. The drawer of his mother's dressing table and the winged Oliver typewriter lurched into his mind. He tasted hunger—why were he and his mother always leaving openings?

Compunction bobbed in his throat, but he forced himself to slip out of bed. In the hallway, he eyed Florry's door, which was ajar, and listened to the XpressFlow rinsing her blood clean. He slipped through the door and waited a few moments until he was sure she was asleep. Then he tiptoed to the wardrobe. Carefully, he lowered the typewriter from the top shelf and held it against his chest.

The cool of it reached his skin through his Henley tee, and he conveyed it to the foot of his mother's king single. Then he heard a whisper, or the rustle of linen, and his mother sucked in a stertorous breath. She slurred something that sounded to his ears like, 'But where did they go?'

He paused, and his heart fluttered behind the typewriter's wings. In the dressing table's mirror, he tried to make out the lump of Florry's form under the sheets. His mother had been awake when he'd stolen her jewellery box; she'd watched him in silence, and for the first time he wondered whether she'd been scared rather than sympathetic.

His throat constricted, and he waited for Florry's breathing to lapse into a rhythm. She hadn't been asking a genuine question, he assured himself; she'd been talking nonsense in her sleep.

He lugged the typewriter through the house and out into the yard, where his mother had hung washing on a foldaway clothesline. In the aviary, five of the lorikeets didn't notice his presence. But the grey fledgling flew maladroitly across the aviary and clung to the chicken wire nearest to him. It trilled its three sweet and sour notes, although he wasn't sure whether they were encouraging or admonishing.

He ignored the bird and hurried around the corner with the typewriter. Beneath the carport, he rummaged behind the domed birdcage and beside the tin of salmon-pink paint. He shifted a sledgehammer aside and created a niche among a pile of oxidising tools. Into the niche he placed the typewriter, before he made an obfuscating barrier of the birdcage and paint tin.

He backed away to check whether the typewriter would be visible on the off chance that his mother were to walk this way to the street. It probably wouldn't be, he decided, and took another step back. Then a thud resounded behind him, and he flinched and about-faced.

At his feet was the loose brick he'd straightened earlier; it lay on the concrete, on a forty-five-degree angle. He knitted his brow at it, and his gaze climbed to the brick-shaped cavity under his bedroom window. The distance between the fallen prism and the wall wasn't more than half a metre. This was great enough, though, to suggest that the brick could not have dropped of its own accord. It had to have been dragged out of place—or forced out from the inside.

To his right, the driveway led to the street where the visitor had placed the red toolbox on the kerb. Benji ran his thumb along his bottom lip. His bones began to rattle, and his breathing quickened. But he added up his mother's slurred words and his discovery of the brick: this was all a guilt-and-anxiety fever dream, he told himself.

To prove it, he knelt and shuffled forward until the fallen brick was against his knees, and he kept shuffling until the brick was parallel with the side of the house. Then he leaned over and peered through the cavity as if through some benighted viewfinder.

Under the house, the crawlspace was pitch-black, and he could spy no more of it than he could the inside of the nesting box. He straightened and picked up the loose brick at his knees. It was heavier than he'd imagined; either that, or he was more enervated than he'd anticipated. He had to use both hands to lever the brick back into position.

In the instant before he slid it into place, something shifted under the house. Light winked off its metal surface, and he heard it slither over the dirt. A still frame of the dream from which he'd been shaken returned to him—it was a smoky image of the curly-haired girl, scribbling on the glinting sheet of paper. The frame was different from his earlier recollection, though: drained of colour, the pencil in the girl's hand had become the white of oblivion.

Then the brick slotted into the cavity and eclipsed both the dream and the house's substructure. Benji stayed stationary. He kept his fingers before his face, almost touching the wall. It occurred to him that he could remove the loose brick and take another peek at the crawlspace. But the fleshy mountain range of his scars burned, and he left the brick alone.

III

His nonna's typewriter obeyed the same gravity as the brick, and in the dim of the pawnshop, Benji struggled to heave it onto the surface of the glass counter.

Behind the counter, the shop's sinewy owner, Mert, cocked his pierced eyebrow. He wore black studs in his drooping ears, and his skin was like butcher's paper that'd been scrunched up and poorly flattened. 'I'd hoped never to see you again, Benji,' he said in his clipped accent. 'In the nicest possible way.'

Benji glanced at the front window. Beyond the dusty electronics and knick-knacks on display, the business's name was painted in yellow. In all the times he'd been here—with and without Sondra—he didn't think he'd ever read it. All he knew was that it began with the scream of several A's in a row. This had never seemed more appropriate than when he'd pawned the jewellery from his mother's box. But it seemed almost as appropriate now.

'Yeah, well, I'd hoped never to see you again either, man, as much as I appreciate your specific brand of'—he returned his gaze to Mert and made a wiping motion—'face.'

Mert prodded at one of the typewriter's pearly keys. 'I assume this is why you're here? To sell me this beast?'

'No, no—not sell it. I'm not gonna sell it.'

Mert had sullied the X key with an oily fingerprint. Benji stared at it. That morning, he'd heard his mother chopping tomatoes while listening to songs of devotion on the radio; he'd fed the lorikeets and polished the typewriter. The loose brick in the wall had watched him. But at least it was quick work—he'd been surprised to find the typewriter agleam. When afternoon arrived, he'd snuck the typewriter along the driveway and let it sit like a child on his lap on the bus ride to the fringe of the CBD.

Stale tobacco wafted from Mert's body to Benji's nostrils. 'And, by the way, that was only a joke about your brand of face, Mert. It's a beautiful face brand you got there. Okay?'

'You're not the first to say that.' Mert chuckled, and his crow's-feet deepened. 'But you are the first to say it in that way.'

Benji pointed at the typewriter. 'This is an amazing typewriter, man.'

'It looks impressive.'

'Looks very damn impressive. As you can see, it's an Oliver. See there?' He gestured at the gold branding, inlaid in triplicate on the typewriter. 'It's a genuine one from the olden days—my nonna used to use it in her shop—and it's got, like, this unique winged design, you know?'

Benji watched Mert lean over the typewriter. Above the keyboard, a central metal piece resembled a tuning fork, or perhaps a bird's stiff carcass; either side of the carcass, striated plastic wings curved upwards as if in flight.

Mert rested his palm on the glass counter. 'I thought it wasn't for sale?'

'Oh, it's not for sale. This *beast* is too rare a breed, man.'

Benji bit his cheek. He'd heard an echo of the sales pitch he'd delivered to the visitor about the grey fledgling. If he hadn't done that, if he hadn't shaken the visitor's hand, perhaps he wouldn't be in this pawnshop with its screaming name. Among these conditionals lurked the smoky still frame from his dream: the curly-haired girl scribbling in futility with her white pencil. But he wondered how far back in time one had to travel to find the root cause of anything.

Afternoon sunshine broke through the dim, and a woman in a bucket hat entered and beelined for a saxophone on the wall. Mert gazed past Benji, but his palm remained flat. 'I don't have much demand for old typewriters. Or much demand for anything, really.'

'Yeah, well, you can sell this one online for, like, a full grand.'

'Why don't you do that, Benji? Get your thousand dollars.'

Benji clucked his tongue. 'I don't wanna sell it, man—I want to use this as collateral for a loan. Say, eight hundred dollars?' He squeezed the fingers of his right hand with his left. 'I'll pay you back in, like, a week, or a month—I'm telling the truth, I swear. If I don't, you can sell this beast and make a couple hundred bucks' profit, easy.'

Mert crinkled his nose, and more creases appeared around his laughter lines. He lifted his palm from the glass. 'I don't know. The jewellery you used last time as collateral—'

'Six hundred?' Benji pressed his stomach against the front of the glass counter and remembered the cool of the typewriter through his Henley tee. On display were gaudy costume jewels and boxy cameras and outmoded video game cartridges from the 2000s. The trinkets he'd stolen from his mother were long gone, and he eyed Mert's palm print fading on the counter. 'Five hundred?'

Mert leaned over the typewriter again. 'If you leave this with me, I can loan you three hundred and sixty dollars.'

The number pinballed through Benji's head: more than what he'd last paid for a gram, and the precise amount the visitor had agreed to pay for the grey fledgling. Perhaps he'd come full circle, and this was the default amount Mert offered him for his goods; Benji couldn't remember. Anyway, it probably wouldn't buy him a Sunday of protection from Raymond. 'That's not enough, man.'

'It's all I can give you. And you'll have to pay it back at fourteen percent interest, within one month.' Mert licked his thumb and erased his fingerprint from the X key. 'Are you sure this is what you want, Benji?'

Benji sighed. He looked to the street and caught sight of a man in a baseball cap and thundercloud suit. The man's features were obscured by the screaming letters on the window. He marched by the pawnshop without a glance, but something about the way he rolled his shoulders made Benji shiver. He looked at Mert and, deadpan, pressed the Y key on the typewriter.

Only minor details about Raymond's house had changed since Benji's last visit with Sondra. The blinds in the upstairs windows were venetian rather than vertical. The double garage doors were metal when they used to be wood, and where there'd been a sensor light at the side entry, an Edison bulb now seemed to burn constantly. But the wattle tree with its yellow puffs of flowers—the 'duckling tree', as Sondra used to call it—still seemed lucent under the streetlight outside, and Benji had lingered long enough to know that the house served the same purpose it always had.

Perhaps some houses were like that: always the same underneath. He bit the inside of his cheek and recalled the glint and slither he'd glimpsed in the crawlspace. Coming back to Raymond's, he'd expected to feel a similar sense of dread; what surged through him instead was a rattly thrill. It was true that the wad of cash he'd received from Mert probably wasn't enough to buy protection. But it might be enough to buy oblivion or escape.

He whistled a quiet self-rebuke. Then he walked to the side entry and rang the bell next to a security door's metal grille.

Soon, a woman appeared; she carried a doleful young boy in one arm. 'What do you want?' she asked.

Benji didn't recognise her, and he rapped his knuckles against the cash in his pocket. 'Is, um, Raymond around?'

Before Benji's eyes, the woman seemed to seesaw.

'Ray used to help me out with stuff,' he continued, 'and I need his help again—with something different this time. Don't worry, he knows me. Like, he knows who I am: tell him it's Benji.'

The woman retreated. 'Raymond doesn't live here anymore.'

'Wait, I can pay. I can pay.' Benji took the cash out and slapped it against the grille. 'See there? And I'm not a cop, man. If I was a cop, I couldn't lie about it, right?'

'No, that's a myth.' The woman began to turn away. 'You should leave.'

'Hold on—wait.'

The woman paused.

Benji hesitated. Then, frantically, he rolled up his sleeve to reveal his elbow. He straightened his arm and displayed his scars. 'I'm not a cop, okay?'

'Old school.'

The woman let him into the house, and Benji pulled his sleeve down.

He followed her and the boy to a murky living room where a group of people lounged around on leather sofas. They were different people from the last time he'd been here. Different, too, was the television that sent bolts of sitcom light through the room and cachinnated over a cockroach on the tiles. A shirtless man whose arms were tattooed with faces got up and kicked the cockroach; it skidded past Benji's sneakers and into the kitchen.

The woman and boy flopped down in the man's spot and stared at the television. 'Kimber?' the woman called out. 'One of Ray's strays.'

Belatedly, Benji noticed a diminutive woman in a long-sleeved shirt sitting at a table in the closest corner. Kimber snacked on a pile of seeds, and the tattooed man positioned himself as sentry behind her.

'What are you eating?' Benji asked.

The man widened his eyes and put on a mad grin. But Kimber continued to snack as if Benji wasn't there. The television laughed, and he glanced at the group huddled around it. He counted four adults, plus the boy, although their places on the sofas seemed to switch depending on what was on screen.

'It's hạt dưa,' Kimber replied eventually. 'Roasted watermelon seeds from Vietnam. I peeled them already; you want to try?'

'Okay—yeah, yeah, I'll try.' Benji snatched up too many seeds and shoved them into his mouth. When he bit into them, all he tasted was char. 'They're good,' he said.

'Mum used to get them from her village when I was a kid. Customs was always so bitchy about it.' Kimber picked at her teeth and looked at Benji. 'We haven't had many of Ray's strays lately. We don't much even sell that specific stuff anymore. It's all cold brew now. You been in jail?'

Benji gulped down the seeds. 'No.'

'Got a new guy?'

'No.'

'So you're a police informant?'

Benji's mouth felt dry, and the room listed like a capsizing ship. He was about to speak when Kimber chuckled. 'It's cool, dude. Wouldn't matter if you were anyway.' She rocked her chair back and placed a seed in her mouth and eyed his wrinkled sleeve. He tried not to move. But someone watching television tittered, and he twitched again. Kimber wagged her finger. 'You know what I reckon?'

The tattooed man draped his arms around her. 'Nah, what do you reckon?'

'I reckon this dude's been living with Jesus since Ray quit.' She pointed at a tacky chandelier dangling lopsided from the ceiling. 'Praise the Lord, am I right?'

Benji pictured his mother, praying while he plugged her into the XpressFlow. 'I've been living clean, man, yeah, but I'm not a Jesus-y kinda guy.' He remembered Paolo and the defrocked priest and the alluring leather satchel at his feet. Then he rubbed his upper arms and realised his skin had gone cold. 'Actually,' he added, 'I'm not here to stop living clean.'

The tattooed man guffawed. Kimber shoved his arms off her and brought her chair legs clattering back to earth. 'What the fuck *are* you here for then?'

The room tipped too far, and Benji worried he was about to topple. 'Can I sit? Do you mind if I sit?'

Croupier-like, Kimber shoved a handful of seeds in his direction. Benji sat across from her and held up a seed and focused on it for balance. 'Me and Raymond—um, Ray, you know?' He sucked air into his lungs. 'We had a good relationship. Like, he was a friend, in a way, and I could ask him for help—not free help, but he'd help me out if I needed it.'

'That doesn't seem like friendship,' Kimber said.

'Yeah, well, that's what me and Ray had with regard to the friendship thing.' Benji tossed the seed into his mouth. He slowed his speech and continued, 'Now Ray's gone, and you're here, and I need a favour. And it doesn't have to be a free favour—I can just pay you, and we can leave it at that.'

Kimber pursed her lips at the faces on the tattooed man's arms. 'How much can you pay?'

'Don't you wanna know what I want?'

Kimber shook her head languorously, and Benji peered at the group lounging on the sofas. The woman who'd let him in had abandoned the boy to the television so she could be entertained by Benji instead. He took the cash from his pocket and placed it on the table. 'I just need some protection, okay? Just one dumb, stupid day of protection—that's all I'm asking for.'

'One day?' Kimber handed the cash to the tattooed man, who counted the notes. 'Then I never see you again?'

'Yeah, yeah, this Sunday, man. Just . . . if you come to my house Sunday before dawn, and maybe be ready to do violence—you know?—if somebody shows up wanting to do violence to me.' Benji pointed at the tattooed man. 'He could do it.'

The tattooed man spoke into Kimber's ear and she nodded. He strode off with the cash, and the dread Benji had anticipated finally arrived. 'Where's he going?' There was nothing to stop them taking his money and booting him out, he realised, as he watched the tattoos disappear through the kitchen. 'Where are you going, man?' he called out.

'Relax.' Kimber snacked on a couple of seeds. 'The problem I see is: we don't have a friendship like the one you had with Ray. I don't know you. You're a stray dog off the street, dude.' A cackle from the television forced her to pause. 'So, before we talk favours, I reckon we have to talk friendship. Don't you agree?'

Benji placed his hands in his lap and squeezed the right with the left. He nodded, and something landed on the pile of seeds before him. For some reason, he figured it was the cockroach and jerked to his feet. But it wasn't the cockroach: the tattooed man had returned and lobbed a tiny red balloon onto the table.

'I don't want that,' Benji said. The dread and the thrill rode the rollercoaster of his blood and rattled every bone of his body. The mountain range on the crook of his elbow felt volcanic, and when the television audience cracked up, he thought of the visitor's fists and the old woman's bell of a voice. 'I don't want that,' he repeated.

'This is how we become friends.' Kimber blinked at him. 'I take your money. You take that good shit. Everybody wins.'

Benji met the tattooed man's eyes. 'What about protection, though—this Sunday?'

Kimber scratched her head. 'Maybe come back later in the week with, say, five hundred, and we'll do your favour for you.'

'But I don't have—'

The tattooed man gripped Benji's nape and stopped him mid-sentence. Kimber snacked, and the tattooed man swept up the balloon and some seeds and pressed them to Benji's chest. 'You talk too fucking much,' he breathed, and marched Benji past the dying cockroach and out of the house.

In his mother's room, Benji tore off his latex gloves—and Florry, who was propped up in bed, passed her gloves to him. 'Thank you,' she said.

'Don't mention it, Mama.'

He eased himself onto the edge of her king single and felt the tiny balloon in his pocket press against his thigh. With mechanical indifference, the XpressFlow pumped and cleaned and backwashed his mother's blood, and his gaze was carried along the tubes that led to and from her wounds and into and out of the machine.

'Benji,' Florry murmured. 'Do you know where my mother's typewriter is?'

Gloves in hand, he tensed his arm. Kimber had accepted his money, and the tattooed man had foisted a gram onto him. But maybe he'd unconsciously asked to buy escape. Perhaps he'd even invited the visitor to harm him and intimated that Father Paolo should reject his plea for help.

'That old thing?' he replied.

The truth: he considered giving it to his mother. He could hug her and explain that this time was different. This situation was temporary, and he'd fix it without him or her or the grey fledgling coming to harm. But he knew what that would sound like, especially off the tip of his particular tongue. Plus, he still needed five hundred dollars to make sure everything would be okay.

'It was dusty, Mama,' he continued, 'and I saw that it was taking up space in your wardrobe, so I put it out with the—you know?—with my stuff under the carport.'

His mother's face seemed wan and fatigued. 'Can you fetch it for me, please?'

'I mean, it's under some things now.' He got up and went over to Florry's dressing table. Then he slipped his hand into his pocket; with his fingers, he worried the balloon's latex and thrilled at the deposit of coarse granules within. 'I'll just have to shunt some bric-a-brac around. Do you need it urgently? I can get it tomorrow maybe, or the day after—I didn't think it even worked.'

'It works well enough for what I use it for.'

The drawer of the dressing table was open, and from its corner his mother's diamond ring winked at him like the slithering object in the crawlspace. His heart thudded, and he continued to worry the balloon.

'What do you use it for?' he asked.

'It's silly.'

'Yeah, well, you're a silly woman—you may as well tell me.'

'I write letters to my mother,' she said. 'No paper or anything. Just me, nattering and typing, typing and nattering. Listening out for her whispers. Sometimes she tells me things, Benji.'

'Oh yeah, like what?'

Distracted, Benji rubbed the balloon more intently. He could use the ring as collateral to get a loan of five hundred—and to bring the typewriter home. On Sunday, of course, his mother wouldn't be able to find the ring. But it was small enough that she might convince herself she'd misplaced it. Sometime later, perhaps, he could return the balloon to Kimber for a refund and scrape together the money to retrieve the ring and drop it on the floor somewhere for Florry to find.

'—they changed,' his mother said, completing a sentence he hadn't heard. 'They changed, and they changed back, and then they changed a final time.'

Benji glanced at the mirror; Florry's reflection appeared distant and lethargic. His eye darted to the sepia photograph of his nonna and the empty spot where the jewellery box had been. Abruptly, he removed his hand from his pocket. 'Who changed?'

Florry's head lolled backwards. 'I need to go to sleep now,' she said.

'Okay, Mama.' Benji slapped the gloves against his palm and stepped into the hallway. 'Do you want the door closed?'

'Never all the way.'

Florry lay down and switched off her lamp. Benji swung the door towards himself and left it ajar. 'I'll come back and check on you in half an hour,' he said.

'I love you, Benji,' his mother slurred, as if in her sleep.

Five minutes later, Benji squatted beneath the carport in front of the obfuscating barrier of the birdcage and the tin of salmon-pink paint. In his fist, the red balloon crinkled like a packet of chips—he'd wrapped it in foil, as much to keep it safe from the elements as to keep himself from caressing its skin. Now he held it above the niche where the typewriter had been and found himself unwilling to let it go.

From the aviary, the grey fledgling trilled its three sweet and sour notes. Then, unbidden, a voice at the back of his head started to compile a list. Another thought nagged at him, too: he'd told his mother that he'd stored the typewriter under the carport. She might come searching for it; she might already be on the lookout for a cap or a gram. He couldn't hide the balloon here any more than he could tape it to the underside of the toilet cistern.

Tablespoon, the list began.

Benji tried to silence it by turning towards the house. His gaze scuttled up to his bedroom window and traced the mortar back down until it found no bonding around the loose brick. The brick seemed slightly more askew than he'd left it, and he recalled the glint and slither he'd glimpsed in the crawlspace. The hairs on the scruff of his neck stood on end, and his nape ached from the tattooed man's vice-like grip.

Bic lighter, the list continued.

So rapidly that he almost skinned his knees, Benji knelt before the loose brick in the wall. He used his free hand and the thumb of his other fist to lever it out of place; the brick fell painlessly onto his thighs and rolled onto the concrete. He peered at it and avoided looking into the crawlspace. Balloon in hand, he stuck his entire arm through the cavity.

One of Florry's syringes, the list went on.

He urged his fist to unclench—to drop the balloon onto the dirt under the house. But his fingers refused to obey. They ached and began to cramp, and he pressed his cheek to the wall above the cavity. He watched the moonlight commingle with the streetlight and illuminate the driveway. Through the bricks, he listened to his pulse.

Florry's rainbow tourniquet, the list finished.

He heard something slithering towards him in the crawlspace and bit the inside of his cheek, but he kept his arm extended and the balloon in his fist. The slithering ceased, and in a beat of undisturbed night, the still frame of the curly-haired girl flashed in his mind. Another detail had altered, he realised. Whereas before he'd perceived the smoke around her to be an amnesiac haze, he now saw that it billowed from the glinting paper on which she scribbled with a white pencil.

Suddenly, Benji felt a spider scratch through his sleeve at the serried contours of his scars, while a second set of arachnid limbs feathered his fist. Again, he commanded himself to drop the balloon. But he didn't, or couldn't, and it was only when another spider landed on the back of his hand and another settled on his wrist that he understood—the spiders had five legs each.

His arm shook violently, and his pulse thundered through the bricks. He pictured four spiders, three limbs of each having been cruelly plucked by two children. Then, in place of the spiders, he imagined the filthy nails of those children creeping along his arm. His bones rattled. But his fist unclenched and dropped the balloon, which sounded as if it landed not on the dirt under the house but on a metal surface.

He yanked his arm out through the cavity and brushed cobwebs off his sleeve and found no spiders there at all. Fumbling with the brick, he shoved it back into position and closed off the crawlspace. Then he rushed into the house and sidled into his mother's room to check on her—and to borrow her diamond ring.

IV

Wednesday arrived, and Benji found himself in the dim of the pawnshop once more. He ran his thumb along his bottom lip and realised that the cuff of his long-sleeved tee was frayed. He hoped his mother hadn't noticed. As much as possible, he'd avoided her and the sight of the loose brick. He'd tickled the grey fledgling's neck and tried to keep the list from his mind. But now the sensation of spiders or nails creeping along his arm returned to him, and he let his hand fall. Immediately his own nails tapped his thigh, and he brought his thumb back to his mouth.

'What do you think?' he asked.

On the other side of the counter, Mert squinted through an old loupe at the diamond in Florry's ring. He set the ring on the counter's glass surface and peered at Benji. The loupe remained over his eye, held in place by his socket; it almost touched the scabby gunk that'd collected on his eyebrow piercing.

'The diamond's a VS2,' Benji said. 'That means not-very-included, I think, according to the internet, but the diamond *is* included with the ring, you know?' Barely visible in the backroom, the winged Oliver typewriter sat atop a pile of unsaleable DVD players. The ring should get the typewriter back, he assured himself, along with the extra five hundred Kimber had demanded. 'So what do you think, man?'

'I think'—Mert plucked the loupe from his socket and rested it upright beside the ring—'that I do not want to buy this ring from you.'

'Oh, come on.' Benji threw his hands out and his head back. 'You know I'm not selling this ring. I'm pawning it. It's an heirloom, okay? An *heirloom.*'

Mert came out from behind the counter. His jeans were ripped, revealing the bony chalk of his knees. 'Benji, I don't see you in two years—more than two years, in fact.' In the middle of the cramped pawnshop, he straightened a stack of celebrity gossip magazines from the 1990s. 'Now you come to my business twice in one week, putting the hard sell on me with your *nene*'s stuff.'

Benji trailed Mert and his stale tobacco cloud to the magazines. 'First of all, again, I'm not hard-selling you anything here, man. The ring's collateral. I'm gonna get the money to pay you for it. Second . . .'

Mert groaned at a celebrity's unblemished face. Then he took off, and Benji followed him to the musical instruments on the wall. The saxophone remained unsold, and next to it hung a mariachi guitar.

'Second,' Benji said, 'this isn't my nonna's ring. My dad gave it to my mum when they got engaged. I don't remember the man, okay? Mean ol' countryman, from what I hear—but you gotta admit he had amazing taste in rings.' He forced out a laugh. That truly was the extent of his knowledge of his father. He'd spurned every opportunity to find out more: what could they offer each other except mutual disappointment?

Instead of replying, Mert took down a violin and ran a finger over a few chips in the varnish. He carried it back to the counter, and Benji stalked after him.

'Why'd you inspect the ring if you're not interested?' He almost crashed into the counter. 'Why'd you look at it with that loupe thingy? Huh?'

Carelessly, Mert tossed the violin onto the counter near the ring. He rummaged through a cabinet and took out a square of sandpaper. 'What happened to that friend you used to come here with? Sondra?' He began sanding the chipped area. 'What happened to her, Benji?'

Benji bit the inside of his cheek. He'd embraced Sondra, at her sister's house, on the night before she passed. Her curly red hair had smelled like the duckling tree. They'd both been clean for a while—had both arrived at step four—and she'd released him and feigned pinching the raw flesh on the crook of his elbow.

'She's dead, isn't she?' Mert said. He stopped sanding and fixed his gaze on Benji.

Benji gripped his right hand with his left. 'No, man. No. She's not dead. She's, like—she's fine, I think. She's . . . okay. She moved in with her sister, or at least that's what people are saying.'

'Don't lie to me.' Mert aimed the sandpaper at Benji like a gun. 'What. Happened. To her?'

'What happened to her?' Benji released his own hand. 'What do you think happened to her?' He knocked over the loupe as if he were conceding a game of chess; it rolled off the counter, and he heard it crash to the floor at Mert's feet. 'We were meant to get sober together, man, and she actually did move in with her sister—and I moved back in with my mum.'

After Sondra had pretended to pinch Benji's elbow, she'd given him a melancholy smile that put him in mind of the first time she'd helped him get on. In her expression, he could see the adolescent-in-pain she'd been when they'd met. He'd asked if she was all right; she'd assured him she was, and he'd believed her. Then he'd been one of six at her desolate funeral in Castlewood Cemetery.

'I visited her the night before,' he told Mert. 'She seemed okay, you know? But . . .'

Mert stared at him a moment longer, before he retrieved the loupe from his feet and stood it up on the counter. 'And what do you need the money for, Benji?'

Benji gripped the counter. 'Look, there was a threat of violence made against my person,' he said, 'and against my mum's person—and I gotta pay to take care of that, you know?'

Mert resumed sanding the violin. 'Did you go to the police?'

'I mean, sort of.' Benji dropped his head. Then he spied his pale knuckles on the edge of the glass counter and, beneath them, the jewellery on display, none of which was his mother's. 'What do you fucking care, anyway?' he blurted. 'You bought our shit for years, man, and you never asked. And you knew, man—don't pretend like you didn't know.'

Mert blew wood shavings off the counter and let go of the sandpaper. His butcher's-paper face seemed to be trembling. 'How much do you need?'

'Five hundred,' Benji shot back. 'And can I have my nonna's typewriter as well, please, Mert?'

The pawnshop owner shook his head. 'I can loan you an extra five hundred,' he said, 'interest-free, as a one-off favour, or I can give you the typewriter back. Either way, you still have to pay off the previous loan at fourteen percent. Okay?'

Mert glanced at the typewriter, and Benji did likewise. 'Okay,' he said.

The sun hadn't gone down when Benji arrived at Raymond's old house the next day, yet the blinds were shut and the Edison bulb was burning. The woman with the boy on her arm allowed Benji in without interrogation. She led him through the kitchen—where ants feasted on the cockroach—and into the living room.

Benji stared at the tacky chandelier and waited for the woman to announce his arrival. Then he startled: she'd left him alone with five hundred interest-free dollars and Kimber and the tattooed man. The pair of them lounged on one of the sofas in front of the television, which sprinkled the room with the muted glow of a murder documentary.

Benji cleared his throat. 'Hey, Kimber. Hey, tattooed guy.'

Indolently, Kimber's eyes shunted his way. 'Who the fuck is this dude?' she drawled.

'No clue.' The tattooed man made his nostrils porcine, as if he were truffling for Benji's scent. 'The fuck are you, dude?'

'Uh, Benji.' Benji tapped his chest and heard the dull knock-knock of nail on bone. 'I don't know if I told you my name the other night, though.' He gestured at the table in the corner, on which were two smeared plates and a digital scale. 'I mean, I told the woman my name—the one who let me in—but I think she just said I was one of Ray's strays.'

Kimber stretched and yawned. 'You here to buy, Ray's stray?'

'No, no—not buy.' He rushed towards the television so that its glow might help them recognise him. 'Actually, I want to talk to you about, maybe, selling you back what you sold me, or returning it—or however that would work.'

Through her yawn, Kimber shot him a bemused look. He flinched and wondered why his words always outran his thoughts and why his thoughts always seemed to travel in a circuit.

'We can come back to that,' he said. 'But you really don't remember me? I ate those, um, burned seeds with you.' He rubbed his nape and saw the faces on the tattooed man's arms. 'And you, man? You grabbed me by the neck and shoved me out.'

'I do that to a lot of people,' the tattooed man replied.

'Yeah, well, you're hurting your customers, man.'

The tattooed man grinned.

Benji moved to stand directly in front of the television. The screen prickled his skin, and he remembered the five-limbed enigmas crawling along his arm towards the balloon in his fist.

'Jesus!' Kimber exclaimed. She planted her soles on the floor, one by one, and rested her elbows on her thighs. 'You're fucking Jesus, aren't you?'

'Jesus?' the tattooed man asked.

'The dude who's been living with Jesus since Ray finished. That's him.'

'No,' Benji said. 'But, like, you did say that the other day.' He indicated the tattooed man. 'And he said I talk too fucking much, but I don't think I do. I mean, yeah, I blah-blah-blah a lot, but only enough to get my point across in the—you know?—in the, um, loquacious manner of speaking that I speak in.'

'Jesus,' the tattooed man repeated, chuckling.

Kimber's eyelids fluttered shut, and she arched her back. 'Did you try that gooood shit I gave you?'

'Nah, I still got it.' Benji cast his eye towards the table and the digital scale. Kimber wasn't on the cold brew she'd mentioned. In his experience, that stuff made you want to tear strips off yourself and those around you; that was why he and Sondra steered clear of it. He took in Kimber's long sleeves and understood what she'd used—why she kept some around—and the static of the television made his scars tingle. 'And like I said,' Benji added, 'I'm hoping to sell it back to you, after the job is done and all.'

'What's he *on* about?' Kimber asked, and the tattooed man shrugged.

'The job.' Benji showed them the five hundred dollars, which was in fives, tens, twenties, fifties. 'Remember? You said to come back with half a grand and you'd do a favour for me.'

The appearance of the cash raised the tattooed man to his feet. He extended a hand to Benji, who hesitated. The expressions on the tattoo-faces shifted with the scenes of the murder doco: one face sneered; another watched on compassionately. Benji found himself relinquishing the money, and the tattooed man retreated to the sofa to count it.

'What favour are you after again?' Kimber said.

Benji stepped away from the television. 'It's like I told you: I just need him, or whoever—even a bunch of you—to come round my house before dawn on Sunday, and stay maybe half the day?' He plonked himself on the arm of the other sofa. 'And if a visitor comes by looking to, like, do some violence to me, you just have to be prepared to do violence in return—at least enough to stop him, you know?'

The tattooed man finished counting and nodded at Kimber. She frowned. 'Why would a visitor want to do violence to you, Jesus?'

'Uh, it's a weird tale, man.' Benji brought his thumb to his bottom lip and wondered where to start. 'Last Sunday, this guy wanted to buy a lorikeet from me—I've got an aviary thing around the Hills hoist in my mum's backyard, okay? And I said, yeah, sure, of course, but he wanted to transport the lory in this, like, toolbox.' He moved his hands about as if rubbing his nonna's crystal ball. 'Anyway, I said no—no way, man. And he said give me the lorikeet next Sunday or—so, yeah, Sunday?'

Kimber seemed entranced by Benji's swirling knuckles, but the tattooed man was watching the murder doco. 'Why Sunday?' he asked.

Benji stilled his hands. 'It's not like his fist was taking questions, man.'

'So, Jesus . . .' Kimber emerged from her trance and narrowed her eyes. 'All this trouble's because you won't sell a lorikeet that lives in a big cage in your mum's backyard?'

He shrugged and copped an eyeful of blood spatter on the television. 'Stop calling me Jesus, man,' he mumbled.

The tattooed man passed the cash to Kimber, who smiled impishly. 'We got your back, Jesus,' she said. 'Just give us your address, and we'll take care of eeeeverything.'

Benji released a slow breath and stood to leave. Relief flushed his veins; it felt almost like a drug, and being called Jesus was no more painful than the sting of a needle. Soon he was on his way home, but not before he'd picked a yellow flower from the duckling tree.

On the street of his mother's house, Benji raised the yellow flower to his nose and inhaled its fragrance. The subtle smell seemed consonant with the setting sun, and he smiled to himself. Then he approached the driveway and noticed a figure crawling beneath the carport. Aligned with his bedroom window, the figure—who appeared to be his mother—moved about on all fours among the potentially useful trash he'd stockpiled there. He tossed the flower onto the lawn under the sign advertising lorikeets and jogged along the side of the house.

'Mama?' he called out.

Florry didn't respond; she wore the nightgown she'd lived in for most of the week, but he couldn't see her face. A sheet of corrugated iron protruded from a hoard of chipped roof tiles and shaded her head. On one side of her, the domed birdcage had been knocked over; on the other, the upright tin of paint pressed against her torso.

He stood between her and the loose brick under his window. Then his spine tingled, as if he'd never abandoned his spot in front of Kimber's television, and he considered the possibility that the figure before him wasn't his mother. But he dismissed this fear and replaced it with a more reasonable one: that Florry had discovered her ring missing. He folded his arms and kept his tone light and said, 'What are you and your bony old butt doing out here, Mama?'

'What am I doing out here?' Florry's voice corrugated through the iron, and she crawled backwards towards him. Her pallid face emerged from the shadows. 'I'm doing what I asked you to do, Beniamino.'

She groaned and moved onto her knees. Then she climbed laboriously to her feet. His instinct had been to help her up. Instead, he observed the frailty of her without unfolding his arms. 'If you wanted the typewriter this bad, like, Mama, you should've just told me. I didn't know it was urgent.'

She brushed her hands together and smoothed down her nightgown. 'I told you it was urgent.'

'You never told me that.'

'I told you more than that.'

He looked down and noticed a hole in the toe of his sneaker and wondered when it'd formed. 'Yeah, well, I don't remember anything.'

'You really don't, do you?' His mother's voice was quiet, and her fingertips traced his hairline. 'My poor, poor Benji.'

The wounds on her arm drifted across his vision. He pictured Sondra with her shivery head on his shoulder when they were homeless and cruising low during the shortage of 2011. Then he overlaid this with the smoky still frame of the curly-haired girl; there was something different about the memory yet again, Benji realised.

Before he could examine it further, his mother removed her fingertips from his hairline. He felt an ache in his skull. Florry seemed as if she were about to ask a question—*the* question, he thought. But a breeze whiffled her nightgown, and she jutted her chin at the items under the carport. 'I almost cut my cheek,' she said.

Benji unfolded his arms and stood beside her. 'On what?'

'On that.' She pointed to the corrugated iron. 'It's dangerous, Benji—you should throw it out.'

'Yeah, well, you're not meant to be crawling around in there.' He stepped past her and righted the birdcage to re-create the obfuscating barrier. 'Unless you're, like, an *arachnid* or something—then you can creepy-crawl all you want, Mama.'

Their positions transposed, he peered at the loose brick behind her. It seemed even more askew than before. The ache in his skull intensified, and he made a fist that held no balloon. He met his mother's eyes and sensed in them compassion and confusion and the one question she couldn't ask.

'I have it under control, Mama,' he said conspiratorially. 'Nonna's typewriter, your diamond ring . . .'

'My diamond ring?'

'They're safe, okay? They're not out here, but they're safe, and we're safe, and I'm taking care of everything.'

Florry gazed at him steadily, and he rubbed his nose. 'I'm not using again, Mama—I'm not,' he said. 'I mean, I went to my old dealer's house, yeah, and I got a gram—but I'm just—okay? Look, look.' He knocked twice on his own chest. 'Remember last Sunday before church—when the hose messed up my shirt? This visitor was in the yard—you saw him, right?'

Florry's lip quivered. 'No.'

'Yeah, well, there was a visitor in the yard, Mama. He came to buy a lorikeet, and I'm telling you, man, he was gonna kill the poor bird. So I refused to sell, like you would want me to do—like Jesus would want me to do—right?' He flinched at the invocation and let out a frustrated guttural sound. 'And, like, he threatened me, Mama—and there's been weird goings-on here, man, or weird goings-on in here.'

He pistolled his index finger at his temple and let his arm fall to his side. 'I needed money to pay for protection, so I sold your—no, no, not sold; I *pawned* some goods—you know?' His voice wavered, and his mother continued to stare at him. 'But it's all under control,' he continued. 'That's the thing I need you to understand, Mama—I got it all under control.' He took hold of his mother's warm hands. 'It's like I promised when I moved back in: I'm taking care of you. I'm taking care of everything.'

He touched his forehead to Florry's. Her irises were huge and her sclera shiny. 'You don't believe me, Mama?' he asked. 'I'm telling the truth, I swear.'

Florry rose onto her tiptoes and kissed his brow. 'I love you,' she half-whispered, 'but that's what you always say'—she released his hands and stepped away—'when you lie to me.'

She walked off towards the back of the house, and Benji felt his mother's warmth recede from his empty hands.

V

Late on Friday morning, Benji placed bowls of wet mix, beans, apples and peas onto the plywood floor of the aviary. He exited through the gate and shut it behind him. Five of the lorikeets glided towards the food. But the grey fledgling fluttered ungracefully to him and gripped the gate with its talons. Benji tickled its neck through the chicken wire. Then he tried to see into the nesting box. He couldn't make out the two eggs or the mother lorikeet, and his own mother's words floated through his mind: *That's what you always say when you lie to me.*

Benji stopped tickling the grey fledgling. He padlocked the gate and ambled over the grass to the house. Near the back door, he let the hot concrete burn his bare soles and listened to the radio inside blaring songs of devotion. Florry would forgive him—would believe him—he told himself, when he retrieved the ring and typewriter.

Sighing, he lobbed the padlock's key into the air and tried to catch it. It fell onto the ground and tinkled like a bell. This reminded him of the voice of the old woman in the ute—how similar her voice had been to Florry's, he thought. He stooped to collect the key and, doubled over like this, saw a face sneering down at him. It wasn't a face, though; it was all skin. The world seemed to seesaw. Then he straightened and understood what he was looking at: one of the faces on one of the tattooed man's arms.

The tattooed man, who wore a sleeveless hoodie, grinned and wandered onto the grass.

The hairs on the scruff of Benji's neck bristled. 'Hey, man, what are you doing here?'

'He's with me.'

The reply came from Kimber, who emerged from around the corner. She was accompanied by a woman in overalls—the one who'd let Benji into the house—although the boy wasn't with her.

'Yeah, well,' Benji replied, 'that doesn't really answer my question, does it?'

Kimber paused before him. 'We came to see where Jesus lives, then we saw your invitation out front and—'

'My invitation?'

The visitor had referred to an invitation as well, Benji recalled, and a knot tied itself in his stomach. 'Do you want to, like, buy a lory, maybe?' he asked. 'Is that why you're here?'

The tattooed man indicated the aviary. 'It is pretty fucking amazing, eh?'

Kimber stepped onto the grass and squinted at it, and Benji positioned himself beside her. He took in his mother's Hills hoist, wrapped in chicken wire, as if seeing it for the first time; it genuinely did look like a gazebo made of knucklebones. 'Um, Kimber?' he said.

'Relax,' she drawled, and smiled at him tranquilly. 'We're here because we got your back. Remember?'

'What does that mean, though?' Benji cast a glance at the woman in overalls. 'What does she mean by that? You're, like, two days early.'

The woman said nothing, and Benji blinked at the back of the house. He could no longer hear his mother's religious radio program; rather, he heard her talking to someone—and he thought he heard a voice whispering in reply. The knot in his stomach tightened, and his heartbeat rattled the padlock's key in his hand. Kimber and the tattooed man were walking towards the aviary.

'I don't need you guys for two days, man,' Benji called out. He jogged to catch up to them. 'Just, you know, like I said—Sunday, dawn, come round, be ready. Did you get the days mixed up?'

Kimber didn't break stride. 'No.'

'Come on, man.' Benji placed a hand on the tattooed man's shoulder. 'What are you guys doing?'

The tattooed man hunched and swerved menacingly in his direction. 'Don't fucking touch me.'

Benji backed off. He didn't stumble, as he had when the visitor advanced on him, but the moments seemed cognate with each other. 'Just tell me what you're doing here, man.'

The tattooed man seemed about to reply when Kimber called out, 'It's locked.'

She tugged at the padlock on the aviary's gate, and the whole structure jangled. Inside, the lorikeets screeched and flapped about in a panic. The noise should've been deafening, yet Benji registered it as a mere vibration in the air. He was calculating what it meant that Kimber wanted to get into the aviary—and he was guiding the key towards his pocket.

But the tattooed man grabbed him by the nape and arrested his arm. Benji felt whiplash, and his larynx, or a muscle adjacent to it, throbbed. The tattooed man squeezed Benji's bicep, and the scars on his elbow burned. He grunted and tried to wrench himself loose. With his keyless hand, he whacked at the tattooed man, but his blows were feeble, and the tattooed man simply absorbed them.

He twisted Benji's arm behind his back; Benji's nerves fired with pain, and he stopped struggling.

'No more of that shit,' the tattooed man breathed. He manoeuvred Benji towards the aviary and kicked him onto his knees in front of Kimber. 'Give her the key.'

Benji looked up at the dealer. Her face appeared to him as if it were melting, and his pain, rather than radiating from his neck or shoulder or elbow, felt like it emanated from within the aviary. The lorikeets hadn't stopped screeching, and his heartbeat still rattled the key. 'Please don't do this,' he begged.

Kimber extended her palm. 'Key.'

'I don't understand.' Benji shook his head. 'I paid for—'

With his shoe, the tattooed man shoved at Benji's back. 'Give her the fucking key.'

Benji let out a sob. The breeze cooled his cheeks, and he understood that he was crying. 'Please don't kill my birds, man.' He blinked to try to get a less liquefied view of Kimber's face. 'Like, I know to you they're worthless, or stupid, or whatever,' he said. 'But to me? To *me*, man, they're my—they're my birds, you know?'

He was blubbering, and his words emerged malformed; it would be impossible for him to explain, anyway. He pictured Sondra pretending to pinch the scars of his elbow and his mother lying awake in bed while he stole her jewellery box. 'And I like—I just need to, like—I need to save—need to fix—just don't kill my birds. Please?'

Kimber leaned forward, and her melting features coagulated. 'We're not going to kill your birds, Jesus,' she said. 'We're going to save you.'

The tattooed man wrestled Benji onto his belly, and he and Kimber worked together to try to force the key from Benji's grip. In a shrill voice, someone cried, 'No,' again and again. Someone called Benji's name. Someone was wailing. Benji wasn't sure who was who.

Then the rattling moved from his fist to his bones: he no longer had the key, and the tattooed man held him in a headlock. He could scarcely breathe as he watched Kimber unlock the aviary's gate. She flung the padlock aside, and in an animal frenzy four lorikeets fled straight away. They soared above Benji's crown, a flock of rainbows between him and the sky, and disappeared into the distance.

A moment later, the grey fledgling made its way towards Benji; unable to fly properly, it paused on the grass. As if through a haze, Benji stared at the bird hopping in an uncertain circle. Beyond it, he could see Kimber shooing the mother lorikeet into flight and making two spiking motions in the aviary. He wheezed, and the tattooed man released him.

'Up you get,' the tattooed man said.

He hauled Benji, semiconscious, to his feet and kicked out at the grey fledgling, which managed to take off and cruise at a low altitude towards the street.

The tattooed man shoved Benji into the aviary, and Kimber slouched against the chicken wire. 'No lorikeets, no trouble: that's what you said, right?'

Benji's tears dripped staccato onto his feet. Around him were bowls of food and bird shit, and he took in the broken shells and spilt yolks of the two eggs that'd been in the nesting box.

'You're welcome, Jesus,' Kimber said.

She and the tattooed man walked away, and Benji realised that the woman in overalls had been restraining his mother on the concrete.

On the aviary's plywood floor, Benji lay on his side among the remnants of his birds. His eyeballs felt crazed and his tears thick as albumen. Reports of burning in his elbow and pain in his neck reached his brain. He imagined the grey fledgling dangling from the drooling maw of the visitor's massive dog. But his lorikeets were gone, and mostly he pictured the galaxy composed of Stars of Bethlehem and his whole world shrinking to the black perdition inside the toolbox. That fate appeared unavoidable now.

Footfalls crunched on the grass, and he became aware that his mother was circumnavigating the aviary. Through his tears, she looked so much like his nonna, and he wondered whether her infirmity had reached some sort of inflexion point. 'You believe me now, Mama?' he asked hoarsely.

'I do.' She walked around out of his sight. 'Who were those awful people, Beniamino?'

'I paid them,' Benji replied. 'I'm sorry,' he cried out in a broken voice. 'I'm so sorry, Mama.'

'No, my son, I'm sorry all of this happened to you.'

For some reason, Benji felt a need to reassure her that none of it was her fault. But he didn't trust his voice and let silence descend. Florry continued to circumnavigate the aviary as if she were performing a sacrament of her own invention. 'She told me they went around, Benji. They went around and then they came around.'

Benji sniffled and scowled. 'Who went around and came around?'

'The children,' his mother said. 'Jack and Lonnie.'

Her voice travelled in a languid arc behind him, before she wandered back into his field of vision. Her trajectory made him woozy, and his nausea swept the heat from his elbow to his cheeks. 'Who told you this, Mama?' he asked, half sitting up. 'And why are you always talking about those stupid children?'

She stopped at the open gate and swayed on her feet. 'You really don't remember, do you?' She turned her gaze to meet his. 'You went missing for seven days, Beniamino.'

The heat in Benji's cheeks dissipated. But the knot in his stomach returned, and the scars on his elbow thrummed.

His mother stepped onto the plywood. 'When you were a boy,' she said, 'I went through a rough patch. Your father left me. I was drinking too much—this was before I found the church properly.' She glanced at the carport beside the house. 'You were riding your bike out on the street when you were . . .' She looked back at him, her face flushed with sorrow. 'Somebody kept you for a week—we still don't know who.' Pensively, she thumbed her bottom lip. 'They found opioids in your system, burn marks on your mouth. You told police there was someone else with you—a little girl—but they never found her. Sometimes, I dream that they never found you.'

Florry swallowed, and Benji watched the ornithological skin of her throat wobble. His pulse rumbled through his temples, and his vision of the present remained hazy. But the smoky still frame of the curly-haired girl sharpened in his memory.

'I always thought you were faking when you said you couldn't remember,' she went on. 'Because why else would you—?'

'No, Mama,' he interjected. 'No more.'

He squeezed his eyes shut. The effort made him rattle, yet he managed to submerge the image of the curly-haired girl in the churning ocean of his thoughts. He pictured Sondra's hair, soaked after a swim at Brighton-Le-Sands in 2010, and the fresh lavender bruises around her track marks. Again, he remembered her helping him get on for the first time, but now he wondered how much of the past his teenage self had already forgotten.

His mother's hand stroked his hairline, and he winced. 'Don't you want to come inside, Beniamino?' she asked.

He shook his head.

'You're just going to lie out here?'

Eyes closed, he waited until he was certain his voice wouldn't betray him. 'Close the gate,' he said. 'All the way.'

It was either a light or the list on the edge of Benji's consciousness that nudged him awake. His side hurt, and he groaned. He wasn't in bed; he'd fallen asleep on the plywood floor of the aviary. Half-awake, he rolled onto his back and parted his eyelids. Above him, the chicken wire that umbrellaed the Hills hoist made an argyle print of the sky. The moon idled between clouds, and Benji recalled his mother's hand on his hairline. He tried to forget everything she'd told him.

Tablespoon, the list restarted in his mind.

The clouds overtook the moon, and from the corner of his eye, he saw an inconstant white light glowing nearer to home. He sat up and peered at the back of the house. It was dark inside. His mother had likely attached herself to the XpressFlow and gone to sleep. The glow he was observing burned closer to the earth, out of sight, somewhere on the carport side of the house.

Bic lighter, the list continued.

Unable to discern the light's origin, he stared at its mesmerising overflow. His stomach growled, and he swallowed his thirst. His mind raced through the rest of the list: *one of Florry's syringes, Florry's rainbow tourniquet*. The list was incomplete, he thought. He'd compiled it with the balloon in hand, and that was now wrapped in foil and hidden in the house's substructure.

The light waned, and he stood and strode out of the aviary. On the grass, he watched the light return and sparkle in the domed birdcage. He broke into a run. The concrete near the back door felt like a sheet of ice, and he slipped. But he caught himself on the corner of the house and careened beneath the carport as the light faded.

In the suburban dark, he halted and took a few agnostic breaths. Then he accepted the sight before him: not only had the loose brick under his bedroom window tumbled into the crawlspace, but several mortared bricks around it had also collapsed. What remained in the wall was a roughly circular hole—a passage in or out of the crawlspace.

The light rose, and he realised that its origin was beyond this passage. Circumscribed by the hole, the light shimmered from somewhere under the house. He blinked and imagined it rising and falling and floating among the foundations. On the periphery of his vision, he saw the street, and an instinct to run gnawed at him. But the list could not be finished without the balloon, and he remained rooted to the spot.

When the light dimmed, he dropped onto all fours and reached into the crawlspace. He patted the dirt around the collapsed bricks and sought the foil-wrapped balloon. Then it returned—the light—and he paused his frantic scratchings. Between him and its origin were brick pillars and time-worn partitions—and in a corner, on the fringe of an unnaturally dense umbra, the visitor's red toolbox glinted.

Benji shivered from his nape to his coccyx; the toolbox was what he'd seen when he'd first levered the brick back into place, he thought. The light twinkled and went out, and from the dark under the house he heard the slither he'd encountered earlier. But with a desperate hand, he reached past the collapsed bricks and felt around for the balloon. His fingertips touched a tiny object. It wasn't wrapped in foil, though, and felt less like a balloon and more like a reptile's discarded skin. *Rattle, rattle—we snakes*, he remembered Sondra whispering.

The light rose again, and the umbra in the corner stretched out to meet him. Just beyond its circumference, the red toolbox had stopped slithering. It cast its own shadow over the snakeskin at his fingertips. He didn't dare to move; he tried to control his shivering and keep perfectly still.

The light flickered and weakened. But in the instant before it went out, he glimpsed the filthy and decaying hands of a child. With sawtooth nails, the hands reached out from the umbra and opened the toolbox. Benji gasped, and his heart pounded. Then the light disappeared, and he snatched up the snakeskin and a mound of dirt in his fist.

He tried to yank his arm away, but the child's hands grabbed him. The nails needled his flesh. He grunted with pain, and the crook of his elbow burned as if a wildfire were spreading through the mountain range of his scars. The light swelled, yet it was mostly obscured by the umbra that had now arrived at his fingertips—and emerging from the lampblack shadow were the child's hands that gripped his arm.

There was another, even smaller pair of hands in the same state of decay, he realised; they shifted the open toolbox from the darkness to the light. On the toolbox's scratched base lay the sheet of foil in which he'd wrapped the balloon. It had been flattened out, and on the foil's surface was burned a bleak spiral.

Benji's entire body quivered, and finally his mind loosed a memory of the curly-haired girl in motion. She hadn't been scribbling with a white pencil on a glinting sheet of paper. Her brown ringlets had curtained her face, which she angled over a shiny sheet of foil. On the foil's surface, she chased a smoking spiral with the white barrel of a pen. Benji could hear her inhalations. Beneath the spiral—beneath the foil—an adult hand held a flaming Bic lighter.

Benji gave another grunt and clenched his teeth against the pain. If he remembered any more, he thought, years of being wasted would be wasted. The light went out, and he wrenched his body back with as much force as he could muster. The first child's hands tugged him towards the umbra; the smaller hands scratched at his wrist. But the children lost their grip, and he fell backwards and slammed his head against the birdcage. A high-pitched noise started up in his ears, and he stood and sprinted to the back door of the house.

Locking himself inside, he caught his breath and peeked out at the yard. He saw nothing but the dark shape of the Hills hoist aviary. Around his elbow, though, his shirt was wet with blood. He unclenched his cramping fist and let the mound of dirt trickle to the floor. What remained on his palm wasn't snakeskin—it was the broken latex of the now empty balloon.

VI

When the sun rose, Benji, unslept, trudged from the back of the house to the hallway. His mother's door was ajar, as ever, and the XpressFlow had finished with her blood. In the silence, he heard her muttering a question as if she were on the phone. But a reply came that sounded like the skittering of dead leaves. On the other side of the door, she would still be attached to her haemodialysis machine—and the winged Oliver typewriter and diamond ring would still be gone.

'Beniamino?' Florry called out.

He almost went into her room. Then he noticed his sleeve, stained with blood, and the broken balloon skin that remained in his dirt-smeared hand. In his bedroom, he found his laundry cleaned and folded on the chest of drawers. He shoved the balloon under the clothes and tore off his shirt and wiped his hand on his pants. Kicking the shirt under his bed, he glanced at the mess of flesh in the crook of his elbow.

Only the floorboards separated him from whatever had clawed at him in the crawlspace. Yet it wasn't this that made his breath catch; it was the recollection of the curly-haired girl, her face curtained by her ringlets, chasing a smoking spiral with the white barrel of a pen.

The floor creaked across the hallway, and he shoved his arms through the sleeves of the collared shirt he'd almost worn to church six days earlier. Before he could begin to do up the buttons, Florry appeared in the doorway. 'Benji?' She looked him up and down. 'Are you going out?'

'Going out?' He fumbled with the buttons of his shirt, from which Florry had erased the stripes of rust. 'At this hour, Mama? Where would I go?'

His mother watched his struggle with the buttons and stepped forward to finish doing them for him. 'We could go away for a while?' She patted his chest. 'To the beach, maybe? Just for a few days.'

Benji grimaced. 'Don't worry about me, Mama.'

She reached out to do the buttons of his cuffs, yet he took over. He felt a sense of fatalism about the visitor's return the following dawn, but perhaps there was still a way to square things with his mother over the typewriter and the ring. The scheme that entered his mind was crude, though, and he hoped a more elegant one would occur to him by nightfall.

Gently, he placed his hands on Florry's shoulders. 'It's like I said, I'm taking care of you, okay? I'm taking care of everything.'

He strode to the kitchen and drank coffee and wolfed down a bowl of cereal. The rest of the morning, he kept himself busy doing odd jobs around the house—like sweeping up the dirt from near the back door and cleaning the XpressFlow and vacuuming his room. Mert wouldn't be in the pawnshop after hours, he told himself; that was when he had to go.

Benji spent the afternoon unwinding the chicken wire from around the Hills hoist. He rolled it into a cylinder and kicked it in front of the hole under his bedroom window. Rather than obscuring the crawlspace, though, this made it resemble an eye staring at him through a prison fence. There was an element of risk in his plan—if he got caught. But he wouldn't get caught. He'd smash his way into the pawnshop and grab more things than he needed and get the hell out of there.

He swivelled and took in the empty niche and the sledgehammer. Then he twitched: what if Mert *was* there after hours? Benji imagined the pawnshop owner aiming a gun at him, as he'd aimed the sheet of sandpaper. He pictured himself swinging the sledgehammer at Mert's eyebrow piercing and perforating the butcher's-paper skin of his face. 'Fucking dumb,' Benji whispered to himself.

But by dusk, no more elegant plan had come to him, and while Florry listened to religious radio and cooked eggplant parmigiana, he crept into her bedroom. Mostly what he noticed was absence: an empty bed and bloodless XpressFlow; a pawned ring and typewriter; a sepia photograph of his dead nonna and a missing jewellery box. He collected a pair of latex gloves and one of Florry's stockings for his head.

In his own room, he stuffed the items into a duffel bag. After a hesitation, he retrieved the balloon's skin and packed that as well. He shoved the bag out through his window and heard it bounce off the cylinder of chicken wire.

Later, he ate cheesy eggplant with his mother and settled her onto her XpressFlow. Later still, he jogged out to the carport and ignored the hole in the wall and added the sledgehammer to his duffel bag. Then he headed towards the street and cast about on the front lawn for the yellow flower he'd earlier tossed aside.

En route to the pawnshop, Benji detoured to Castlewood Cemetery and hurdled the fence and found Sondra's grave. The duffel bag weighted down his shoulder, and he stared up at the night sky. In his mind, the smoky image of the curly-haired girl eddied into a memory of Sondra jabbing a needle into his arm for the first time. Then he pictured Sondra, twenty-something years older, alone, loosening her tourniquet for the last time. He felt dizzy and squatted and placed the yellow flower, half-wrapped in the balloon's skin, against the base of her headstone.

A breeze made the long grass genuflect, and Benji lingered graveside until his surrounds stopped spinning. Then he walked along one of the cemetery's roads and paused before an ornate family vault. In the zero-hour dark, its pentagonal facade and the cross attached to its gable roof seemed familiar. Its courtyard even housed a statue of the Virgin and a marble bench. Instinctively, he shambled towards the bench and sat.

The breeze chilled his arm, and he became aware that his wounds had opened again: from his elbow to his wrist, his collared shirt was mottled with blood. His first thought was of the enormous bleeding Jesus in Sacred Innocents' Church; his second was of his fear that Mert would be in the pawnshop after hours. He held his face in his hands, and the stench of his blood wafted to his nostrils. There'd be so much more of that smell, he thought, when the visitor returned.

Through his fingers, he clocked the duffel bag to his left and the hole in his sneaker. Then he broke out in goosebumps: a pair of black brogues was planted on the ground next to him. Between the brogues lay the alluring leather satchel he'd seen outside the church.

Benji lowered his fingers and looked to his right. Dressed in a black suit, the defrocked priest was sitting beside him with his head bowed and his hands in his lap. The priest's profile seemed pixelated and unfixed and barely discernible. Benji couldn't say how the priest had gotten there, or if he'd already been there when Benji had sat. But a strange compulsion to confess lodged itself in his throat. 'They let my lorikeets go,' he mumbled.

For a while, the defrocked priest made no reply. Then in a quiet voice he said, 'That doesn't sound so terrible.'

'They might not survive in the wild.'

'Ah.'

'And Kimber, and the tattooed guy: they're not gonna help me, man. And under the house, and my mum . . .' Benji tried to wrangle the words. 'And now I have this—this dumb, stupid plan to rob a pawnshop.' He clasped his right hand with his left. 'And tomorrow's fucking Sunday, man. And I came here, and I, like—I don't even know what I'm looking for.'

'Yes you do.' The defrocked priest did not move; his voice was a sibilant rush. 'That is why you did not go to the church.'

'What? Wouldn't you want me to go to the church?' Benji glanced at the squat silhouette of a tree on a hill in the distance. 'Aren't you, like, a priest or something?'

'Aren't you a junkie?' The defrocked priest spoke the words without intonation, and the old woman's bell of a voice tolled in Benji's head.

He glared at his inquisitor. 'You know, man, people are saying you had something to do with those children.'

'Which people?'

'Most people.'

'Ah.' The defrocked priest gave a slight nod. 'Most people understand that everything they want in this life has a cost. What they do not appreciate is that it is not always the buyer who must bear it.'

Benji considered this. 'So, you do know something?' he said.

The defrocked priest shut his eyes meditatively. 'Something of what?'

'Something of—something about the children, man.'

'Most people know something of the children, but most nobody knows everything.' A smile appeared to play at the corners of his mouth, and he opened his eyes. 'Wouldn't you rather talk about why you are here with me?'

The defrocked priest turned to Benji, and in the gloom, his eyes seemed to move out of sync with the rest of his features.

He might have been smiling, or perhaps wearing a rictus grin, and static crept down Benji's spine. But he neither budged nor looked away. Vaguely, he was aware that the defrocked priest's hands, as if operating without a master, had lifted the satchel onto his lap.

'Everything you desire,' the defrocked priest said. 'You can have it, Beniamino.'

Benji wanted to ask how the priest knew his name, but before he could speak, a faint whistle sounded somewhere within the cemetery—and the priest's irises drifted. Benji dragged his own gaze to the statue of the Virgin and remembered Florry crawling under a sheet of corrugated iron in search of the typewriter he'd pawned. 'How much will it cost?' he asked.

'All you have to offer,' the defrocked priest replied, 'is your name.'

'My name?'

Again Benji met the man's eyes, and the defrocked priest withdrew a dog-eared exercise book from his satchel. He flicked through pages of scrawled writing that was difficult to decipher. *The children went into the cave and smashed up some stars*, Benji read. Then the priest found the page he was seeking and passed the book to Benji, as well as a pen with a white barrel and black tip. 'Write,' he commanded.

Benji rumpled his chin; the only marking on the page was an imperfect circle. 'But you already know my name.'

'You must tell it to the book. Write your name'—he extended a middle finger, missing a nail, and pressed it to a blank space in the circle's centre—'here.'

His finger retreated, leaving a dimple in the exercise book. This depression was where Benji touched the page with the pen. Ink bled into the paper. The whistle sounded again, closer this time, and he thought he recognised it. He peered out over the crenellations of the headstones. But he could spy nothing sentient, and surrounded by the dead, he thought of how infirm Florry had seemed when she'd circumnavigated the aviary.

Tears pressed at his eyes. 'I just have to, like, write my name?'

The defrocked priest nodded, and Benji produced the down stroke of the first letter of his name. Haltingly, he drew the upper semicircle, followed by the lower one. A tear dripped onto the letter, and the whistle reverberated through the cemetery. This time he was certain he recognised it: the whistle was composed of three sweet and sour notes. His pen skidded off the page, and he blinked at the tree on the hill.

Without a glance at the defrocked priest, he placed the exercise book and pen on the bench between them. He removed the weight of the duffel bag from his shoulder and stood and exited the vault's courtyard. He strode to the tree—a bottlebrush—and caught sight of the grey fledgling hopping about on the lowest branch.

'How'd you get all the way out here, man?' Benji asked. He wiped his tears and raised a horizontal finger towards the lorikeet. 'Come on down, Grey Ghost,' he said. 'Come on.'

This was the first time he'd given one of his birds a name, and Grey Ghost responded by leaping from the branch onto his finger. He tickled the bird's neck, and the bird trilled its three sweet and sour notes once more.

Benji spotted what he thought was a filament of bottlebrush among the grey plumage of the bird's chest. But when he tried to remove it, he realised that it was attached. Grey Ghost had sprouted the frangible beginnings of a single red feather.

'Technicolour,' Benji muttered.

He snickered and sniffled and rubbed the bird against his cheek. It bobbed up and down, and he lifted it above his eyeline. Grey Ghost took off and flew, almost competently, through the cemetery and into the night.

Benji turned back to the family vault and the bench on which he'd abandoned the exercise book and his duffel bag. The defrocked priest sat there and waited for him. But Benji hunched his shoulders against the breeze and strode off in the direction of home.

Benji walked a circuitous route and felt as if he roamed for hours. Yet the night stretched on, and somehow, the family vault loomed before his bleary eyes. He blinked and sought out Sondra's grave among the headstones. Then he realised that the headstones were actually terrace houses: he was on the suburban street on which the church stood.

This did not diminish his expectation of finding the defrocked priest sitting on the marble bench. But the courtyard was vacant, and he wandered along the laneway where he'd seen his mother. Soon he approached her house and read the sign on the lawn that advertised the sale of lorikeets. Both Kimber and the visitor had called it an invitation, and he'd come to accept it as such.

He hung his head. Dawn was approaching, and he pictured the typewriter and ring he'd failed to retrieve. He thought of the panting of the massive dog and the visitor's ineluctable fists. Perhaps there was no such thing as making things square, he thought; perhaps there was only ever more payment and more debt.

When he reached the driveway, he became aware of a sparkling in the chicken wire by the side of the house. The wire was no longer obscuring the hole in the wall, though; the cylinder had rolled back against the domed birdcage. He moved closer and drew a ragged breath.

A lambent light shone from the crawlspace, its origin hidden somewhere among the house's foundations. Its overflow illuminated a small figure—a girl with curly brown hair—who stood with her back to the street. She obscured his view of a kneeling woman whom he'd have assumed was his mother but for a glitch in her motion. Beneath his bedroom window, the woman clasped the decaying hand of another child—a boy—who was climbing out of the crawlspace.

Benji shuddered; madly, he wondered whether the boy was him. Then the light flickered and began to fade, and he remembered the sawtooth nails that had clawed at his arm and showed him the spiral burn on the foil. He strode towards the lawn—and as if registering his presence, the kneeling woman glitched like a video played in reverse and turned her face to him.

He'd been right: she was not his mother. She was his nonna, exactly as she appeared in the photograph on Florry's dressing table. His nonna whispered something to him, but he couldn't hear her. He did not wish to hear her; he did not wish to see the children's faces. The light snuffed itself out, and he hurried across the lawn and into the house.

In the hallway, Benji bolted the front door and nudged his mother's bedroom door wide open. Quietly, he stepped into Florry's room. He listened to his mother's gentle snores while the XpressFlow worked, and he let himself be soothed by their harmony.

At the foot of her king single, he slipped off his sneakers. He padded in his socks to the side of the bed opposite the XpressFlow and eased himself into a seated position. Then he leaned back against the headboard, and the exhaustion of the week embraced him. The cave of Florry's wardrobe and the drawer of her dressing table and the advertisement for his nonna's business swam in the darkness. He yawned, and Florry stirred.

'It's only me, Mama,' he said.

'Beniamino?' she croaked. 'Are you okay?'

'You're asking again?' He tried to cough out a couple of laughs. But the coughs were more like whimpers, and he placed one ankle on top of the other. 'No, Mama, I'm not okay,' he replied. 'Like, not so far, but maybe someday—if I make it.' His mother's form shifted under the sheets, and he blinked hard. 'I couldn't get your typewriter and ring back for you tonight.'

'That's okay, Benji.' His mother fell silent for a few moments, before she asked, 'You didn't hurt anyone trying, did you?'

Benji recalled the defrocked priest turning to him in the cemetery and the sole letter that he—Benji—had inscribed in the circle. 'No, Mama,' he replied.

Florry rolled onto her side, and the sheet rustled. 'I don't think I need the typewriter anymore.'

'Because Nonna whispers to you?' He could make out the tubes in his mother's arm that anchored her to the XpressFlow. His eyelids drooped, and he pictured his nonna helping the boy out of the crawlspace while a curly-haired girl waited nearby. 'What's the latest with the children?' he asked.

'The word has gone quiet on that,' his mother said.

'People aren't talking?' Benji yawned again. 'Not speculating?' The outline of the dressing table sharpened slightly, and he realised that he could see the contours of his face in the mirror. 'It's almost dawn, Mama, and my lorikeets are all gone.' He swallowed. 'So that visitor might come back and . . .'

He peered at his mother. She lay still, and her breathing began to take on the cadence of sleep. 'Why don't you rest, my son?' she murmured.

'Yes, Mama.'

He lay down with his head on the same pillow as his mother. Her warm hand found his and squeezed it, and he let his eyes drift shut. He thought he heard a ute's engine roar and idle on the street outside. Then, behind his lids, he observed a serenely pulsing light. But whether it was white or red or another colour altogether, he couldn't really say.

Interlude

Amma

Twenty-four years earlier, a sleeping puppy twitched in the corner of its raised perspex cage. Its rear legs pumped and paddled and became covered with the hay that lined the cage's base. At the pet store's entrance, Amma Corban shifted her head and looked for the soft pads of the puppy's paws. But her view was obstructed by the hay and the pea-sized holes, arranged in a circle, that'd been punched in the perspex to allow oxygen in.

She rested her forehead against the cage and blinked unevenly, on account of the skin tag taking shape on her left eyelid. The puppy stopped twitching; it breathed peacefully, its paws buried in the hay. She glanced through the cage at her son. A scrawny kid in a baseball cap, he reached into a miniature enclosure off to the side of the pet store. She yanked at the elastic around her wrist and let it go; it snapped back, and she winced.

The patter of footsteps approached, and she lifted her forehead from the perspex and looked over her shoulder. A girl was sprinting through the sparse crowd of the shopping centre. She was trailed by a woman in a denim jacket who had just emerged from a chocolate shop across the way. The girl stopped next to Amma and stood on her tiptoes to peer into the cage.

Then the woman in the denim jacket caught up to the girl. 'See the little doggy?' she said. 'It's sleeping.'

The puppy's legs twitched, and Amma got a clear view of its paws. But she noticed that the girl was staring at her. Amma smiled at the girl and strained not to blink.

The woman in the denim jacket cleared her throat. 'I like your hair,' she said to Amma.

'You mean that?' Amma replied.

'Yeah, it's got so much volume. And the waviness—I love it.'

Amma blinked, rapidly and unevenly, and fingered the split ends that hung over her shoulder. 'My ex-husband didn't like it. He dragged—'

'Well I do,' the woman declared. Then she grimaced and led her protesting daughter away.

Amma watched her and yanked again at the elastic at her wrist. She took hold of the ends of her hair and twisted them around and around like a corkscrew. The twisted hair she coiled into a bun, which she secured at the back of her head with the elastic.

She saw the woman in the denim jacket glance back at her before she disappeared around a corner. Then Amma caught movement in the pet store. Her son stepped away from the miniature enclosure; he let his arms fall to his side and stood dead still. She strode over to him and followed his gaze.

Her eyes widened. In the picket-fenced enclosure were a doll's house and bowls of food and a pair of rabbits. The brown rabbit was nibbling on something, but the white rabbit was lying still. It neither twitched nor breathed peacefully, and Amma had the impression it'd been dropped onto the floor like a bag of butcher's meat.

She looked about in a panic. The shop assistants were chatting with a customer beside a display of kittens, and Amma scooped up her son and fled the pet store. Then she carried the boy through the shopping centre, in the opposite direction to the woman in the denim jacket. She checked behind her, but no one had followed.

Outside a music store, she slumped onto a bench to catch her breath. She met her son's eyes beneath the brim of his cap and gave him a kiss on each cheek. Then she hugged him and peered down at her shoes. Planted on the floor beside them was a pair of black brogues, and between the brogues lay an alluring leather satchel.

She raised her head. Seated next to her was a man who looked as if he were once a priest—or rather, a man in a black suit and shirt that seemed to be missing a clerical collar. He had his head bowed and an accounting ledger open on his lap. One of his hands rested on the left page and mostly obscured the name of the account holder written in the top corner. In the credit and debit columns, though, she could make out other names and tallies of various animal species.

She felt the brim of her son's cap dig into her neck and moved her eyes to the right-hand page. On it was inscribed an imperfect circle that roughly resembled a halo.

Part Four

Nera

I

The first night she spent in the farmhouse, Nera Pahlavi peered out the kitchen window and saw only her reflection and shuddered. Storm clouds had gathered, and nothing outside gave off even the faintest glimmer of light. She pressed her face to the glass, which fogged with her breath, but still she could see none of the acreage that now belonged to her.

Somewhere on the land she knew there to be an unbroken silver mare, probably wandering its paddock to test the fence for weakness, and two alpacas—a brown female and a white gelding—grazing or sleeping or doing whatever it was alpacas did at night. She wished she could see these creatures now, although she understood that if they loomed out of the darkness it would undo whatever remained of her calm. Plus, if it were the horse she saw, then it had freed itself of its paddock and she'd have to phone its owner, Reese Mundine, the taciturn neighbour who'd subdivided her property and sold Nera the lesser half.

That might not be so bad, Nera thought. At least it would mean company.

She retreated to the living room and breathed hot air onto her fingertips. One of the drainpipes juddered, as if it were trying to swallow, and she had to remind herself that this was what she wanted—or, rather, that this was what she'd convinced her husband she wanted. Nasser had been sceptical of her desire, particularly after his hair fell out the first time. She'd shaved the tufts that remained and kissed his bald head and protested that not all her dreams were about him.

But this dream was. She saw how it made him smile—that they imagined the same future—and how it reassured him that they were kindred spirits, and the more she gave up on him the more she embellished, with promises of livestock and fresh eggs and self-sustenance. Better to live that dream now than admit herself so hollow.

There was no reason to suffer in silence, though. She switched on the television, and it filled the house with a jingle for a regional car yard. She loathed its off-key pride. But it was catchy, so she turned the volume up and hummed her way to the bathroom. From the cabinet, she fetched herself a couple of Solnox pills while the television began to recite the late-night news.

Back in the kitchen, she poured a glass of cabernet and tossed the shell-pink pills into her mouth. She washed them down and remained stationary until she was sure her airways were clear. Then she wandered into the living room and watched the television over the rim of her wineglass.

'One year ago today, the children went missing from this workers' club car park,' a reporter said, hands clasped at her navel. 'Their mother had gone inside to play the pokies and returned to the alarming discovery of an empty car.'

The reporter's voice was pitched somewhere between sympathy and judgement. This irritated Nera more than the jingle, probably because its tone reminded her of her work as a family lawyer. She could almost hear herself counselling a woman whose nails were chewed to the quick, and she muted the television.

A low-resolution photo of the missing children appeared on the screen. An olive-skinned boy in a grey hoodie sat at a school desk beside his younger sister, who wore her sharp cheekbones and faded yellow t-shirt uneasily. The children had their chins on their chests, as if they'd just been reprimanded, and their eyes were shaded in defence against the camera's flash.

'Look up,' Nera whispered.

The children in the photo did not look up. They kept their heads bowed, and the news moved on to a story about a blaze in an asbestos-lined warehouse. Nera downed the dregs of her wine. She yawned and switched off the television. The warehouse fire went out; the Solnox kicked in.

She rinsed her wineglass in the kitchen sink, and at the end of the hallway the front door rattled. Then, from the darkness, she heard a sound, quavering and high-pitched, like the lament of an ungreased hinge. She caught sight of herself in the window again. Her reflection shivered. She took a few paces towards it and pressed her face to the glass and made it disappear. Then she exhaled, slow and stuttering, and the fog of her breath crept over the windowpane.

Through it, she saw a glow in the distance, vague and located to her right. Slowly, the glow became more defined—there was motion and order to it. Two swarms of light, discrete and graceful, danced and fizzed and made sublime patterns against the darkness.

She breathed shallowly, and the fog ebbed on the pane. The lights began to spiral skywards, to cycle up towards the firmament, and the sound came again—more guttural this time, more prolonged, less like rusted metal and more like the plaintive cry of a human voice. Nera gasped and stepped back, and her reflection stepped further out into the darkness.

In the morning, the storm clouds had cleared, and she emerged from the farmhouse and gazed warily at the land. Framed by the driveway and dirt road, the front lawn was short and strewn with alpaca shit that was either congealed like greasy pine cones or piled like a collection of pebbles. The freshest shit glistened in the sunlight, and the female alpaca sniffed the ground and grumbled. It raised its head and spat towards Nera, who searched for the gelding.

Her eyes drifted left, to a wired-off field in which she might one day keep cattle—although she'd made no plans to do so. The land was too large and unwieldy, and she missed the bounds of her beachside home in Sydney's Bronte. She pictured the narrow driveway where, after a long day of work, she'd sometimes be lulled to sleep in her car by the sound and scent of the ocean, until Nasser would knock on the window and wake her. She thought of the walled courtyard where he would sit and smoke cigarettes and read the newspaper, long after most people had given up both.

She looked beyond the lawn to the large pasture that included the paddock in which the silver mare nosed its timber fence. To the right of the paddock, a little way off, was a copse of shrubs and stunted bloodwoods that huddled together in a circle. In front of this she caught sight of the gelding; it was sprawled on a tussock of grass, sunbathing, or asleep maybe, which was how she'd discovered both alpacas the day before.

She strode towards it with the intention of shooing it away. It disquieted her that the gelding lay beneath the spot where she'd seen the lights. Perhaps it was this animal that had uttered the prolonged guttural cry. But her disquiet was hasty and irrational, she scolded herself. She wasn't sure that *was* the spot and, besides, the strangeness of the previous night may not have happened—not really.

It may well have been a wine-and-Solnox-induced hallucination. She'd had one of these before, in the months after Nasser's death, and she remembered it in fragments, or in sensations, if such a thing were possible. She'd held her daughter's hand. The girl had led her down to the beach, and together they'd stepped into the warm ocean.

Nera had roused from her reverie alone in the moonshine, with the water of Bronte Beach very real and very cold around her ankles. She and Nasser didn't have a daughter. They had tried; he'd always said he wanted a girl and a boy, but she'd never truly wanted either until the moment of her hallucination, about which she'd confided in nobody. Sometimes, she even told herself that she only mixed wine and pills in the hope of dreaming of her daughter's face again.

Close to the mare's paddock, she stumbled over a knotted root. The horse approached the timber fence and flared its nostrils and snorted at her. It galloped around its enclosure and skidded to a halt at the gate. A sympathetic impulse to free it welled inside Nera, but the horse brayed and kicked up dust. If she freed it, she thought, it'd probably stomp all over her.

She cleared her throat and approached the gelding and waved her arms about. Then she slowed. The long grass of the tussock swayed; its green blades were flecked with red. The gelding lay there in the sun with its throat slashed open. The wound looked like a lurid neckerchief, and the animal's white fur was matted with blood. Insects crawled and flew. A blowfly, stuck in the incarnadine mess, did neither, and all the hairs on Nera's arms stood on end.

Reese was less affected by the sight of the dead alpaca, perhaps not affected at all. Nera had called her to come and look, and she was doing just that. She bent towards the carcass. Then she straightened and removed her wide-brimmed hat. She smoothed back her greying hair. Nera's own hair had gone grey twenty years earlier. But it was only now—having shuttered the law firm and moved to the country—that she'd grown lazy about dyeing it.

'You think someone did this?' Nera asked.

Reese placed her hat back on her head and slapped it down with her palm. She licked her parched lips and glared at the shrubs and bloodwoods. Her shoelace had come undone, and for a moment Nera felt an odd kinship with her. She'd stood like that once, beside her bed, which was stained with Nasser's vomit—his body had already been removed. Her shoelace had been untied, and through the blinds, rays of sunlight had sliced across her face.

Reese killed the moment of kinship with a cluck of her tongue. She marched towards the bloodwoods, and Nera trailed her. Reese stopped by one of the trees and ran her hand along its scabrous base. Bark crackled off and fell to the ground. The trunk oozed its red kino.

'What are you looking for?' Nera asked.

'Blood,' Reese replied.

She ducked into the copse, and rather than follow her in, Nera waited in the daylight. Reese's footsteps crunched over dry leaves; the soil beneath sounded miry. Then for a while all Nera could hear were the trees, swishing like the ocean. She walked around the copse until she glimpsed Reese's muddy boots and callused hands: her neighbour had paused to tie her shoelace.

'Find anything?' Nera asked.

'Hard to tell.' Reese emerged and offered Nera a weak grin. 'Pretty fucking bleak in there,' she said.

They returned to the tussock, their gaits too aligned for Nera's liking. The bloodied grass rippled around the dead alpaca. The living alpaca now grazed near the mare's paddock.

'You don't think it was a person?' Nera asked.

'Could be,' Reese said. 'Some kids, not happy you've taken up residence.'

'Why not happy?'

'Don't respect sea changes, I guess.' Reese brushed leaves and dirt off her pants. 'You see something to make you think it was a person?'

Nera pictured her reflection backing away into the darkness. She thought about the lights that swam skywards and the guttural cry. None of those things was evidence, and most of those things had probably not even happened. The only matter of relevance was the cut on the gelding's neck, which seemed to her like a knife wound. But what did she know? She shook her head.

Reese scratched her cheek. 'More likely than kids, your male here just got unlucky.'

'How?'

'Snagged his neck on a sharp bit of tree. Poked his head where he shouldn't have. Who knows?'

'But there's no blood trail,' Nera said.

Reese shrugged. 'There's blood here somewhere,' she said. 'But I wouldn't worry about it. What I would worry about is where we're going to bury this bastard.'

Nera chose a spot behind the bloodwoods, invisible from the house, on a green hillock that resembled an ancient barrow. She and Reese spent the better part of the afternoon digging a grave there. Reese did most of the work. She stripped down to a singlet; her bronze biceps developed a sheen, and the wrinkles on her brow filled with dirt.

Around sunset, they used a tarpaulin to drag the dead gelding over to the barrow. It was heavy and stiff and attended by insects keen to accompany their host into the ground. Out of breath, Nera made sure she shovelled dirt fast over the carcass to make up for all the effort Reese had put in. Then she brought Reese a hand towel to dry herself off.

'Get yourself a new alpaca when you can,' Reese said, from behind the towel.

'I'm thinking of getting cattle,' Nera replied.

'And if your other alpaca goes,' Reese added, as if Nera hadn't spoken, 'get yourself a gun.'

It might have surprised Reese to learn that Nera already had a gun—an exceedingly serious-looking Winchester rifle, complete with scope. Had Reese learned about it, though, she might have guessed that Nera would take the rifle out of its safe as soon as she was alone. Instead, Nera chased a couple of Solnox down with a glass of wine and lowered herself into a bath of Epsom salts to soothe her aching muscles. She didn't need to get her gun, she told herself; what she needed was a decent night's sleep.

But the weather was hardly on her side. Through the frosted bathroom window, Nera could see the approach of an electrical storm. On the horizon, the night sky sparked and scintillated as if it were about to start a bushfire. None of its warmth reached her, though. She shivered in the bathtub and lifted her pruned fingers from the water and flexed them individually, counting the seconds to determine how far away the storm was.

She got to ten before she accepted that there would be no thunder. Neither was there the drumbeat of rain. There was only light and silence. She sank into the tub and submerged her chin and felt a pang in her lower back. The ends of her hair floated from her nape, and the gooseflesh of her bare form swayed before her—an optical illusion caused by the bathwater, which seesawed ever so slightly. She shut her eyes.

When she opened them, the electrical storm was right outside, but there was still no rain. Behind the frosted window, light appeared to dance and spin. Then the storm was overhead, and lightning stripped everything in the bathroom of colour and shape. Where reality had been, plain and unremarkable—chequerboard tiles, a wineglass, concealer spilled on the vanity—there now hung a brilliant sheet of light.

For a protracted moment, this sheet was all Nera could see. She stood and heard a splash. Bathwater dripped from her body. She placed two fingers against the skin of her neck and felt its clock-like tick. That and the chill of the air assured her that nothing had been destroyed.

The moment ended; the bathroom returned.

Nera got out of the tub and hurried to the hallway. The white sheet of light passed through the living room and the kitchen, and she was reminded of a photocopier and an X-ray machine—of what had been her life for some years. She pictured a boy in her office, with his battered mother, wiping snot and tears from his face. Then she imagined Nasser at the hospital, in his nurse's uniform, slogging his way from the children's ward where he worked to the chemo ward where he would become a patient.

The storm moved beyond the house, and she rushed to the kitchen window. She ignored the pain that shot through her; she ignored her reflection, which showed her naked and dripping. Her breath fogged up the glass, but she could see through it clearly enough.

Outside, two swarms of light drifted low through a cloudless sky. They orbited each other, the lights, and turned everything directly underneath them pure white for just an instant. They flew past the front lawn and onto the pasture where the female alpaca slept.

They were the same lights Nera had seen the previous night. But this time they did not cycle skywards. Rather, they glided over the tussock and began to plummet. Towards the copse they spiralled, these dancing lights—slowly now, slowly, slower still—until they descended beneath the bloodwoods' canopy.

Nera could no longer see them, yet she did not look away. A droplet of water or sweat leaked from her hair and trickled along her spine. Then from the copse there emanated an explosion, or an electrical pulse, that spread over the land and made everything lucent. The grass glimmered, and the mare glowed ghostly and wandered its ghostly paddock. The wire fence sparkled, and the timber posts seemed chalky and ablaze.

It was as if everything were dead, as if Nera were witnessing the spectral truth beneath the world. Her own hands were radiant, she realised, her sunspots lustrous. Even the alpaca shit on the front lawn shimmered.

On the glistering tussock, though, something wasn't shining: there were two figures there. They were blurred and difficult to make out. But they had the contours of human beings, and Nera had the impression that they were watching her.

The skin of her neck ticked faster, and she was suddenly conscious of her nudity. She covered her chest with her forearm. Thunder arrived, belatedly, and reverberated through the land. She felt the rumble within herself, and everything began to flicker. Sound and light grew weak together and faded away, along with any sign of the figures on the tussock.

II

Daylight carried Nera to the town centre of Morningvale and its pharmacy, a cobwebbed store that seemed to be going out of business. Its display window was blanched, and its roller door was only partially raised, as if to discourage customers. She passed beneath it easily enough and greeted the bald, stooped pharmacist who stood at the register.

'Morning,' he replied, biting at a hangnail.

Nera made a show of searching one of the aisles and wincing at the pain in her back. She stretched and reminded herself that only three real things had happened overnight: she'd done further damage to her muscles and hidden the rifle among the boxes under her bed and double-dosed her medication.

Whatever had happened before that—the spiralling lights and disconcerting figures—were mere projections of her mind. In the coming days, she'd need a fresh supply of Solnox to calm it. But she didn't know the pharmacist, and in her experience it was best to make nice before returning to present such a heavy prescription.

'Do you have any heat gel?' she asked. 'My back is killing me.'

'No surprises there,' the pharmacist said. 'Old girl like you starting to farm.'

Old girl? she thought indignantly. He was older than her fifty-one by at least ten years.

He limped out from behind the counter and squeezed past her down the aisle. The shelves were dusty and one-item deep, and he quickly found what he was after. He placed a white tube of cream in her hand and closed her fist around it and patted her fingers.

Nera watched, bemused, as if it were not her he was touching. Yet she could feel the arid whorls of his fingerprints and the yearning of his damp palm—along with the subtle creep of anger within her.

'Cream's cooling, not heating,' he said. 'But soothing? Definitely.'

His teeth were yellow and sticky with toffee, and the breaths that flowed through them were little whistles. She withdrew her hand and tried to prevent any connection between him and her husband from solidifying in her mind. But she was too late. All they had in common were those breaths, though, and Nasser only breathed like that at the end.

The pharmacist limped back to the counter. 'You're the lady solicitor who's bought half Reese Mundine's place,' he said.

'Guess the rumours are true.'

He went behind the register and coughed into his hand. 'Gonna run cattle on it?'

'Hopefully, once I've gotten used to the place.'

With a tissue, he wiped the mucus off the thin skin between his thumb and forefinger. Then he dumped the tissue and unwrapped a toffee. 'Just you on your lonesome?'

He crumpled the wrapper and tossed the sweet into his mouth.

'Friends come up from Sydney all the time,' Nera said.

She nudged the white tube across the counter and eyed a pile of newspapers on the floor. An inset on the cover promised a profile of a former detective who'd saved the life of a teenage girl and her baby. Beneath that was an editorial about the dangers of poker machine addiction, and beneath that were ads for cheap airfares and sports betting.

'Did you hear all this from Reese?' she asked.

'Don't know Reese that well'—the pharmacist sucked on the toffee—'except by reputation.'

'What reputation?' Nera said. But it occurred to her that she didn't want to engage in gossip about her neighbour, so she added, 'She's really helped me to settle in.'

'I'm sure she has,' the pharmacist replied. 'Paper?'

'What?'

'Saw you eyeing the newspaper.'

He paused expectantly, and she felt obliged to lean over and appear as if she were considering the purchase. It was unusual for a pharmacy to sell newspapers, she thought, and anyway she hadn't bought one since Nasser's subscription expired.

'No, thanks,' she said. She arched her back, and a bolt of pain shot through it. 'You don't carry codeine, do you?' she asked.

'Codeine's prescription only,' the pharmacist said.

'Since when?'

From his shirt pocket, he drew a pair of spectacles that seemed to be made of copper wire. He put them on and jabbed at some buttons on the register. 'Oh, a few years back now.'

She wanted to ask if he could spare a couple, for pain and suffering, but thought better of it. 'How come you don't open the door all the way?' she said. 'Is it broken?'

'Roller door's at five foot eight,' he replied. 'Gives a good impression of height—in case anyone's thinking of robbing the place.'

That night, in the middle of it, Nera yanked her front door open all the way and aimed her rifle at her land. Someone had knocked, twice, and remained silent even after she'd warned them that she had a gun. But now the doorstep stood empty.

From the threshold of the farmhouse, she scanned her property. The tree line, barely visible on the horizon, did not mark its end.

The dirt road bisected it and passed over undulating farmland and stretched on into oblivion. Blood surged behind her temples, and she regretted not taking the last of her Solnox. Still, she composed herself and stepped outside.

A blur of motion seized her attention, and she swung her rifle towards it. In her trembling sights was a young girl, wearing a yellow t-shirt. The girl sprinted through the alpaca shit on the front lawn and continued onto the pasture. She was running towards a boy—taller, in a grey hoodie—who ambled away from her. The girl ran, and the boy ambled, and both went in the direction of the tussock where the female alpaca was sprawled.

Nera lowered the rifle; she'd seen the children before, she thought, yet she couldn't place them. Then she noticed something glinting in the boy's hand. It might have been a lolly wrapper or a coin—or perhaps it was a knife. Reese had said that the gelding's throat might have been slit by children. These children appeared too young, and too familiar, to be alpaca killers. Plus, the girl had knocked on the door, twice, and might've been frightened off by Nera's warning that she had a gun. But if the boy did have a knife, the children were dangerously close to the female alpaca.

'Hey,' Nera shouted. 'Stop.'

The children did not stop. The girl caught up to the boy and took his hand, and they went together towards the tussock.

Gripping the rifle, Nera began to give chase. She cut through the lawn and the alpaca shit, which was dry on the outside but released its moist fetor once trampled. The stench was in her nostrils; the shit caked her soles and got mushed between her toes. She ran on. Soon her back started to complain, and her head made a gyre of the land. Dizzy, she sucked in breaths that scraped at her throat.

She reached the tussock, and the land ceased its spin. The children were not there, and the female alpaca was fine. Sprawled on the ground, listless, it chewed a clump of grass stained with the gelding's blood. Its throat was exposed—there to be slit—and it stared at Nera with the mournful gaze of a fatalist. The week before his death, Nasser had tripped over a living room rug and stared at her like that, with his throat exposed; she'd helped him up and told him they'd move to the countryside soon enough.

She blinked back tears and peered around in an attempt to discover where the children had gone. At the gate of its paddock, the mare waited. Its eyes gleamed like two obols, but they were not trained on Nera. They were fixed upon the bloodwoods.

There, she saw moonlight wink off the knife—or whatever it was in the boy's hand—and slip off the dew on the girl's ankle. The children vanished through the shrubs and tree trunks and into the Stygian darkness of the copse.

Nera caught her breath and approached cautiously. The treetops swished; all else was quiet. She trudged along the perimeter and searched for signs of life. She listened for the crunch of dead leaves, for footsteps sinking into the soil. But she heard nothing. 'There's nowhere to go,' she called. 'Why don't you just come out? I'm not going to hurt you.'

She made her way to the other side of the copse and paused to take in the barrow. The dirt of the alpaca's grave had settled somewhat, and the moon hovered above it like the gibbous cap of a monument. She looked again to the bloodwoods. She could end this by entering the copse. *Just go in,* she urged herself. *Go in.* But the prospect of doing that filled her with inexplicable terror.

'Okay,' she said, as if to herself. 'I'll be waiting.'

She walked to the mare's paddock, from where she had a good view of the copse, and sat against the timber fence with the rifle in her lap.

Nera woke to find Reese on her haunches in the driveway near her mud-spattered four-wheel drive. Under the mid-morning sun, Reese cast her eye over the front lawn. She turned to the open door of the farmhouse and considered it. Then she looked to Nera and doffed her hat and went to unlock the four-wheel drive's boot.

Nera shifted, exhausted, and the rifle slipped from her lap. She saw that her feet were caked with alpaca shit, and she stood up and felt her cheeks burn. The female alpaca meandered near the tree line; the mare trotted in its paddock, and the bloodwoods swayed in the breeze. Everything seemed so ordinary that she was more than certain that the children had fled.

With as much poise as she could muster, she carried the rifle towards the house. She did not set foot on the front lawn. In the driveway, she passed her neighbour, who was pulling a rope and dirty blue tarpaulin from the boot. Nera walked on and heard the boot slam shut behind her.

'Morning,' Reese called out.

The greeting was neither unfriendly nor sarcastic. Still, Nera considered feigning temporary deafness. The farmhouse was so close. She could slip inside quietly and pretend none of this had ever happened. But her neighbour might not pretend, or might take the discourtesy as a slight. Nera's shoulders slumped and, resigning herself to judgement, she faced Reese.

Reese looked her up and down. She lingered on the rifle and raised an eyebrow at the sight of Nera's soiled feet. Rather than judgement, though, what Nera saw on her face was a flicker of something else—affinity, or even the kinship she'd felt previously. In the twitch of Reese's mouth, too, she sensed a calculation of one kind or another.

'Sometimes I don't sleep well,' Nera said.

'Me neither,' Reese replied, with a weak grin. She slung the rope over her shoulder. 'Was hoping to break the mare in some more today. If you don't mind.'

'That's fine,' Nera said.

'I'll be out there'—Reese aimed a crooked finger at her own heart, yet Nera understood she was pointing through herself to the paddock—'for quite some time.'

Reese gave two restrained nods with an interval between them, as if there were an invitation to be inferred from the pause. She grimaced at the front lawn and lumbered off, and Nera decided that when she was presentable, she'd tell her neighbour about the children.

Showered and changed, she made two cups of tea and headed back outside. In the paddock, Reese had the mare on a rope and was leading it around in a tight circle. She swung the dirty tarp at its flank, and the horse kicked out and tried to wrench itself free. Reese allowed it to turn again in a tight circle.

'Progress?' Nera asked.

She planted a booted foot on the fence's lower rail and offered Reese a cup.

'A bit,' Reese replied. 'But see how she's reacting to the tarp? She'd hoof me in the guts if I gave her a chance.'

She whipped the horse with the tarp. The mare kicked out and almost caught her in the hip, and she dropped the tarp and released the rope. The horse jerked away and Reese ducked out through the fence. She clapped dirt from her hands and accepted the cup of tea from Nera. They both watched the mare stomp its hooves and trot to the far side of the paddock.

'It's afraid of the tarp,' Nera said.

'Maybe she saw one with a dead alpaca on it.'

Reese slurped at her tea and frowned with distaste. Nera took a sip of her own tea, without slurping, and singed her tongue. But she'd already made up her mind to speak.

'Last night,' she said, 'I saw the two kids who killed the white alpaca. A girl and a boy. They were here.'

Reese removed her hat and wiped sweat off her forehead. 'What'd they look like?'

Nera had a vague impression of the children's backs and shadows and clothes—an indistinct image of their bowed heads or of the bowed heads of children like them. 'Younger than I expected,' she said. 'I didn't get much of a look.'

Reese fanned herself with her hat. 'What'd they do?'

'They just knocked. Ran. Hid in there.'

Nera indicated the bloodwoods with a lazy sweep of her arm. Reese angled her body to the front lawn and leaned back against the fence. Her armpits were wet. Behind her, the tarp flapped about, and the mare nickered and fled from it once more.

'You chased them through the alpaca crap on your lawn?' Reese asked.

'Yeah.'

'Barefoot? With your gun?'

Nera hesitated. 'I thought they were going to kill the brown alpaca. The female.'

'How come?'

Nera went over the night's events in her mind. The girl had knocked on the door. Nera had gotten her rifle. She'd seen that the boy might have a knife in his hand, and the children had fled into the copse. All of that had happened—really happened. Yet somehow, it didn't seem enough.

'Were they Koori kids?' Reese asked.

Nera glanced at her sharply. 'No, I don't think so. Like I said, I didn't get a good look.' She knuckled sleep from the corner of her eye. 'I was sure I saw something,' she muttered.

'Yeah, I know the feeling.'

One-handed, Reese replaced her hat on her head. She put her teacup down on the timber rail and ducked through the fence into the paddock.

'You don't like the tea?' Nera asked.

'Don't take milk,' Reese called out over her shoulder. 'No sugar, either.'

She collected the tarp and untied the agitated mare. Then she jogged back to Nera with the tarp in one hand and the rope in the other. 'Why don't you come round mine for dinner tomorrow?' she said. 'I'll make us a stew.'

'Sounds good,' Nera replied.

They sauntered over the pasture, their footsteps again too aligned for Nera's liking. This time, she unsynchronised them by stuttering her step.

Reese climbed into her four-wheel drive.

'You don't think I should be worried about these kids?' Nera asked.

'You got yourself a gun,' Reese said. 'Besides . . .'

She didn't finish her sentence; she just glanced at the front lawn and got the engine going and drove away.

When Reese had moved beyond the tree line, Nera squatted and took up the exact position her neighbour had occupied earlier. The front door of the farmhouse was closed. The kitchen window overlooked the lawn, and through the alpaca shit a single set of bare footprints headed in the direction of the tussock. A single set. There was no second pair of prints, let alone a third. The children had left no mark on the land whatsoever.

The lack of other footprints felt even more ominous once the sun set on it, and Nera drank cabernet from the bottle and took the last of her Solnox to help her fall asleep. She couldn't tell whether this worked, although it certainly calmed her. She lay in bed with her eyes shut. Her heartbeat slowed, and her mind drifted.

It was only later that she realised she could hear breathing that wasn't her own. It was in the bed, right next to her: a wheeze with a whistled undercurrent. It was so familiar that she couldn't say how long it'd exhaled solace into her ear before she became conscious of its presence. When she did, though, whatever solace it provided evaporated. Its tremolo put her in mind of the pharmacist—or something more eldritch that she did not wish to name.

She shivered and clamped her eyes shut. The breathing beside her shrilled in and out, and she did not move a muscle.

Then one of the drainpipes juddered, and the wheeze and whistle stopped. Goosebumps spread over Nera's upper arms. She hushed her own breathing. What she heard next was a wretched series of glugs. The sound of vomit in a throat—*glug*. The horror of sick going nowhere—*glug*. Neither travelling up nor down—*glug*. And the pain of a final attempt to dislodge the blockage—*glug, glug, glug*.

Nera whimpered, and a weight without breath shifted in the bed, as if someone had just risen. The intimation of a shadow caressed Nera's face, and she shut her eyes even tighter. She listened to footfalls hitch and shuffle through the bedroom. They continued heavily down the hallway and faded towards the front door.

Her eyes finally opened at the click of the lock being turned. Frantic, she patted the space beside her. It was empty, and the sheets were cold and damp. She scrambled out of bed and reached beneath it for the rifle.

In the hallway, she aimed the rifle at the front door. But it was still closed, and there was no one to be seen. She swerved into the living room, where the empty bottle of cabernet slept on a wine-stained blanket on the couch. The television was off, and its screen reminded her of how absurd she must have appeared to Reese—how much more absurd she must appear now.

She made a sudden turn towards the kitchen: someone was there. An emaciated figure stood at the sink with its back to her. Her pulse thudded in her wrists and sent a tremor through the rifle. Her vision clouded, but she managed to place one foot in front of the other and advance to the kitchen.

On the edge of the tiles, she steadied the rifle. The figure was a man whose bald head was bowed but whose eyes, she sensed, were gazing out at the land. His hands rested on the counter either side of the sink, and his slender fingers were splayed. He wore scrub pants with no shirt. She could see his rib cage expand and contract and the constellation of moles around his scapula. 'Nasser?' she said, shakily.

The man raised his head. But he continued to gaze at the land, or so it appeared to her. His breathing grew more rapid, as if he were hyperventilating, and with no small amount of effort, with impossible sluggishness, he began to turn towards her. The curve of his jawline came into view, followed by the nub of his cheekbone.

She could almost see him; she was about to see him.

Then to her left, at the end of the hallway, the front door flew open. She heard the feather-light patter of footsteps growing louder, getting closer. Possessed of no instinct to scream or aim the rifle, she stood and watched the yellow and grey blur of the children—the girl and the boy, the latter with a shiny object in his hand—sprint along the hallway and out into the night.

She blinked at the empty doorway. Her pulse thudded in her wrists again, and the rifle fired. She heard its whipcrack and the ping of a bullet passing through glass. Confounded, she kept staring at the doorway until the slap of skin against tile forced her attention back to the kitchen. Nasser must have fallen, she thought. But when she looked down, she recoiled. The rifle slid free of her grip—it would be of no use to her, she understood.

On the kitchen floor, where Nasser might have collapsed, lay the dead gelding. It was decomposing and covered in the dirt she and Reese had shovelled over it days earlier. The gash on its throat was crusted with congealed blood, and larvae made no distinction between the wound and the remainder of its flesh. A blowfly zipped from the carcass to the window and crawled out through a jagged bullet hole in the pane. Beyond her bloodless reflection, Nera saw the children run past the tussock and return to the copse.

III

Nera had been parked across the road for hours when the pharmacist raised the roller door to a height of exactly five foot eight. Her eyes in the rear-view were craterous—sleep had not visited her for the remainder of the night. She'd rummaged manically through the boxes beneath her bed for her Solnox prescription and clambered into her car. Pre-dawn, classical music had been her soundtrack; now that it was daylight, the radio was tuned to some AM talkback show.

'This so-called mother,' a caller fumed, 'abandoned her children while she was on the bloody pokies. And she's the one who's responsible for their—'

Nera pulled the keys from the ignition and strode into the washed-out store. The pharmacist was behind the register, his lips sealed over a toffee. She could tell from the way he tilted his head that her walk was jittery. But she marched directly to the counter.

'Cream help with the muscles?' he asked.

'Yeah, it did.'

He flipped the sweet in his mouth, and she imagined it in a sink full of saliva. She could picture it on her kitchen tiles, covered with dirt and crawled upon by insects. She could see it cracked in two. Bile rose in her throat, and she forced it down behind an insipid smile. Then she laid the prescription on the counter.

'I need this filled, please.'

The pharmacist smiled back at her and made no effort to pick up the prescription. 'Farming tougher than you figured, old girl?'

'I'm not really farming yet,' she said. 'Just getting acquainted with living here.'

The light above her plinked and drew the pharmacist's gaze. Fatigue dragged the smile off her face. She scratched at an old scar on her shoulder and rotated the prescription on the counter so that its cursive was upside down to her.

Still the pharmacist didn't touch it.

'How's Reese Mundine treating you?' he asked.

Nera shrugged with more vigour than she intended. 'Neighbourly,' she said. She searched for something gossipy to add, but nothing came to her. 'She's breaking in a horse on my property, so she's got an easement for the next little while.'

'Has to come feed it, doesn't she? Get it used to her presence?'

'She does.' Nera tapped the counter with her nails. 'Can I get this, please?'

The pharmacist sucked on the toffee and put on his copper spectacles. He held the prescription at arm's length. *'Nera Pahlavi,'* he read. 'Where's that name from? Got some Indigenous in you, do you?'

'It's Hebrew,' she said. 'Look, I'm in a bit of a rush. Can you—?'

'What are you rushing for?' He placed the prescription on the counter again. 'You're not farming.'

'I have . . .' Nera threw her arms out, a little uncontrolled. 'Some friends are coming to stay, and I have to prepare. Can you just give me the medicine, please?'

She felt more jittery than when she'd entered, as if something was beginning to come undone. She could hear this in her voice and feel it in her chest.

'Prescription's out of date,' the pharmacist said.

He held it out, and she snatched it and inspected it. He was right—the prescription was three hundred and sixty-six days old, and it wasn't a leap year.

'By one day?' she scoffed.

'That's the short of it.'

'You can't overlook one day?'

'Rules are rules, old girl.'

The pharmacist swallowed the sweet, and she wished he'd choke on it. She wished he'd choke, and she could step over his corpse and collect the prescription herself. He opened his mouth, and the whistle returned to his breaths.

'Can't you just give it to me anyway?' she said.

'Listen, if I overlook the date for you, you'll—'

'Can't you just give it to me?'

The fluorescent light plinked again, and the pharmacist whistled in a deep breath. 'Nera, if I overlook the date for you—'

'Just give it to me, okay?' she said quietly. 'Just stop being a fucking prick and give it to me.' She shut her eyes a moment and pitied herself. 'Can't you just help me? Please? I only just buried my poor husband.'

The pharmacist removed his spectacles and positioned them on the rim of the register. Then he gestured limply at the exit.

🐇

The rest of the day fizzled through pubs and cafes and roadside diners, and at dusk Nera waited beneath a light bulb on her neighbour's porch. She blinked at a barn in the middle distance, where a massive dog sat panting behind the overloaded tray of a Dodge Ram ute. Unnervingly, the dog appeared to be staring at her—until a farm worker in a red baseball cap ushered the canine into the ute's cabin and got in himself. The engine roared, and the ute scudded along the only road that led to and from the property.

Then, hatless, Reese opened her front door and squinted at Nera as if the bulb above her were a flare.

Nera could smell herself, a malodour of booze and sweat. She could feel her desolation, or whatever it was, as a dryness of skin and eyes and mouth. Her neighbour must be able to sense it, she thought. But Reese simply stuffed a hand into the pocket of her sweatpants. 'C'mon in,' she said.

Nera followed her into the rustic kitchen-cum-living room. Only the kitchen half of the space was illuminated, and Nera lingered by the dining table, on the brink of darkness.

'Rough day?' Reese asked.

She went to the stove and stirred a pot with a wooden spoon. The grimy rangehood sucked up the steam, but the house was already infused with the aroma of beef and tomato and bay leaves.

Nera's head throbbed. 'No, I just didn't sleep well. Again.'

'Can take some adjustment,' Reese said. She knocked the wooden spoon against the pot and rested it on a saucer. Then she turned and regarded Nera. 'Like when I first came out here,' she said, 'I heard that big bastard of a boulder out front—did you see it?'

'No.'

Reese opened the door of the refrigerator in the corner. 'Anyhow, I heard it creeping round at night. Heard it *rumbling* near my bedroom.' From the refrigerator, she took out an oversized carton of wine and put it on the edge of the kitchen bench. 'Glass?'

'Please.'

Reese grabbed two whisky glasses from a cupboard. 'Turns out the boulder? Not creeping round at all—I'd gotten that out of some old bedtime story.' She filled the glasses with chilled cask wine and, at the dining table, handed one to Nera. 'Can be a mean and lonely country,' she said, 'if you let it be.'

Nera sipped at her wine and felt the syrupy stuff coat her palate. She was tempted to invite Reese to come take a look at the disinterred alpaca in her kitchen. But she worried that in her diminished state she might say too much, or that the animal had somehow been reburied during the day. Plus, she feared that if Reese somehow learned of her trips to the pharmacy, her credibility would be shot. Maybe it already was.

She shielded her eyes. 'You wouldn't have any codeine, would you?'

Reese clucked her tongue. 'Advil do?'

'Don't worry about it.' Nera sighed. 'I just need . . .'

Her heart thumped dully in her head. She made forlorn eye contact with Reese, who swilled her wine and went behind the kitchen bench. 'Have a lie-down,' Reese offered.

'I couldn't.'

'Sofa's comfy, and the food'll still be a minute.'

Nera glanced at the sofa in the dark living room. 'I'll just sit for a second,' she replied.

She plonked her glass on the coffee table and sat on the sofa. Its pillows were soft, and its springs had lost all resistance. Reese refilled her own whisky glass with wine and took a quick sip.

'How long have you been by yourself?' Nera asked.

'Well, you saw,' Reese replied. 'I got a few hairy blokes working for me Monday to Saturday, so I'm never alone for long.'

She rinsed a cabbage at the sink, and a yawn tumbled from Nera's mouth. 'No, I mean here,' she said. 'Living here. By yourself.'

Reese got out a chopping board and knife. 'Going on a decade now, I guess.' She began to slice the cabbage, and there was a strange interval between the sight of the knife bobbing up and down and the rat-a-tat of blade against wood. 'Was married before that,' Reese added.

Nera yawned again. 'Yeah?'

'Couldn't hack it in the end. Got divorced and moved out here. You?'

Reese returned to the stove, and Nera heard the pot lid clang. Her neighbour gathered up the sliced cabbage and let it fall through her fingers into the stew. On the coffee table was Nera's perspiring glass of wine. She knew it was impolite to put her feet up next to it, but she found herself stretching out her legs. Then she shut her eyes.

'I'm a widow,' she said. 'This life was my husband's dream.'

The night went quiet, except for the kettledrum inside her head. Then the warble of Reese's voice broke through to her, and she opened her eyes. In the light, Reese was an unfathomable smudge at the kitchen bench. She might've been sipping at her wine or biting at an apple—it was hard to tell.

'What?' Nera asked.

'Said that makes it sound like you died.'

This confused Nera, and she let her eyes close once more. 'Not me,' she said. 'My husband died.'

'How'd he pass?'

The question was muffled and faraway, and to the timpani inside Nera's head were added cymbals and a snare: the pot lid again, she thought, or the clangour of something coming undone completely. 'He choked to death,' she murmured. 'But by then I'd already given up on him.'

She'd never said that to anybody before, and she wasn't sure that she'd spoken it aloud now. Her voice was an echo, and in the pause between sentences she felt a dread that seemed to surge for hours.

Someone was tugging on her boot, and she kicked out and caught Reese in the hip. She was still seated on her neighbour's sofa, with her feet up on the coffee table, but all the lights in the house were off. 'What are you doing?' she asked.

Reese held a hand out in apology. She was in a nightgown, and the silhouette of her body was visible through the gauzy fabric. 'Just thought you'd be more comfortable,' she said.

Nera cleared her throat. 'What time is it?'

'Past midnight.'

Nera planted her boots at the base of the coffee table. Only one shoelace was untied, she saw; the other remained firmly knotted. 'I'm going to go,' she said.

Reese didn't protest, and Nera headed for the door.

'Did I tell you how my husband died?' she asked.

Reese scratched her cheek. 'No.'

'Good,' Nera said.

IV

Nera accelerated past the big bastard of a boulder out the front of Reese's property and wished her neighbour had just let her sleep. She could've slept; in the morning, she could've assessed the situation more rationally and determined what her next move should be. She could've told Reese all she needed to without fear of saying too much. Now she was adrift and agitated, with a potholed road unfurling under her high beams.

It wasn't long before her property appeared on her left. The entrance loomed, an open-gated gap in the wire boundary fence. She stopped the car and surveyed the land. From out here, the view was different—more serene, or peaceful, maybe. The grassland undulated over patches of murk and moonlight, and the dirt road snaked through it all and pierced the tree line in the distance.

Nothing beyond that was visible. She was left to imagine the mare in its paddock and the children in the copse and the quiet farmhouse with the dead gelding in the kitchen. Or perhaps the gelding wouldn't be there. Maybe she'd find the farmhouse empty and the animal returned to its grave on the barrow.

Nera swallowed. She had no desire to be back on her property, yet where else could she go, in her state, at this time of night? She allowed the car to crawl towards the entrance and flicked on the indicator.

Then she heard a sound, quavering and high-pitched, like the lament of an ungreased hinge—the same sound she'd heard on the first night she spent in the farmhouse. A shudder went through her, and a breath seeped from her mouth. She pressed hard on the accelerator; the engine grunted, and the car picked up pace.

The indicator stopped blinking, and she drove past the entrance. She'd drive all the way back to Sydney, she decided, and the first thing she'd do was visit a twenty-four-hour clinic and get herself a new prescription. She'd hole up in a motel with Solnox and wine and stay in bed for a few days. After that, she'd start to put her old life back together.

But the acreage of her property was not behind her—not yet—and through the windscreen she caught sight of an animal. Its shape was vague at first, but soon its elongated neck and brown fur became apparent. Its legs pumped ferociously on the edge of her land.

The female alpaca bolted towards the boundary fence. Then it launched itself over the wire and landed, not without elegance, on the roadside. Nera couldn't comprehend what she was witnessing. Her heart buzzed, its beats undifferentiated. She hit the brakes and wrenched the steering wheel anticlockwise. The car skidded in the direction of the alpaca, which continued to sprint into its high beams.

The bumper slammed into the animal, and momentum scooped it onto the bonnet. Its neck twisted. Its head smashed into the glass. Nera's own head pitched forward. Her hairline connected with the top of the steering wheel and her cheek with the centre. A moment too late, the airbag ballooned and shoved her back, and at the wire boundary fence the car screeched to a halt.

In the silence, Nera sat in the driver's seat. Her whole body trembled, except for her hands, which gripped the steering wheel. Smoke curled around the car. She could smell burned rubber and taste metal. The airbag was deflating, and the windscreen had a crack in it. Her high beams illuminated the land.

There was an ache in her head and neck and lower back. She turned her face, with impossible sluggishness, and peered at the side window. Her reflection peered back at her, shivering and faint. Blood crept down her brow. Her cheek was cut and swollen.

Through her reflection, she saw the alpaca sprawled by the roadside. The creature's crown was blotched and its throat lacerated such that, if it threw its head back in morbid laughter, the wound would yawn open.

For a long while, neither human nor animal moved. Then the alpaca grumbled, and its legs twitched. It began to pant, and its moist eyes darted around madly. Nera willed it not to thrash about. But it did. Its throat came apart, slowly, as if it were being unlaced. Blood poured from the wound—*glug*. Pink cables of flesh were extruded—*glug*. And the animal's body jerked for a final time—*glug, glug, glug.*

Nera prised her hands from the steering wheel. Her fingers quivered, and she brought them to her lips. She covered her mouth and screamed—a prolonged, guttural, plaintive cry, like the one she'd heard on her first night in the farmhouse. Reese was right, she thought: she was living the dream of a dead man, and what did that make her? She let her chin drop onto her chest and listened awhile to her own breathing.

Eventually, she raised her head and looked out through the windscreen. Where she expected to see the land, she saw something else—her home; her real home in Bronte. Her high beams shone in the narrow driveway, and the scent of the ocean was in her nose.

She must have been lulled to sleep after work again, she figured. But Nasser wasn't there to wake her. Instead there was just this curly-haired young girl in the back seat, with her hand resting weightlessly on Nera's shoulder.

The girl reached out and stroked a lock of grey from Nera's clammy brow. Nera startled, and the girl frowned. 'What's wrong?' she asked.

Nera wasn't sure how to respond. Her heart was filled with something that might've been terror, or love. With her faded yellow t-shirt and sharp cheekbones, the girl looked somehow different from how she remembered. But this was her daughter, she decided; it had to be. 'It's so good to see you again,' she said.

The girl smiled and sat back, and Nera noticed that she wasn't alone. Beside her was a boy, slightly taller, who gave the impression that he'd just climbed in, feet first, through the window. He wore a grey hoodie and had his eyes fixed on a shiny object in his hand.

Nera exhaled unsteadily. At first she didn't recognise the boy. Then it came to her that he was the girl's brother and therefore had to be her son. 'Hey,' she said.

The boy raised his eyes sheepishly. 'Hey.'

'What've you got there?'

The boy made no reply. He closed his fist over the shiny object, and the children exchanged a mischievous grin.

'Can we go to the beach?' the girl asked.

Nera peered at the night around them. 'It's too dark, sweetheart.'

'It is not,' the girl replied.

'It's getting light,' the boy added. 'Look.'

Nera realised that the children were telling the truth. Around the girl and the boy she could sense the faintest of glows, an aura in anticipation of the sunrise. Her own hands had it as well, this glow, this aura, and so did the car seats. It was as if she were witnessing her own sudden contentment reflected in everything. 'Okay,' she said. 'Let's go.'

They got out of the car, and the children bounded ahead of her and left her staggering along the road in their wake. She passed a dead alpaca sprawled by a wire fence; its throat was slit open, and flesh spilled from the wound. She had the sense that she was meant to feel something for this creature, but all that stirred beneath her contentment was a faint anxiety, and that was for the children, who'd darted through an open gate and into—what was it? An alley?

'Wait,' she called out. 'Come here and hold my hand, please. I don't want you two getting lost again.'

She didn't know why she'd said that. Still, the girl returned and took her hand straight away. But the boy sulked and refused and waited defiantly at the alley's entrance.

'You don't have to hold my hand, if you don't want,' Nera said. 'Just be careful, okay?'

The boy screwed up his face. Then he grasped her hand, and she felt the shiny object press into her palm. She walked hand in hand with the children down the undulating alley, which was bordered on both sides by featureless houses. They exited through a tree line and stepped together onto the shimmering sand of the beach.

Nera found the tree line out of kilter with the city, and she couldn't feel the sand underfoot. But this didn't matter to her. She'd seen her daughter's face once more; she'd even gained a son. She was at the beach with the children, and everything was glorious and glowing.

It was only when the children dragged her to the shoreline that she hesitated. The ocean was dark, and out in the water was a grassy island that resembled an ancient barrow. On its slope was an empty grave, which flooded with seawater when the tide flowed in. She stared down at her boots—the laces of which were loose—and watched the tide arrive and recede without touching them.

The children tried to tug her towards the shallows, but she resisted. 'I can't go in,' she said. 'I'm wearing shoes.'

'That's okay,' the girl replied.

'It's going to be cold,' Nera said.

'You have to come,' the boy said. 'We already paid.'

The children pulled at her hands and took a step forward themselves. When she failed to budge, they exchanged a glance and shrugged and let her go.

The shiny object the boy had pressed into her palm remained there, and she examined it under the moonlight. It was a special-issue coin, an eccentric one—something a child might prize. A blowfly and larvae were engraved on its face, near the perimeter, which was in mint condition. But the centre of the coin was charred and blackened, as if it'd been struck by lightning.

She glanced up from the coin and saw, or imagined she saw, that a gloomy copse of shrubs and bloodwoods had grown right at her feet. She blinked, and the copse disappeared, although the tree trunks, oozing their red kino, left a sinister afterimage on her irises.

Then from somewhere she heard a horse let out a long, terrible squeal. Behind her, a little way off, a silver mare galloped wildly around its enclosure on the beach. The mare kicked up sand with its hooves and slid to a halt at the gate and waited to be freed.

Closer to Nera was a reedy patch of beachgrass that swayed in the breeze. Its blades were stained with blood. She scanned the beach and noticed in the distance a smattering of oily animal shit and a farmhouse sinking into the sand and a wired-off field.

These strange sights placed a thought at the margin of her consciousness, and she turned to the water once more. The children had waded to where she couldn't reach them—and the ocean, having pushed out beyond her reckoning, now gathered itself on the horizon.

A wave rose up from the earth to the sky and started to approach the shore. Inside the wave were two discrete swarms of light. They orbited each other—the lights—and swam back and forth from one side of her vision to the other. A squid-like double helix, they danced and fizzed, full of grace, and made sublime patterns against the darkness.

Nera's skin tingled; her heart thrummed. The thought at the margin of her consciousness was swept to the centre, where a profound sense of bereavement settled. She remembered the car crash and fell to her knees. The alpacas were both dead, she recalled, and her husband had passed. The children were not even hers: the girl was not her daughter; the boy not her son. But this only doubled her sense of loss, and she began to weep.

She wept, and the wave advanced, soundless and brilliant, towards the children. She wept, and the wave obliterated the grassy island and the empty grave. She wept—the wave was about to claim the children, who only bowed their heads in response, as if they were being reprimanded. She wanted to call to them, to warn them. From the shoreline she reached for them, desperately, holding the tarnished coin in her hand.

'Look up,' she whispered.

But the children in the ocean did not look up. The girl took the boy's hand, and they went together towards the wave of light.

Interlude

Sue

Detective Inspector Sue Maric rode her motorcycle along the main street in Morningvale. She cruised by a faded pharmacy, the roller door of which was shut, and zoomed down roads lined with acres of tillage. A truck heading in the opposite direction blasted its horn, and she leaned over her handlebars and sped up.

It wasn't long before she slowed at a scene where a crew worked to remove a crashed car from the road. The car's windscreen was cracked and its airbag deflated and its bonnet smeared with blood. On the asphalt nearby, an alpaca lay with its throat yawning at a pool of yet more blood. Sue nodded at the crew. Then she rode on and turned through an open-gated gap in a wire boundary fence.

On farmland now, she let the motorcycle's wheels roll over a dirt road and beneath the shadow of a tree line. She emerged on the other side and took in the land. A lonely farmhouse that must have been recently built or renovated loomed in the distance. In its driveway, a police car and unmarked sedan were parked near two vans.

She accelerated over the dirt road and past a mare in a fenced paddock. The horse's gaze was fixed on a copse of bloodwoods and shrubs, in and around which a team of forensic investigators worked. They wore masks and disposable body suits and headlamps; they wielded equipment that they used to unearth and examine and record—to reduce the unfathomable to its quotidian details.

Between Sue and the forensic investigators loitered three police officers in gumboots and the junior detective in a suit and shoe protectors. He raised a latex-gloved hand in greeting, and she revved her engine and parked outside the house. She dismounted and removed her helmet and unzipped her black jacket.

On the front lawn, a set of footprints ran through pebbles of shit that glistened in the sun. In the house's front window, a tiny bullet hole winked at her; she could hear flies buzzing inside. The junior detective jogged over the pasture between them, and she brushed hair from her brow. She strode towards him and jabbed her thumb over her shoulder. 'What's that about?' she called out.

'What do you mean?' he called back.

She waited for their paths to meet. 'There's a bloody bullet hole in the window.'

'Yeah, there's . . .' He exhaled and adjusted his horn-rimmed spectacles. 'I figured forensics should focus on the main site first.'

He passed her pairs of fresh shoe covers and gloves, and she sighed. 'Just make sure nobody goes in there. Maybe tape it off.'

'Will do,' he replied.

But he didn't make any move in the direction of the farmhouse, and Sue pursed her lips. She rested a hand on his shoulder and put on the shoe covers. Then she wandered towards the copse while dragging on the gloves. The junior detective walked alongside her—something glinting in his grip—and they approached a tussock of grass flecked with blood. Sue pointed at it.

'Animal, apparently,' the junior detective said. 'Anyway, I thought you might be interested in this.'

He offered her an evidence bag. Inside the bag was an eccentric special-issue coin with blowflies and larvae etched onto it. The centre of the coin was charred. 'What am I looking at?' she asked.

'The homeowner told paramedics she found it when she went digging—in there.'

'Actually, there's a question.' Sue gave the coin back to the junior detective and glanced at the copse ahead of them. 'What made her go digging in there?'

The junior detective shrugged. 'We're lucky she did.'

'Lucky,' Sue repeated.

She shook her head. Then she and the junior detective walked by the three uniformed officers, who looked as if they yearned for acknowledgement but did not expect it. Near the circular copse, Sue halted. The junior detective did likewise, and Sue stared at the ring of trees. Red kino oozed from their trunks. Beyond them, she could only glimpse the headlamps of the forensic investigators roving around like coastguards on a night-time ocean.

'This must be the place,' she muttered. She reached into her jacket pocket and withdrew a dog-eared photograph she'd carried with her for the last year. It was the square photo of the simple two-panel painting, marked as evidence.

She extended her arm and raised it before her. Ignoring the left panel, she focused on the right, which depicted two children holding hands in front of a bloodied tree that wore a halo. 'Do you know what this is?' she asked the junior detective.

'A potential threat?' Next to her, he fidgeted with the coin in its bag and raised his eyes from the painting to the sky above the bloodwoods. 'Or a religious offering? That's what you told me, anyway.'

'Yeah, it's both of those things. And now'—she slipped the photograph back into her pocket—'it's also an admission.'

'An admission?' The junior detective glanced at her sharply. 'By who?'

Sue sighed again. 'Go tape off the house, will you?'

The junior detective seemed as if he were about to demur. Instead he retreated, and his footfalls crunched over the grass. As they faded, one of the forensic investigators emerged from between the trunks of two trees. 'You haven't moved them yet, have you?' Sue asked.

The forensic investigator lowered her eyes; her hair and most of her face were covered. 'We were waiting for you,' she replied. Solemnly, she turned and retreated into the copse.

Sue took a few paces forward and stopped with the tangled roots of a bloodwood at her feet. She shuddered and inhaled a final clean breath. Then she followed the forensic investigator into the darkness.

Part Five
The Children

1

The children stared at their mother from the back seat of the orange Datsun. But Jack cast his gaze towards the parking brake long before Lonnie looked away. She watched Ilene disappear into the lobby of the Casus Hill Workers' Club—and she kept watching, her dark brows low, until her eyes appeared tearful and her lids fluttered.

'She's not coming back,' Jack said. 'We should just go.'

Lonnie reached over and picked a speck of fluff off the side of her booster. 'It's only been *one second*.'

Her brother squeezed his unwashed body through the gap between the front seats. The side of a seat pressed against his jumper, which pressed against his bandage, which pressed against the wound on his abdomen. He sucked in a sharp breath. Lonnie rubbed her forefinger with her thumb, and the speck of fluff drifted onto her yellow t-shirt. She almost smiled. Then she swept the fluff onto the carpet.

'What are you doing?' she asked.

Jack lounged with his head against the driver's door and his sneakers on the passenger seat. 'You know what I reckon we should do?' He grabbed the steering wheel and rotated it a tick. 'We should just take the car and drive away.'

'We'll get in trouble, Jack.'

'We're already in trouble.' Jack sat up. A hatchback drove by with its headlights on in the daytime. 'I'm saying we go and go and go.' He flopped down and bumped his head against the wheel, although he showed no outward sign of pain. 'We go so she never finds us again.'

'You don't know how to drive.' Lonnie moved forward and positioned her head between the two front seats. 'Do you hate her?'

'No. She hates *us*, Lonnie.'

'Does not.'

Jack turned his face from his sister. No keys dangled in the ignition, and he traced the angular keyhole with his nail. Tautness showed across his jaw. But when he faced Lonnie again, he opened and closed his mouth to produce a sound like bubbles popping.

Lonnie adjusted herself so she could see her blank expression in the rear-view mirror. 'She didn't do it.'

'You don't understand *anything*. We should just go.' He sat up again and brought his knees towards his chest. 'Maybe she just hates me.'

Lonnie broke eye contact with herself. 'Who could hate you?'

Jack grinned at Lonnie, who smiled back and showed her pointed little incisors. Then she forced her way through the gap between the front seats and tumbled onto the passenger side.

'You know what was cool?' Jack's grin widened. 'When you bit his face.'

'Yeah, he was a bully.'

'He scratched me and called you a black hen.'

'He deserved it.'

'So I gutted him like a fish!'

'And I bent down'—Lonnie leaned over so that her crown almost touched the glove compartment—'and I chomped his face!'

She gnashed her teeth gleefully, and Jack laughed. Then she reached down to the footwell. Her hand patted a sticky film of iced coffee on the carpet and grasped a small cardboard roll under the headland of her seat. She straightened up and pouted at it.

'What's that?' Jack asked.

Lonnie held the roll upright and sniffed her palm. 'It's coffee money,' she said.

'Coffee money?' Jack shuffled closer and extended his arm over the centre console. In the console was a miniature ziplock bag with traces of powder in it. 'Lemme see.'

Lonnie passed him the roll of coins. He flipped it over as if it were an hourglass. 'It's not coffee money,' he said. 'It's real dollars.'

'How much dollars?'

'Now we should really go.' Jack raised his mischievous eyes. 'We can afford it. We can go and go and never need her ever again.'

'Ja-ack.'

Lonnie exaggerated a slump of her shoulders. Jack smirked. He turned away and opened the driver's door and climbed out of the car.

'Where are you *going*?' Lonnie said.

The door slammed, and she craned her neck and watched Jack saunter along the side of the car. She lost sight of him at the boot, and he didn't reappear on the passenger side. Frantically, she scanned the car park. Mostly what she saw was asphalt and other cars dulled by an overcast sky. Leaning against a distant SUV, though, stood a wiry man in a black suit who carried a leather satchel over his shoulder. Her eyes went wide. But the man paid her no attention at all, and she let her gaze drift away from him.

Then Jack popped up at her window, and she startled. 'That's not funny,' she protested.

Jack kept smirking. He tapped at the window with the roll of dollar coins. 'Come on,' he said. 'Let's go.' Lonnie sank into her seat and ignored him. He cupped his face and pressed it against the glass. 'Let's go,' he repeated, through the side of his mouth.

After a moment, Lonnie opened the door a fraction. Jack tugged at the handle, and as the door swung on its hinge, he pretended to stagger backwards while keeping his face pressed to the glass. Then he skipped to Lonnie and offered the roll of coins to her as if passing a baton. 'I'll let you buy whatever you want.'

Lonnie sighed. 'I just don't think we should go *forever*.'

'She's not coming back, Lonnie.' Jack waggled the coins. 'And we have money now.'

'Oh-kay.' Lonnie accepted the coins and planted her feet on the asphalt. 'If we run out of dollars, we come back, right?'

Jack's face contorted. 'Why should we come back when she's not going to?'

Lonnie didn't take a step.

'Fine,' Jack said. '*If* we run out of dollars, and *if* you still want to come back, we come back.'

'Promise?'

'I promise.'

Lonnie nodded and walked past him.

'But we'll never run out of dollars,' he yelled. He jogged ahead of her and leaped victorious into the air. 'We have enough dollars to last forever!'

Lonnie laughed. She and Jack wandered away from their mother's car towards the main road where, unheard by them, a vehicle that had been biding its time started its engine.

The vehicle remained out of earshot when they reached a street that was at once suburban and a minor thoroughfare. They passed a liquor store on the corner, adorned with a poster of a blonde actress reclining on a beach. She gazed lovingly over her champagne flute at the children shambling by.

Lonnie gripped the roll of coins. 'Do you think she has more dollars than we do?'

Jack shrugged. 'What do you wanna buy first?'

Lonnie walked backwards for a few steps so she could stare at the actress. 'I wanna go to the beach.'

'You can't buy the beach.'

'I don't wanna buy the beach—I wanna *go* to the beach.'

'We're nowhere near the beach. Pick something to buy.'

She spun about and walked on. The liquor store faded into the background, and the children drifted by houses that seemed too damp and deserted for noontide. At a roundabout, the children waited for a sedan to turn right.

Jack flicked his grey hood up onto his head and crossed the road in front of Lonnie. 'What do you think Dad said to Mum?' he asked over his shoulder.

'When?'

'Today.'

'Um, I think he said that he loves us,' Lonnie replied, with an upward inflection. 'And Mum said she loves us too.'

'How come he didn't come to the car?'

Jack stepped onto the kerb. He kept going, and Lonnie jogged to catch up. 'Because,' she said.

'Because why?'

'Because he's'—Lonnie touched the coins to her chin—'not ready yet.'

'You're such a *baby*.' Jack fixed his eyes on the uneven pavement. 'I reckon he said he wants us both to get lost.'

He jabbed at the wound on his abdomen and scrunched up his nose. Then he shoved his hands into his pockets while Lonnie whacked the roll of coins against her open palm. Beside them, nondescript houses flickered by; ahead was a railway bridge.

Lonnie stopped walking abruptly and patted Jack's upper arm. 'That!' she exclaimed. 'That's what I want to buy first.'

He stopped next to her. Between twin cramped residences squatted a second-hand clothes store. Its display consisted of mannequins dressed in fake furs and pleather jackets. One mannequin wore flares and a flannel shirt and straw hat; its face was featureless except for a handlebar moustache that was peeling off. The lettering on the window, which had once announced the shop's name, now consisted of a game of hangman.

'Cool,' Jack said, and lowered his hood.

Together, he and Lonnie approached the shop's door and saw a handwritten note gummed to it. The shopkeeper would be back in half an hour, the note announced, although it gave no indication of when it had been penned.

'It's closed?' Lonnie asked.

'For thirty minutes.'

'Maybe it'll be open when we come back?'

She walked on, and Jack groaned. 'Stupid shop,' he muttered. He kicked at the door, without any particular force; it shifted a little and betrayed that it was unlocked. 'Hey Lon,' he called out. 'Wanna see some magic?'

Lonnie turned back to him, and he shoved the door open. Her face lit up. She skipped over to the entrance. 'We have to pay for whatever we want to take,' she said.

Jack gave one big nod. He followed his sister into the store, which, from the higgledy-piggledy look of it, may as well have been shut for a decade.

At the back, they found a smattering of children's clothing. The selection was moth-eaten and reeked of must. But Jack changed into a pair of chinos—the cuffs of which he had to roll up several times—and a loose-fitting collarless shirt. Lonnie pulled a corduroy pinafore embroidered with flowers over the top of her school uniform. They posed side by side in front of a mirror and inclined their heads towards each other.

'How do I look?' Lonnie asked.

'You look nice,' Jack replied. 'How about me?'

'You look nice as well.' Lonnie waved the roll of coins at him. 'How much dollars do you think we should leave?'

Jack searched his outfit for a price tag. There wasn't one. He eyed the hoodie and the trackpants of his uniform on the floor. 'I'll take care of it.'

Lonnie handed him the roll of coins, and he went behind the counter to the till. He tried to remove the cardboard wrapping from the coins; it wouldn't come off, so he banged it on the corner of the counter until it split near the top. Lonnie joined him and turned a bronze key in the till's drawer. It shot open with a ping. Inside were a few notes and plenty of coins.

'Do you think this is the same like Mum uses at her work?' Lonnie asked.

'Who cares?'

Jack counted out five dollars and placed them one by one into the till. He grabbed a fresh plastic bag from a shelf. Lonnie shut the till and locked it. Jack collected his old clothes from the floor and stuffed them into the bag. Then the children, both in their new second-hand clothes, left the store.

The clouds grew less ominous, and soon the children came to a street that was predominantly lined with restaurants. Many of these were closed until dinnertime. But they walked by an open Thai restaurant that pushed the perfume of coconut milk and lime leaf onto every pedestrian. Jack sniffed the air, and his stomach growled.

Beside him, Lonnie hummed and surveyed the street ahead. A motorcycle roared past, but the vehicle that'd been biding its time was nowhere to be seen or heard. In the distance, a pizza joint touted its wood-fired bona fides. Lonnie's eye lingered on the business next to it—a faded salon that said it specialised in 'Afro-Jamaican styles'. She stroked her curls, some of which were matted to her brow.

'Can I get my hair cut?' she asked.

'Your hair's fine.' Jack tapped her shoulder with the three-quarter roll of coins and swung the bag of his old clothes back and forth. 'Anyway, it's my turn to choose. And I say we buy something savoury.'

'What's savoury mean?'

'Food.'

They drew alongside a gelato shop, its white tiles separated from the pavement by a thin strip of aluminium. Inside, the gelato on display was piled high and adorned with macarons and cookies and wafers. The scent of ice cream cones wafted to the children. Lonnie turned her questioning gaze to Jack, who fixed his on the chewing gum that freckled the concrete at his feet.

'No,' he said.

'Ice cream is food.'

'It's not savoury.'

'Why not?'

He shrugged. 'Just isn't.'

They wandered on, and Jack inspected the facades of the cafes and restaurants. He hesitated outside a charcoal chicken shop in which a huddle of adults on their lunchbreak screamed their orders. Then he and Lonnie kept walking. A bit further along they paused outside a bar that bore a picture of a burger drooling cheese. But a sign with the number 18 circled and crossed out made the children march on.

'What if . . .' Lonnie began. 'What if Mum comes back to the car with savoury for us?'

Jack rolled his eyes. 'She won't.'

'What if she does?'

Jack stopped walking. Lonnie continued for a moment before halting. She faced her brother, who stepped towards her and jabbed the coins in her direction. 'Get it through your thick skull,' he said. 'Mum's not coming back.'

'But I'm *starving*.' Lonnie fingered the flowers embroidered on her pinafore. 'Maybe we should go back and get ice cream.'

'We're not turning around.' Jack poked the wound on his abdomen with the roll of coins. 'We don't go back unless we run out of dollars, remember?'

Lonnie's mouth was shaped like the upper half of a hula hoop. 'Where are we gonna eat, Jack?'

He scanned both sides of the street and spotted a neon sign with a chilli outlined on it. Then he aimed the roll of coins over Lonnie's shoulder. 'Right over there, sista.'

He gave this answer as if the sign had always marked their destination, and he brushed past Lonnie and headed to it. Lonnie trailed him into an Indian diner with harsh lighting and a range of curries and naans on display. Jack stood at the counter and stared at the plump deep-fried pyramid of a samosa.

A distracted young woman emerged and took his order and the four dollars he counted out. She put the samosa in a paper bag that the grease instantly made transparent. Then she gave Jack the bag and fifty cents change before retreating to the back room once more.

Jack exited the diner and sat on the kerb between two parked cars. He placed the roll of coins and plastic bag of clothes at his feet. Lonnie smoothed down her pinafore and sat next to him. With the paper bag in his lap, he removed the samosa and broke it into two almost equal pieces. Steam rose from the split-open snack, and he rested it on the paper to let it cool.

'You don't remember that night, do you?' he said.

'Yes I do.'

'What do you remember?'

'I remember'—Lonnie stared across the road—'that Mum helped us out of the water. And she hugged us. And she said she was sorry.'

'I don't think she said she was sorry.'

Lonnie squinted and rubbed her knuckles on the flowers of her pinafore as if she were scrubbing them. The samosa in Jack's lap stopped steaming, and he handed her the larger portion. They held each other's gazes and bit into the samosa simultaneously. Jack was the first to grin. But Lonnie's smile was bigger than his.

'This is so yummy.' She took another bite. 'It's better than ice cream,' she said with her mouth full.

Jack's mouth was also full. 'That's because it's savoury.'

They ate the rest of the samosa without speaking and licked the grease from their grimy fingers.

II

The children turned onto an avenue bordering the train tracks and followed it for several minutes. Jack hauled himself onto the painted brick wall outside a housing estate and shuffled along unsteadily, as if on a balance beam. Then Lonnie insisted on detouring onto an undersized cricket field. She stood on the concrete pitch, which was covered in green cloth that was torn on the diagonal.

Jack waited on the grass. 'Looks like a bedsheet coming off.'

'I wanna lie down,' Lonnie replied.

'Yeah, but what do you wanna buy?'

Jack twirled the half-roll of coins and swung the bag of clothes in a full circle—a yo-yo going around the world. Lonnie traipsed on, and he trailed her back to the avenue. Soon they came upon a cottage with a front yard full of garden gnomes. She waited at the gate while he tiptoed into the yard, exaggerating his sneaky movements for comic effect. He rested the coins and bag on the ground and struggled to lift one of the gnomes by its samosa-shaped cap.

'We can't steal anything, remember?' Lonnie stage-whispered.

He released the gnome, and it clattered onto its side. Its head popped off and rolled to his feet. Jack mugged at Lonnie, and she smiled. Then a grumble and a crash emanated from the cottage.

Jack collected his things and took off. Lonnie did too, and a moment later they were sprinting over the pavement and losing a race to a train that sped along the tracks beside the avenue.

Outside the station, the children stopped to catch their breath. 'Do you think,' Lonnie said, 'that a giant gnome lives in the house?'

Jack guffawed. In front of the children was a T-junction. The avenue that followed the train line was mainly residential, but the cross street—the one that terminated at the station—had several businesses on it.

'Come on,' Jack said. 'Let's have a rest.'

The children entered the station's tunnel. Jack tried to get Lonnie to climb the stairs, but she ran to an elevator and pumped the button. The elevator arrived, and they rode it up to the platform. Lonnie jogged to a bench and sat. She eyed a man wheeling a bike along the platform and tapping his travel card against a digital reader. Jack joined her on the bench.

'How do you get one of those cards?' she asked.

'You buy one.'

'From where?'

'The card shop.'

She rested her temple against his arm. 'You don't have to know everything,' she said.

'But I do know everything.'

'Like about Mum and Dad?'

Jack crinkled an eye. He and Lonnie rested until a train rolled into the station. One of the carriages opened in front of them, and Jack hopped off the bench. 'Hey, Lonnie, you want to get on? We could go *anywhere*.'

Lonnie blinked as if she'd been asleep. 'We didn't buy a card.'

'So?'

'What if the train knows we don't have a card?'

'How can the train know?'

'Trains are smart these days—like TVs and stuff.'

Jack scoffed. But he creased his brow and looked along the platform. A flock of passengers, having alighted, scurried towards the stairs. The man with the bike guided it onto the train, and Jack gestured at him. 'Bet his bike doesn't have a card.'

'His bike's a bike, Jack,' Lonnie replied.

'What do *you* know?'

A three-note sweet and sour melody played, and all the doors of all the carriages slid shut. The train pulled out from the station, and Jack watched it head towards the horizon.

'I'm thirsty,' Lonnie said.

'Let's get a drink then.' He passed her the half-roll of coins. 'It's your turn to choose anyway.'

The children plodded down the stairs and through the tunnel. At the front of the station was a busker with an acoustic guitar. He wore a leather vest and sang with his eyes closed, his voice sweet as nectar. Jack and Lonnie paused at the busker's open guitar case, which was strewn with coins. They watched his mouth and listened to his song. The lyrics had him leaving behind his gambling days and yearning to cruise down five final highways. He finished the song and made eye contact with the children.

'Where'd you learn to sing like that?' Lonnie asked.

The busker tuned his guitar. 'In the shower, mostly.'

Lonnie fiddled with the half-roll of coins in her hand. Jack slipped the plastic bag onto his wrist and dropped the fifty cents he'd received as change from the samosa into the guitar case. The busker nodded and strummed a note of thanks. Then Jack and Lonnie crossed the avenue that ran parallel to the railway tracks, and the busker serenaded them as they strolled along the street lined with businesses.

One of the first they happened upon was a tobacconist with a melting facade and dismal interior. Through the window, Lonnie inspected the ornate shisha pipes. 'What's a toe-bax-honest?'

'A place that sells bad stuff,' Jack replied. He peered at his and Lonnie's reflections superimposed over the pipes in the window. They were warped and unrecognisable, and behind them the warped and unrecognisable vehicle circled past. Jack scratched his eyebrow. 'You're thirsty, right?'

He took Lonnie's hand—the one with the coins in it—and led her into a newsagent. A digital bell announced their arrival, and he released her hand. He ignored the shelves of magazines and last-minute birthday cards and beelined past a display freezer to the drinks fridge. Lonnie diverted down the first aisle and plucked a magazine off the shelf. On the cover was a glossy photo of a mansion surrounded by verdant lawns; a fountain that looked to be made of meringue gurgled in the foreground, and sugar pines crowded the fringes of the shot.

Jack turned to look for her and saw a small woman behind the counter reading a newspaper. The woman lowered her reading glasses, and the hairs on Jack's arms stood on end. Lonnie was mostly obscured by the shelf, but still he positioned himself between her and the woman.

Lonnie showed the magazine to him. 'Do people really live in houses like this?'

'Rich people.' He closed the magazine and returned it to the shelf. 'Anyway, I like our house.'

'You like it more than a castle?'

Lonnie followed Jack to the drinks fridge.

'Yeah,' he said. 'It's not a house's fault that—'

'You kids buying something or killing time?' the woman behind the counter interjected.

She'd taken off her reading glasses and flattened both palms on the newspaper. Lonnie's chin dropped. 'We have dollars,' she murmured.

'We're killing time,' Jack announced. He arrived at the drinks fridge and squared his shoulders. 'But we're also gonna buy a drink'—he opened the fridge for Lonnie—'*and* ice cream.'

'Yeah!' Lonnie said.

Jack snatched a can of lemonade from the fridge, and Lonnie ran the few steps to the freezer. She pointed the half-roll of coins at a choc-hazelnut ice block wrapped in silky plastic. Jack glanced at the price and pouted. But he opened the freezer and took out the ice block, and the children carried the items to the counter.

The lipstick on the woman's mouth smiled. 'Anything from among the confectioneries?'

Jack examined the chocolates and candies on the shelves attached to the counter. He fingered an individually wrapped Thunderhead Super Sour. Lonnie's attention was elsewhere. On the back wall, a collection of hula hoops hung from a hook. She nudged Jack and pointed.

Behind the counter, the woman followed their eyes. She gestured at the coins in Lonnie's hand. 'You don't have enough, sweetie.'

The woman charged them seven dollars for the ice block and lemonade. Lonnie held out the half-roll of coins, and Jack peeled away more of the cardboard wrapping and counted out dollars until their cache was almost depleted.

The children walked away from the newsagent, and the distant murmur of the busker's singing filled the space between them. Distracted, Lonnie held her untouched ice block in one hand and the diminished roll of coins in the other. Jack slipped the loops of the plastic bag onto his wrist again and opened the can of lemonade, which clicked and let off some of its gas.

'Did we win?' Lonnie asked.

Jack raised his eyebrows. 'When?'

'Just now.'

Jack allowed an elderly couple with a fluffy dog to pass before he reached into his pocket and retrieved the Thunderhead Super Sour. 'I reckon we won.'

Lonnie sighed, albeit without conviction. 'We said no stealing.'

'Come on—she deserved it.'

Lonnie said nothing, and Jack rang the noiseless lolly as if it were a bell. The corners of his sister's lips curved upwards. 'Yeah, she deserved worse,' she said.

'She deserved some *hula*,' Jack added.

Lonnie thrust the coins forward like a fencer. She bit into her ice block and peered at the street corner looming before them. Then she knocked what was left of the roll of coins against her pinafore. 'Jack, are we running out of dollars?'

He ripped the Thunderhead's wrapper with his teeth. 'No way.'

'But the lady said—?' Lonnie turned her pleading eyes to her brother. 'Does that mean we get to go back soon?'

'I told you: we're never going back.'

'You promised we'd go back when we run out of dollars.'

'*If* we run out of dollars.'

Jack tossed the lolly into his mouth and sucked on it and attempted to stare Lonnie down. But his lips puckered, and his eyes began to water. He stood on the spot, behind a woman on crutches using an ATM, and soon his face resembled a lemon.

'What's wrong?' Lonnie asked.

'Sour,' Jack wheezed. 'Sour.'

He arched his back and poured lemonade into his mouth. Lonnie watched on, and there was an instant or two of calm: Jack's expression grew less citric; the woman at the ATM received her cash.

Then the soft drink fizzed and foamed at Jack's lips. He rushed to the kerb and disgorged the lemonade and Thunderhead into the gutter. Some of it sprayed onto his shirt, some onto his shoes. The lemonade trickled through a metal grille and dripped into the underworld of the street. The lolly bounced beneath the tyre of the vehicle that was biding its time; it indicated and reversed into a parking space.

Jack wiped his mouth and faced Lonnie. Without judgement, she extended her arm. 'Ice block?' she said.

He swapped the soft drink for the ice block and gnawed at the choc-hazelnut. Lonnie took a swig of lemonade and belched in the direction of the woman on crutches. Then she glanced at the vehicle—a maroon ute with a horned ram's head badge on its tailgate. She saw a massive dog panting in the cabin. But she could only see the hands of the figure in the driver's seat, which had only a loose grip of the wheel.

III

The sun broke through the clouds, and the children rounded the corner onto an undulant road. No quiver of the busker's voice reached them, and neither did the maroon ute seem to be following. This road had more of an industrial bent than the ones they'd travelled to get to it. Lonnie swigged at the lemonade and dinged the roll of coins against a pole outside a store that sold car batteries. On its front wall, photos of batteries were arranged into a grid that looked more like a spot-the-difference puzzle than an advertisement.

Ambling alongside her, Jack ate the ice block and swung the plastic bag and toyed with a button at his navel. Lonnie saw the faint lemonade stain on his shirt. 'It's your turn to choose what to buy,' she said.

The children walked in silence for a while. They took turns eating the ice block and drinking the lemonade until their victuals were all finished. Then the road began to slope up, and next to a cheerless assortment of warehouses and factories they slowed to climb the hill. One of the factories bore graffiti of a cartoon woman spray-painting the crumbling facade of a building; a cartoon man acted as lookout before an empty doorframe, and the X of some barricade tape flapped at his back.

'Did you do that painting?' Lonnie said.

Jack eyed her sidelong. 'Which one?'

'The one Mum showed us near the school.'

'Nope.'

'Me either.' On every second step, she pushed down on her thigh with the empty can. 'We shouldn't have cut the hula hoop.'

Jack stuck the bare popsicle stick into the side of his mouth like a cigar. 'Yeah we should.'

'It was mean.'

'*She's* mean.'

'We can be mean sometimes, too.'

Outside an office with windows covered by blinds, they paused at a skip full of rubbish. Jack threw the popsicle stick in. 'We're only mean to people who are looking for mean.'

Lonnie put the can to her lips and slurped at nothing. 'Am I looking for mean?'

Jack shook his head. He switched the plastic bag from one hand to the other and rushed off up the hill. Lonnie threw the can into the skip. Then she chased after her brother.

'You're not looking for mean either, Jack,' she called out. She caught up and tried to match his strides. 'And you're not mean to me.'

'I know that.' He kept his solemn eyes on the pavement, but he laughed to himself. 'I know everything, remember?'

Lonnie placed her hand on his shoulder. They neared the top of the hill, where a repair shop of some sort spilled its goods onto a brick-floored courtyard. Flaxen weeds sprouted in the cracks, and garbage bags piled up in a corner. The smell of rot filled the air. But that didn't stop Lonnie from gasping. A claw crane machine with a crack in its front pane rested against the shop like an abandoned phone box. Not far from it was a kids' rocking ride in the guise of a mouldering horse.

'Can I?' Lonnie asked.

Jack's gaze traced the electrical cables of the machine and the horse. Both were plugged into a duct-taped power board, the cord of which ran beyond the garbage bags and into the murky passage by the side of the shop.

'Oh, wait.' Lonnie removed her hand from his shoulder. 'It's your turn to choose.'

She gave him the roll of coins, and he felt the ridges in the cardboard that delineated each dollar. There were four dollars left. With his untrimmed thumbnail, he levered the edge of one coin up and offered it to Lonnie. 'I'll give you my turn,' he said.

His sister held out her palm, and he flicked the coin onto it. She ran to the machine and sought out the slot where she should insert the dollar. Jack wandered past; the claw machine was filled with plush toys—some brown, some white—that looked like strange woollen giraffes. He went to the mouldering horse and sat in its saddle.

Lonnie inserted the coin and grabbed the joystick. She rotated it, and the claw responded by dangling in a haphazard circle. Then she hit a backlit button, and the claw descended towards the plush toys. It clutched at thin air and returned to its origin.

Lonnie strode over to Jack. 'Can I have another dollar, please?'

He hesitated before he flicked a dollar from what remained of the cardboard wrapping onto her palm. Unbidden, a second dollar tumbled out after it. Lonnie glanced at her brother's face. He opened his mouth as if about to ask for the second dollar back. But he twisted his lips into a smile. 'Go,' he said, nodding like an adult. 'Have fun.'

She returned to the cracked machine and inserted the first dollar. This bought her about three seconds of play: the claw hovered above one of the brown plush toys; she punched the backlit button, and the claw dived and came up empty.

Jack climbed off the horse, and Lonnie fed the second dollar into the slot. This time she focused on manipulating the claw, on guiding the joystick through a robotic spiral. She lowered her eyebrows. Her tongue poked out of her mouth. With the side of her fist, she punched the backlit button.

The claw descended and picked up a white plush toy and carried it towards Lonnie. She bounced happily on the balls of her feet. The claw dropped the plush toy into a chute. Lonnie squatted and shoved her hand into the chute's other end. But the plush toy wasn't there.

Jack came over and peered through the cracked pane. The toy's elongated neck was snagged on some jagged perspex, and it remained in the belly of the machine. 'It's stuck,' he said.

Lonnie stood on her tiptoes and looked through the glass. Then Jack saw her height diminish as she flattened her feet on the bricks. 'Gimme another dollar,' she said. 'I can win a brown one and knock the white one free.'

Jack prodded the last dollar from the cardboard wrapping. It was shinier than the others, except for a charred spot in its centre—and rather than featuring a mob of kangaroos, it had an enormous fly and what seemed to be maggots etched onto it.

He looked from the special-issue coin to Lonnie. She dug her fingernails into her upper arm as if it were bruised and extended her beggarly hand. Her pinafore bunched at her chest, and his eye drifted to the flowers embroidered on it. 'I think I'm gonna keep this one,' he said.

He let the breeze take the cardboard wrapping and held up the last dollar to display its tail to Lonnie. She gave it a cursory inspection and released her own arm. 'Oh-kay,' she said, and they exited the brick-floored courtyard.

The children left the undulant road. They roved across a sward of grassland that separated two rocket-ship-like apartment complexes; they meandered along hushed streets. When they came to a fork in a randomly chosen road, Jack stopped at a line on the pavement. He made a turnstile of his arm in front of Lonnie, and the plastic bag swayed against her.

'Heads or tails?' he said.

A cloud passed over them, and Lonnie raised her eyes to the clearing sky. 'Are our dollars all gone?'

'What do you think this is?' Jack balanced the special-issue coin on his thumbnail, against his forefinger. 'Heads or tails?'

Lonnie sighed. 'Tails.'

Jack flipped the coin and caught it and sighted the monarch's profile. He led Lonnie along the path to the right. Then they took turns to make further decisions about where to go, which streets to explore, until they approached the roundabout near the second-hand clothes store and the railway bridge.

Lonnie pointed at the bridge. 'Are we going back to . . .?'

'We're going in circles!' Jack shouted. 'I should never have listened to you—we should've just gotten on that train and *gone*.'

'We didn't have a card.'

'We didn't *need* a card.'

He stomped away from the roundabout in the direction from which they'd come. But Lonnie remained. Suddenly, she tore off the pinafore and fixed up her hair and t-shirt. A truck barrelled along the road and blew smoke over her head.

'What are you doing?' Jack called out.

'It was itchy.'

Lonnie scratched her neck and craned it to look at her brother. He waited a distance behind her, and she peered not at the second-hand clothes store but towards the liquor store with the poster of the actress at the beach. She couldn't quite see it from where she was.

'You coming?' Jack called out.

Lonnie filled her cheeks with air and then let them slowly empty. She draped the pinafore over the wrought-iron fence of a house and trudged to Jack. The children retraced their steps for a while. Then they came to a side street and diverted onto it without discussion. The street was lined with short houses and tall trees, and the dappled shade made the afternoon flit from hot to cold.

About halfway down, the children came upon a leafy park tucked away between an alley and an electrical substation.

Jack strode to the park's gate. He unlatched it and shoved it open and heard its creak. Almost bowing, he gestured for Lonnie to go in. She wandered into the park, which was filled with the flecked metal of play equipment. A pair of swings hung on the periphery. Close by was a seesaw with a fading rainbow bird painted on it. There was a slide in the back corner, next to a wooden fence, and in the park's centre a copper-coloured merry-go-round sat dormant.

'Jack,' Lonnie said, 'you promised if we run out of dollars, we go back to the car.'

Jack took the special-issue coin from his pocket. 'But I still have a dollar.'

He grinned, and Lonnie folded her arms. 'That's *cheating*.'

'Anyway, life isn't about having dollars, Lonnie.' He pocketed the coin and shut the gate. 'Wanna go on the swings with me?'

She unfolded her arms and headed for the swings. Indolently, she sat in one and shuffled back and forth on her tiptoes. Jack dropped the plastic bag onto the dirt and sat in the swing beside her. He put all his effort into animating the swing, and within seconds he was whooshing through the air. Lonnie observed him for a moment. Then she bent and straightened her legs, and soon she was whooshing through the air herself.

After a minute, though, Jack slowed his swing and Lonnie brought hers to a standstill. She held on to the chains and sat without movement or expression. 'I remember how they drove us to that water thing,' she said. 'And Dad watched us. And Mum helped us get in. And then she almost let us go.'

Jack leaped off his swing. 'You remember all that?'

'But she didn't let us go, Jack. She saved us.' Lonnie sought out his eyes. 'She loves us.'

Jack blinked at the electrical substation next to the park. 'Does she love me?'

'You know she does.'

'I know she's trying her best.' He swallowed. 'And I know we have to go back to the car.'

'You know *everything*,' Lonnie said.

'No, I don't.' Jack returned his gaze to Lonnie. 'Like, what if we deserve more than her best?'

'What do you mean?'

'What if she can't do it by herself?'

'We'll help her.'

'What if she deserves *mean*, Lonnie?'

'Oh.' Lonnie got to her feet. 'If I ever catch her looking for mean, I'll chomp her face.'

She gnashed her teeth and stumbled over a clump of dead leaves. Jack caught her, and they fell into an embrace. 'And I'll gut her like a fish,' he mumbled. Lonnie released him, and they shared a sad smile. He picked up the plastic bag. 'Guess I should change again before we go, huh?'

🐇

Jack went behind the slide to change into his old clothes, and Lonnie strolled to the copper-coloured merry-go-round in the middle of the park. Its ridged metal surface was pieced together from a circular central plate surrounded by four annular sectors; near the perimeter of each sector, an arched rail was bolted down at both ends.

Lonnie skimmed her fingertips over the warm metal. She sat between two of the arched rails. Then she lay with her back flat on the merry-go-round and let her legs dangle off the edge. Somehow the day had grown piercingly bright, and she shut her eyes and hummed the first tune that the busker had sung.

It wasn't long before Jack returned, wearing the grey hoodie from lost and found. He slammed the plastic bag of second-hand clothes onto the slide. It skidded along and tumbled onto the dirt. He booted the bag and strode towards the merry-go-round.

Lonnie heard his footsteps approaching, and she stopped humming. 'Jack?'

'I'm here.'

He squeezed himself into the space between his sister and an arched rail and lay shoulder to shoulder with her. Longer than hers, his legs also dangled off the edge. She rested her cheek on the merry-go-round, facing Jack, and opened her eyes.

'How do I look?' he asked.

'You look like you.' She squinted at her own t-shirt. 'How about me?'

'You look like you as well.' He drummed his fingers against the wound on his abdomen. 'Ready to go?'

Lonnie sat up. In the park, the swings weren't swinging; neither was the seesaw seesawing. The collarless shirt appeared to be crawling out of the plastic bag Jack had kicked, but no breeze troubled its cotton.

'Can we spin the merry-go-round one time before we go?' Lonnie asked.

'Mm-hm.' Jack propped himself on his elbows. 'You'd better hold on.'

Lonnie planted her feet on the copper-coloured surface and casually clasped an arched rail. Jack stepped onto the dirt, and his shoes crunched over some dead leaves. He gripped the same rail as his sister and adopted a standing-start race position. 'Ready?'

He made the merry-go-round wobble, and Lonnie stumbled. She gripped the rail more firmly and copied her brother's stance. 'Set,' she said.

'Go!'

Jack ran in an anticlockwise direction and dragged the arched rail along with him. The merry-go-round squealed like an animal and spun reluctantly. Jack put his head down. He pumped his legs as hard as he could.

On the slow-turning merry-go-round, Lonnie looked like she was surfing; on the dirt, Jack looked like he was wading through water. But, in time, the merry-go-round picked up pace and allowed him to build into a sprint.

It spun faster and faster and faster until it seemed to move of its own accord. Lonnie could barely hold on. Jack was almost run off his feet. The strain showed on his knuckles, and he clung desperately to the rail. Then he leaped, still clinging on, and flew for a moment before he landed, elegant and upright, on the metal surface beside his sister.

Lonnie raised her eyebrows, but Jack played nonchalant. He hunched to make himself more aerodynamic, and the children spun around and around. The wind rose and swept through their hair. It whiffled their clothes and howled in their ears; it obscured the creak of the gate, which opened and shut as the figure from the ute entered the park.

The figure was too tall to be their mother, too pale to be their father. Unlike both, it had returned to them and would never leave. It walked its massive dog and wore a red baseball cap and the face of a man.

But Jack and Lonnie didn't even see the figure, for where the merry-go-round should have been slowing, it only accelerated. The park around them accelerated too, turning in the opposite direction, erasing its details as it went along. The swings lost their contours. The slide was ironed out. The seesaw grew hazy. Beyond the merry-go-round, the world reduced itself to a rotating wall of colour—and the figure was nothing but a vermilion streak on that wall.

And the merry-go-round kept spinning, faster and faster, and the children kept going around and around. Jack held on to the rail. He spied the vermilion streak now, but his face betrayed no fear. There were so many other colours to look at, and his awestruck gaze flitted about to take them all in.

Next to him, Lonnie widened her eyes. She moved them from the base of the rotating wall to its very top. The wall reached all the way to the firmament, and she watched day accelerate into night. Then the top of the wall glowed yellow, like a halo, and carved the visible sky into a dark circular mirror.

An image loomed in the mirror, and Lonnie leaned back and peered at it. Jack glanced at her and followed her gaze. But the children did not see themselves reflected in the sky. Rather, they saw an upside-down image of their mother. Her crown was aimed at them and her feet planted on the stars. Then the halo pulsed—and Ilene seemed to react to it. She gazed up, or down, and appeared to look directly into their eyes.

Lonnie reached out and held Jack's hand. 'We're coming home, Mum!' she shouted.

'Yeah,' Jack yelled. 'We're . . . we're coming home!'

He held Lonnie's hand and blinked at the sky. Then the image of their mother dissolved. She disappeared, from head to toe, and the stars at her feet coalesced into a strange white light which outshone the halo that described the dark circular mirror.

The light gained shape and form, and Jack and Lonnie could not look away. It was a shimmering double helix—two intertwined strands of radiance that twirled around each other and slow-danced and floated gracefully towards the children.

Around Jack and Lonnie, the wall of colour accelerated. On the merry-go-round, they spun ever faster. The light revolved on the same axis, in the same direction, but it travelled at its own serene speed. It shone unevenly and continued its unhurried descent. Then it settled over the circular plate in the centre of the merry-go-round. There it hovered, rotating slowly, drifting up and down as if it were afloat on an invisible ocean.

Jack and Lonnie were still holding hands. He looked at her; she looked at him. The light illuminated the sheen on their innocent faces, and the children smiled at each other. They were going home.

ACKNOWLEDGEMENTS

I would like to thank: Kirsty Wallace-Hor, without whom this novel could not have been written; my children, Jude and Tessa; David Goldberg and Ella Roby for being generous, insightful, critical readers of my work; my wonderful publisher, Robert Watkins, for believing in my novel; Ali Lavau for her excellent editing; George Saad for designing a beautiful cover; Alisa Ahmed and everyone at Ultimo Press; Benjamin Paz and Caitlan Cooper-Trent of Curtis Brown; Create NSW and Varuna Writers' House; Marie Maroun of Mushroom Studios; Roland Fishman, Jo Symonds, Richard Cornally and Kathleen Allen of the Writers' Studio; and my parents, the rest of the Gamieldien family and the Wallace-Hor family for their love and support.

Zahid Gamieldien is an author, screenwriter, editor and writing tutor. His short fiction has been published in literary journals including *Overland*, *Meanjin*, *Kill Your Darlings*, *Island Magazine* and many others. His work was listed for the Richell Prize and selected for inclusion in the 'best of' fortieth anniversary edition of *The UTS Writers' Anthology*. His screenwriting has been listed for awards, and as an editor and writing tutor, he's helped several authors get their work into print. Most recently, he received funding to undertake a residency at Varuna House and a major grant from Create NSW to write his next novel.